T0359410

# HISTORICAL

*Your romantic escape to the past.*

## A Marriage To Shock Society

Joanna Johnson

## The Scandalous Widow

Elizabeth Rolls

MILLS & BOON

DID YOU PURCHASE THIS BOOK WITHOUT A COVER?
If you did, you should be aware it is **stolen property** as it was reported 'unsold and destroyed' by a retailer.
Neither the author nor the publisher has received any payment for this book.

A MARRIAGE TO SHOCK SOCIETY
© 2024 by Joanna Johnson
Philippine Copyright 2024
Australian Copyright 2024
New Zealand Copyright 2024

First Published 2024
First Australian Paperback Edition 2024
ISBN 978 1 038 94182 4

THE SCANDALOUS WIDOW
© 2024 by Elizabeth Rolls
Philippine Copyright 2024
Australian Copyright 2024
New Zealand Copyright 2024

First Published 2024
First Australian Paperback Edition 2024
ISBN 978 1 038 94182 4

® and ™ (apart from those relating to FSC®) are trademarks of Harlequin Enterprises (Australia) Pty Limited or its corporate affiliates. Trademarks indicated with® are registered in Australia, New Zealand and in other countries.
Contact admin_legal@Harlequin.ca for details.

Except for use in any review, the reproduction or utilisation of this work in whole or in part in any form by any electronic, mechanical or other means, now known or hereafter invented, including xerography, photocopying and recording, or in any information storage or retrieval system, is forbidden without the permission of the publisher, Harlequin Mills & Boon.

This book is sold subject to the condition that it shall not, by way of trade or otherwise, be lent, resold, hired out or otherwise circulated without the prior consent of the publisher in any form or binding or cover other than that in which it is published and without a similar condition including this condition being imposed on the subsequent purchaser.

All rights reserved including the right of reproduction in whole or in part in any form.
This edition is published in arrangement with Harlequin Books S.A..

This is a work of fiction. Names, characters, places, and incidents are either the product of the author's imagination or are used fictitiously, and any resemblance to actual persons, living or dead, business establishments, events, or locales is entirely coincidental.

MIX
Paper | Supporting responsible forestry
FSC® C001695

Published by
Harlequin Mills & Boon
An imprint of Harlequin Enterprises (Australia) Pty Limited
(ABN 47 001 180 918), a subsidiary of HarperCollins Publishers Australia Pty Limited
(ABN 36 009 913 517)
Level 19, 201 Elizabeth Street
SYDNEY NSW 2000 AUSTRALIA

Cover art used by arrangement with Harlequin Books S.A.. All rights reserved.

Printed and bound in Australia by McPherson's Printing Group

# A Marriage To Shock Society

Joanna Johnson

MILLS & BOON

**Joanna Johnson** lives in a little village with her husband and too many books. After completing an English degree at university, she went on to work in publishing, although she'd always wish she was working on her own books rather than other people's. This dream came true in 2018 when she signed her first contract with Harlequin, and she hasn't looked back, spending her time getting lost in mainly Regency history and wishing it was acceptable to write a manuscript using a quill.

**Books by Joanna Johnson**

**Harlequin Historical**

*Scandalously Wed to the Captain*
*His Runaway Lady*
*A Mistletoe Vow to Lord Lovell*
*The Return of Her Long-Lost Husband*
*The Officer's Convenient Proposal*
"A Kiss at the Winter Ball"
in *Regency Christmas Parties*
*Her Grace's Daring Proposal*
*Their Inconvenient Yuletide Wedding*

Visit the Author Profile page
at millsandboon.com.au.

## Author Note

The first inkling of *A Marriage to Shock Society* came while I was rereading my favorite Jane Austen novel, *Emma*.

I always felt Miss Woodhouse's friend Harriet was a far more interesting character than the heroine. Where Emma was brought up in luxury, illegitimate Harriet Smith was raised as a "parlor boarder" at a school for young ladies, not learning the identity of her father until much later in the novel. By some lucky chance, she was taken under Emma's wing and so was exposed to Society, which given her station, she couldn't have accessed otherwise. But it left me wondering what would have happened to "natural daughters" who lacked such sympathetic (and well-bred) friends.

Emily Townsend is one such unclaimed daughter. Her background is similar to Harriet's, spending her childhood at school with no knowledge of her parentage, although sadly she lacks Miss Smith's influential mentor. Unwanted and unloved, it seems her destiny is to be sent far away from the town she grew up in, to take a job where nobody knows her shameful origins...

Until she meets Andrew.

Although now the Earl of Breamore, Andrew Gouldsmith understands what it's like to live on the fringes, and he doesn't want a wife from among the *ton*. Emily piques his curiosity from their very first meeting, as a young woman very different from those he knows, although the mystery of her parentage poses problems he hadn't expected. He fears for his new countess's happiness if she insists on trying to find her father—but much like Emma Woodhouse, Emily will not be deterred once her mind is made up!

For Sissy

# Chapter One

Staring up at the intimidating frontage of Huntingham Hall, Emily Townsend knew there was no turning back.

The five-mile walk from the neighbouring town of Brigwell had taken longer than she'd anticipated and she feared she looked dishevelled, pushing aside a limp strand of hair and wishing the back of her neck wasn't quite so damp from the summer sun. She had to be at her very best when she finally worked up the courage to knock at the door and, taking a deep breath, she peered up once again at the biggest house she had ever seen.

It was hewn from the same pretty Warwickshire stone as the school she had lived in since birth, but any scant similarity between the two buildings began and ended there. Miss Laycock's establishment comprised little more than a largish cottage, the second floor reserved for the parlour boarders that included Emily. Despite the lofty claims of advertisements placed in the Brigwell Gazette it was neither particularly exclusive nor prestigious. It had never truly felt like *home*, even though she had never known any other, and the smallest flutter of excitement stirred now despite her jangling nerves.

If she was right…

The flutter grew stronger and Emily tried her best to check

it. If she let herself get her hopes up too high it would be even more painful if they were then dashed, especially with so much at stake. It had been made abundantly—and abruptly—clear that there was no longer a place for her at the Laycock School for Young Ladies and she'd been left with no choice but to act, now throwing all her faith in what she'd seen on a smudged piece of paper more than twelve years before.

The hand she raised to the ornate bellpull shook uncontrollably, and she swallowed rising apprehension as she listened to the chime. In a matter of moments the door would open and she'd step inside, mere minutes away from a scene she'd imagined countless times, and then—

And then—what?

He'd be delighted to see her, this stranger whom she'd given no warning she was coming...wouldn't he? If he wasn't, she might die of shame right there in Huntingham Hall's no doubt magnificent parlour, but she had no choice. There were no other options left to her, and as the door opened Emily forced a smile, clasping her hands together to hide how they trembled.

'Good morning. I would like to see Lord Breamore. Is he at home?'

She spoke with as much confidence as she could muster, glad of the hours she'd spent rehearsing before her bedroom mirror when the newly emerged butler bowed instead of immediately turning her away.

'Yes, ma'am. Please come inside.'

The man withdrew and with one final glance over her shoulder Emily followed. She'd succeeded in getting past the front door and that in itself felt like a victory, although any triumph was rapidly replaced by awe as she stepped over the threshold.

The entrance hall alone was bigger than Miss Laycock's entire drawing room. High ceilinged, gleaming with marble and lit by sunshine cascading in through tall windows, it was more a palace than a house and she'd never felt so out of place in her life as she removed her faded bonnet and handed it to a waiting maid. Even the servants were better dressed than she was and hurriedly Emily tried to hide a visibly mended hole in the palm of one glove. If the other parlour boarders could see her now they'd be amazed at her nerve in daring to set foot in an Earl's home, somewhere a person of her position had no right to *think* about let alone visit, and she prayed for the frightening gallop of her pulse to slow as the butler turned back.

'I shall inform His Lordship of your presence. What name may I give?'

'Miss Townsend. Miss Emily Townsend.'

She watched keenly for his reaction, but it seemed her name meant nothing to him.

'Thank you, ma'am. His Lordship will be down directly.'

Emily attempted another smile, although her limbs felt like water as the maid began to lead her away. Her nape was still too hot and her heart still flung itself against her ribs and, when she was shown into what seemed to her the grandest parlour on earth, she all but fell onto a sofa rather than sat.

The maid withdrew, leaving Emily alone and at the mercy of her thoughts.

*'His Lordship will be down directly.'*

Another surge of excitement rose and again she attempted to master it. She'd dreamed of this day since she was nine years old, when she had forced open the forbidden drawer of the late Mrs Laycock's desk to hunt the secrets she knew lay within, and what she'd found had turned her world on its head. Many questions had been answered by that piece of paper, none of which her guardians had shown any intention of addressing themselves then or since, but the biggest still remained and Emily's heart leaped into her mouth as she heard footsteps approaching and knew the final piece of the puzzle was about to fall into place.

She sprang to her feet, hardly breathing as the door swung open. A man stood on the threshold, his face momentarily hidden by shadow, but then he stepped fully into the room and Emily felt as though she had been kicked in the stomach.

'Good morning. Miss Townsend, is it? I am Lord Breamore. I believe you wanted to see me?'

The Earl smiled, the unfeigned warmth of it reaching his dark eyes. He was tall enough that she had to lift her chin slightly to look into his face—a pleasant one, as she might have been more aware if a crushing weight hadn't just come slamming down across her chest.

*But he's far too young. Surely this can't be right?*

It was like being doused by a shower of cold water. Every trace of excitement vanished instantly, all tentative hope draining away as she gazed up at the man who wasn't who she wanted him to be, and the first words she spoke to him came far more bluntly than she'd intended.

'You are Lord Breamore? The *only* Lord Breamore?'

His almost black eyebrows raised a fraction at her forthrightness, but so did one corner of his mouth, a half-smile that even Emily couldn't miss.

'I'm afraid so. There's generally only one of us at a time.'

He seemed to consider for a moment. 'Perhaps you were expecting my uncle, Ephraim Gouldsmith? The previous Earl?'

Emily swallowed, the sudden dryness of her throat almost choking her. 'Perhaps.'

'In that case I'm afraid I have bad news. He died two months ago.'

The unexpected Earl gestured for her to sit and Emily found herself folding back down onto the sofa she had sprung from so eagerly. Dismay and confusion crowded her, although from somewhere she managed to dredge up the only socially acceptable response.

'I'm sorry, sir. My deepest condolences.'

The Earl inclined his head. He seemed unmoved by the recent bereavement and Emily wondered fleetingly at his coolness before reality returned to eclipse all else.

*I'm too late. If Ephraim Gouldsmith was indeed my father I'll never know him now...and we'll never have the happier future together I hoped for.*

The weight in her chest shifted to make room for a shard of ice. For *years* the only thing that had made her sad existence in any way tolerable was the dream of one day meeting the father nobody wanted to tell her anything about. No one at the school, where she'd been deposited as a newborn, had ever truly cared for her. Mrs Laycock had occasionally bestowed a tight smile or stiffly encouraging word, but after she died and her daughter took control even that meagre approval came to an end. *Miss* Laycock was even more austere than her mother, never hesitating to use the cane in her attempts to shape Emily into a respectable young woman, although it seemed illegitimacy was a stain no amount of rapped knuckles could erase. The only future deemed appropriate for such an unfortunate creature was as a governess for a family prepared to overlook her dubious origins in exchange for a pittance, a grim prospect she'd been informed was now imminent. A position had been found for her with a family almost a hundred miles away from Brigwell, practically on the other side of the country and far from everyone and everything she'd ever known, and to evade that fate she'd finally played the single winning card she thought fate had dealt her.

*But I left it too late.*

Vaguely she heard the Earl ring a bell by the fireplace and then seat himself in a chair to one side of her sofa, the tread of his boots muffled by expensive rugs. Each one must have cost as much as her board and schooling did for a year, and she stared blindly down at the woven designs, despair washing over her like a chilly breeze.

Was this really the outcome of all that time spent looking forward to this day? The paper in Mrs Laycock's desk had stated her anonymous mother was deceased, dying in childbed and leaving Emily behind, but to discover she had a father still living had given her nine-year-old self the strength to go on. A maddeningly placed smudge had obscured his surname, leaving only his title exposed alongside a smeared impression of a coat of arms courtesy of his ink-spattered signet ring, but that had been enough. There was only one Lord living near Brigwell and that was Breamore, and without ever having laid eyes on him Emily knew it *had* to be his signature scrawled on the dotted line. Who else could not only afford to pay for her lodging and education in advance but would take the trouble to do so, spending what must have added up to a small fortune by the time she'd come of age?

Such generosity had been enough to convince her that he cared, and as the years had passed that certainty had taken root in her lonely, affection-starved heart, which cherished the notion of her distant papa until she'd built him up into an almost mythical figure for a girl who had nothing else to cling to. In her desperation to belong somewhere she had seized on what she ached to be true, a fiercely held conviction she'd reminded herself of every time her cold life at the school grew too much to bear—that fathers existed to love their daughters, even if they couldn't always keep them, and that one day hers would come to take her away from the bleak situation he must have had good reason for making her endure. He had invested money and effort in placing her with the Laycocks, surely proof he wanted to know where to find her when the time was right, and only the looming prospect of forced servitude had made her abandon her patient waiting and seek him out for herself.

There was a loaded pause. Clearly her unwitting host expected some kind of explanation as to why he had a silent, obviously unhappy woman in his parlour, but when it became plain one was not forthcoming, he leaned forward.

'We've established I'm not the one you want, but can I assist you anyway? Perhaps if you told me why you'd come to see my uncle?'

Emily glanced up. He was watching her with interest, and for the first time she noticed the liveliness of his eyes, dark but simultaneously alight with intelligence and good humour. He was attractive, she realised now she looked at him properly. Twin grooves beside his mouth suggested he smiled often and the line of his jaw could have been shaped by a sculptor's knife. His nose was slightly crooked, broken and mended long ago, but the small flaw lent character to what could otherwise have been a far blander kind of handsomeness. In all he was a man it was no hardship to look at, which only managed to make her current position feel even worse.

The only possible justification she'd had for calling at Huntingham Hall had been the belief her father lived there and now her audacity had no basis at all. She ought to leave at once, running away before the new Earl realised what kind of woman he had allowed into his home, but to her horror she wasn't sure she could. Despair had sapped her strength and made it all but impossible to stand, pinning her to the sofa while Lord Breamore politely waited for an answer she was powerless to find.

What was she supposed to tell him? That she had come to ask if his newly buried uncle was her absent papa, the only person who could save her from being sent miles from home to slave for pennies it was assumed an illegitimate girl ought to be grateful to receive? It wouldn't paint either of them in a particularly flattering light—his uncle as an errant father and herself as the secret, unwanted product of an indiscretion—and she fumbled for an answer that wasn't an outright lie.

'I understood he was a friend of my mother's.'

*That might have been true*, she reasoned uncomfortably as she watched Lord Breamore's brows knit together.

There must have been *some* kind of relationship between her poor nameless mama and the previous Earl, even if only the most transient. A child could be made in a matter of moments, one of the older school boarders had told her once, and although at the time Emily hadn't been *entirely* sure what the other girl had meant, she now had enough of an idea for her current blush to deepen another three shades.

'You say your *mother* was a friend of his? That's...interesting.'

The corners of his mouth turned down. There was a small cleft in his chin and he rubbed it thoughtfully, his uncertainty making Emily hold her breath. 'I wouldn't have thought he ever had a single friend in his life, let alone a woman.'

He hesitated, clearly choosing his next words carefully. 'He wasn't known for his regard for ladies. I take it you never met him?'

The question struck at the very centre of Emily's unhappiness. 'No, sir. I never had that pleasure.'

'Well. It might be best to consider that a blessing.'

The Earl's mouth twisted and Emily felt herself frown. What could he mean by that? There was now no chance of her meeting Ephraim Breamore and his nephew was her only link to him, the sole person who could tell her anything about the man she'd never had the opportunity to know.

'Wasn't he a pleasant man?'

To her surprise Lord Breamore gave a short laugh. It rang hollow in the room, and at her obvious confusion he held up an apologetic hand.

'Forgive me. It's only that there are many words that could have described my uncle, and *pleasant* wouldn't be one of them.'

He nodded towards a painting hanging against one richly papered wall. 'See for yourself. Even in his portrait he glares, and that's nothing to how he would scowl when he was alive.'

Emily turned at once. She had no idea what the former Lord Breamore had looked like and she braced herself to come face to face with him, even if that face was rendered in oils rather than flesh and blood. Perhaps their noses had been the same shape, or they'd shared the same unusual reddish-gold hair? It was a chance to see whether her imaginings of him had any root in fact, and she almost forgot she was being watched as she craned her neck to take a better look.

She'd expected to find at least some resemblance between herself and the man in the ornate frame…but there was none.

It was as if the artist had been tasked with creating a subject the opposite of her in every conceivable way. The painted face was square where hers was rounded, his skin olive-toned in place of her pink and white, and the thick hair waved in a much less distinctive mid-brown. His eyes were dark too, in stark contrast to her own blue, and the expression in them was exactly as his nephew had described. Ephraim Gouldsmith glowered down at her, dislike etched into every painted line, and for the first time she felt a glimmer of doubt.

*Was I wrong?*

There was absolutely no likeness whatsoever, not even the most tenuous. Between uncle and nephew there was an undeniable similarity, their colouring and jawlines clearly passed down through the generations, but for herself there might have been no family link at all. If it hadn't been pointed out to her which painting was Ephraim she never would have guessed he was the man she suspected of being her father, and the longer she gazed up at him the stronger her sudden doubts became.

*But if not him...?*

Out of the corner of her eye she saw her host likewise studying the portrait. There was little affection in his expression and, when he spoke, she heard a note of distaste loud and clear.

'I don't believe he ever thought well of anyone. If your mother was the exception, she must have been a singular woman indeed—he thought ladies a waste of time only fools pursued, which was why he never troubled himself to marry. His money was the only company I ever knew him to enjoy.'

He gave his uncle another lingering look before turning away, and Emily followed his lead. Meeting Ephraim's painted eye made her feel cold. His gaze was too hostile, as if angry with her for daring to enter his home, and the lack of anything approaching a paternal resemblance...

Was a man who apparently disliked women so much likely to have fathered an unwanted child? To hear Lord Breamore speak of him, the former Earl had been more concerned with his fortune than pleasure-seeking. Between his disinterest in the fairer sex and his looks so opposite her own, the evidence against him was mounting, and Emily's confusion grew likewise.

*First I thought he must be my father, then I discover he's died, and now I'm not sure he was my father at all. For years I was so certain, but now...*

There was too much to process while sitting in such a luxurious parlour, a place she was growing ever more uncomfortable to have invaded with every second that passed. She needed to go away to think and it was an immeasurable relief to find some of the strength had returned to her legs as she prepared to stand.

'Thank you for your time, my lord. I've taken up far too much of it. I'll bid you good day now.'

She saw him lean forward as if about to speak but the opening of the parlour door beat him to it. A servant with a tea tray appeared and set it down on a nearby table, answering the Earl's murmured thanks with a neat bob before silently leaving the room.

He smiled as the door closed again. His face had taken on a tightness when viewing the portrait but that seemed to have passed, the upward tick of his lips effortlessly catching Emily's eye, and she had no time to wonder at herself for noticing such a thing, at such a time, before he reached out.

'If you've decided to leave, at least have some tea first. Without wishing to sound rude, you look as though you need it.'

In what might be considered an uncharacteristic move for an Earl, Andrew picked up the teapot himself, simultaneously stealing a glance at the mysterious Miss Townsend's downturned face. She was pale again now, the pretty flush replaced by a curiously unhappy pallor, and he couldn't help but note the way her fingers shook when she unconsciously pushed back her hair. It was a striking colour, somewhere between russet and blonde, and he wondered again why such an attractive young woman had come to Huntingham Hall.

He poured out a cup and pushed it towards her. She did indeed look in need of a drink, although perhaps of something stronger than tea. When he'd first entered the room she'd looked as though she was about to fall over, her blue eyes wide with shock that had rapidly turned to obvious dismay, and he was no closer to understanding why. The only thing that was plain was that she had come expecting to see Uncle Ephraim, and the news of his passing had affected her far more than the old devil deserved.

'Oh… Thank you, sir. You're very kind.'

He saw how she hesitated before reaching for her tea. Her thoughts were evidently elsewhere and he took the opportunity to let his own unfold as she stirred a fragment of sugar into her cup.

Had she and Uncle Ephraim been having some kind of liaison? Was that it? The idea made him want to grimace, the thought of such a soft-spoken young woman in that gnarled grasp not an agreeable one, but then he dismissed it out of hand. She had never met the previous Earl, and besides, what he'd told her was the truth. His uncle had never looked at women with desire, only ever disdain, and the likelihood of him being interested in her even if they'd crossed paths was surely less than zero.

*She claims her mother had been a friend of his but that has to be a lie. All Uncle cared for was money, and it's very clear this Miss Townsend has none.*

Her clothes were clean but mended, and the soles of her shoes were worn thin, he saw with the empathy of one who had once been in a similar position. His uncle had only ever been able to tolerate those with wealth, as though poverty was contagious… as Andrew knew all too well.

As if sensing he was trying to puzzle her out, Emily looked up, colouring slightly when she met his eye. She shifted uneasily on the sofa and Andrew was glad she hadn't caught him in his survey of her dress, aware she must already be feeling ill at ease in his grand home.

*Just as I did as a boy, whenever Uncle deigned to summon me here. It always felt more like entering a viper's nest than a house, hoping he wouldn't notice how my cuffs were frayed and my shirts always slightly outgrown.*

It was a memory he didn't particularly want to examine at that moment, and instead he sipped his tea while pretending not to observe his guest. Every now and again she took a surreptitious glance around the room, apparently marvelling at the costly furniture and rich velvet curtains at each window, and eventually he couldn't restrain his curiosity any longer.

'You said my uncle knew your mother, but not why *you* came here. Are you quite sure there's nothing I can do?'

He'd expected her to jump for another unconvincing lie but instead she merely shook her slightly bowed head, gazing steadily down into her cup.

'No, thank you. It doesn't matter now. I think I made a mistake.'

Her voice was carefully neutral, but the tiniest quiver of a muscle near her mouth gave her away. For some reason she was both upset and trying to conceal it. Despite his piqued interest, Andrew's conscience pricked him to change the subject.

'I hope you didn't come too far. It's warm today and I assume from your dress that you walked here.'

'Yes, sir. From Brigwell.'

His eyebrows rose. Brigwell had to be at least five miles away, across a patchwork of fields and lanes too rough to be called roads. To reach it was more of a trek than a stroll, and one that only an individual with a real purpose would set out on…which brought him once again to the lingering question of *why* Miss Townsend had thought it worth the bother.

'That's some distance away. I feel a gentleman would send you home in his carriage.'

For the first time since he'd entered the parlour Emily granted him a smile, small but immediately drawing his attention to the shape of her lips.

'No gentleman should ever trouble himself on my account, my lord. I enjoy walking. A couple of miles is no hardship for me.'

She sought refuge behind her teacup again, her blue eyes hidden by the sweep of her lashes, and it struck Andrew that whatever she might be thinking was as mysterious as her appearance at his home.

What he *did* know was that he liked her answer. The days where *he* had to walk everywhere were gone now, of course, vanished the moment Uncle Ephraim had taken his last breath, and part of him missed the freedom of setting out across a field and feeling the sun shining down on his upturned face. Venturing among the forests and fields had been one of the few pleasures in his old life. His new duties now took up much of his time, the title he'd so recently inherited a heavy responsibility alongside the many privileges—and adjustments—it brought.

*Not that I'd wind back the clock, however. Not after what Mother and I endured to bring us to this moment.*

More for something to occupy his hands rather than out of any real desire for one, Andrew poured himself another cup and drank it in three gulps, wishing it was port or wine or anything better equipped at helping him outrun unwanted memories.

Andrew's father had been Ephraim's intended heir, and when a fever carried him away the Gouldsmith inheritance had transferred to his then barely five-year-old son. Most people would have assumed Lord Breamore would make some arrangements to care for his poor sister-in-law and her now fatherless child, stepping in to support and comfort them in their grief, but that had not been the case. Uncle Ephraim never lifted a finger to help in the dark days following Father's death and, even now, over twenty years later, Andrew could still picture his mother's tear-stained face as they'd been forced to pack their things and leave the home they could no longer afford. Mother's widow's jointure was small, and in the absence of any other family to turn to she'd had to make it stretch, dismissing servants and selling trinkets until only the bare bones of her once luxurious existence remained. Andrew might have been in line for an earldom, but anyone looking at him in those lean years would have struggled to believe it, and any pride he might have felt at the prospect had faded while he was still a child.

The old Earl's only interest had come later, when advancing age had made him demand occasional visits from his reluctant heir, although such calls gave neither party much satisfaction. Ephraim had been displeased with his nephew's lack of regard for wealth and status, and Andrew frustrated by his uncle's obsession with both, and it was always a relief to leave for his home in Derbyshire again, even if the roof sometimes leaked and the doors squeaked on their hinges with every strong wind.

A movement from Emily's sofa stirred him. She had set down her cup and looked as though she was about to stand, and Andrew firmly pulled himself back into the present.

'You're preparing to take your leave. Joking aside, you'll allow me to call for my uncle's—for *my* carriage?'

Rising, Miss Townsend shook out her skirts. She hadn't touched any of the dainty biscuits arranged on the tea tray so there could be no crumbs to dislodge, giving the distinct impression she was instead trying to avoid looking at him. 'No thank you, my lord. I'm very happy to walk, although even if it was a distance of twenty miles I couldn't accept such a generous offer. It wouldn't be right.'

'Wouldn't it? Why not?'

The careless question slipped out before Andrew thought the better of it. At once he realised his mistake, watching the colour in Emily's cheeks deepen into a crimson flush.

Of course she wouldn't accept his offer of a carriage. A woman like Miss Townsend would be painfully aware of the difference in their stations and never want to give the impression she'd forgotten her place, even if he was still struggling to come to terms with his own.

To Emily's eyes he was privileged and wealthy and existing in a world far removed from hers, even if he knew there was more to his position than the obvious. Doubtless he had more in common with his slightly shabby uninvited guest than with the refined young ladies that showed him such interest when he set foot in a ballroom, although to tell her so would be absurd. She was a stranger; given their opposing social circles it was very unlikely he'd ever see her again, and it would be foolish to behave as though nothing had changed, when in fact his life would never now be the same again.

His mother had tried to prepare him. Since he was a boy she'd told him of the grand inheritance he stood to gain and the title that would be bestowed on him, doing her best to ready him for a world his father's death had excluded them from so mercilessly, but still Andrew felt like a fraud. Lady Gouldsmith had done as much as she could to mould him into an Earl-to-be, teaching him to dance and play cards and grasp the varying subtleties of upper-class etiquette, and yet the lower sphere their poverty had forced them to enter had influenced him more than anything else.

His playmates as a child weren't the offspring of knights and baronets as they would have been if his father was still alive. They were apprentice clerks and rectors' sons, respectable enough but with no prestige, and it was alongside these pleasant but ordinary young men that he'd become a man himself. He'd even sought employment as a tutor once he was old enough, something the *ton* would have considered an unthinkable humiliation, but he'd taken satisfaction in knowing the money he presented to his mother each week was honestly earned. For years he'd lived as a simple gentleman, never rich but at least comfortable in the modest existence he had carved out for himself, and when the black-edged letter had come that announced Ephraim's death he had felt as though the rug had been pulled sharply from beneath him.

'Very well. If you've made up your mind.'

A flicker of relief crossed Miss Townsend's face. It seemed she was eager to make her escape, and he had no wish to detain her, the feeling of having just put his foot in it not one he wanted prolonged.

He bowed. ‘It was a pleasure to meet you, Miss Townsend. I’m only sorry I couldn’t be of more help.’

Another of those eye-catching smiles was his reward for such gallantry, though it struck him that perhaps this time it was a little forced. ‘Please think nothing of it, my lord. I ought never to have imposed in the first place. I apologise sincerely for troubling you.’

Solemnly she dropped into a low curtsey, her knees almost touching the carpet, and began to withdraw. She walked with admirable poise and Andrew realised he wanted to carry on watching her as she turned back, dipping him one final curtsey before she left—to return to wherever she had come from, disappearing, without him knowing why she had come at all.

# Chapter Two

Emily kept her attention firmly on her plate as she forced down her breakfast of thin porridge. If she hunched in her seat, and made herself small and quiet, perhaps Miss Laycock wouldn't notice her, sparing her conversation she was in no mood to entertain.

Or perhaps not.

'Are you ill?'

A sharp voice issued from the head of the table and, looking up, she found herself fixed by an equally sharp pair of eyes.

'No, Miss Laycock. I'm quite well.'

The school mistress didn't seem convinced. The stern eyes narrowed and Emily braced herself as they swept over her. It was true she probably did look ill, a night spent trying to untangle what had transpired at Huntingham Hall not allowing much sleep, although she would rather have bitten her own tongue than confess what was troubling her. If Miss Laycock learned one of her charges had dared stray near a *ton* house she would have boxed the girl's ears for having ideas above her station, and even at the grand age of twenty-one Emily suspected she wasn't immune to receiving the back of a righteous hand.

'You haven't said a word since you sat down. Are you bilious?'

'No, ma'am. As I said, I am perfectly well.'

Out of the very corner of her eye she caught two of the other parlour boarders exchange nervous glances. Miss Laycock was not a woman to rile, and Emily felt a flutter of apprehension as she was skewered with another pointed look.

'I'm glad to hear you aren't sickening for anything. The timing would be unfortunate, given I received another letter from Mrs Swanscombe this morning.'

A folded sheet of paper lay beside Miss Laycock's plate and she tapped it with a deliberate finger. 'She requires you to attend her no later than the fifteenth of this month. It seems each of the three previous governesses left after a short time and without much notice, and she is keen for the children's education to begin again as soon as possible.'

The flutter in Emily's insides spread its wings more forcefully. 'The fifteenth? But that's hardly more than a week away!'

'Correct. Now that your appointment is settled, neither Mrs Swanscombe nor I saw any reason to delay.'

Miss Laycock casually dabbed her napkin to her mouth as if she hadn't just changed the course of Emily's life in a few scant sentences and Emily herself could only stare with mute horror as the other girls diligently studied their laps.

Barely a week before she had to leave behind everything she knew and take up a position she hadn't wanted in the first place? The thought filled her with dread, coming to rest like an anchor in her chest, already heavy with the confusion and disappointment of the day before. Her visit to Huntingham Hall had been supposed to save her from being sent away, not make the prospect seem even more unescapable, although of course her reason for venturing there hadn't been solely to thwart Miss Laycock's plans.

If Lord Breamore *had* been her father, she would finally have found the family she'd always longed for. After a lifetime without affection she wanted nothing more than to be loved, to be held in a safe pair of arms and know she was valued and cared about, and for all her dreams to have fallen flat was almost more than she could endure. The old Earl was dead, and even if he had been her father—which she now doubted—she'd never have the chance to know him, everything she'd hoped for slipping through her fingers like bitter sand. Her life stretched ahead empty of all hope, the shining figure of her papa she had conjured to ward off her loneliness turned to a shadow, and the loss of that comforting warmth made her feel hollow right down to her toes.

A lump had risen in her throat and she tried to clear it with a sip of lukewarm tea, aware Miss Laycock was watching her. Those gimlet eyes were all-seeing, however, and she knew she was in danger when the school mistress pursed her lips.

'You might show a little more gratitude. It isn't everyone who would take on a governess with your background.'

Her tone was severe, setting the younger girls sitting around the table huddling lower into their chairs. From force of habit Emily jumped to make amends.

'I am grateful, ma'am. It's just… It's almost a hundred miles away. I shall know no one, and you said the house is somewhat remote…?'

'It's true there are no immediate neighbours nor a directly adjoining town, but what does that matter? Mrs Swanscombe has six children, all of whom she describes as "spirited". You'll be too busy to think of recreation.'

Miss Laycock spoke with the authority of one used to being obeyed, and Emily clamped her teeth together, wishing she knew how to argue back.

The prospect of her employment sounded worse with every added detail. She was to be marooned in a house in the middle of nowhere with nobody to talk to, attempting to wrangle six ill-disciplined children who had managed to chase off at least three other governesses, and all for a wage of next to nothing. It would be a living nightmare and one it seemed more and more imperative she avoid, especially now her first idea for doing so lay in tatters. If she'd found her father he would have taken her in, of course, but now she was entirely without help she would just have to find a way out of her situation alone.

'It isn't that I don't appreciate your efforts on my behalf, ma'am, but surely there must be an alternative? I realise money doesn't grow on trees and fully intend to pay my own way. If I could just find a position closer to Brigwell, nearer home—'

'You do not have a home.' Miss Laycock's reply was like a whipcrack. 'You were brought here because there was nowhere else for you to go and my mother was paid to take you. Since you are now of age, the money for your board has ceased and I do not operate a charity. Mrs Swanscombe has offered you paid employment and frankly you should be glad of it, considering nobody in this town is likely to want someone of your origins beneath their roof.'

A tense silence fell over the room.

The desire to know more about the *origins* spoken of so cruelly stirred, but for perhaps the thousandth time Emily dismissed it, her stomach clenching into a tight ball. She'd asked so many times she'd lost count, begging to be told about her parents and the reason they had surrendered her, but neither Mrs Laycock nor her daughter had ever been moved to answer. Either from spite or a misguided sense of duty, every question had always been met with blank refusal, and there seemed little hope of that changing now, not when it was clearer than ever that Miss Laycock couldn't wait to be rid of her.

To her dismay she felt a tell-tale stinging behind her eyes. The absolute last thing she wanted was for anyone seated around the dining table to see her cry, and she rose swiftly from her chair.

'Please excuse me. I find I have little appetite this morning.'

One or two of the other girls peered over their shoulders at her as she slipped away, but Miss Laycock was the only one to call after her, the hard voice cutting in its indifference.

'Sulking won't achieve anything, Miss Townsend. You'd be much better employed in going to your room and starting to pack.'

Emily didn't go up to her room. Instead, she moved blindly for the side door into the garden, biting the inside of her cheek to stop her tears from beginning to fall.

A gate was set into the hedge that bordered the garden and she pushed through it, too intent on escaping to think where she was going. To the right a lane led to Brigwell's main street, while the left opened into the countryside beyond and instinctively she turned for the latter. In the fields she could be alone, although Miss Laycock's words rang in her ears every step of the way.

*'You have no home.'*

*'There was nowhere else for you to go.'*

*'Someone of your origins...'*

She plunged onwards for what could have been minutes or hours, paying scant attention to which direction she was heading in. Her insides had drawn into an unhappy knot and she blinked hard, her stubbornly restrained tears scattering shards of light before her eyes. They made her vision blur, the grass and hedges all around her reduced to indistinct green smudges, and by the time she realised a thick tree root lay sprawling across her path it was too late to prevent it from snatching at her foot.

The ground came up to meet her with a thud, knocking the wind from her as she landed in a heap of skirts and outstretched arms. Sharp stones grazed her palms, but it was a stab of pain in one ankle that was the final straw, the tears she'd been holding back at last springing free.

'Damn it. Damn it, damn it, *damn it*!'

She finished on a dry sob, shakily pushing herself up to sit back against the trunk of the tree. The root had torn her stocking and she looked down at it despairingly, seeing it was ruined beyond mending. It had been darned three times already, and the knowledge that she couldn't afford a new pair clawed at her already tight throat. She had nothing and no one and now she even had to leave Brigwell behind, and in spite of her determination not to, Emily dropped her face into her hands and cried.

The tears poured down her cheeks, hot against her skin. The pain in her ankle echoed that in her heart and for some minutes she was helpless, only able to lean against the jagged bark as the weight of her sorrow held her down. Now the tears had started she feared they might never stop, but eventually she found the strength to lift her head and roughly wipe her eyes.

'There's no use crying about it. I might be impoverished, unwanted and quite possibly orphaned, but I can still attempt to keep at least some small measure of pride.'

She took a deep breath, holding it until her lungs ached before exhaling slowly. Allowing Miss Laycock to see the effect of her callous words was out of the question. It would give her satisfaction Emily had no intention of granting. She closed her eyes briefly as she wondered whether she could get back in time to avoid being missed. If she was gone for too long her absence would be noticed, and she braced herself to stand, gritting her teeth when a fresh crackle of pain arched up from her ankle.

'Come on. Get up.'

With a grimace she managed to lever herself off the ground, still leaning against the tree for support. An attempt to put her foot down was met with another sharp stab and she choked out a gasp, her fingers digging into the bark. It seemed that if she loosened her grip she might fall and it occurred to her that, short of crawling back on her hands and knees, she had little hope of returning the way she had come.

She glanced around. Perhaps there was a branch she could use as a walking stick? With growing concern she looked about her, seeing nothing of any use—although a large shape coming into view around the corner of the lane made her suddenly forget everything else.

A man was riding towards her on a great grey horse, the tails of his green coat flying out behind him. Even from a distance she could tell he was well-dressed, and as he came closer she felt her stomach plummet down to her scuffed boots.

She lurched backwards, pressing herself harder against the tree. He hadn't yet seen her. If she moved quickly she might just be able to hop out of sight, probably making her ankle hurt even more but the pure mortification of the alternative not worth considering. With any luck he would ride right past her, disappearing over the fields in the opposite direction, and if she waited a few minutes he'd be long gone before she tried to hobble back to the school.

Edging into the shadows as hurriedly as she could she heard the beat of hooves come closer. They grew louder and louder, horseshoes ringing out against the dry mud—and then to her alarm they slowed to a stop, halting dangerously close to where she stood with the bark digging into her spine.

'Ma'am? Are you there?'

If she'd had any doubts as to who the rider was before, there could be none now. His voice was one she'd heard very recently, deep and cultured and not easily forgotten, and as she forced herself to peep out she wished the ground would open beneath her feet.

'I thought I recognised the colour of your hair. Good morning, Miss Townsend.'

The Earl was far too polite to ask *why* she was endeavouring to hide behind a tree, but Emily could tell he was thinking it as she peered upwards, feeling all her blood vacate the rest of her body to come rushing into her cheeks.

It would have to be Lord Breamore who saw her in such a state, she thought dismally as he gazed down at her, the sunlight scattering bronze threads among his dark hair. *Of course* it would be the most elegant man of her acquaintance who would witness her tear-mottled countenance and puffy eyes. After her entirely inappropriate visit to his house she would have been quite happy never to see him again, still mortified to have strayed into a place where she didn't belong, and the fact he was even more handsome than she remembered didn't help matters one straw.

'Good morning, my lord.' She attempted a curtsey, her face glowing hotter when all she could manage was an ungainly squirm. 'I would not have expected to see you here.'

High up in the saddle the Earl smiled, a slight quirk of his lips that did something uncomfortable to her already twisted insides. 'It's thanks to you that I am. Your visit yesterday reminded me how pretty the countryside around Brigwell is, and I made up my mind to come here on my morning ride.'

He waved one gloved hand at the sunlit lane bordered with swaying trees, although when he looked back at her he was frowning.

'Forgive me, Miss Townsend, but is something wrong?'

'Wrong, sir? No. Why should you think that?'

She'd never been a good liar, and Emily knew he had come to that conclusion himself when he immediately brushed her denial aside.

'Because the evidence is here in front of me. I don't pretend to be an expert, but I believe even I can tell when a woman has been crying.'

The Earl fixed her with a direct gaze. Clearly he was too much of a gentleman to remain unmoved by a lady's distress, although the lady in question wished he'd ride off again instead of prolonging her discomfort.

'You're kind to ask, my lord, but it's nothing I would have you trouble yourself about.'

'With respect, that wasn't what I asked.'

In one smooth motion he unhooked his foot from one stirrup and slid to the ground, landing in front of her before she had time to blink. The slight heel of his riding boot made him even taller, and for the first time Emily noticed his height was well matched by the width of his shoulders, broad enough to invite a second and perhaps even a third glance. He didn't come any closer, although he didn't need to for her to be able to look into his eyes. They were warm and brown, filled with concern so genuine it took her by surprise, so unused to anybody showing her sympathy that for a moment she forgot they were from two different worlds.

'I'd received some bad news—twice, in fact, in little more than a day. Crying won't help anything, I know, but I confess I found myself momentarily overwhelmed by things I cannot change.'

Even as the final word escaped she regretted having spoken it. Why had she given him even the vaguest idea of what had upset her? He was an Earl and she was nobody, and she shouldn't have bothered him with her troubles even though he had asked…

Lord Breamore studied her face, his gaze lingering on the red marks framing her eyes. 'I'm sorry to hear it. I can see whatever it was must have been unwelcome indeed.'

He paused, one hand resting on his horse's neck. The mare snorted softly and he absently rubbed her nose, not seeming to care that it might leave a smudge on his pristine kid gloves.

'I wonder, Miss Townsend… Would I be correct in thinking

at least part of your unhappiness relates to your visit to Huntingham yesterday?'

Emily stiffened, feeling the ridges of the bark behind her pressing through her gown as he went on.

'Learning of my uncle's death certainly seemed to affect you more than I might have imagined, considering you'd never met. Is it fair to assume that was part of your unwanted news?'

He watched her closely, giving her nowhere to hide. There was still concern in his eyes, but a spark of curiosity had joined it. Emily found herself wanting to back away, into the shadows of the trees or anywhere else he couldn't fix her with the look that made it so tempting to tell him the truth.

'I—'

The words caught in her throat, halfway between escaping and being swallowed again. Admitting that the death of Ephraim Gouldsmith had indeed dealt her a bitter blow would make his nephew wonder why she cared so much, and she shrank from the prospect of explaining herself. The Earl might—*would*—think the worse of her to learn she wasn't even sure of the identity of her own father, and for some reason the idea of his disapproval helped her make up her mind.

With as much conviction as she could summon, Emily forced a smile, hoping it would be enough to cover a breakneck change of subject.

'I must return home, sir. I didn't tell anyone I'd gone out walking and they must be wondering where I am.'

Giving him no chance to reply she gave another awkward attempt at a curtsey and abruptly turned away, managing only one ungainly step before her ankle ruined her escape.

'Ouch!'

She sucked in a harsh breath as pain lanced up from her boot. It felt sharper than it had even a few minutes ago, and she knew she was trapped as the Earl came towards her, cutting off any hope of flight.

'Are you hurt?'

'Just my ankle. I caught it on a root and gave it a wrench. It isn't anything serious.'

There was a different kind of concern in his face now, although every bit as appealing as the variety that had gone before it. 'Perhaps not, but evidently too painful to walk on.' He shook his head decisively. 'I can't leave you here like this. If you'll allow me, I'll take you home myself.'

Emily started. He couldn't take her back to the school—he just *couldn't.* Miss Laycock would be furious she had inconvenienced someone of such high rank and would probably banish her to Mrs Swanscombe's even earlier than planned. It was an unthinkable imposition for one of her standing, and she was trying to find the words to refuse when another of those eye-catching smiles stopped her in her tracks.

'I know what you're thinking, but don't worry. I'm not offering you a carriage this time—just Constance.' He nodded to the mare beside him and Emily saw how even the horse's bridle gleamed in the sun, the leather soft and more expensive than all her clothing put together.

'It isn't so much the carriage, my lord, as being in your company. If someone saw…'

'What would they say? That you should have turned down my offer in favour of staying here, clinging to a tree?' He laughed, the deep note one she realised she could have gladly listened to all day. 'There can be no impropriety for you in accepting my help. If anyone has a problem with either of our actions they can take it up with me.'

He smiled again and Emily knew it was hopeless. Surely resisting that handsome face was impossible and, when combined with the most kindness she'd been shown in a long time, she had more chance of jumping over the moon than refusing him. She ought to say no but it just wouldn't come, and when the Earl held out his arm she took it.

'Here. Lean on me.'

Her breath caught as he carefully helped her out from the shadows, his forearm solid beneath her fingers. Each hopping step jarred her ankle, but somehow the pain faded when he drew her to him, her head scarcely reaching his shoulder and the rich green wool of his coat almost brushing her ear. It was the closest she'd ever been to a man, she realised with a jolt. Most girls had attended at least one dance by the time they reached her age, but Miss Laycock would never countenance such frivolity, and so, instead of dancing, it was to raise her onto his horse that a gentleman first placed a hand on her lower back.

'You'll permit me?'

She nodded wordlessly, not trusting herself to speak. Lifting her seemed the easiest thing in the world: he swept her up as though she weighed nothing, that first touch by a strong pair of hands unforgettable. With expert gentleness he placed her into the saddle and she clung to the pommel, with what felt like an entire swarm of butterflies taking wing in her stomach as he climbed up behind her.

'Settled?'

Another nod was all she could muster. The hard breadth of his chest lay flush against her back, warm despite the layers of clothing between them, and Emily feared she might combust when a firm arm wound around her to anchor her in place.

'Good. Let's get you home. By the by—where is that, exactly?'

There was hardly anything to her, Andrew realised as he tightened his arm around Emily's waist and tapped his horse into a brisk trot. She was all angles and unpadded bone beneath another drab gown, but her hair smelled of wild flowers and sunshine and he had to curb the impulse to breathe it in as it stirred just beneath his nose, the breeze making her red-gold waves move as though they were alive. Her head was uncovered and she wore no gloves, something unheard of for any respectable young lady venturing outside, but he was too distracted by other things to spend much time wondering why.

The headache that had been his constant companion since he woke had eased a little since riding out from Huntingham Hall, some of the cobwebs blown away by the summer air. It had been a mistake to drink so much the night before and he was paying for it now, but Lady Calthorpe's ball had been so crashingly dull he'd had to make his own entertainment. It had been filled with people just like Uncle Ephraim—rich, self-important and humourless, on the whole—and he couldn't say he'd particularly enjoyed dancing with the unending succession of young ladies who had been dangled before him like beautifully dressed carrots on sticks. A new, youthful Earl was a fine thing for every mama with an unmarried daughter, and he'd been harried since the moment he'd stepped into the ballroom, forced to twirl one debutante after another with nothing much to say to any of them. As the highest-ranking man in the room it would be assumed he had much in common with these well-bred ladies, but that assumption was misguided as ever, and as Emily shifted in the saddle Andrew felt his interest in her return full force.

'How's your ankle? I hope the movement isn't hurting you?'

'Hardly at all, sir. I'm just thankful for your assistance.'

Her voice was little more than a murmur above the thudding of hooves and he had to lean down to catch it, sitting sharply back again when his cheek accidentally brushed her ear. With each of the horse's long strides she swayed against him, her slim waist undulating under his palm, and it was becoming difficult to deny he found himself infinitely more attracted to her than any of the women he'd danced with the night before.

*But why, though?*

He tensed as his horse stumbled slightly, the movement throwing Emily even harder against him as though to test his restraint.

*Is it because there might be some scant similarity between us, given the years I spent with barely a penny to my name, or because she seems so determined to remain a mystery?*

That was a distinct possibility. She still hadn't told him what had upset her so clearly, what she'd been doing out in the fields or even where she lived. His earlier enquiry as to the latter had produced the distinctly unhelpful reply of 'Brigwell, sir,' with nothing more to go on than that, and he had to wonder if she was doing it on purpose.

*She could just be odd, I suppose. Why else would she have been attempting to hide behind a tree when I stumbled across her?*

Perhaps she'd felt so uncomfortable after their first unexpected meeting that she hadn't wished to see him again, resorting to diving into bushes to avoid him? For his part, it was true that one motivation for stopping to help her was concern, but he couldn't deny another reason followed closely behind. Ever since she'd left his parlour he hadn't been able to stop trying to guess why she'd been there in the first place, and it seemed almost serendipitous he now had a chance to find out.

They reached the end of the lane and, in the absence of any direction from his passenger, Andrew spurred the horse straight on. The overgrown trees swept down too low for him to ride along the footpath Emily must have taken from town, and he found he was glad of the landowner's negligence—the obstruction meant taking the long way round. Although if he wanted to satisfy his curiosity, he realised time was running out.

Careful not to let his face graze hers again, he leaned down.

'What if I told you that my assistance came at a price?'

He felt her stiffen. Already seeming to consist solely of ribs and sharp edges, she became even more tense, her spine hardening as if encased in armour.

'I would have to ask you to set me down here and now, my lord. I regret I have nothing with which to pay you.'

'Not money, Miss Townsend.'

Aware of his poor phrasing, Andrew hurried to correct it. 'My price would be the true answer to a question.'

The smallest whisper of tension left Emily's iron backbone, but not much, and there was an uncomfortable pause before her reply was almost lost in the wind.

'I suppose I'd say yes, sir. You've been far kinder than I'd have expected. It would be ungracious of me to refuse.'

She waited, her sunlit hair sliding over her shoulders. It had come looser and looser from its knot as they'd ridden along, sprinkling pins into the dry mud behind them, and now it hung freely around her like a silken cloak. Its natural perfume was more enticing than ever and it tempted Andrew to abandon his questioning, instead feeling the urge to bury his face in its waves…

'Why did you really go to see my uncle?'

He covered his lapse of good sense with a blurted query. If the mere scent of her hair was enough to distract him it didn't bode well for when she got down from his horse and he saw her face again, disarmingly pretty even when streaked with dried tears. A shabby gown did nothing to set her at a disadvantage. If anything, it made her shine all the more brightly, like a precious jewel half hidden in rubble and waiting to be found, although the image faded when he heard her sigh.

The deep breath seemed to come all the way up from the very soles of her mended boots. 'I suppose it makes little difference now. I'll be gone from Brigwell in a few days and then my foolishness won't matter.'

She rearranged herself slightly, tucking her elbows closer against her sides. A glance over the top of her head showed her hands had tightened on the pommel, and Andrew felt the rigidity in her back return with a vengeance.

'I'm not altogether sure where to start.'

He kept silent as she gathered her thoughts, her slender fingers never loosening their vice-like grasp of the saddle.

'I've been a parlour boarder at Miss Laycock's School for Young Ladies since the day after I was born. Neither Mrs Laycock nor her daughter, when she became mistress, would ever tell me anything about my parents or why I was placed there, other than to make it clear there was nowhere else for me to go.'

Emily turned her head slightly to the side and he saw the curve of her cheek glowed a brilliant crimson. Reading between the lines she had just admitted to being born on the wrong side of the blanket, and he heard the raw edge of shame in her voice, already difficult to catch above the wind in his ears but now even lower still.

'When I was nine I found the papers regarding my admission. I discovered my mother had died in childbed and my father was *Lord* someone, although I was unable to learn either of their names. My board and education were paid for in advance, obviously by my father, and I was always convinced he would return to claim me.'

There was a moment of silence, broken only by the horse's heavy breaths and the swishing of wind-stirred trees. Emily's iron spine had bent a little. She hunched now as if she had a pain in her belly, her shoulders rounded where previously she'd held herself so firmly upright.

'After my twenty-first birthday it seems the money for my keep ran out, and a few days ago Miss Laycock informed me she'd found me a position as a governess a hundred miles away, far from what I consider my home. She wouldn't countenance any refusal and so I sought to find my father, thinking to throw myself on his mercy until I found a position more to my liking, but it did not…turn out as I had hoped.'

'That's why you tried to see my uncle? Because you imagined *he* might be the man?'

It was a good thing Emily couldn't see his face, Andrew thought as he watched her give a single, tentative nod. It was all he could do to keep his hands steady on the reins, shock spreading through him like wildfire.

*She thought Uncle Ephraim...?*

The very idea was impossible. Of all the men in the world, the late Lord Breamore had been the very least likely to create a child, his disdain for women and people in general rendering that an inarguable fact. Ephraim Gouldsmith had never looked kindly on a lady in his life, and certainly never with enough lust to seduce one, his cold heart moved only by money and the unceasing desire for more. Miss Townsend couldn't have been more wrong in her assumption, and Andrew had to marvel at the extent of her error—but that didn't make her current dismay any less real. For whatever reason she'd convinced herself Ephraim was her father, and her reaction to learning of his passing now made perfect sense, the inaccuracy of her belief taking nothing away from the pain she must have felt to discover he was gone.

'I see.'

Taking great care to keep his voice level, Andrew cast about for the right words, wishing the education his mother had scraped to afford had taught him how to manage unhappy young women as well as Latin. 'And I, like a fool, dropped the knowledge of his death on you with no warning. I'm truly sorry for that.'

Emily's answering shrug set a surge of pity rising inside him. 'You needn't apologise, my lord. How could you have known?'

She huddled into herself, perhaps regretting laying herself so bare, and Andrew cursed himself for forcing her to it. His curiosity had made her admit things she probably wanted to keep locked away, private loss and unhappiness he was ashamed to have caused her to relive.

He would have to break the truth about Uncle Ephraim to her gently. She couldn't be allowed to carry the old wretch in her heart when he didn't deserve to be there, the thought of the old Earl's reaction to her if he'd still been alive making Andrew's jaw harden. The late Lord Breamore would have rained humiliation down on her for daring to have ideas so above her station and Andrew tried not to imagine it, the picture of Emily's tear-stained face when he'd found her that morning flashing before his eyes.

'He wasn't a man much interested in women, Miss Townsend. I see no resemblance to him in your face or temperament… You also said the money stopped when you were twenty-one?'

'Yes, sir. My birthday was just last week.'

'In that case I'm afraid he really can't have been your father. My uncle lived in Italy for a few years around the time of your birth. He wouldn't have been in England to meet your mother or to secure your place at school.'

Bracing himself for despair, arguments or perhaps even more tears, it was a relief when instead Emily simply shook her head.

'In truth, sir, I had already begun to doubt it myself. As you say, there is no resemblance between us, and when you spoke of his distaste for women it seemed unlikely that he might have…'

There was no need for her to finish. Both parties knew what went into the making of an illegitimate child, and the sliver of Emily's profile he could glimpse behind her hair was still flushed a deep, unhappy pink.

'Of course, any financial assistance would have been very much appreciated but it was the man himself I truly wanted to find. I suppose I'll have to reconcile myself to it and accept my new position with Mrs Swanscombe—there are worse fates than living among strangers, even if it wouldn't be of my choosing.'

'You'll leave town? Is there no other way?'

'I think not. I must make money to support myself and Miss Laycock has made it very clear to me there are few in Brigwell who would countenance a woman of my standing having care of their children.'

Her bare hands looked as though they were carved from ivory as they held onto the saddle, so stiff and white they might have belonged to a statue. One glance at them told Andrew her face must be much the same, tight and pale aside from the flare of shame in each cheek, and as they drew closer to town he realised he hadn't the faintest idea of how to reply.

The stigma of her illegitimacy would indeed be a problem. He'd seen similar in his village in Derbyshire, with a young woman widely rumoured to have been fathered by a passing tradesman. It was supposed that as her mother had been loose so must the daughter be, and the local men had barely given the poor girl a moment's peace until at last she'd eloped with the baker's son to the horror of his parents. A woman's reputation could be her glory or her downfall, and the unfairness of it didn't affect the truth, someone like Emily placed at a disadvantage while still in her swaddling clothes.

He opened his mouth—and closed it again just as quickly. An offer to help her had pushed forwards and very nearly made its way out, although at the last moment he managed to snatch it back.

*Be sensible. Think before you speak.*

How could he be of help to her? He had no children of his own in need of a governess, and giving her money would be a mistake. It would suggest she'd done something to earn it and he knew exactly what that *something* would be, an act that would fan the unkind whispers already swirling about her until they burst into flames.

'Can you not ask this Miss Laycock for more information? Surely she would have records, documents…?'

He caught the smallest breath of a laugh. 'I've tried, sir, many, many times. Either she doesn't know or has made up her mind to tell me nothing—there's no hope of learning anything there.'

'I see.' He thought for a moment. 'And the paper you found? It gave no hint as to his identity, other than his title?'

'No. His name was covered by an ink blot, leaving only the *Lord* exposed. There *was* a smudged crest alongside his signature, as though his signet ring had brushed the ink and left a stamp of sorts, but it was so smeared I could hardly tell what it was supposed to be without the original to compare it to.'

She lapsed into silence and Andrew didn't attempt to draw her out again. There seemed little else for her to add, or at least little she *wanted* to, and neither spoke again until eventually she tentatively cleared her throat.

'You can set me down here, please, my lord. I'm sure I can walk the rest of the way myself.'

Caught up in his thoughts he'd barely noticed they were on the edge of town and he reined his horse in abruptly, bringing her to a stop at the end of the lane that led to the market square. There was nobody around, but it seemed Emily wanted to take no chances, slipping out from beneath his arm and sliding to the ground without waiting for him to hand her down.

He heard her draw in a pained hiss as she straightened up, but at his move to dismount she held up a hand.

'There's no need, sir. As I said, I can walk from here quite easily.'

'Really? With that ankle?'

'Hobble, then.' She smiled up at him, a false smile, but one that emphasised her pretty cheekbones nonetheless. 'But it's best I'm not seen with you. You understand.'

She stepped back, slightly lopsidedly but still managing some of the poise he'd so admired as she left his parlour. Clearly the education her mysterious father had paid for had focused heavily on deportment, although when she raised her chin to look at him she didn't quite meet his eye.

'Thank you for your help, sir. I don't doubt it was a small thing for you, but for me it was a moment of kindness when all seemed bleak indeed.'

The spot of colour in each cheek blazed brighter and Andrew suspected her unsteady curtsey was a ruse to hide her countenance—a reprieve for which he found he was grateful.

His earlier suspicion had been proved right. Looking into her face again did nothing to lessen the fledgling attraction to her that had begun at first glance, and when coupled with her gratitude he found he had nothing to say, his chest oddly tight as he gazed down at her bowed head.

For such a small act to mean so much to her she must have led a cold and empty life. He'd had his own struggles, but at least he'd always known he was loved, his mother taking great pains to teach him money was not the most important thing to strive for. A secure home and the chance to understand herself were all Emily wanted, things even the lowest farmhand took for granted but she had been denied, and there was a strange heaviness around Andrew's heart as he tipped his hat to her and turned to ride back the way he had come.

# *Chapter Three*

A light was still burning in the Dower House's window when Andrew returned from Captain Maybury's dinner party, the single lamp casting an eerie glow over the drive. It was past midnight, but his mother clearly had not yet retired to bed, and he gritted his teeth on a yawn as he took a detour from Huntingham's front steps to knock at her door.

It was no surprise that she answered it herself. Old habits died hard, and although she could now have afforded an army of servants she preferred only two maids to live in, young girls who would have been sent to their beds some hours before, while their mistress sat up to keep watch.

'You're back earlier than last week. Was the music not to your liking this time?'

She let him into the shadowy hall, the candle she held throwing strange shapes against the wall. With a white shawl over her nightdress and her greying hair in a plait there was a touch of Shakespearean ghost about her, and Andrew felt as though he was following a spectre as she led him down the corridor and into her parlour.

'The music was fine. I just wanted to leave.'

He dropped into a chair beside the fire, stretching his legs out towards the blaze. 'I wish you wouldn't wait up for me.

It's not necessary now we live in a respectable neighbourhood again. What do you think might happen to me when I'm taken everywhere by carriage?'

'I don't know. I suppose it'll just take a while for both of us to adapt to the change.'

Lady Gouldsmith settled into the chair opposite, drawing her shawl around her shoulders in another relic from the years they'd spent living in draughty houses. 'How was it?'

'The same as always.'

'Oh. As enjoyable as that?' His mother gave a wry smile. 'Was Mrs Windham there again?'

'Yes.'

'And Mrs Forsythe?'

'Yes.'

'And their daughters, of course?'

'Of course.'

Another yawn was building and this time he let it out with an audible crack of his jaw. It had been another long and tedious evening and he wanted to go to bed, weary from the effort of juggling two ambitious mamas both vying for the same thing—himself.

'I wish you'd come to these dinners too, Mother. You're always invited. It would help divert some of the attention from me.'

'I'm afraid the presence of an old widow couldn't do that. Until you've taken a wife you'll be the most interesting man in the county, and there's nothing I or anyone else can do about it.'

The fire had died down and Lady Gouldsmith leaned over to take up the poker, deliberately looking away from her son as she prodded the flames. It was glaringly obvious what she was about to ask, and Andrew wondered how she'd phrase it this time, the same question as always but delivered in a hundred different ways.

'So...still nobody has caught your eye?'

He'd meant to laugh at her predictability but tonight it caught in his throat. For the first time since they'd arrived back in Warwickshire he might have answered *yes*—although the woman on his mind for the past two days had not been among those seated around Captain Maybury's grand dining table.

Miss Emily Townsend would never receive an invitation to such a gathering, Andrew thought, as he watched his mother cast a length of kindling into the fire. Captain Maybury and his fine friends would never have heard of her, far too refined to know anything of unfashionable Brigwell or its residents, and even if they had she would *not* have made the guest list. In her faded gown she wasn't anywhere near smart enough and her plain speech would amuse them, and the fact she didn't even know who her father was placed her miles beyond the pale.

*And yet to me none of that seems to matter. If anything, it makes me like her all the more.*

He let his head rest against the back of his chair, gazing up at the firelight moving over the ceiling. The image of copper-gold hair and flushed cheeks had lingered ever since he had left Emily at the side of the road. It flickered before him now, a pair of bright blue eyes joining the attack. They had been made raw by crying and the sympathy he'd felt then came again as—not for the first time—he allowed their meeting to replay itself through his tired mind.

It wasn't just money she'd wanted from her father, he was certain. It had been to know the man who bore half the credit of making her, someone that, despite the passing of more than twenty years, he still felt his own loss of every single day. The initial wound had closed over but a scar remained, and he knew how easy it would be to tear it open again, grief fading into the background but never fully going away. Miss Townsend had known her own unhappiness and that made them the same, in a way, and he suspected that they could have grown to understand each other if only they'd had the chance to try.

*But we won't have one.*

Andrew frowned up at the ceiling, surprised by the sudden intensity of his disappointment.

*She's leaving Brigwell in a few days and then I shan't see her again.*

He sat forward, hoping his mother had missed the pinch of his brows. 'My circle boasts many young ladies now, all of them amiable, but there's nothing on which to build a connection. Our lives have been too different to find much common ground.'

Lady Gouldsmith nodded as she propped the poker back in its place beside the hearth. 'A solid foundation is important for a successful marriage. I would not have you wed where you couldn't agree, even if the lady was the richest woman in all of England.'

'Money doesn't come into it. I've enough now to last several lifetimes—I can't see that I need any more, even if to say that would make my uncle turn in his grave.'

At the mention of Ephraim a shadow crossed his mother's face. The previous Lord Breamore had strongly disapproved of his younger brother's choice of bride, determined that any marriage should have been to the advantage of the family coffers. Mother's only fortune had been her face and good nature, however, and Ephraim had never forgiven her for it, his decision not to help her after Father's death rooted in resentment he'd carried until his very last day.

'How that man and your father were brothers I shall never understand. I'm glad a woman's money matters little to you. Your father was the same, and although we paid the price for it later I wouldn't have had him any other way.'

'Nor I.' Andrew slowly shook his head, thoughts of Emily still lingering. 'It was difficult at times but I'm grateful for what that taught me. I don't need carriages and expensive clothes to be content, and I'd like the same to be true of my wife.'

'That would be a fine thing. As your mother I only ever want you to be happy…although, of course, as the latest Lord Breamore, it's also necessary for you to produce an heir.'

Lady Gouldsmith slid her son a hesitant glance from beneath the lace edge of her cap, the dark eyes they shared glinting with reflected firelight. 'Your father and I weren't granted time enough to provide you with siblings. Unlike your late uncle you have no nephew to save you from matrimony, and it would be a shame indeed if your father's name were to die out.'

She spoke lightly but Andrew could hear her sincerity. Uncle Ephraim had done little to garner admiration, but Father had been a good man. He deserved for his legacy to live on, and besides, it would be a wonderful thing to have a family again. The five short years he'd had with both his parents had been the happiest of Andrew's life, and he found he wanted to recreate it himself, the building of a better future perhaps the best cure for a sad past.

The romance of his parents' relationship was something he would have liked to experience, although now a love match was out of the question. As mere Andrew Gouldsmith he'd had the luxury of time, able to wait for as long as it took to find a woman who could capture his heart, but for the Earl of Breamore duty must come first. He owed it to his father's memory to wed quickly, setting his own desires aside for the sake of the man whose life had been cut so tragically short. All that remained was for him to attempt to find a wife, among those with whom he was supposed to feel more commonality than his early years meant he ever could.

'I've no intention of letting it. I'll marry as soon as I've found a woman with whom I feel at least some accord.'

He pressed his fingers against his eyes, feeling some slight relief from an ache growing behind them. He'd drunk too much again. It was beginning to be a pattern, and not one he wanted to continue, his dislike of the Society events he was obliged to attend making him seek solace in the bottom of his glass. If he wasn't careful he might end up doing something unwise next time and then he'd be known as the scandalous Earl rather than the desirable one, although the idea of escaping the determined mamas that hunted him was almost enough to make him consider downing an entire bottle.

'I'm going to bed. You'll go to yours now too, I hope?'

'Yes. I'll be able to settle now I know you've returned.'

His mother rose and Andrew followed her back to the front porch, pausing briefly to stoop and kiss her cheek before stepping out into the night. The door closed behind him and he heard the scrape of a key in a lock, and then the single light in the Dower House window was extinguished, leaving him alone in the dark.

For a moment he didn't move. The moon hung above him in a silvery arc and the stars winked back as he gazed up at them, enjoying the cool air on his skin. Captain Maybury's dining room had been loud and stifling and he relished the silence that surrounded him now, only the faraway cry of a fox interrupting the peace of the night. In the darkness he wasn't an Earl or a gentleman or anything else someone might label him. He was just Andrew, standing still looking up at the stars, and he found himself wondering if Emily was doing the same.

*Of course she's not. She's far too sensible to be loitering outside at this time, catching her death of cold.*

He'd definitely drunk too much if that was what he was thinking, he rebuked himself as he turned towards the Hall. Miss Emily Townsend would be tucked up in bed by now, her beautiful hair probably bound up in a braid and her eyelashes sweeping down onto smooth cheeks, and for a split second the mental picture made it difficult to concentrate on climbing the front steps.

She might be softer, somehow, in a nightgown, less stiff than when she'd sat in front of him on the horse and he'd locked an arm around her waist. That hadn't made the experience of holding her against him any less enjoyable, of course. She was still warm and the secret sweep of her waist was still unmistakably womanly, and when the curve of her backside had fitted so neatly into the space between his thighs—

He grabbed the front door handle and pushed it open. It wasn't a gentlemanly thought and he tried firmly to leave it outside, attempting to turn his mind in a more respectful direction as he nudged the door shut behind him…

And then, quite without meaning to, he stumbled onto an intriguing idea.

The sound of a pianoforte being tortured floated up from the floor below as Emily folded her spare nightgown into a neat square, her bedroom window open to the fresh morning air. The rest of her belongings were already packed into the small trunk that lay open on her bed, and she placed the nightgown on top, her meagre possessions barely filling it halfway. All that remained was to fetch her books and winter cloak and that would be everything, a whole life able to fit in a case with room enough to spare, and as she straightened up she wished she could stow her unhappiness inside it too.

There was a brief pause in the strangled Mozart. Probably Miss Laycock had just brought her fan down sharply over the knuckles of whichever unfortunate girl was currently struggling her way through and, despite her despondency, Emily felt a flicker of sympathy. Music lessons with Miss Laycock were often fraught affairs and her own knuckles had paid the price more than once, although at this moment she would have gladly suffered the same thing again if it meant she didn't have to leave. In two days she would board a post carriage, and then another and another, riding a whole chain of the uncomfortable, rattling things until she'd left Brigwell far behind. And once at Mrs Swanscombe's house she'd face loneliness worse than any she'd known before.

The despair that was never far away placed its hand on her shoulder and she was powerless to shrug it off. The only positive she could think of was that her ankle felt better that morning, the stabbing pain now reduced to a slight ache, although even that scant silver lining ebbed when she recalled who had helped her at its peak.

With a sigh she sat down on the edge of her bed. Had she been right to tell Lord Breamore the truth? After his kindness to her she could hardly have refused, and surely his opinion of her hardly mattered. Even if she'd stayed on in Brigwell, an Earl wouldn't care about the life story of someone like herself. He'd been curious, no doubt, rather than truly interested, and would forget all about her now they were destined never to meet again. If he thought badly of her after hearing about her shame then it should make no difference…

So why, then, did she seem to care so much?

One corner of the trunk was digging into her back and she pushed it away, passing a hand over her face when she heard something inside it fall over.

She had other far more pressing concerns than what a near stranger thought of her. Her entire life was about to change and it was a waste of time to daydream about a man so hopelessly out of her reach, with his kind, dark eyes and hands strong enough to lift her into a saddle without breaking a sweat. Men like that weren't meant for women like her, and she'd be a fool to imagine he'd given her a second thought once she'd slipped down from his horse, their worlds so far apart there was no hope of bridging the gap.

A brisk knock brought Emily's head jerking up. She hadn't realised she'd placed it in her hands, and she stood up hurriedly as a face appeared around her bedroom door.

'There you are. You've a visitor waiting in the back parlour.'

The other young woman seemed almost as surprised by this development as Emily herself. In all her twenty-one years at the school nobody had ever come to call on her, and she frowned as if she'd just been told a particularly difficult riddle.

'What? Who is it?'

'A *man*. Andrew somebody. I didn't catch his last name.' The messenger paused, took half a step into the room and lowered her voice. 'If you come down quickly Miss Laycock might not see. I don't think she heard the bell above the din of Jane's playing and you could speak to him without her knowing.'

She raised her eyebrows meaningfully, although Emily continued to stare at her without any understanding whatsoever.

The only Andrew she knew was the local butcher's son. They'd exchanged perhaps ten words in as many years and even then only about a side of beef. Why he would come to see her was a mystery, but definitely one she preferred to solve without Miss Laycock breathing down her neck. Male visitors were strictly forbidden and her caller would be dismissed as soon as he was discovered, the doctor the only man ever allowed to darken the Laycock door.

'I'll come down now. You said he's in the back parlour?'

At an affirming nod Emily left the room, slipping silently out onto the landing. The sound of murdered Mozart showed no sign of stopping and she was glad of its cover as she crept down the stairs, careful to avoid the creaking tread at the bottom. The back parlour was situated behind the kitchen, in a leftover from the times a housekeeper had ruled the domain instead of Miss Laycock, and Emily felt her heart begin to beat faster as she stole down the corridor and tentatively—still unsure of what she might find—pushed open the door.

It was fortunate she wasn't holding anything. If she had been there was no way she wouldn't have dropped it when the man standing by the empty fireplace turned around, his face familiar but most certainly not the one she'd expected.

'Lord Breamore!'

His answering smile set her already skipping heart bounding even faster. 'Good morning, Miss Townsend. I hope you'll forgive me for calling unannounced.'

He bowed, as casually as if finding an Earl in the second-best parlour was an everyday occurrence. 'I thought it would be better not to use my title. For myself I couldn't care less whether the whole school knows who I am, but I guessed you'd prefer discretion.'

Lord Breamore—*Andrew*—smiled again but Emily didn't return it. The question of what he was doing there was so overwhelming it drowned out everything else—aside, perhaps, from the wish she'd thought to tidy herself up before leaving her room, acutely aware of a tea stain on the front of her apron. By contrast the Earl looked as immaculate as ever, his boots gleaming and hair perfectly arranged, the healed break in his nose the only flaw in his features and yet somehow managing to enhance them rather than the reverse…

A particularly discordant note from the distant pianoforte brought her back to her senses. Miss Laycock would be furious if she realised rules were being broken. Emily stepped into the room, hastily shutting the door behind her.

'It's an honour to have you here, my lord, but I'm afraid I'm not allowed male visitors. The headmistress will be finishing her lesson soon and if she catches me with you she'll be severely displeased. Was there something you needed from me?'

What could have brought him there was impossible to guess. In his beautifully tailored coat and silk cravat he seemed as out of place as a thoroughbred in a field of ponies. She wasn't sure where to look, suddenly shyer in his presence than she'd ever been before.

*That's because you know how strong his hands are now,*

a little voice in the back of her mind piped up helpfully. *And how it feels to have his arm around you. It was firm and unyielding, and more muscular than you might have expected a gentleman's to be—*

Fortunately, Andrew didn't appear to have noticed how heat had rushed into her cheeks. He was still beside the unlit fire, the arm she was so enamoured of resting on the mantle, and to her surprise he now seemed somewhat ill at ease himself.

'If time's short I won't waste it. I came with a proposition—or, more precisely, a propo*sal*.'

'Of what kind?'

He glanced at her, a swift flit of his dark eyes that sent a thrill skittering down her spine. 'Perhaps you'd like to sit before I continue?'

'I'd rather stay here by the door, sir. If I hear Miss Laycock coming I can intercept her while you slip out through the kitchen. I know from experience that her lessons can end abruptly.'

Andrew inclined his head, a slight crease appearing between his straight brows. His air was definitely bordering on the uncertain now. He gave the impression of one teetering on the brink of something, one finger unconsciously tapping the top of the mantlepiece.

'Very well. It's a proposal of the usual kind a man might make a woman.' The Earl paused for a moment, his finger abruptly ceasing its restless twitch. 'Marriage.'

Emily blinked.

*How funny. I could have sworn he just said 'marriage'.*

'I'm sorry, my lord. I must have misheard you.'

'No. I think you heard me perfectly.'

She felt her face slacken into blank incomprehension. Her ears had caught the words, yes, but she couldn't grasp what they meant, and she stared at him, wondering what other definition of marriage he could possibly be referring to. It couldn't be the one *she* knew, with the church and the rings and the 'til death us do part, and her confusion only grew when he came closer, and slowly, as if being careful not to frighten her into running away, reached out to take her hand.

'I'm in earnest. If you'll have me, I'd like to make you my wife.'

His hand was bare, she realised dimly, and warm where hers was cold. He must have removed his glove at some point and his skin against hers set fireworks wheeling through her insides, each one trailing countless sparks. On the day he had lifted her onto his horse she'd felt the power in his grip, although now it was gentle, allowing her to pull away if she chose, but as she looked up at him and saw the honesty in his eyes she knew that she would not.

'But...*why*?'

It was the only response she could think of, and one Andrew seemed to have been expecting, a ghost of the smile he'd flashed when she'd entered the room reappearing to draw her attention sharply to his mouth.

'That's a fair question. I think I'd say the same if someone I'd only met twice before offered me their hand.'

He still held hers and Emily felt herself begin to burn, aware his palm was big enough to eclipse her fingers within it.

'Do you want to be sent a hundred miles away?'

His unexpected bluntness startled her into honesty. 'No, sir.'

'Would you rather stay in Warwickshire and perhaps continue the hunt for your father?'

'Why...yes.'

'If you decided to marry me, I could help you with both of those things.' Andrew's voice was level, neither wheedling nor pushy and speaking with the quiet frankness of a man telling the truth. 'You said your father was a Lord. As my Countess and the mistress of Huntingham Hall you'd have access to every high-ranking man in Warwickshire and could easily carry on your search. For my part I am in need of a wife and, having met many, *many* of the young ladies in this county, I've come to the conclusion that my best match would be you.'

He nodded as if to emphasise his point and Emily watched him, hoping her face wasn't that of the simpleton she currently felt. He was offering her everything she wanted in the whole world and yet she couldn't make herself understand, her mind working at a far slower pace than her racing heart.

'I don't… How could I possibly be a good match for you? For an Earl?'

'As I said, I've met many young ladies since I came to take my inheritance. In general they've been pleasant, accomplished and credits to their families, but that is not what I want.'

A shade flitted over his handsome face, half a second and then it was gone, a nameless emotion Emily saw with shock-glazed eyes. 'You see an Earl when you look at me, but I didn't grow up with wealth. My mother and I knew what it was to count every penny and, as such, I feel little kinship with those who might be thought of as my peers. I don't place great value on having a new carriage every year and I'd like my wife to be the same—someone who has lived in the real world and understands it, and is grateful for things money can't buy.'

He looked down at her, serious now, with no trace of a smile, and Emily felt something twist.

Surely the whole thing was folly, still so unlikely she half suspected she was dreaming. She couldn't marry an Earl no matter what he said—it just wasn't *done*, the chasm between them too wide and too dark for anyone of her station to cross. For all his sweet words and the undeniable attraction that had her in its thrall, he was still above her, from a sphere entirely separate from her own, and the sudden desire to abandon all good sense and go along with his madness was only just held in check by the equally strong knowledge that he would regret his choice as soon as it was made.

'I can't.'

Her throat was dry. 'I thank you for your offer, my lord, but I can't accept. It would shame you to marry me. I couldn't allow your reputation to suffer for my sake.'

Andrew shook his head, his brows knitting together again in a frown so determined she wanted to trace it with her fingertips.

'I don't see why it would. Nobody outside of Brigwell knows you, and certainly none of my new circle. You'd have the chance to reinvent yourself, should you choose. Whatever version of Emily Townsend you wished to be would be up to you.'

Very gently he increased the pressure on her hand, drawing

her towards him, and Emily found she couldn't stop herself from allowing it.

For all her conscious mind's warnings, her baser instincts cut through the fog of her sluggish mind, instructing her to obey the quietly insistent pull of Andrew's fingers. It was magnetic, unfightable, and when she stepped near enough for him to take her other hand she thought her leaping heart might burst out through her ribs.

'Do you really think I could stand beside you and feel shame?' he murmured, his gaze holding hers and refusing to let go. 'Knowing your circumstances makes me respect you more, not less. If I can look past your station, past the things about yourself you cannot change, do you think you could do the same for me?'

His face was very near to hers. Probably she should pull away, some tediously puritanical part of her thought, pretending offence that he presumed to get so close, but such a thing was impossible. If he leaned down just a fraction more he could kiss her, something no man had ever done before, and only the most untimely of interruptions stopped Emily from losing her head entirely and rising up to kiss *him* instead.

Far too late she realised the pianoforte had stopped its tuneless tinkling. The door behind her had opened and she hadn't even noticed, too spellbound to focus on anything but Andrew's scandalously enticing mouth, but Miss Laycock's cry sent her flying back from him as though she'd been scalded.

'What is this? Who is this man?'

Even the Earl seemed slightly taken aback as the headmistress stormed into the room, although Emily had to marvel at how quickly he recovered.

'Good morning, Miss Laycock. My name is Andrew Gouldsmith.' He gave a sweeping bow, the very image of well-bred charm. 'Please forgive my calling. There was something I needed to speak to Miss Townsend about that was too important to be delayed.'

At the mention of his name Emily felt her stomach drop, already writhing like a bag of snakes. If Miss Laycock realised she had somehow crossed paths with an Earl there would be hell to pay, but the schoolteacher merely primmed up her mouth, evidently failing to connect the name with the title it disguised.

'It didn't look much like speaking to me.'

Turning her back on him she reached to take hold of Emily's arm. 'Come away at once. This is a disgrace. You'll return to your room and stay there until the carriage comes for you, and I don't want to see your face downstairs again before you leave.'

Angry fingers brushed her sleeve but Emily pulled away, for the first time in years failing to jump to do as she was told. Miss Laycock stood on one side of the door and Andrew on the other, and Emily took a step towards him, the same magnetic pull that had drawn her into his grasp guiding her again to move closer to his side.

She risked a glance up at him. He was watching intently as she made her choice, his eyes never leaving her face, and the unspoken encouragement she saw there made everything fall into place.

She'd never expected to marry. The lonely life of a governess was all she'd ever envisioned for herself, on the off-chance Lord *Somebody* never came to claim her, and it had seemed foolish to aspire to more when Miss Laycock had always made it seem so inevitable…but with Andrew things could be different. For the first time in her existence she could have a real home and help to find her father, at last able to know his love as she'd yearned to since she was a neglected child, and with growing wonder at her uncharacteristic defiance, Emily lifted her chin.

'Please give my apologies to Mrs Swanscombe, but I won't be taking the position of governess. I hope she won't be too inconvenienced.'

'What? Whyever not?'

Miss Laycock's eyes flashed. Beside her Emily felt Andrew move and then the snakes in her stomach turned to butterflies as his finger traced the lightest of reassuring touches across her wrist.

'What do you think you'll do instead? If you think for one moment you can stay here, you can't. I've told you before I don't offer charity.'

The headmistress glared but somehow her displeasure had

lost its power to make Emily shiver. There was nothing to fear from that wrath any longer, she realised, not now Andrew stood so close beside her, that smallest of touches enough to make her want so much more—and she could have it, if only she was brave enough to say the words out loud.

'I don't want charity, ma'am. I'm still leaving, but of my own choice. I hope you'll be happy to hear I'm going to be wed.'

# *Chapter Four*

Staring up at the unfamiliar ceiling of an unfamiliar bedroom, Emily wondered if she'd taken leave of her senses.

A maid had come to help her dress—*another* unfamiliar development—but she hadn't yet gathered the courage to go downstairs. Once she set foot outside her new bedroom she would have truly begun her first day as a resident of Huntingham Hall's Dower House, and the bizarreness of the fact seemed to have rendered her unable to stand up. She wasn't sure exactly how long she'd spent lying fully clothed on top of the most comfortable bed she'd ever experienced, but it was probably too long, the clock on her bedside table ticking the minutes away accusingly, and it took all her self-control not to bury her head beneath her pillow and stay there.

Instead, however, she forced herself to sit up. Lord Breamore's mother would be at the breakfast table and it would be unforgivably rude to keep her waiting, especially as she'd been gracious enough to take a stranger into her home. Her face had been a picture of shock when her son had brought Emily to her door the previous evening, but to Lady Gouldsmith's credit she had collected herself quickly, any surprise hidden behind hospitality that Emily couldn't quite tell was genuine or forced.

'Either way, you can't stay up here all morning,' she mumbled now towards the ceiling's elaborate cornicing. 'Like it or not, it's time to go down.'

A mirror hung above her washstand and, finally dragging herself to her feet, she glanced at it, immediately wishing she hadn't when her eye fell upon the sleeve of her gown. She'd neatly repaired a small rip in it but the mend was still visible, and she grimaced to wonder whether her hostess would notice. Lady Gouldsmith would be dressed impeccably, no doubt, drawing more attention to the difference between them that the Earl seemed so determined to overlook, and once again Emily questioned whether she had made a catastrophic mistake.

*He said he didn't grow up with wealth, but surely what one considers wealthy is subjective? An Earl might consider himself impoverished if he only had three footmen instead of ten, without ever knowing what it's really like to live on slender means.*

The one thing he had decided they had in common wasn't really true at all, she thought as she tried to tuck a stray thread out of sight inside her cuff; and surely as Lord Breamore got to know her he'd come to that conclusion himself. Every moment she spent with him would be an opportunity for him to realise his mistake, which was unfortunate, considering that to spend more time with him was exactly what she wanted.

*I'll have to be more careful.*

Getting carried away would be unwise, she tried to tell herself as she headed for the stairs. The Earl had thrown her a lifeline and she was grateful for it, but she shouldn't let that gratitude—or the attraction to her bewildering new fiancé, which showed no signs of diminishing—cloud her judgement. Lord Breamore had made his offer to her based on an assumption and she had accepted out of necessity and temptation, and that was not a firm enough foundation for anything more. Until both of them had a better understanding of who they were marrying it would be sensible to exercise restraint, although as Emily reached the bottom of the stairs she couldn't stop her heart from making a sudden, excited leap.

Voices were issuing from the dining room, one of them so deep and delightful she recognised it at once. Clearly the Earl had come to take breakfast with them and Emily stopped in her tracks, caught between running back the way she'd come and pushing on into the room. The door was slightly ajar, the low conversation taking place beyond it *just* audible, and without intending to she found herself listening as she groped for the courage to go in.

Lord Breamore's voice came alongside the clink of metal against China. 'How is Emily this morning?'

'I couldn't tell you. She hasn't yet been down.'

'Perhaps she didn't sleep well.'

'Perhaps. Such a drastic change of surroundings would make it difficult for anyone to get much rest.'

There was a pause in which Emily barely breathed, still unable to move either forwards or back. She'd hardly spoken to Lady Gouldsmith since arriving at the Dower House, pleading exhaustion as an excuse to retire early the night before, and with such scant acquaintance it was hard to tell whether the other woman's remark held any kind of reproach.

It seemed the Earl was wondering the same thing. 'You disapprove?'

'Of course not. She seems a sweet girl, if entirely out of her depth—which is why I'd urge caution.'

A sensation not unlike a trickle of icy water crept down Emily's back. She *was* out of her depth, and the situation *was* strange enough to require caution, and to hear it said out loud made her feel as though the Earl's mother had found a window into her mind.

'You know the *ton* only care for their own,' Lady Gouldsmith continued, entirely unaware Emily now hung on her every word. 'Your uncle was furious when your father married me, a gentleman's daughter with a modest dowry, and Miss Townsend's background is far more uncertain than that. If you bring her into this world I hope you're prepared to protect her from what might follow, especially given the disadvantage from which she begins.'

For a moment there was quiet.

'If anyone asks about her past, we'll tell the truth.' Lord Breamore's deep voice was level. 'That she lost her parents as a child and was brought up by respectable people. There's no need to go into more detail to satisfy idle curiosity.'

'You might find that easier said than done.'

A gentle splash suggested Lady Gouldsmith was pouring herself a cup of tea as well as dispensing wisdom. 'Just be sure to take good care of her. It would be sad indeed if she found herself having escaped one unfortunate future only to stumble into another.'

Emily drew back from the doorway, not wanting to hear any more. Her heart was beating hard enough that she could feel it in her ears, and a knot sat in her stomach like a fist, clenched so tight the idea of eating breakfast held no appeal at all.

Clearly the Earl had already shared the private details of her background with his mother. He would have had to eventually, of course, but somehow knowing the elegant woman on the other side of the door was aware of her shameful origins made the fist grip harder still. Lady Gouldsmith evidently had her reservations about the match and, although she'd spoken kindly, she hadn't *quite* given it her blessing, managing to shoot an arrow directly into the centre of all Emily's uncertainties.

Before she could consider the matter further, however, a movement behind her caught her attention. A maid was crossing the hall and quickly Emily stepped back towards the door. The servants were probably already whispering about her, and being seen eavesdropping wouldn't help make a good impression, something that currently seemed very important as she squared her shoulders and—reluctantly—tapped on the door.

The voices on the other side ceased immediately. There was a short pause and then a chair scraped against a wooden floor as someone got to their feet, boots coming nearer as the unseen person came to answer her tentative knock—

The door swung open and for the briefest of beats the Earl's smile chased away all her fears.

'Ah. Good morning.'

He gave a slight bow, his crisp white shirt dazzling in the sunlight streaming through a window at his back. She couldn't see past him, his tall frame filling the doorway, although even if they'd been the same height his face made it impossible to look anywhere else.

'You don't have to wait to be allowed in. Until the wedding, we'd like you to consider this your home.'

At Miss Laycock's establishment the girls had been required to knock before entering any room, probably to stop them from becoming too comfortable, but Emily didn't tell him that. His welcoming smile had fleetingly loosened the vice in her innards, but it tightened again at the thought of the school, the place she *should* have woken that morning if the world hadn't been turned upside down.

'I'm sorry, my lord. Force of habit.'

'Andrew. I'm not "my lord" or "sir" any longer. I'd like you to call me by my name, if that's acceptable to you?'

He looked down at her in polite inquiry. He was very close and she could see where he had recently shaved, the skin of his jaw slightly pink from the razor's edge. The cleft in his chin she'd noticed the first day they met was more obvious when he was freshly shaven, and she realised she'd been looking at it for a fraction too long when the lip above it began to curve.

Hurriedly she nodded. 'Of course.'

'I'm glad to hear it. Will you sit down?'

Andrew stood aside and she scuttled past, careful not to brush against him. A place had been set for her at the table and, with a curtsey to Lady Gouldsmith, she sat down, intensely aware that Andrew's chair was right next to her own.

His mother smiled, genuinely, as far as Emily could tell. She'd been just as kind the night before and it seemed she was keen to put her guest at ease, even if she harboured doubts not intended to be overheard.

'Good morning, Miss Townsend. Or, following Andrew's example, perhaps you'd prefer I call you Emily?'

First names were less formal and therefore marginally less frightening, and Emily nodded at once.

'Yes, Lady Gouldsmith. Please do.'

'Oh, but we must be fair. There's no need to use my title around the breakfast table, surely. We'll be Emily and Eleanor here—although once you're wed, of course, you might find you *like* being called Lady Breamore.'

She smiled again and Emily tried to return it, although her face suddenly felt as though it were carved from marble.

*Lady Breamore.*

Even Andrew taking his seat beside her, accidentally brushing her arm as he sat, couldn't entirely distract her. Somehow in all the confusion of the past few days she hadn't fully grasped exactly what becoming his wife would mean, and for a moment she felt almost dizzy, the change from an illegitimate girl to a Countess far too huge to take in one leap.

'I can guess what you're thinking.'

Eleanor was watching her, one eyebrow raised knowingly. 'I wasn't born Lady anything either. I gained my title on marriage, just as you will, and I remember how strange it felt the first time someone said it. You'll get used to it, though, and more quickly than you'd imagine.'

With an encouraging nod she reached for a tray of cold ham, leaving Emily to stare down at her own empty plate. There were plenty of things with which to fill it but she couldn't bring herself to take any, anxiety making her feel unable to eat so much as a crumb.

'Can I pass you something?'

Andrew's voice was very close to her ear. There was something unexpectedly reassuring in it—more the depth than the innocuous question, and she busied herself in spreading her napkin over her lap as she tried to rein in her nerves enough to answer.

As Lady Breamore she would have a much better chance at finding her father, she reminded herself firmly. Wasn't that why she'd taken this path in the first place, to meet the one person she had long since convinced herself loved her as she had always wanted to be loved? Andrew was a risk, an attractive one she doubted could ever turn into something more, but her father was a far more certain prospect. Even if her husband ended up regretting her, she was sure her papa never would, and now that she had taken the first steps on this unexpected journey she had to stay the course.

She glanced to the side, feeling her nape prickle when she met Andrew's eye. He was waiting for her to say something and she quickly scanned the table, seizing on the first thing she saw despite not being hungry in the least.

'Yes, please, my lo—Andrew. Perhaps a piece of toast?'

She hardly took more than a mouthful, Andrew saw as he sat back in his chair and drained the dregs of his coffee. Few remnants remained of his own breakfast but Emily's plate still held almost all of her toast, crumbled to appear smaller, although the definitive way she set down her knife suggested she'd finished. Either she always ate like a bird or something had stolen her appetite, and he realised—with slight discomfort—he didn't know her well enough to tell which was the truth.

*And yet we're to be married.*

It was still a good idea despite some small uncertainties, he told himself. The reasons he'd given her for their match were sound even if he felt some natural hesitation now that there was no turning back. Emily wanted a home and the chance to find her father, and he wanted a sensible wife who understood money wasn't a God-given right, and they had both made the right choice given the limited other options available to them.

Hadn't they?

Unwilling to dwell on the question, it was a relief when his mother posed one of her own.

'Do you have any plans for today?'

'I thought I might show Emily the grounds.' He turned to her with as careless a smile as he could manage. 'If you wanted to see them, that is?'

'Yes. I'd like that.'

She nodded, her piled-up hair swaying slightly as she moved. It was dressed more neatly than he'd seen it before, a few curls artfully arranged around her face to show her features to their best advantage, and he made a mental note to reward whichever maid was responsible. The style emphasised the almond slant of her eyes—the same soft blue as a hydrangea in full bloom, he'd already decided—and when she fixed them on him he felt his prior reservations waver.

Their rapid engagement would be even more difficult for her to adapt to than for himself. Leaving his modest life in Derbyshire and taking his place among the *ton* was an uncomfortable adjustment for him, but he had at least known it would happen eventually, aware of his position as Ephraim's heir since he was a child. For Emily there had been no such time to prepare. Blindsided by his proposal, she had agreed to become his wife without any real understanding of what she was agreeing *to*, acting out of necessity above anything else, and it was now his job to make sure she didn't come to regret it. Wedding a stranger was a gamble for both of them but she had more at stake, her decision to marry him catapulting her into a world she'd never set foot in before. He ought to spend less time contemplating his feelings and more time trying to help her with a transition that must have been like something from a dream.

'Good. If you'll excuse me for a short while, I have a letter to finish. Shall I call for you again in an hour?'

Another nod was his cue to rise from the table. Pushing back his chair he prepared to stand—but a warm touch on the back of his hand made him stop dead.

'I'm sorry. I was trying to move out of the way.'

Emily shuffled in her seat, the leg of her chair somehow caught on his. In attempting to detach herself, however, she instead leaned closer still, her arm brushing his hand again and her flushed face suddenly so near he had to act quickly to curb the first thought that came to mind.

He was still too late.

In the school's back parlour he would have kissed her and the picture came to him now, flaring vividly in spite of his attempt to hold it back. With her chin tilted and eyes wide Emily had been the most tempting thing he'd ever seen—and what was more he could have sworn she'd *wanted* him to bend his head and claim her, her lips slightly parted and breath coming shallow and fast. She might only have accepted his proposal as an alternative to exile, but in that moment at least she had felt something stir, he was certain of it, and if he'd managed it once there was hope he could do it again. A marriage of convenience didn't necessarily have to mean a marriage devoid of desire—although that wasn't something to consider in detail while his mother sat opposite, watching with amusement barely concealed behind her teacup.

At last, after what felt like far too much of a struggle, Andrew unhooked his accursed chair and stood up. Emily was far too busy rearranging her cutlery to return his bow but his mother smiled up at him...perhaps slightly too knowingly, he thought uneasily, not entirely comfortable with the expression in her dark eyes as she watched him leave the room.

Emily was already waiting for him when he had finished his letter an hour later, the hairstyle he so admired now hidden beneath a shabby bonnet as she hovered in the Dower House's porch. If she was to be a Countess she would have to be dressed like one eventually, although that was a concern for another time. Today he would begin by easing her into what was to be her new home, starting with the prettily unthreatening grounds, and Andrew made sure not to let his eyes wander to her more frayed edges as she descended the front steps.

'Ready to survey your new domain? Or the outside of it, at least?'

'Yes. I'm looking forward to it.'

She followed him to the gate that separated his mother's more modest garden from Huntingham Hall's sprawling back lawns. They reached out seemingly endlessly, punctuated with manicured hedges and paths bordering flowerbeds filled with colour, the grass sloping gently downwards until it met a line of trees at the very edge of the park beyond. To one side an artificial lake reflected the clouds gathering overhead, the sunshine that had been present at breakfast now fast disappearing, although even the increasingly brooding light couldn't dim the beauty before them as Andrew paused to allow Emily to savour her first glimpse of what she would soon call her own.

'What do you think?'

Her petal-blue eyes were round. 'This...all of this...is yours?'

'That's right. The parkland behind those trees makes up the rest of the estate.'

'The rest of the estate? There's more?'

'Yes. Just a few hundred acres.'

She'd risen on tiptoe, peering around her from the paved patio that afforded an elevated view down to the water, and for a moment he feared she might lose her balance.

'A few hundred? A few *hundred acres*?'

'It used to be much more before my great-grandfather inherited. Apparently his tastes ran to expensive women, wine and horses and he had to sell off some farms to cover his debts.'

Emily's lips parted in wordless disbelief. Her amazement couldn't have been more different from the feigned nonchalance of the young ladies of the *ton*, and he found he much preferred her willingness to show what she was really thinking. It was an impressive sight and he was glad she didn't try to pretend it wasn't, still just as struck by it himself even after visiting year after year.

Her enthusiasm made his own rise to meet it.

'Come with me. I'll show you my favourite place when I was made to come here as a boy.'

He led her down a set of stone steps towards a path between two hedges, winding away from the shadow of the Hall. It reared up behind them like a mountain carved from pale yellow stone, its windows dulled beneath the clouds but still as magnificently many-eyed as a peacock's tail. Emily peeped back at it as they walked, as if she was worried it might rise from its foundations and come after her, and he was glad to have something up his sleeve as a distraction.

'In here.'

They turned into a kind of courtyard, the walls made from well-tended hedges that stretched above even Andrew's head. In the very middle of the gravelled space was a raised pond with a statue standing guard over it, some kind of Grecian figure he had no clue how to name, and he let Emily go ahead of him to look down into the water.

She leaned over the elaborately carved edge, at first not seeming to see anything, but then she gave a gasp.

'What—?'

'Uncle Ephraim's prized collection. Goldfish, imported all the way from Portugal.'

Emily glanced at him over her shoulder, eyebrows raised beneath the worn brim of her bonnet.

'Goldfish?'

At his nod she twisted to sit on the edge of the pool, one hand trailing at the surface of the water. Several bright, metallic shapes followed the dabbling movement and he saw her face light up when a greedy little mouth fastened on one fingertip, her delight so unselfconscious he couldn't look away.

'I've never seen anything like them. Then again, I suppose I shouldn't be surprised even your uncle's *fish* were gold.' She paused. 'I'm sorry. That was impolite.'

'But not uncalled for.' Andrew shrugged, unwilling to allow Ephraim to spoil the moment. 'He was extremely proud of them. Anything with even the slightest suggestion of value interested him very much indeed.'

He moved to stand beside her, watching as the gleaming fish cut effortlessly through the water. If he looked closely he could make out Emily's face reflected back at him, distorted by ripples, but the sudden soberness of her expression clear all the same.

'I feel I should apologise.' She traced a finger through a knot of pondweed, apparently either unmoved by its unpleasant texture or too set on her own thoughts to notice. 'For suggesting he was my father, I mean. I shouldn't have made assumptions about someone I never knew, and in doing so implying his conduct was not always…gentlemanly.'

Andrew shook his head. 'There's no call to apologise. If anything, to be considered was a compliment he didn't deserve.'

Emily didn't look up, her face still turned to the water. The rippling mirror showed she was frowning, and he sought to change the subject before the late Lord Breamore could spread even more unhappiness from beyond the grave.

'It should be me saying sorry. I haven't yet asked after your injury. With everything that's happened since it occurred, I realise I neglected to enquire.'

Still perched on the edge of the pond Emily flexed her foot, Andrew not quite managing to stop himself from taking an admiring glance at the flash of slender ankle. 'It's much better. Only a slight ache now rather than real pain.'

'I'm glad. I can't imagine you'd want to limp down the aisle.'

'Down the aisle.' She repeated the words slowly, more to herself than to him. 'How soon will that be?'

'It depends. To read the banns takes three weeks, but with a common licence we could wed within days.'

He tried to sound casual but knew he'd failed when her gaze flickered over him, towards and away again, as quickly as blinking. It was a conversation they had to have at some point, but he hadn't expected it quite so soon and he had no idea how to go about it. Planning a wedding was not something he'd imagined he'd be doing even a few days before.

'What would be your preference? As the bride-to-be?'

'I hardly know. If we waited for the banns that would at least give you more time.'

'More time for what?'

There was a pause, and then a deliberately downward tilt of her head hid her face from him, even her reflection now concealed by the peak of that blasted bonnet. 'To change your mind, should you wish.'

'Change my mind?' Andrew frowned. 'I have no intention of it. Unless...?'

A unpleasant sensation crept over him. Was she speaking of her own thoughts rather than trying to guess his, wanting to break their engagement almost as soon as it was made?

He leaned down, trying to see beneath the straw brim. She kept her eyes fixed firmly on the goldfish, however, refusing to allow him to read anything in them, and he was just about to press harder for an answer when he felt the first raindrop land squarely on the top of his head.

'Oh!'

Evidently Emily had just suffered the same experience. She jumped up as the pond's surface broke out into countless dimples, the fish turning to golden blurs as the rain began in earnest. The downpour was as heavy as it was sudden, and within seconds Andrew felt dampness beginning to spread over his back, his light summer coat ill-equipped for the barrage crashing down on their heads.

Emily squinted up at him. 'Should we run back to the Dower House?'

Her worn old bonnet was little match for the deluge. Already the curls around her face had darkened to bronze rather than gold, and she held her hands above her head in an ineffectual umbrella, the rain spattering onto her gown to mould the thin muslin to her shoulders.

'No need. There's a folly just through here we can shelter in until this passes.'

He turned for the far corner of the courtyard where another path led beneath a stone arch, Emily scurrying behind him. Beyond it a mock-Gothic ruin stood among a small knot of trees, its walls intentionally crumbling but the roof intact, and he waved her inside just as the first rumble of thunder sounded somewhere far away.

Leaning against one wall he watched her trying to catch her breath. Her chest rose and fell rapidly and he had to make himself look away, her damp bodice clinging to her like a second skin. For all her angularity there was still a distinctly feminine curve to the swell of her bosom, and he turned his attention firmly to the ceiling, all too aware that a large part of him was reluctant to make the change.

For a short time neither spoke, only the drumming of rain on the roof breaking the silence between them.

Perhaps she was thinking about what she'd hinted at beside the pond, Andrew mused, studying a spider spinning its way down from a beam. He certainly was. His stomach felt as though someone had kicked it, an unsettling mixture of disappointment and unease. It had definitely seemed as though she was having second thoughts and he wondered at how instantly he had wanted to reassure her, his first reaction being the desire to talk her round…

'This is a beautiful little place. Did your uncle build it?'

He looked down. Emily was examining the arched windows, following the winding progress of a rose climbing through one empty frame. She seemed entranced, and not even the laughable idea of Ephraim being responsible for something so fanciful as a folly was enough to distract Andrew from her expression, no longer hidden by the bonnet she had removed while he was diligently looking elsewhere.

'No. My grandfather commissioned it for my grandmother as a wedding present many years ago. My uncle had no patience for anything even slightly romantic or whimsical—it's a miracle he never had it knocked down.'

'I'm very glad he didn't.'

She lifted her head to peer up at the ceiling, the movement revealing the pale line of her throat. It shone pearl-like in the grey light and Andrew found himself gripped by the desire to touch it, perhaps running one finger from her ear all the way down to the dip between her collar bones.

'If you like it that much, consider it yours.'

The air hung heavily, warm and richly scented with wet soil. All around them the sound of rain on the roof came in a constant pitter-patter like the rapid beating of a heart, mirroring Andrew's own as he turned to face her full on.

'So, Emily. Do you?'

'Do I what?'

'Intend to change your mind. As you suggested *I* might.'

He saw her throat move as she swallowed. A stray ribbon of damp hair hung at her ear and, without stopping to think, he reached out to brush it aside, his chest tightening when he heard her take a shaky breath.

Her eyelashes swept down but the rosy flush of her cheeks gave her away. They glowed almost as pink as her lips, her mouth drawing Andrew's gaze like a moth to a flame, and despite the overwhelming temptation to drop his head and kiss her he forced himself to hold back. If she was having doubts as to their marriage, then trying to kiss her would be the very worst thing he could do...but that didn't make it any easier to fight the urge, every fibre of his being now trained on that downturned face.

At last, she put him out of his misery.

'No.'

Her voice was low and not entirely steady. 'I think I made

the right choice. My only fear is you might come to think otherwise.'

'That's a worry you need not entertain.'

It was a struggle not to allow the relief that threaded through him to show on his face. She wasn't thinking of fleeing, then—only feeling the kind of natural uncertainty he himself had experienced that morning, although the depth of his relief gave him pause. Already it seemed he was set on the marriage going ahead, far more strongly than he'd realised, and he wasn't entirely sure how to feel at the knowledge his mind was apparently so firmly made up.

The rain continued to patter gently on the roof, the occasional droplet slipping through a gap to splash onto the floor. With Emily so close by the desire to kiss her lingered, and with great difficulty he stepped away, peering out of the window at the full-bellied clouds. It didn't seem as though the sun would be reappearing any time soon and they would have to make a run for it eventually, she back to the Dower House and he to the Hall, although soon there would be no need for them to part at two separate front doors.

The thought spurred him into action.

'Will you come to the Hall tomorrow afternoon?' He looked back at her, attempting not to notice how her damp gown still clung so tightly. 'I think it might help ease your mind if you were more familiar with it before moving in. My greatest wish is that in time it will start to feel like home—both to you and myself.'

'I'd like that.' Slowly, and far more endearingly than Andrew knew she intended, Emily smiled—still slightly uncertain but determined to be brave. 'I very much hope you're right.'

# Chapter Five

The moment she saw him at breakfast the next morning Emily knew something was wrong.

Andrew's fingers seemed to have a life of their own, tapping distractedly on the tabletop, his teacup and against the salt-shaker, and no sooner had she sat down than Lady Gouldsmith confirmed Emily's suspicions.

'You're fiddling. What's the matter?'

He looked up from his misuse of an innocent butter knife. For half a second he glanced at Emily, piquing her apprehension, but then he addressed his mother. 'Do you recall the date?'

'The fourteenth, I think. Why?'

'Ah. It seems that you, much like myself, forgot what that means.'

His hair was more disordered than usual, perhaps indicative of having an agitated hand pushed through it, and Emily only had a moment to note how such dishevelment suited him before he went on.

'Monroe just reminded me I'm supposed to host a card party this evening. Only a small one, something I agreed to weeks ago and subsequently disregarded given far more important things, but I can't back out of it now.'

He turned to her, the butterknife still balanced between two fingers. 'I'm sorry. I can imagine this is the last thing you want so soon, but I'm afraid my guests already know you're here.'

Emily felt herself pale. 'You wish me to attend a *ton* party? *Tonight?*'

Out of the corner of her widened eye she saw Lady Gouldsmith purse her lips. 'I forgot how quickly news travels when you have a lot of servants. It was only ever a matter of time before rumours began, and unfortunately an Earl's engagement is like manna for gossips.'

'But I can't.' Horrified, Emily looked to Andrew as if he might save her instead of being the one throwing her to the wolves. 'All those high-ranking people… I wouldn't know where to begin.'

'I'm truly sorry. If there was any way of avoiding this situation I would take it. We could say you were indisposed, but—'

'But that wouldn't lessen their curiosity one jot.' Eleanor finished her son's sentence with grim understanding. 'If you wanted to minimise the scrutiny around your engagement, as for certain delicate personal reasons I believe you would prefer, then we must try to avoid making you a point of interest. There are few things more intriguing than someone else's secrets, and if it seems as though Andrew is keeping you hidden away people will wonder why.'

Emily stared down at the tablecloth, trying to master her panic. In only a few hours she would have to walk into a room filled with the best and brightest of Warwickshire Society and pretend she belonged? Two days ago the only member of the *ton* she'd so much as said 'good morning' to had been Andrew, and now she was expected to be centre of attention for a whole crowd of them. The idea of having so many well-bred eyes on her made her want to shrivel in her chair.

'I thought I'd have more time to learn how to be a real lady before I had to be one in public. Such people will see immediately that I'm not one of their kind.'

The moment she set foot in the Hall her origins were sure to show themselves in a multitude of ways she didn't even know existed, probably from the way she spoke right down to the way she held a spoon. Tongues would wag and speculation begin in earnest, and all too soon Andrew would realise he'd made a mistake in bringing her there, the idea of causing him embarrassment making her insides feel like tangled rope.

Another realisation added the final touch to her unhappiness.

'All that aside, I have nothing fit to wear.'

Shame stole over her to admit it out loud, but it was the truth. Her limited wardrobe was comprised of dresses that had been made over so many times they were more patches than gown. Beside Andrew and Eleanor she would look like a scullery maid, and she felt her face grow hot to realise they must be thinking the same thing.

'Don't worry about that.'

Lady Gouldsmith came to the rescue, cutting through Emily's inner turmoil with genteel ease. 'I have dresses I'm certain will fit you. With a few tweaks I'm sure you'll outshine us all.'

There was a clatter as Andrew finally laid down the knife.

'Would you excuse me? There are things I need to see to before tonight. With your permission, we'll postpone your tour of Huntingham until another day.'

He stood up without looking at her, vaguely bowing to the room at large before striding to the door and disappearing. Emily watched after him with the knotted rope of her innards pulling tighter still.

She heard Lady Gouldsmith sigh. 'Off he goes. As I knew he would.'

'He did leave rather quickly.' Trying to sound calmer than she felt, Emily made herself take a slice of toast, although she knew there was scant hope of choking it down. 'I hope he wasn't angry that I had reservations about the party?'

'No, no. He would never be upset with you for that.' Eleanor shook her head, her face sombre as she reached for the teapot. 'You're not the only person wishing they didn't have to go this evening. Andrew dreads these occasions too and won't be easy until it's over and done with.'

'Is that so?'

Emily's surprise was met with a wry half-smile. 'Oh, yes. I think he feels almost as out of place among these people as you do. He might be an Earl now, but for years he considered himself quite the nobody.'

Carefully stirring a piece of sugar into her cup Eleanor gave another sigh, barely audible above the gentle clinking of her spoon.

'Sometimes, you know, I'm not sure which state he preferred.'

Night had fallen before Emily saw her fiancé again, by which time a transformation had taken place.

Andrew's eyes flickered wider as she ascended Huntingham Hall's front steps and came towards him, walking beside Lady Gouldsmith as stiffly upright as a jointed doll. Her borrowed dress was the most beautiful—and expensive—thing she'd worn in her life, and the fear of tearing it made her already heightened anxiety shoot skyward. Only the frank admiration in Andrew's flame-lit face stopped her from fleeing back to the safety of the Dower House.

'You look—'

He broke off as if finding the right word was momentarily beyond him. His eyes never left her, however, sweeping from the top of her befeathered head to the gauzy hem of her gown, and only his mother discreetly clearing her throat prompted him to try again.

'Forgive me. I know it's rude to stare, but I'd defy anyone to resist if they were to see you now.'

He bowed and Emily only just remembered to curtsey in reply. In the light of the torches on either side of the Hall's front door Andrew's features had taken on a new sharpness, the lines of his cheekbones and jaw thrown into relief by the shadows of the flames, and she marvelled that it was even possible for him to become more handsome than before. For herself she knew she had the borrowed gown to thank for any improvement in her appearance, giving it full credit for Andrew's flattering reaction, but it would be churlish to scorn a compliment just because it wasn't strictly deserved.

It was as if he'd read her mind.

'It isn't the dress every man in the room will be admiring

tonight, if that's what you imagine. You lend your charms to the gown—not the other way around.'

Andrew's smile was almost as dangerously delightful as his words. The two together nearly succeeded in making her already weak knees give way entirely, and it was only the timely intervention of Lady Gouldsmith that prevented an accident on Huntingham's front steps.

'Goodness. I had no idea I'd raised such a smooth-talking gentleman.' She arched an amused eyebrow at her son before squaring her shoulders like a soldier marching to war. 'I'll go in and mingle, shall I? I suppose at least one of us should pretend to be pleased to see your guests.'

She sailed inside, her voice rising to greet someone, leaving Emily and Andrew alone in the warm night air.

Unsure what else to do with herself, Emily smoothed down her skirts. They glistened in the torchlight, falling from just below her bosom in a cascade of pistachio silk that contrasted strikingly with the copper-gold of her hair. Every time she moved her head she could feel the strange weight of the ostrich feathers on top of her curls, a feat of engineering it had taken two maids to achieve, and she wondered how Society ladies could bear having so many pins sticking into their scalp. She might *look* more like one of them now but she *felt* as much a stranger in a foreign land as ever before, although some of her misgivings retreated into the background when Andrew held out his arm.

'I'm sorry for being so inattentive to you all day. I promise that from this moment on I won't leave your side.'

*That* was an agreeable prospect indeed, and she tried not to seem too eager as she slipped her fingers into the crook of his elbow and allowed him to draw her towards the door. It was a secret pleasure to be so near him again. His shoulder gently brushed the curls at one ear, setting the nerves there tingling, and the breadth of his forearm under her fingertips reminded her of the strength in his hands. Even the smell of him tempted her to take a deeper breath, soap and a woody undertone she didn't recognise, but was so unmistakably *him* that she found herself wanting to bottle it, although a swift glance at his face brought her growing fancies up short.

A casual observer might have missed the set of his mouth or faint hardness around his eyes, but to Emily both were plain as day. They hinted at unease, manfully concealed but impossible to hide completely, and as they stepped over the threshold and into the entrance hall her mind reeled back to recall what his mother had said only that morning.

*He doesn't want to do this either.*

Clearly he didn't feel quite at home among the *ton*, just as Eleanor had told her. She'd been sceptical when he had declared they had that much in common, but to look at him now she could see he'd been in earnest, catching a glimpse of the real man behind the glossy façade of an Earl. Something had happened to make him feel that way, and she wanted to know what it was, his life before he'd come to Warwickshire something she suddenly burned to understand. Whatever had occurred had forged a link between them that surely wouldn't have existed otherwise—but now was not the time to ask. The parlour door was before them, opening to show a roomful of faces turning in their direction, and all other thoughts were chased away when Andrew bent to murmur into her ear.

'This wasn't how I wanted your introduction to Huntingham Hall to be, but there might be a silver lining. You'll meet some of the highest-ranking men for miles around here tonight—one of which could be your father.'

The smile she'd managed to force froze painfully in place. Somehow that idea hadn't occurred to her, although at present she had no chance to consider it. The moment she entered the room it seemed as though everyone in it swung round to stare, strangers breaking off their conversations to peer at her, and the fact there were probably only twenty people in the parlour didn't stop it from feeling like a crowd of hundreds.

'Don't be afraid. As I said—I won't leave your side.'

Her fingers still lay in his elbow and her heart leapt as she felt him give them a reassuring squeeze. Evidently he was determined to set his own feelings aside to focus on hers, and

Emily found her throat had grown tight, unable to speak as the first of his acquaintances came forward.

In all the years she'd lived at Miss Laycock's mercy nobody had ever put her wellbeing above their own. She had never expected it, unsure how to grasp the notion, but that one gentle squeeze said more than any words. Andrew knew she was uncertain and afraid and was inviting her to rely on him, a prospect so perilously wonderful she didn't dare accept.

*You're not married yet.*

He'd said he wouldn't change his mind, that day in Huntingham's gardens when they'd sheltered from the rain—but how could he be so sure? There had to still be a risk, even if only a small one, that he could rethink their engagement before they were wed. A young lady of his own rank would be far better placed to help him fully find his feet among the *ton*, someone who could support him rather than the other way around, and until she had a ring firmly on her finger it wasn't safe to allow her hopes to carry her too far.

'Sir Montfort. May I introduce my fiancée, Miss Townsend?'

A man had materialised through her distracted haze and she made herself focus on him as he sank into a flourishing bow.

'A pleasure, madam.'

He straightened up, his silk cravat gleaming in the light of a chandelier swaying above them. 'We were surprised to hear of your sudden engagement, Breamore, but now I think everyone will understand why you had no desire to delay.'

The elderly knight nodded gallantly at Emily and she smiled weakly in reply. If the other man had known the truth, she was certain he wouldn't have spoken so approvingly, although it seemed he was by no means the only one intending to pay her the courtesy of an introduction. Over Sir Montfort's stooping shoulder she saw another man hovering, flanked by three women and a stylish couple who looked her up and down with undisguised interest, and she was very glad Andrew's arm showed no sign of loosening its grip on her hand.

'The Earl for less than two months and already you've bested your old bachelor of an uncle. Very well done.'

Sir Montfort clapped Andrew on the shoulder and withdrew,

his place taken immediately by a mother and daughter, who dropped into curtseys so deep Emily wondered how they kept their balance.

'Good evening, my lord. Thank you for inviting us to Huntingham.'

'You are always most welcome, Mrs Windham, and of course Miss Windham.'

Mrs Windham smiled tightly. Both she and her daughter were frighteningly fashionable. Their gowns must have cost a fortune, and despite the relatively informal occasion they glittered with jewels, earrings and necklaces that caught the light, making them twinkle like fallen stars. There was such glamour in their finery that Emily had to remind herself not to examine them too closely, so splendidly turned out that they reminded her of a pair of exotic birds she'd once seen in a travelling show.

As if sensing Emily's awe Miss Windham glanced across at her. She was extremely attractive, with golden hair and the effortless elegance of a woman who knew she was admired wherever she went, and Emily shrank slightly from her cool green gaze. Beside such a creature she felt more out of place than ever, like a child dressing up in her mother's clothes. Surely Miss Windham was the kind of young lady Andrew ought to have proposed to, a far better match for an Earl than she herself could ever be—although it seemed he still disagreed.

'Please allow me to introduce you. This is Miss Townsend.'

To her amazement, she thought she caught a trace of pride in his voice as he subtly brought her forward, refusing to allow her to half hide behind him. 'You may have heard we are recently engaged.'

'Indeed we did.'

Mrs Windham sounded far less pleased about the situation than Andrew. She allowed Emily a smile, a chilly stretch of her mouth that didn't reach her eyes. 'We heard a rumour, although as the news only reached us through a third party we weren't entirely sure it was true.'

If there had been pride in Andrew's voice, Mrs Windham's held ice. Evidently she was most put out to see undisputable evidence that her daughter would not be the next Lady Breamore, and it was left up to Miss Windham to smooth over her mother's obvious disapproval.

'Clearly it is, Mama. Congratulations my lord, Miss Townsend.'

With a neat curtsey Miss Windham took her mother's arm and drew her away, their skirts whispering behind them as they retreated, and Emily watched them go, the unease already sitting in her stomach beginning to flutter harder.

'I think perhaps Mrs Windham will not be a friend to me.'

'I think perhaps you might be right. But never mind.' Andrew shrugged, pausing to nod politely to a guest passing towards the card tables. 'She was once intent on marrying Uncle Ephraim, many years ago, so I'm not sure her opinion is worth much.'

The parlour door opened and closed repeatedly. More people arrived, the room growing hotter and louder as the evening progressed, and acquaintance after acquaintance came forward to meet their soon-to-be hostess. Every time Andrew waved towards her, with satisfaction that she could hardly dare to believe was genuine, introducing her to what felt like a never-ending stream of ladies and gentlemen, whose names she forgot almost as soon as they were revealed. It was like being in another world, the effort of playing the part so exhausting that her head began to ache, and only the knowledge that Andrew was pushing through his own discomfort to help with hers gave her the courage to carry on.

He was true to his word. He didn't leave her alone for so much as a moment, remaining a constant and reassuring presence at her side. Even when talking to someone else she could sense his awareness of her, never allowing himself to be distracted by anyone in the room, which was more than Emily could say for herself.

Andrew took up the vast majority of her focus—but not quite all of it.

She'd determined within the very first half-hour that there were four men in attendance who were the right age to be her father. Two of them she discounted at once, one whose hair was much too dark and the other with a complexion the handsome olive of the Mediterranean, although neither of the remaining two filled her with much confidence. One gentleman was fair, although the shape of his face was nothing like her own, and the last contender seemed too shy to have spoken to a woman in his life, let alone father an illegitimate child. On the whole she doubted any of the men beneath Huntingham's roof were who she was looking for, and her disappointment was bitter, not even a glass of sweet punch able to wash it away.

'Will you join us for a game of whist, Miss Townsend?'

A voice at her shoulder made her turn. A young man stood behind her, some baronet's son whose name she had been too nervous to absorb when told, and her worry piqued sharply at what should have been an innocuous request.

*Heaven help me. What do I do now?*

Was this how she was to be caught out? By a friendly game of whist, of all things? It was the kind of thing well-bred young ladies were born knowing how to play, probably, but she had no idea of the rules. Miss Laycock had frowned upon card games of any kind, believing them to be a gateway to gambling and sin, and for a moment Emily wondered if it was too late to turn and run. Any second now he'd realise she hadn't a clue, would think how odd it was for an Earl's fiancée to have such a gap in her accomplishments, and would begin to wonder why…

'Ah. I was actually just about to ask Miss Townsend if she would play for us,' Andrew cut in smoothly. 'There's a pianoforte just through there. You'd be out of sight, I'm afraid, but we'd still be able to hear you.'

He gestured towards a half-open door on the other side of the room, flicking her the briefest of glances that left her in no doubt that he understood her predicament, and she seized the lifeline at once.

'I'd be glad to. If you'd excuse me, sir?'

The nameless baronet's son bowed but she didn't stay to see it. The choice between being looked at by the *ton* or merely listened to was an easy one. She crossed the room as quickly as elegance allowed, for the first time in her life grateful for Miss Laycock's insistence that all her girls were forced into music lessons whether they liked it or not.

Slipping into the adjoining room she felt herself relax slightly.

The curious eyes that had tracked her all evening couldn't see through walls, and as she seated herself at the pianoforte—an extremely expensive looking instrument and definitely the handsomest she'd ever seen—some weight lifted from her chest.

It was unfortunate that none of the men present were likely to be her papa, but that didn't mean her search was a lost cause. To stumble across him during her very first foray into Society would have been unlikely, surely, and today's failure didn't necessarily mean more would follow. She would just have to keep her nerve, keep forcing herself not to hide from the prospect of being seen by the very people she was afraid might see *through* her, and eventually she would find the missing piece she knew could make her whole.

She placed her fingers over the ivory keys, appreciating their cool smoothness before she took a breath and began to play.

The hum of conversation from the next room grew quieter. For a moment the only sound was melodic tinkling before the talking and laughter resumed, lower now to allow her audience to listen as they bent over their cards. Somehow knowing a roomful of landed gentry could hear her was less frightening than being required to play whist, and Emily let herself be borne away by the music, not realising someone had entered the room behind her until they came to sit beside her on the pianoforte's upholstered stool.

Startled, she looked up from her busy hands, although she knew instinctively who she would see.

'Don't stop playing. I just thought you might need someone to turn the page for you.'

Emily nodded, not quite trusting herself to speak. The stool wasn't large and there was no way for Andrew to stop his leg from touching hers, the long line of his thigh pressing against her skirts. To reach the music book he had to lean across her slightly, and she almost fumbled a wrong note when his cheek was suddenly before her, clean shaven that morning but now dusted with the lightest suggestion of stubble. The urge to see what it felt like rose so sharply she could barely hold it back.

It was essential she say something to break the tension building inside her, tension she knew must be one-sided. Andrew had come because he'd promised to stay by her side, not because he'd *wanted* to, and she grasped for the first thing that came to mind as she struggled to remember that dampening truth.

'I've been thinking. I'm not sure any of the gentlemen here tonight could be my father.'

She kept her voice down, her hands still moving with unthinking skill. For Andrew to hear her he had to lean closer, something that did nothing to help regain control of her wayward thoughts. 'None of them bear any resemblance to me in any form. I've looked and I really don't see any likeness at all.'

Out of the corner of her eye she saw him incline his head thoughtfully. 'I agree. I don't believe any one of our guests could claim the credit for your beauty.'

Emily's fingers slipped, a jarring note ringing out.

'I'm sorry.' Andrew sounded mildly amused, although there was an undercurrent of something else. 'Was that too forward?'

'No. I didn't… I don't mind.'

She stared down at the keys as if her life depended on it, not looking up even to read the music.

He could have said whatever he liked. The truth was that his mouth was so close that even curse words would have sounded sweet issuing from it. But he had instead called her beautiful, and she was in danger of swooning off the stool.

Her body had unconsciously begun to curve towards him, wanting to shrink the already slim gap between them down to nothing at all. One of his hands lay on his lap, the other raised waiting to turn the page, and she bit her tongue against the desire to feel them on her. With his leg still pressed against hers, and the edge of his cheek so near, she felt as though she was burning, only the necessity of keeping her fingers on the keys helping her to fight the feelings coursing through her like a flood; although no amount of Bach could drown out the insistent thought that ran unchecked through her head.

*I wish he'd kiss me. At this moment there's nothing I want more.*

*Don't kiss her. Do not kiss her.*

Andrew tried to concentrate on following the music, anticipating when to turn the next page, but it was damned difficult when half of his brain was busy with far more interesting things.

Every time Emily moved her arm grazed his, a continuous light touch that was impossible to ignore. She was all but sitting in his lap, the pianoforte's stool smaller than he'd anticipated, and he wasn't sure how much longer he could contain the ache to slide an arm around her waist. She seemed focused on the ivory beneath her fingers, now apparently determined not to look at him, but even that didn't make much difference. Her profile was just as pretty as when she faced him full on, the soft curve of her lips mere inches away, calling out to be kissed, and he clenched his jaw as he prayed for the strength to resist.

He was supposed to be shielding her from whispers rather than exposing her to them, he reminded himself, trying to heed his own wisdom as Emily's elbow accidentally caressed the inside of his arm. They might be engaged, but it would still draw comment if anyone were to look into the room and find them intimately entwined, and besides—hadn't he decided to take things slowly?

She'd expressed doubts as to their match once already and he didn't mean for it to happen again. In both appearance and behaviour her presence at Huntingham that evening had convinced him he'd made the right decision in choosing her above any highborn lady, and he found he was more determined than ever to see their engagement through.

If he hadn't already known she was uncomfortable to be among the *ton* he wouldn't have guessed. Her nervousness on entering the parlour had seemed the kind any young lady might feel on meeting a roomful of strangers, mostly concealed behind good manners almost as polished as those honed at court. For all her faults it seemed Miss Laycock hadn't stinted on lessons in decorum, and he'd felt an absurd amount of pleasure to see Emily receive the admiration she deserved, none of his guests suspecting for a moment that she was anything other than one of their kind.

*But she isn't.*

He dared a sideways glance at her, noting the perfect petal-like smoothness of her cheek as she kept her eyes trained immovably on the keys.

*She feels like me, an outsider acting a part. And unless I'm much mistaken I believe she's worked that out already.*

Probably his mother had hinted at the truth, but it wouldn't have taken Emily long to figure it out for herself. He hadn't wanted to attend this party either, despite it being under his own roof, and he had the feeling he'd done a poor job of hiding it at the breakfast table that morning. He had meant for his presence to be a comfort for *her*, not the other way around, but something about her hand on his arm made it easier to slip into the impenetrably well-bred shell of an Earl. The usual sensation of being the odd one out was absent with Emily beside him, no longer feeling like the only one in the room who had experienced life's harsher shadow, and as she came to the end of the piece, the pianoforte lapsing into silence, he considered if he ought to tell her so.

*I think not. Or at least not yet.*

There was a smattering of applause from the next room. Emily flexed her fingers but didn't resume playing, and he sensed her hesitate.

'Should I go on?'

'Please do. You play extremely well.'

A trace of colour crept into the cheek closest to him, pink against the strawberry-blonde ringlets at her ear. 'I don't know about *extremely*, but I'll continue if you wish.'

She lifted her arm to shuffle a new sheet of music to the front, the feathers in her hair waving as she moved. The maids must have spritzed her curls with rose water, the subtle floral sweetness tempting him closer still, and he wondered briefly if he would have to resort to sitting on his hands.

The smell of her, the barely perceptible warmth of her leg against his… It was a delight and a torment to sit so near yet be unable to touch her, and when he heard a light cough from the doorway it was almost a relief to stand up and move away.

'Andrew? A few of your guests are wondering where you went.'

Lady Gouldsmith's countenance was impassive as she withdrew again, for which Andrew was grateful, although Emily's face when she finally looked at him properly was enough to throw the innocence of the situation into doubt.

Her cheeks were flushed, for all the world as though she'd been caught doing something she shouldn't, and the thought almost brought him to his knees.

*Stop. Control yourself.*

'Do you want me to stay?'

He half hoped she would say yes, although he supposed the shake of her head was far less dangerous. 'You need to attend to your guests. I think I'm safe enough in here.'

'Very good.'

She gave him the smallest of smiles as he stepped back, turning her attention almost immediately to the sheet of music in front of her. There was a short pause, a rustle as she adjusted her skirts, and then the sound of the pianoforte beginning again ushered Andrew from the room.

He barely saw her again for the rest of the evening. She continued to play until refreshments were served, although by that time it seemed she had relaxed slightly. She no longer looked quite so worried when spoken to, and when his guests began to leave she even managed a convincing smile, perhaps not completely genuine but close enough for a passing glance.

'You don't have to do that.'

Leaning against the fireplace, Andrew watched her rearranging the cushions on the now empty sofa, fastidious as any well-trained maid. His mother had retired to bed shortly before and they were alone, the parlour quiet aside from Emily's well-intentioned—but entirely needless—attempts to tidy up.

'I can't help myself. At the school there would have been hell to pay if we'd left a room like this.'

She smoothed down an embroidered throw on the back of a chair, her practical domesticity at odds with the ostrich feathers and silk dress. Evidently it would take more than one card party for her to make the transition from school boarder to future Countess, although in Andrew's opinion that wasn't necessarily a bad thing.

'Was this evening as you'd feared?'

'No.' Straightening a stray antimacassar, Emily shook her head. 'Most of your acquaintances were very pleasant. I'm not certain whether they'd be quite so welcoming if they knew my true background, but they were by no means as frightening as I imagined.'

'I'm glad. I wouldn't have you distressed in what will soon be your own home.'

A large, tasselled cushion had fallen onto the floor near the fire, and slowly she moved to pick it up, bringing her closer to where Andrew leaned against the mantle.

For a moment she fiddled with the fringing, running her fingers through it as if untangling invisible knots. 'Miss Windham in particular was charming. Very pretty, too. And extremely well-dressed.'

Andrew nodded absently. She was within arm's length now, he estimated, close enough for him to see how her sandy eyebrows had drawn together slightly, her face angled away but her cheekbones glowing in the dying candlelight.

'I suppose she is.'

'Are you still quite sure…' She stopped, even her fingers pausing in their phantom unpicking.

'Am I quite sure…?'

'That you wouldn't prefer someone like her? Miss Windham?'

Her eyes were averted but he could sense her full attention was fixed on him. 'I know you said you had no intention of changing your mind, but now that I've seen the kind of woman you might have chosen…it makes me wonder.'

From beneath her lowered eyelashes Andrew thought he caught a flash of blue dart in his direction, but he was too preoccupied to pay it much mind.

*This again? Surely, after tonight…?*

He stood up properly, no longer lounging against the fire. At the movement she turned towards him, now looking at him rather than that damned cushion, and he felt the same desire to move closer to her he'd been fighting all evening stir with renewed vigour.

He took half a step towards her—and she didn't back away.

Hadn't she guessed he had no interest in any woman but her? He'd been trying so hard to control himself, but he wasn't made of stone, and as he looked down into Emily's uncertain face, now perhaps only a hand's breadth from his, he realised he had reached the end of his endurance.

'Never mind. Forget I said anything. Goodnight.'

Hurriedly she turned to leave the room—but his hand on her wrist brought her spinning back again.

For a split second confusion flared in her eyes, but they closed the moment he pulled her towards him, the cushion falling forgotten onto the floor as he bent to bring her mouth to his.

Her lips were warm and yielding and he swallowed a groan to finally taste them, scarcely able to breathe as he heard her feather-soft sigh. Of their own accord his fingers moved from her wrist to the sweep of her waist and he felt her sway against him, his blood heating as she seized hold of his shirt to steady herself. Tentative at first, her lips moved more forcefully, opening to allow the very tip of his tongue to delve inside, and it was almost more than he could stand when she ventured to copy him, hesitance turning to boldness that set his skin ablaze.

Emily's hands were braver now, pulling him down, and he was happy to obey, his own palm pressed flat on the curve of her lower back and tilting her body to his. Probably she'd be able to feel how much he wanted her, inexperienced but certainly no fool, but he couldn't manage to feel ashamed that she might guess how for him their wedding night couldn't come soon enough.

The thought of it was the only thing that could have brought him to his senses. Before there was a wedding night there had to be a wedding, and against every desire he pulled back, breaking the kiss but unable to loosen his vice-like grip on her waist.

'Do you still think I have even half a thought to spare for Miss Windham? Or any of the others you might meet?'

Her eyes were glassy and her lips still parted as she looked up at him, flushed as a poppy in a field. It seemed she was either unable to speak or had forgotten how, as she merely shook her head in a dazed little quiver that made him want to pull her to him all over again.

'Will you stop questioning now whether I know my own mind?'

This time his question was met with a fervent nod.

'Good. Because next time I might have to kiss you properly to make my point.'

At last she managed to find her tongue, although her voice was little more than an unsteady murmur. 'That wasn't properly?'

'No.'

He gazed down at her, feeling the pounding of his heart all the way down to his boots. It raced as though he'd been running, and it was only the refusal to push her too far, too fast that stopped him from showing her exactly what he meant.

'Not even close.'

# *Chapter Six*

Arriving at the Dower House the next morning, Andrew almost tripped over a large parcel sitting in the middle of the hall's floor. It was wrapped in brown paper with no label attached, but that didn't stop him from knowing at once what was inside.

The morning room door opened and his mother appeared, Emily a few paces behind. Lady Gouldsmith's interest seemed fixed on the mysterious package, but he saw Emily cast him a swift glance, her eyes lingering briefly on his mouth before she looked away again. The memory of their late-night entanglement must have been just as fresh in her mind as it was in his, he realised with a stir of interest somewhere too intimate to mention, and he was relieved to see he hadn't frightened her away with his reckless declaration that there was much more to come.

'We've been waiting for you.' His mother poked the package with her foot, making the paper rustle. 'That was delivered at the crack of dawn this morning. What is it, and why is it in my hall? As I'm not expecting a delivery myself I believe it must be yours.'

'It's not exactly mine.' Andrew raised what he knew she'd think was an annoyingly enigmatic eyebrow. 'And if I'd told you to expect it, it would have ruined the surprise.'

He turned to Emily, for the first time noticing she wore another borrowed gown. The sage-green morning dress was pretty but didn't fit her as well as one made with her in mind, and the secret anticipation already forming climbed another notch.

'Do you recall I went away to finish a letter on the morning I showed you Huntingham's grounds? Just after breakfast?'

She nodded cautiously, a rosy trace appearing now he addressed her directly. 'Yes. Why?'

'I was writing to my man in London, asking him to send me this.' He jerked his head towards the parcel. 'It's for you.'

'For me? What is it?'

'If you open it, you'll find out.'

He smiled, trying to ignore a loose thread of uncertainty. Surely any woman would be pleased with what he'd arranged for her. But he couldn't know for definite until she unwrapped it, and there was a distinct air of hesitation in the way she came forward and knelt to untie the strings.

With its bindings undone the brown paper fell open.

Andrew felt a twinge of relief. The wooden chest standing among its wrappings was just as handsome as he'd hoped. Made from oak it was larger than he'd expected, with mother-of-pearl flowers on its lid that he thought would delight its new owner, who at present looked as though she didn't understand.

'For your wedding trousseau,' he clarified, seeing the need for an explanation. 'I thought we could go to Leamington today. The shops there are far better than those in Brigwell and you can fill this chest with whatever you like.'

Kneeling on the floor beside the mess of crumpled paper Emily's eyes widened. She didn't speak, however, and he felt the thread of uncertainty unravel a little more.

'It's my understanding a bride usually has a chest of clothes and other things to bring with her when she weds. Forgive me for assuming, but I didn't think you already had one. Would you be willing to let me correct that?'

She'd reached for the inlay of the lid, her fingertips hovering over a pearlescent petal. It seemed she didn't quite dare make contact, and she retracted her hand again without touching, instead smoothing her skirts down over her lap in the unconscious gesture Andrew knew meant she wasn't sure what else to do.

There was a pause.

'I don't know what to say.'

'A simple yes would suffice.'

'But it's so generous.' Emily shook her head slowly, the morning sunlight coming through the still-open front door making her hair gleam with the movement. 'I never would have presumed anything like this.'

'I know you wouldn't. That's in large part why I'd like you to accept it.'

That bewildered shake of her head spoke of a need for greater persuasion. Clearly there was a danger she might reject his offer out of some kind of unnecessary modesty, and with a meaningful glance over the top of her head he summoned reinforcements.

Lady Gouldsmith leapt in at once. 'You're in need of clothes befitting a woman of the station you'll soon occupy. As fond of you as I am, you can't wear mine for ever, and you'll certainly need something to wear for the wedding.'

It appeared his gift was easier to accept when put in more practical terms. At the prospect of no longer being a burden on her hostess's wardrobe, Andrew thought he sensed Emily reconsider—still doubtful, but at least not refusing it outright.

'Thank you.' She rose to her feet, dipping a small curtsey as she stood up, and then his heart lurched sideways to see a ghost of a smile. 'Your kindness means more to me than you know.'

That hardly perceptible upward curve was all the reward he could have wished for. He wasn't sure what it made him want to do more, stare at her lips or taste them again, but as he could currently do neither he settled for a polite nod of his own.

'Don't speak of it. I wouldn't be much of a man if I begrudged my future wife some gowns.'

Her spectral smile flickered a fraction wider. The idea of a new dress was agreeable, it seemed, and he was glad of it, her initial reluctance only reinforcing what he thought he already knew.

She didn't *require* fine things to be content. Emily would value her expensive clothes and never take them for granted, just as he himself was conscious of the need to be appreciative of what he had. The lean years of his youth had taught him that lesson, and it made him feel warm inside to think she shared his sentiments—perhaps the common ground between them even fertile enough to allow something more to grow in time.

Evidently, with her acceptance of his gift, her nerve had increased. She allowed herself to touch the pearl flowers now, following the iridescent line of a stalk with wonder he loved to see.

'I know that usually a young lady's family provides the trousseau.' Carefully Emily lifted the petal-shaped clasp that held the chest closed. 'I'm certain that when we find my father, he'll pay you back for providing what he couldn't at the time.'

She opened the lid to peer inside, Andrew suddenly thankful her attention was elsewhere so she might miss his involuntary frown.

*What? Is that really what she thinks?*

Did she truly believe her father was likely to take such an interest? Discomfort nudged in beneath what had previously been uninterrupted satisfaction. Surely she couldn't be that naïve. When he'd agreed to help her find her father he'd assumed it was for the sake of answers, not affection, and that she was prepared for the cool—at best—reception she would receive from a man who had never made any attempt to know her. Now it seemed Emily's hopes were much higher than he'd realised, and his concern grew as he caught his mother's eye, Lady Gouldsmith looking as worried as he was beginning to feel.

*Perhaps I should try to talk her into lowering her expectations.*

She would be hurt to discover her father's apathy if she was expecting anything more, and Andrew felt a sharp stab of something at the thought. An unhappy Emily was a sight he'd seen once before, when she'd attempted to hide her tear-stained face beneath the shadows of Brigwell's trees, and to imagine her in such a state again made him harden his jaw.

*I'll have to say something. As much as I'm coming to care for her, it would be a miracle if her father felt the same.*

The niggling unease at the back of his mind didn't subside for the duration of the carriage ride to Leamington, a distance of about ten miles, which that morning felt like much more.

It wasn't only the disquiet of his thoughts that were responsible for the dragging passage of time, however. Emily sat beside his mother on the seat opposite him, her face turned to the window so he could see the crescent of her profile like a pale waning moon, and he couldn't help but watch how the sunlight played over it as the carriage rattled down the dusty roads. The morning was warm and the subtle flush at the base of her throat was mesmerising, reminding him how her skin had burned beneath his hands the night before, and the desire to touch her again—but knowing he could not—made the journey seem very long indeed.

*Simmer down. There are other things that require your attention.*

Andrew tapped his fingers against his knee as he tried to order his thoughts. How could he broach a subject that she would no doubt find upsetting *without* upsetting her?

There was a simple answer—he couldn't.

However he tried to approach the topic of her father, Emily would end up distressed. She was already lacking in confidence—something for which he credited Miss Laycock—and to suggest her father might not be overjoyed to meet her would do nothing to help build her up. He had imagined she wanted to find this mysterious Lord to satisfy her curiosity and fill in the gaps in her history, not because she believed it would be possible to cultivate a relationship with him, and when he inevitably didn't want to know, her feeling of rejection would be complete.

The rapidity of Andrew's tapping increased, and not even a warning look from Lady Gouldsmith could stop it.

To bring his own father back he would have done anything, and he could well understand why Emily had deceived herself in pursuit of her own. She only wanted what so many never gave a second thought...but it wouldn't happen. The man who had signed her into the school's care hadn't wanted her when she was a newborn and he wouldn't want her now, and no amount of optimism on her part would change that inescapable fact.

'Is something the matter?'

Emily's question wasn't one he particularly wanted to answer. He could hardly look into her eyes and lie, that hydrangea-blue gaze holding him prisoner from the other side of the carriage, but at the same time he couldn't quite manage the truth.

Fortunately luck was on his side.

'Look. We've arrived.'

The carriage was beginning to slow as the traffic increased. Rows of tall white buildings had risen on either side of the road, houses and gleaming shop windows welcoming them as they passed, with well-dressed people thronging the pavements. In comparison with Brigwell, Leamington had all the polish and sophistication of London, and Andrew saw Emily had forgotten she was waiting for him to answer as she peered out of the window, her nose all but pressed against the glass as she drank it all in.

'Have you ever been to Leamington before?'

'No. Miss Laycock mistrusted towns larger than Brigwell.'

'I see.' Despite his unease he had to hide some amusement at the headmistress's interesting world view. 'Don't worry. We'll make sure nothing untoward happens to you.'

The carriage had come to a halt and he opened the door, not waiting for the footman to do something he was more than capable of doing for himself.

*Still not half as Earlish an Earl as Uncle Ephraim was—but then, I hope I never am.*

He handed his mother down the carriage steps and then Emily, her fingers resting lightly in his palm. It was the slightest contact, over and done in a matter of seconds with two pairs of gloves in between, but still he felt his pulse increase. The last time she'd willingly put herself in his hands had been moments before he'd kissed her, when she allowed him to map out the landscape of her body like an explorer in a new world, and from the tiny breath he heard her snatch as his hand grazed hers, he guessed she had made the same connection.

Surrounded now by crowds that made it difficult to move, Lady Gouldsmith took charge.

'We'll be knocked over if we keep standing here in the middle of the street. Ought we begin with dresses? If you'd like, I can show you to the best modistes.'

'Yes, please.' To Andrew's regret Emily moved away from

him to take his mother's outstretched arm. 'Left to my own devices I'm certain to get lost.'

Without further ado Lady Gouldsmith began to lead her away, cutting through the mass of fashionable shoppers with elegant ease. Andrew followed, his thoughts still bound up in the troubling matter of Emily's unlikely hopes—although that didn't stop him from noticing the subtle sway of her waist as she walked in front of him, something he found himself quite unable to ignore.

Allowing herself to be measured for what felt like the hundredth time, Emily tried not to focus on the ache in her legs. Almost a full day of trekking from dressmaker to milliner to dressmaker again had left her exhausted, but she still couldn't sit down, currently stripped to her shift and keeping obediently still as the latest modiste's assistant laid a measuring tape against her back. Her feet were sore and she was in desperate need of a cup of tea—and yet she couldn't remember ever having been so happy in all her life.

All afternoon Andrew had insisted on buying her anything she so much as glanced at, the number of gowns and bonnets and ribbons and *everything* mounting by the hour, but it wasn't the gifts themselves that had had lit such a spark inside her. His consideration was responsible for that, the offer of a trousseau rooted in kindness she valued more than any silk dancing shoes, and as the modiste regarded her with an expert eye she wondered how she had stumbled into such an impossible dream.

For years the only person she'd ever thought would care for her had been her mysterious father, but now...was there a chance Andrew might, too?

That he desired her she now had no doubt—not since he'd shown her so plainly only the night before, the memory making her heart flit faster beneath the scant cover of her shift. His grip on her had been strong but his mouth so gentle, drawing her into an embrace that had engulfed her in flames, and all day it had been difficult to meet his eye without blushing. To provoke a physical reaction in the man who would be her husband was one thing, however, while appealing to his heart was another;

and perhaps it was too much to hope for that an Earl marrying for convenience might leave the way open to anything more.

'How are you getting on in there, Emily?'

Lady Gouldsmith's voice came from beyond the fitting room door. She was seated just outside, although Andrew—as a male and therefore an intruder in such a feminine space—was relegated to a quiet corner of the shop, tucked away where no customers might take fright at his presence. Apparently he had tea and a comfortable chair in which to drink it, and until his pocketbook was required it seemed he had little to do but relax.

'Well, I think?'

At her questioning look the modiste, the intimidatingly stylish Mrs Sedgewick, nodded authoritatively. 'Very well indeed. If I could just ask you to turn the other way?'

Obligingly Emily turned to face the wall behind her, well used by now to what was required. When she'd woken that morning she'd never visited a Society dressmaker in her life, and yet now she felt like an old hand, still scarcely able to credit she would soon be wearing gowns fit for a queen in place of her old mended muslins.

At last the endless measuring finished. The assistant rolled up her tape and Mrs Sedgewick returned to the helm.

'I'll show you some fabrics now. Once we've decided which colours suit you the best we can move on to embellishments.'

It seemed there was little scope for Emily to disagree. The assistant was despatched to fetch the samples, although it was only a few moments before she returned.

'I can't find them, Mrs Sedgewick.'

'What do you mean? You know where the swatches are kept.'

'Yes, ma'am, but they aren't there.'

The modiste sighed, catching Emily's eye in the mirror to offer an apologetic smile. 'Would you excuse me for a moment, Miss Townsend? I shall return directly.'

Shooing her assistant in front of her, Mrs Sedgewick left the fitting room, pulling the door firmly closed behind her. There were murmurs on the other side as she relayed the situation to Lady Gouldsmith, then the sound of footsteps retreating down the corridor that separated the fitting room from the rest of the shop.

Left alone, Emily stretched her aching back. It was a pity there was nowhere to sit down. The only things in the small room with her were an armoire and the elaborate mirror leaning against one wall. Idly she watched herself straighten her shift, the thin linen hardly preserving her modesty. Thanks to Andrew's generosity she had another ten on order, and she found herself wondering if he would ever want to see what he had paid for.

*Stop it. You know that's not something you should think about.*

Her subconscious spoke sense—but there was something in the idea of the Earl seeing her in only her under things that made being sensible seem very difficult indeed. It wasn't unreasonable to imagine a man might have certain expectations of his wife, and the hint he had dropped the previous evening, that the kiss she had found so thrilling hadn't even been at its full power, made her feel suddenly warm. Even a marriage of convenience could have passion, or so Andrew had implied, and she couldn't deny she was growing ever more curious to know for sure.

*If he ever did see me like this...would he like what he saw?*

The question posed itself without her permission, and she saw her mirror image flush to realise what she wanted the answer to be. He managed to bring out the most scandalous side of her, although she hurriedly reined herself in as she heard the fitting room door handle turn.

The door rattled on its hinges but didn't open. The handle turned again and Emily waited for Mrs Sedgwick to appear, mildly puzzled when the door still didn't move. There was some low muttering and another round of rattling, and then Lady Gouldsmith's voice came from the other side.

'My dear? Are you all right in there?'

'Yes,' Emily called back, puzzlement beginning to turn to slight alarm. 'Why?'

There was a brief pause and some more scuffling.

'Not to worry you, but we're just having a little trouble opening the door.'

A second voice followed the first. 'I'm so sorry, Miss Townsend. This door sticks sometimes, although my carpenter assured me it had been fixed.'

'No need to be concerned, however,' Eleanor finished reassuringly. 'We'll get you out...somehow...'

Emily's chest tightened.

*They can't open the door.*

Ever since she was a child she'd hated being confined in small spaces and, now she knew she was trapped, the fitting room suddenly seemed very small indeed. There were windows but they were too high to see out of, giving only thin slivers of bright blue sky and offering no hope of climbing through. Until the door opened there was no way out, and she felt her heart begin to flutter, the muffled voices in the corridor not filling her with much confidence as the walls seemed to draw in around her.

The muttering ceased abruptly, which didn't come as much comfort either. There was a shuffling noise, as if several long skirts were being swept out of the way, and then another sound made Emily's already cantering heart break into a full gallop.

'Can I be of assistance?'

Andrew's polite enquiry held a world of suppressed amusement. Probably from the outside there *was* something to laugh at—three elegant ladies scrabbling at a door that refused to open—although Emily's sense of humour had temporarily evaporated. She was stuck in a small room dressed only in her shift, with a handsome Earl waiting just outside, and she couldn't recall ever having been in such a mortifying situation in all her life.

There was some murmuring as the predicament was explained, and then:

'Stand back, please, ladies... Further than that. I don't know if the wood will splinter.'

Emily's eyes flew wide. Surely he wasn't going to—

'Move away from the door, Emily. I'm going to force it open.'

Alarm hurtling skyward she looked wildly about the fitting room. For all her scandalous daydreams she couldn't *re-*

*ally* allow him to see her in such a state of undress, and yet her gown seemed to have disappeared into thin air. The only place it could be was inside the armoire, and she lunged towards it with desperate haste, her fingers closing around a handle and tugging open the first drawer—

But she was too late.

With a crack of breaking wood Andrew stumbled into the room, the door sagging off its hinges beneath the force of his heavy boot. He swiftly regained his balance and looked around, visibly relieved when he saw her now leaning against the far wall.

'Are you all right?'

He moved as if to come towards her…but something stopped him in his tracks.

Perhaps he hadn't realised immediately what she was wearing—or *not* wearing, Emily thought vaguely as she watched him grow very still, the relief in his face changing to a different thing entirely that made her breath hitch in her throat. His eyes swept over her, seeming darker than ever in their intensity, and with boldness she hadn't known she possessed she made no attempt to hide from them. She couldn't seem to move. Covering herself had felt so important seconds earlier, when he had been on the other side of the door, but now he was before her the hairs of her nape stood on end at his inability to look away. He probably meant to, usually too polite to stare, but there was real hunger in the way he gazed at her, sudden tension in the small room stretching like a rope about to break, and Emily had no idea what might have happened if Mrs Sedgewick hadn't come hurrying in to dampen the embers that had begun to smoulder somewhere shamefully low down.

'Miss Townsend! Are you hurt?'

'No.' With difficulty Emily dragged her eyes away from Andrew's, slightly breathless beneath the weight of his stare. 'I'm quite well.'

'I'm so very, very sorry for such an unforgivable ordeal. I'll speak to the carpenter at once. He'll think twice about carrying out such shoddy work in the future…'

Mrs Sedgewick went on but Emily hardly heard her. Over the

modiste's shoulder she saw Lady Gouldsmith had entered the fitting room alongside the hapless assistant and outnumbered by ladies, Andrew took his leave. Without a word he withdrew to the ruined doorway, slipping out unnoticed by the others—apart from Emily, whose stomach turned over at the glance he gave her before he disappeared.

*At least I have an answer to my question.*

Under cover of Mrs Sedgewick's threats towards every carpenter in England, Emily laid a hand over her chest, feeling how it rose and fell as rapidly as if she'd just run a mile.

*It certainly seemed as though he liked what he saw.*

# Chapter Seven

Lady Gouldsmith's birthday fell less than a week after their visit to Leamington.

She had loved the theatre for as long as Andrew could remember, and even during their meagre years had managed to take him to see something every Christmas that had delighted her as much as him. He could afford now to take a private box as a gift to her and was touched by her excitement, although the presence of Emily, currently sitting across from him in the carriage as they drove into town, made the excursion more… complicated.

He kept his eyes firmly on the window but even that didn't help. He could still see her reflection in the darkened glass, the nights drawing in now that autumn had begun, and he wished he could ask her to stop swaying in her seat. The movement reminded him of dancing—or something more intimate—and he gritted his teeth as he tried to focus on the moon instead of the ghostly outline of her face.

*I shouldn't have broken that door down. I should have let the carpenter come instead of bursting in.*

He hadn't known a moment's peace since he'd gone crashing into the fitting room, and he was still paying for his heroism even now. Nothing he tried seemed to work, the image of her in the thinnest of linen shifts appearing before him at the most inopportune times, and he was half afraid he might be losing his mind.

Eating breakfast?

*Emily in her shift, the pallor of her skin clearly visible through the almost transparent fabric.*

Gone for an early-morning ride?

*Emily in her shift, her secret curves all but laid bare.*

Enjoying a brisk walk out on the estate?

*Emily. In. Her. Shift.*

Belatedly he realised he was drumming his fingers against the leather seat, and he made himself stop before his mother noticed. She'd know at once something was bothering him and he had no intention of explaining what it was, Emily's constant unconscious movements in time with the carriage catching at the corner of his eye.

*I have to keep a clear head.*

Deliberately he checked his pocket watch, although he already knew the time. Turning it over in his fingers gave him something to do other than let them resume tapping, and he watched the second hand jerk its way around the dial as he attempted to curb his wayward thoughts.

Until he'd spoken to her about her father he couldn't let himself be carried astray. His attraction to her was becoming difficult to hide—if indeed he had hidden it at all—but he *couldn't* allow himself to do anything more. She tempted him so much it was hard to think straight, and that was just what he needed to do, the conversation he was putting off too important for him to attempt while distracted. The longer he took to gently help her see reality, the longer she would have to build up her expectations, and then her pain when she found her father had no interest in her would be even greater than before.

How she had managed to deceive herself was entirely understandable. Growing up in such a cold and loveless environment she must have been desperate to believe that someone cared about her, and her relentless desire to have her father as part of her life was one Andrew sympathised with wholeheartedly. The void his own had left could never be filled. Like an itch he couldn't quite scratch, it needled at him, more a dull ache now than the fresh agony it had been at first, but still one he carried with him every day, and it was easy for him to see why Emily was so keen to escape the same thing.

'Are you looking forward to the play?'

At the sound of her voice he instinctively looked up, although she was addressing his mother rather than him.

'Very much so. Are you?'

'Yes…'

'You don't sound sure.'

Even in the semi-darkness of the carriage Andrew saw Emily shuffle in her seat. 'Oh, I am. It's just my first true public outing among the *ton*. You said the theatre is one of the places people go to see and be seen, and I'm not sure I like the idea of the latter.'

She tucked a non-existent strand of hair behind her ear, the gesture betraying her nerves. It was a feeling he well understood. The desire to make his mother happy chafed against the knowledge that half of Warwickshire Society would be staring at him as soon as he entered the theatre and he didn't want to be gawped at either, even if having Emily at his side somehow managed to subdue the worst of his unease.

'Don't worry too much about that.' He leaned forwards, wishing he hadn't when he caught the faintest hint of the rose water on her hair. 'We'll be sitting in a private box. Once seated you'll be able to look at other people as much as you like without them being able to see you in turn.'

'That's a relief.' Emily's shoulders dropped and he realised she must have been holding them tense, whether knowingly or otherwise. 'I must confess some hypocrisy, however. While I don't relish the prospect of being studied myself, I'm intrigued to look around to see if any of the gentlemen there might be my father.'

She smiled, although she didn't hold his eye for long. Ever since that fateful moment at the modiste's shop she hadn't seemed to know how to behave in his presence any more than he did in hers, something unspoken now passing between them he didn't dare try to unpick. But for once the shy lift of her lips didn't make him entirely forget everything else.

'There are certainly likely to be more than a few lords in attendance,' he conceded cautiously. Apparently her apprehension wasn't enough to stop her from pressing ahead with her plans, and his own concerns returned sharply to the fore. 'We won't know all of them well enough for introductions. Even if there was someone you thought could be a possibility, it would be better to wait until you were sure.'

The carriage turned a corner, the squeak of the wheels and beat of the horses' hooves making her quiet reply almost imperceptible—but not quite—and Andrew felt his heart sink at what he only just caught.

'I've waited twenty-one years already. I'd rather not hold on for much longer.'

The theatre was packed to the rafters.

In every direction silk and satin gleamed in the light of countless candles—jewels and gold thread sparkled at necks and knuckles and everywhere in between. The moment Andrew steered his mother and Emily through the doors, the noise and heat hit them like a brick wall, the raised voices and press of cloying bodies not serving to take the edge off his disquiet. It seemed his prophecy had been correct. Most of Warwickshire's upper class thronged the room, affecting to take their seats but in truth hoping to show off their finery to the envy or admiration of everyone else, and he had never been more grateful that Uncle Ephraim's avarice now allowed his reluctant heir the luxury of a private box away from the crowds.

Looking down to check neither his mother nor Emily were being crushed as they fought their way towards the stairs, he saw her eyes were round. She was staring this way and that—at the velvet curtains around the stage, the candelabras hanging from the ceiling, the glittering splendour of the gowns and waistcoats on all sides—and he felt his stomach contract. Was she simply admiring her surroundings, or had she already begun the hunt he feared could only end in tears?

He leaned down so she might hear him above the buzz of

conversation. 'Are you all right? Not too anxious among all these people?'

'I'm fine.' Her fingers tightened on his arm, only slightly, but the momentary pressure still shot straight to his chest. 'Are you?'

Her glance was swift but searching, and Andrew wondered whether she was remembering the card party he had hosted against his will.

'Of course. You never need worry about me.'

It was only half a lie. He couldn't pretend to be enjoying the curious glances in his direction, as ever drawing more interest than he liked, although now there was a difference. When he'd first come down from Derbyshire he'd had to weather those stares alone, but now he didn't have to. Emily walked at his side with elegance any Society lady would strive for, resplendent in a silvery new gown he had paid extra to have made in half the time, and an ember of pride kindled inside him. She looked every inch the Countess-to-be, and he couldn't imagine anyone better suited to the role, her outside lovely but the feeling her presence gave him more valuable than any pretty face.

'Up here. Our box is on the very top balcony.'

With girlish excitement Lady Gouldsmith let go of his arm to ascend the stairs, Emily close behind. Candles set in alcoves along the stairwell walls cast a glow over her every time she passed one, her curls shining gold beneath a crown of gilt flowers he privately thought made her look like a fairy queen. With every floor they climbed the number of people grew smaller, until they reached an ornate door, which at a nod from Andrew was thrown open by a waiting servant.

Lady Gouldsmith sailed in without hesitation, but Emily stopped dead on the threshold.

If Andrew had thought her eyes were wide downstairs then now they were like saucers. 'This is just for us?'

'Yes. Just the three of us.'

She stared at the extravagantly upholstered seats turned towards the front of the box, where an uninterrupted view of the stage stretched out before them. A rich carpet underfoot and gold tassels on the curtains were lavish touches he had to admit added to the general splendour, illuminated by candles in gilded sconces that wouldn't have been out of place in a palace. As if to underscore the air of luxury a bottle of champagne stood in a bucket of ice that Emily went immediately to dabble her fingers through, her face alight with amazement it was a pleasure to behold.

'It's *wonderful*.'

She crossed to stand beside his mother, leaning over the railing to look down at the crowds below. In such skyward seclusion nobody on the lower floors could see them unless they specifically craned their necks upward, but that didn't stop Emily from being able to peer down on *them*. If any man resembling her enough to pique her interest was there she was sure to spot him, although as he caught another glimpse of her delighted face Andrew considered whether his worries might have been premature.

Perhaps he wouldn't have to caution her. Perhaps her enjoyment would make her forget the task she had set herself, the one he feared would make her more unhappy than she'd been before. He could only hope so, as well as do his best to distract her. All without getting too distracted himself, of course, the memory of her beneath the negligible cover of her shift never far from his mind.

Emily sat very still, hardly blinking as she watched the actors move across the stage. Anyone looking at her could have been forgiven for thinking she was entranced by the tragic scene unfolding before her…but appearances could be deceiving.

In truth her focus was trained on Andrew, his seat very near to hers. Each time he scratched his chin or touched his mouth she knew he was going to move before he even raised his hand, so attuned to his presence that even the steady rhythm of his breath sounded loud in her ear. His leg was almost touching hers, her skirts *just* brushing his knee, and the tension of wondering whether his next stretch would bring them into contact made her feel as though she was balanced on the edge of a knife. Since their visit to Leamington she had half feared he'd been avoiding her, but there was no chance of him doing so while they were corralled in the same box, now so close together he could only have escaped her if he shut his eyes. He certainly seemed as though his attention was fixed on the stage rather than on her, although her heart slammed into the front of her bodice when he suddenly turned his head.

'Are you enjoying yourself?'

His voice was lowered and the deep pitch sent a delicious shiver down the back of her neck as she nodded, hoping he hadn't noticed she'd instinctively leaned closer.

'Yes. Even more than I imagined.'

Seated on her other side Lady Gouldsmith's gaze never left the actors. One of them was now lamenting the death of another and a tear glinted on Eleanor's cheek, clearly moved by the action Emily had been too distracted to absorb. She was indeed enjoying her first ever visit to the theatre, although not necessarily for the reason Andrew had in mind, and she sat up a little straighter in her seat.

*This won't do. I'm supposed to be watching the play and looking out for my father, not trying to get as close to Andrew as I can without climbing into his lap.*

Trying not to make her intent too obvious, she let her eye wander over the audience seated below. There had been no attempt to extinguish the candles even after the play had begun, and she could see the other patrons as clearly as if it had been daylight, their clothes and faces brilliantly lit by innumerable flames.

The distance between them was another matter, however. From her lofty seat she couldn't make out the details of their faces, illuminated but too far away to clearly distinguish one from another. Someone she knew well could have been among the patrons clustered below and she wouldn't have recognised them, her place up in the rafters an obstacle she hadn't foreseen.

Disappointment prickled through her.

*First the card party and now this.*

Once again her hopes had been built up for nothing. For the second time she had strayed into the *ton's* natural territory, summoning all her nerve to try to pretend she belonged, and for the second time there was nothing to show for it. Her father might have been in that very room and she'd never know. The disappointment wending through her took on a sharper edge as she considered an unwanted possibility.

What if she never found him?

If she never found her father she'd forfeit the love she'd hoped to gain—for where else could she obtain it? As much as Andrew seemed to like her, he was still marrying her for their mutual convenience above anything else. He had already committed to giving her a home and a lifestyle more comfortable than anything she'd ever dreamed of, and to delude herself into thinking he might offer his heart on top of that would be folly. He'd needed a wife and she'd needed shelter, and if she never reunited with the one person she was certain already loved her then she would have to go the rest of her life without.

Her throat tightened and she made a conscious effort to swallow the aching lump. Just because her own feelings for Andrew were shifting didn't mean his were doing the same. Friendship interspersed with some fleeting desire seemed to be the extent of it, and even for that she ought to be grateful… A difficult concept to hold onto when he leaned forward in his chair, the candlelight casting shadows over his face that made his jawline look like it was chiselled from stone.

The activity on the stage seemed to be reaching a crescendo. Too intent on her inner turmoil to understand what was happening, she followed the audience's lead when they stood up, the curtains pulling shut to the sound of thunderous applause.

'Wonderful. Wonderful!'

On her feet like everyone else, Lady Gouldsmith daintily blotted her eyes with a lace-edged handkerchief, giving Emily a watery smile. 'Look at me, moved to tears! I only hope the second act will compare.'

'The second act?'

'This is just an interval, for people to move around after sitting for so long.'

As if to illustrate her point Eleanor waved over the side of the balcony to where the audience were in a state of flux. But then her eyes narrowed. 'Andrew, is that Lady Sandwell? I *think* I see her—over there, in the box opposite. I don't know who else would wear such an unusual hat. I've been meaning to speak with her about her recommendation for a new gardener—if you'd excuse me.'

Before her son could either confirm or deny the presence of Lady Sandwell and her hat, Lady Gouldsmith disappeared, vanishing through the box's door in a swathe of lilac silk, and abruptly Emily and Andrew found themselves very much alone.

From the balcony Emily returned to her seat, aware of a new unsteadiness in her legs. She hadn't been on her own with him for the best part of a week. Not since she had been so brazen as to allow him to admire her in her shift, and she hardly knew what to do with herself as she pretended her insides weren't swooping like a bird in flight.

Andrew remained at the railing for a moment. Whether he was watching the crowds below or just affecting to she didn't know, although when he turned to her his face was carefully blank.

'Would you care for some champagne?'

He nodded to the bottle still lying in its bath of melting ice. It was already open—Lady Gouldsmith had required refreshment after a particularly gruelling scene—but Emily hesitated.

'I'm not sure. Like everything else the *ton* seems to enjoy, I've never tried it.'

'Do you want to?'

'Perhaps a drop. If I like the taste, I might have a real glass afterwards.'

Andrew inclined his head. Taking a glass from beside the bucket he poured out a thimbleful, seeming to pause before he moved towards her.

The theatre was noisy. Laughter and a hundred different conversations made a clamouring din, but somehow the only thing she could hear was the soft swish of his coat as he leaned down to place the glass in her hand. He was easily close enough for her to touch him, and she willed her fingers to stay still as she took the champagne, staring fixedly at the bubbles rather than his too-near face.

He stepped back—again his footsteps the only thing her ears saw fit to register—just as Emily took her first tentative sip.

'What do you think?'

The bubbles tickled her tongue but the taste wasn't unpleasant, and when she informed Andrew of the fact he gave a dry laugh.

'It improves on further acquaintance. Will you have more?'

'Please.'

She held out her empty glass, bracing herself when he came forward again and bent to fill it.

For all her efforts she realised her hand wasn't completely steady. The surface of the champagne rippled slightly, betraying the tremor inside she was trying so hard to disguise—and when his fingers brushed her knuckles she couldn't help the sharp breath that escaped her parted lips.

Andrew's eyes locked with hers.

If he had been within touching distance before, now he was closer still. He was so much taller that he had to bend almost double to reach down to her chair, still towering over her but his face now all she could see. He seemed to have forgotten the bottle in his hand. He'd ceased pouring the moment he heard her gasp, and she felt heat climb up from her neck when his gaze swept from her eyes to her mouth with the same dark intensity as a few days before.

Andrew didn't move, and neither did she; and yet somehow the champagne bottle was set down, and the glass vanished from her hand, and when Andrew fell into his seat Emily somehow fell with him to end up in his lap.

His lips were sweet with the taste of passion and champagne and she never wanted him to stop, his kiss deep and powerful and chasing out everything else. Her hands were in his hair, pulling him towards her, his grip on her so firm she almost couldn't breathe, half suffocated by her desire to be pressed against him even more. His tongue danced with hers, delving, exploring, twisting, only to break away as he trailed kisses down the length of her neck, burying himself beneath her chin to nip where her pulse bounded at the base of her throat.

It seemed Andrew's pent-up longing was just as great as her own. He cupped her cheek, tipping her head back so he could reach the sensitive jut of her collarbones above the neck of her gown and graze them with his teeth, scattering stars in front of Emily's glazed, half-open eyes. Whatever spell the burning tension of the modiste's fitting room had cast on them was unstoppable, and now the thread had been broken it couldn't be repaired, unable to hold back even in the knowledge that they were in public. All the aching, all the desire to touch him, the fight against doing so abandoned as Emily's fingers tightened in the short hairs on the back of his neck, and her heart sang to hear him swallow a guttural groan. It was impossible to tell where he ended and she began, a seamless melding together that set her alight…

'Wait. Wait.'

Andrew pulled back, his cheeks flushed and eyes as dark as coals. He was breathing like a hunted animal and Emily felt her throat clench as he released her from his grasp, shakily slipping from his lap to collapse back into her own seat.

She huddled into the chair, trying to slow the wild pounding of her heart. Her blood felt like fire in every vein, and she suspected Andrew's was the same as he pushed back his hair, looking as winded as she felt.

'The *ton* would think Christmas had come early if they'd seen that.'

He passed a hand over his face—but when he looked at her his smile sent a static shock crackling in its wake. 'I don't want to give them anything to use against us. Engaged or not, I don't think it would be a good idea to do that again…however much I might want to.'

Emily's already heated blood all but burst into flames. Her hair had come loose on one side and she twisted it back, aware her fingers were almost too nerveless to move. Her mouth was dry and her mind drawn a near perfect blank, too pleasure-drunk to work properly, although from somewhere a single sensible observation cautiously raised its head.

'Them? You talk about the *ton* as though you weren't one of their number.'

'That's because I still don't truly feel as though I am.'

He gave her another of those heart-stopping smiles, although this time she thought she caught something lurking underneath.

She took a deep breath. For the most part all she could think of was the scalding pressure of Andrew's mouth, her neck still tingling where he had branded it with kisses, but her curiosity managed to find a crack to slip through. His past was as much a mystery as ever, and she might never be gifted such an opportunity to ask as now, when his defences were down and his vulnerability was as exposed as his desires.

'Why is that? You've never really told me.'

He was straightening his cravat—his hands not looking entirely steady either—and at the question he paused. For a moment Emily wondered if he would pretend not to have heard her, but then he slid her a sideways look, as ever the meeting of their eyes making heat spark in her stomach.

'I will, but not right now. It grieves my mother to speak of it and she'll be back at any moment.'

With perfect timing—or perhaps imperfect, depending on who was asked—the door to the box opened. Lady Gouldsmith came inside, granting a vague smile to her son and soon-to-be daughter-in-law, although it was Andrew's low, gravelly murmur as his mother turned to close the door behind her that caught Emily's attention like a butterfly in a net.

'Besides...there are other things I'd *much* rather think about at present than sorrows of the past.'

# *Chapter Eight*

There was a slight crack in the flagstone closest to Andrew's boot.

He looked down at it, trying to ignore the sensation of a belt being tightened around his chest. The church was uncomfortably warm but he knew it wasn't the heat that had caused the neck of his shirt to feel damp, his silk cravat tied perfectly but somehow feeling like it was slowly strangling him with every breath. Even above the drone of the organ he could hear the slight shuffling and murmuring of the few guests who had been invited to witness his marriage, and he wondered if they could tell his state of mind from the back of his head, certain even his hair must look slightly tense as he waited for his fate to be revealed.

'Any moment now. She won't be much longer, I'm sure.'

The Reverend Figsbury peered expectantly down the aisle towards the open front doors, but Andrew continued to stare directly ahead. He wished he had the reverend's confidence. Until he actually *saw* Emily walking towards him there was still a chance she might not show, a possibility that pulled his innards into a hard knot.

She had nobody there to support her, after all. The bride's side of the church was empty—she had no family and the necessity of concealing her origins meant her few friends from among Miss Laycock's boarders weren't invited. The only people she'd know were his mother and himself, and if she'd changed her mind there was no one to stop her from bolting, perhaps running from the Dower House before she had to make the change to Huntingham Hall…

Still staring at the back wall of the church he unconsciously shook his head.

She wouldn't run. How could she? She had nowhere else to go, which was the very reason she had agreed to marry him to begin with, and he shouldn't forget it. If he was looking forward to seeing her every day he shouldn't tell her, nor should he admit how much he liked the idea of her making Huntingham her own, introducing the feminine touches his uncle's tenure had deliberately wiped out. To walk into a room and find Emily sitting beside the fire or perhaps catching sight of her picking flowers in the garden was a prospect that made him happier than he thought safe, worry nagging at him even as far more appealing things tried to distract him from what he knew he still had to do.

*But there's no point in thinking about that now.*

Andrew glanced down at his pocket watch. The conversation regarding her father was something he would only have to fret about if she actually came to the church—and she was now fifteen minutes late.

His unease stirred harder. If he turned his head a fraction he could just see his mother alternating between watching him and the door, a constant twist that must have made the person sitting behind her dizzy. She didn't seem worried yet—surely it was every bride's prerogative to arrive a little late—but the reverend was peering over Andrew's shoulder with more and more concern, and he became aware a low muttering had broken out behind him, the guests becoming restless as the wait went on.

'Ah. There she is.'

Reverend Figsbury broke into a beaming smile—and Andrew felt as though his heart had been shot out of a cannon.

He didn't mean to turn around. The previous night he had determined not to watch her walk down the aisle, not wanting to add to the nerves that were sure to be making her weak at the knees, but now the moment had arrived his resolve deserted him. As the organist launched into the wedding march he realised he was moving, spurred on by some force he was powerless to fight, and without knowing quite how it had happened he found his eyes suddenly fixed on Emily's approach.

Time stood still.

She was coming towards him, the sunshine streaming in through the door, swathing her in a halo of light. It lit up the copper brilliance of her hair to shine as though it was on fire, a circlet of flowers somehow sitting atop the flames without catching alight, although beneath it her countenance was pale. The pearly sheen of her skin was offset by a gown of the lightest grey that moved like mist around her and was hardly more substantial, her skirts brushing the ground in a trail of silvery lace more like a spider's web than anything made by hand. If he hadn't been there to witness the sight for himself he never would have believed a woman could look so beautiful, like something from a fairytale come to life, and he could no more have dragged his eyes away from her than he could have found words to describe his awe.

It wasn't her beauty that struck him the hardest, however.

Her steps were every bit as unsteady as he thought they would be, each one clearly costing her great effort. She tottered slightly as if she was walking the deck of a pitching ship, and Andrew's breath seized as he watched her draw nearer, the dirge of the organ suddenly too loud. She looked so small and vulnerable all alone beneath the church's great domed ceiling, every face turned towards her while her own was cast down to the floor, and he knew what he was going to do even before his mind came to a conscious decision.

Without stopping to allow it to catch up, he strode towards her, the wedding guests taking a collective breath as he walked past them down the aisle. Emily looked up at him, apparently startled to find him so suddenly close, but she didn't step back when he held out his hand.

'Here. We'll walk the rest of the way together.'

The murmurs from the pews around him grew louder but

he didn't spare them a glance. Emily was all he could see, her white face tight with strain, and he knew that if she took his hand now he would never want to let go.

She would need someone to rely on. If she found her father she would need a friend to help her through the pain of rejection that must surely follow. She might only be marrying him for security, but that was something Andrew knew he was happy to provide.

His cravat felt tighter than ever as he waited to see if she would place her hand in his. He took a half-step closer, bending slightly so Emily was the only person to catch his murmured words. To his delight she swayed as his breath tickled her neck, but he hardened himself against the urge to follow it with a kiss, the memory of that heated moment in the theatre's rafters streaking through his mind.

'This is how it will be. From this day on, if you wish it, you'll never have to face anything alone.'

Her eyelashes flickered, fluttering over cheeks that now glowed the ready pink he so loved to behold. She seemed to be looking down at the floor, or perhaps at the toes of her dainty new slippers; but then those hydrangea-blue eyes locked on his and the church around him fell away as Andrew felt her fingers settle in his palm.

Afterwards, Emily had no idea where she'd found the nerve.

To enter the church all alone and stand at the top of the aisle, knowing everyone had swivelled to stare at her, was one of the most frightening things she'd ever done. Her heart had been slamming against her breastbone and her stomach had churned nauseatingly, and with every step she'd felt as though she was about to vomit or faint.

But then—Andrew.

She cut him a sidelong glance. The familiar shape of his profile was sharp against the Dower House's drawing room wall. He was talking to yet another person she didn't know, the receiving line at her own wedding breakfast made up of strangers, but for the moment at least she wasn't afraid. All her fear had fled at the first touch of his hand; strong and warm and steady enough for the both of them, and as he had led her to the altar she'd known that he wouldn't let her fall. She was his wife now and he was her husband, and despite a world of uncertainties and concerns for the future she'd never been so glad of anything in her life.

Someone was talking to her and, with immense difficulty, she dragged her attention away from Andrew. What she really wanted was to continue to stare at the man she had just married, still hardly able to believe what she'd done, but her guest was not to be deterred.

'My lady. May I offer my most sincere congratulations.'

Sir Montfort, whom she vaguely remembered from the card party Andrew had held all those weeks before, rose from an elaborate bow. 'A wonderful event. I'm sure I'm not the only one pleased to see a Countess Breamore at Huntingham Hall once again.'

'Thank you, sir. I hope in time to prove myself worthy of the honour.'

Such a thing was impossible, she knew even as she spoke the obvious lie, but what else could she have said? The fact she was now the mistress of a nine-hundred-acre estate, a truly enormous house and the bearer of a centuries-old title was still so bizarre she might have given a hysterical laugh if a fingertip hadn't suddenly traced down the back of her bare arm, sending a rush of blood directly to her head.

'I have no doubt my wife will make the perfect Countess.'

Andrew's smile was charming, although Emily couldn't help but suspect he'd guessed exactly what she'd been thinking. 'I can't imagine anyone more deserving of a life of comfort and privilege than the woman I have been fortunate enough to wed.'

She managed a smile in return, hoping Sir Montfort was too short-sighted to see how she'd flushed.

*'The woman I have been fortunate enough to wed.' Fortunate...*

Probably he was merely being polite...but that didn't stop a secret thrill from tingling down her spine.

He had kept his word until the very last. He'd assured her he wouldn't change his mind about marrying her and he hadn't, their fates bound together now by the ring gleaming golden on her finger. It was the most costly thing she'd ever worn—more expensive even than her cloud-hued gown—but the price didn't dictate its true value. The ring on her third finger represented reliability and trust, the mark of a man she could place her faith in, and she could barely credit that somehow the quest to identify her father had resulted in something so unexpected instead.

*Not instead.* Resolutely she corrected her mistake. *As well as. I'll find my father as well as having gained a husband—of that I'm still sure.*

Andrew was immersed in conversation with Sir Montfort, and for a moment she watched him without being seen. He couldn't have been truly interested in what the old knight was saying—something about rebuilding a chimney, having moved on from compliments—but his polite pretence was convincing. He would never want to offend or hurt anybody's feelings, one of the things she liked best about him, although now his kindness left a bittersweet taste on her tongue.

Until she tracked Lord *Somebody* down she wouldn't have answers as to who she really was—and she wouldn't be loved, either. The consideration Andrew showed her was the same he showed everyone else, and yet she yearned for more, still missing the unequivocal acceptance and approval she'd wanted since she was a child. It was a gap only her father could fill and she knew she shouldn't lose sight of that fact, even if the temptation to hope Andrew might step into the breech grew stronger every day—and wasn't likely to diminish now they were joined together until death did them part.

The afternoon wore on in a whirl of eating, drinking and relentless good wishes. Lady Gouldsmith had outdone herself as hostess for the newly married couple, with cakes and ices and fruit of every description piled high and champagne flowing, and the guests took advantage with full glasses and faces that grew pinker and pinker as day turned into evening. Having barely slept the night before, Emily felt herself beginning to flag as the candles were lit, although when Andrew came to find her, sitting in a chair half hidden behind a curtain, she found herself suddenly wide awake.

'Well, Lady Breamore? As you appear to be falling asleep in your seat, shall we go home?'

The upward curve of Andrew's lips was distracting—half courteous, half amused, and so wholly absorbing that Emily could barely find a reply as he helped her to her feet, his strong grip once again lighting fires beneath her skin.

'It sounds so strange to hear you call me that.'

'I'm afraid you'll have to get used to it. From now on you are a Countess, the equal—or perhaps better—of everyone here.'

He glanced around the room, his eye lingering over their guests, and to her puzzlement the smile segued into abrupt seriousness.

'No matter what the future brings, nobody can ever take that from you.'

His solemnity was short-lived. Perhaps he remembered a wedding was supposed to be a joyful occasion, or he thought whatever had just flitted though his mind was a matter for another time. Whatever the cause he hitched the smile back into place, and only one looking very closely could have noticed it didn't seem entirely effortless.

'I imagine you've long been desiring to leave the party. What do you say to sneaking out unobserved?'

At her nod Andrew held out his hand—and Emily took it without hesitation.

It was easy enough to creep away without being seen. The amount of champagne the wedding guests had ploughed through was impressive, and Emily doubted whether some of them were now even capable of recognising the bride and groom as they crept towards the door, keeping to the shadows thrown by crystal chandeliers. They moved stealthily until Andrew took hold of the door handle and eased just enough of a gap for her to slip through, following close behind and shutting the door again with the softest, most inaudible of clicks.

Out in the corridor the sounds of laughter and voices were dimmed, but it seemed Andrew didn't intend to linger. Still hand in hand, Emily's heart scurried faster as he led her to the entrance hall and through the open front door, the evening air just beginning to hold a crisp note. Above them the moon hung among countless stars, but all she could focus on was the warmth of his palm pressed against hers, walking quickly to keep up with him as Huntingham Hall loomed tall and magnificent out of the darkness.

At the bottom of the steps, Andrew paused.

'Wait.'

He turned to her, at last releasing her hand. 'I only intend to marry once, so I need to do this properly.'

The question of *what* he needed to do balanced on the tip of her tongue—but it fled when he swiftly bent down and scooped her off her feet.

'Isn't it tradition for a man to carry his new bride over the threshold?'

All her breath exited in a squeak of surprise as he drew her against his chest, cradling her as easily as if she'd been a paper doll. With one arm around her back and the other behind her knees she could feel his strength, as solid and unshakeable as the trunk of a tree, and she was too shocked to do anything but lean closer as he climbed the steps and kicked open the Hall's front door.

The butler must have left it unlocked or else Andrew's boot sent the bolt flying. With another of those bone-melting smiles he carried her inside, the smooth linen of his shirt pressed against her ear as she huddled against him, not wanting him to let go. Somehow her arms had found their way around his neck, bringing their faces almost level, and she gave an involuntary shiver when she felt the trace of stubble on his jaw rasp against her temple. The entrance hall was dark. In all the excitement the maids must have forgotten to light the candles, and to find herself alone in the shadows, held tightly against her new husband's chest, was like something from her most scandalous dreams.

Andrew showed no sign of putting her down. Instead he carefully adjusted his grip, splaying his fingers wider at the small of her back, the accidental—or deliberate—caress sending a wave of sensation that drenched her from head to foot.

'You seemed tired earlier. Are you still?'

His voice was low, a deep rumble in her ear. There was something in it she couldn't quite identify, something barely restrained; but she didn't have to know its name to know she felt it too.

Slowly she lifted her head. He was watching her, even in the darkness the gleam in his eye dangerously clear, and with all the brazenness she possessed she shook her head.

'No? That's a shame.' He raised an eyebrow—and Emily's breathing raised its pace. 'I was about to suggest we go to bed.'

Her throat contracted, immediately dry.

What happened on a wedding night wasn't a mystery. The thing she struggled to understand was how Andrew could make her so weak with just one word—*bed*—spoken with such intent that she could give no answer but to slide a hand up to the back of his neck and guide his face downwards.

He needed no other instruction. Even as his mouth found hers Emily felt him moving, knowing without opening her desire-heavy eyes that he was heading for the stairs. Clearly he could walk and kiss at the same time, pressing her against himself as tightly as if trying to fit her beneath his clothes, chest to chest and both aching to get somehow closer still. With tongues dancing and breathing ragged they stumbled upwards, wrapped together in building heat, her first glimpse of his bedroom a single snatched glance as he kicked the door shut behind them and broke the kiss to lift her higher against his mouth.

She sucked in a gasp as his lips sought the neckline of her gown, ghosting over the lace edge to scald the skin below. His hands were gripping her so forcefully it almost hurt, but she didn't want him to loosen them, her palm at his nape pressing him to her with scarcely any room left to breathe. Any thought of restraint or modesty vanished as he gently nipped along her collarbone, still holding her high off the ground, and her fingers curled into his hair when the tip of his tongue delved down into her bodice.

They were moving again, towards the bed now, Andrew parting the curtains with one knee to lay her down on the coverlet. Above her head a canopy of red damask stretched out like a scarlet sky, gleaming in the light of a fire roaring in the grate, but she had no interest in *that*. Her husband was beside her on the mattress, leaning down to kiss her again, and she pulled him to her so the darkness of his smile was the last thing she saw before her eyes fluttered closed once more.

He bore down on her, pressing her into the bed, but the feel of his body flush against hers filled her with the most wanton delight. If her hands skimmed lower she could feel the muscles of his back, and she seized hold of his shirt, pulling it up so her fingertips could graze his skin. He felt as good as she'd imagined, or better—taut and toned and burning at her touch, something she wanted to savour as she dared to slide one hand beneath the waistband of his breeches…

'If you go much further, you'll unman me.'

Andrew's voice was a growl in her ear, hot and urgent as his lips fastened around her lobe and struck sparks of pleasure somewhere much lower down. Somehow he had managed to slide her gown off one shoulder and his mouth went there at once, kissing from her throat to the soft peaks now almost escaping from their bounds. He was everywhere at once, his mouth and his hands, the scent of him all around her and the blazing heat of his skin taking her closer to the brink. She wanted him to do and say and touch *everything*, leaving no part of her a stranger, and although she had no words to express her longing Andrew seemed to know exactly what she meant.

With deliberate slowness he trailed a hand downwards, his fingers lingering on the inside of her leg to force a whine from deep in her throat. She thought she felt him smile against her neck and dug her fingernails lightly into his back in retaliation, triumphing when she heard him groan in reply—but her victory didn't last for long.

He'd reached the hem of her gown and she gritted her teeth to feel him stroke a long line from her ankle to her knee, lifting her skirts along with it until they pooled around the tops of her thighs.

His hand dawdled there, drawing lazy circles across her skin, and only when she thought she might burst or run mad did he lean back on his elbow, positioning himself so he could look down at her as he lay close to her side…and then he dragged his hand the last most essential fraction higher, and began to show her exactly how delicious being married to an Earl would be.

## *Chapter Nine*

A bird was singing somewhere, the only sound in the quiet of the morning, but Emily didn't open her eyes.

She huddled deeper into the bedclothes, drawing the covers around herself more tightly as she waited to awaken fully. She couldn't remember the last time she'd slept so well. There was a slight soreness in her muscles and the secret depths of her core, but she felt loose and limber and more *alive* somehow than she'd ever felt before, realising belatedly that she had awoken with a smile on her face.

The cause of her happiness was obvious; but when she finally cracked open one eyelid, finding an empty pillow beside her made the smile fade.

Pushing herself up she saw she wasn't wearing her nightgown. She wasn't wearing anything at all, in fact, a discovery that made her already warm cheeks flush, although that was the least of her concerns.

Where was Andrew?

On his side of the bed the covers had been thrown back and the hangings were partly open, allowing her a narrow view of the rest of the room. It had been dark when they'd stumbled into it and she hadn't noticed the pretty wallpaper or ornate fireplace that greeted her now, just visible in the dim light that crept in beneath the heavy curtains. Last night Andrew had taken up her entire focus, his hands and the insistent press of his body blocking out everything else, and it was slightly disconcerting to wake in a room she had no real memory of entering. Her husband's—*husband's!*—touch was all she could recall, how he had made her writhe and gasp and finally, breathlessly, fall apart beneath him, and as she combed her fingers through her disordered hair she felt a pang of disappointment.

After all that, had he simply got up, dressed and gone out?

The night before had been wonderful, but not *just* for the things he had done to make her call out his name. Falling asleep in his arms, listening to the steady beat of his heart against her ear, had filled her with such peace she'd wished she could stay awake to hear it for longer, although eventually exhaustion had won. The very last thing she remembered before sleep claimed her was how much she had always wanted to be held like that, safe and warm and content in the knowledge that the strong arms around her would never let her down. It was the feeling she'd longed for since she was a child, and to encounter it from the man she was now tied to for the rest of her life was not something she had foreseen…

There was a noise from the other side of the closed bedroom door. It sounded very much like someone—a maid, probably—intending to come in, and she hastily pulled the bedclothes higher, clutching them to her as the door creaked open.

'Ah. You're awake.'

A loaded tea tray was borne into the room, but not by a servant, and Emily felt her heart turn over as she watched Andrew come towards her.

In the low light she could see his bare chest scattered with the dark tangle she'd run her nails through the night before, snaking down in a line over his taut stomach to disappear beneath the waistband of his unbuttoned breeches. They hung loose around his hips as if they might be persuaded to drop at any moment, and she found she couldn't look away from the matching pair of indents on either side of his navel, razor sharp diagonal lines that pointed the way to the fascinating part of his anatomy she had so recently discovered.

He set the tray down on a small table beside the bed, his smile bordering on wolfish. It seemed she wasn't the only one struggling not to stare. His eyes lingered on her bare shoulders peeping out above the coverlet, and she had to fight the sudden shameless temptation to let it slip lower.

Instead she wrapped the cover around herself more firmly, secretly delighted by the fleeting disappointment that flitted over Andrew's face.

'What's this? Do you usually bring up your own tea?'

She tried to appear offhand, although she wavered when he sat on the edge of the bed, his broad shoulders now directly in her eyeline. It was only a few hours ago that she had gripped them so tightly he had sucked in a harsh breath, and she flushed now to wonder if she'd left a mark, perhaps a series of tiny crescent moons where her nails had dug into the skin.

'Sorry. I should have told you. I gave the servants the day off.'

He leaned forwards, the muscles of his bare back moving distractingly as he passed her a cup. 'I thought that on your first day as mistress of Huntingham Hall you might like the place to yourself…apart from me, of course.'

The wicked curve of his mouth widened and Emily looked hurriedly down into her tea, not daring to meet his eye. If she did he was sure to read the unladylike thoughts currently swirling, and she felt she ought to at least *attempt* some pretence at decorum, even if the bedclothes were currently the only things preserving her precarious modesty.

Surreptitiously she watched him tending to his own cup, wielding the teapot with more skill than one might expect from an aristocrat with servants to attend to every whim. As could describe her too now, she supposed, the ring on her third finger gleaming as she lifted her hand to take a sip. It was her first day as a Countess and yet she didn't feel very different, her new title paling into insignificance beside the other things currently crowding her thoughts.

Andrew sat back again, his shifting weight pulling slightly at the bedclothes, and Emily had to move quickly to prevent herself from revealing more than she intended. It was awkward to hold a cup with one hand and the covers in the other, and she was left with nowhere to hide when he fixed her with those dark, inviting eyes.

'How did you find yesterday, in the end? Was the wedding as you'd imagined?'

He raised his cup to his lips but didn't look away, his direct gaze holding her captive until she answered. Thinking clearly was difficult when he was sitting so close, his warm, bare chest easily within arm's reach and she struggled to block out a sudden skin-tingling memory of it bearing down on her.

'It was less frightening than I'd anticipated...apart from when I first walked into the church, of course.'

She saw him nod, probably remembering her pale, terrified face. Until he had come striding down the aisle to rescue her she'd been almost too afraid to move, nobody sitting on her side of the church to support her and every set of staring eyes belonging to a stranger. There had been no familiar figure to give her the courage to go on, apart from that of Lady Gouldsmith and the groom himself, and despite her current happiness the sting of that knowledge still remained.

'I would have liked to have had some guests of my own. Most brides are given away by their father at the very least.'

She shrugged as though it was of little consequence, but Andrew didn't seem fooled.

'Their father.'

There was something in the way he repeated her words that she didn't quite understand. His eyebrows drew together and he studied the gilt rim of his cup, his scrutiny abruptly leaving her face.

'This desire to find him. I understand it. After I lost my own I would have done anything to get him back again. But...'

His words tailed off into uncertainty, the furrow of his brows deepening. It wasn't often that he seemed discomforted, but he was now, and even the enticing ridges of his chiselled abdomen couldn't distract Emily from wondering why.

After a moment he tipped his head back, addressing the canopy spreading above the bed instead of her. 'It wasn't easy, but I've learned how to live without him. I'm certain, given time, you could do the same regarding yours.'

Emily realised she was frowning likewise. 'What do you mean? I'm already without him. That's what I'm looking to change.'

She saw his fingers tighten on his saucer. There was something teetering on the tip of his tongue, she could tell, but then he shook his head.

'It doesn't matter. Forget I spoke.'

Still without looking at her he drained his cup, placing it back on the tray with a sharp rap of China against metal. It was a restless movement and didn't help to convince Emily that nothing was amiss, although his evasiveness nagged at the back of her mind.

There had been another time recently when he had said less than she knew he'd been thinking—and perhaps now, with the ghost of their perfect night together still hanging in the air, was the time to ask.

Carefully setting her own cup aside she leaned forward, aware the cover of the bedclothes became more and more perilous every time she moved.

'Speaking of things you've had to learn…'

Andrew half turned towards her. Unless the low light was playing tricks on her, his expression was slightly guarded, although his tone was even as ever.

'Yes?'

'That night at the theatre. You said you'd tell me about what happened when you were younger, but not when your mother might overhear and be upset. Surely there's no danger of that now?'

To her surprise he laughed. 'No. She's far too tactful to think of visiting newlyweds the day after their wedding.'

For the briefest of moments he paused, then stood abruptly, pacing over to the window to twitch aside a curtain and look out.

'It's a beautiful day. I think I'd like to show you the maze.'

Caught off balance by the rapid change of direction, Emily blinked. 'The maze?'

'Some Lord Breamore of yesteryear designed it. It's on the other side of the ornamental gardens, somewhere I fancy you've yet to explore.'

Andrew tweaked the curtain a little wider, a slice of sunshine cutting across the floor. If she didn't know better she might think he was trying to avoid the subject she had just raised, although she had no intention of letting him off so easily.

They'd known each other for so long now, were *married*, for goodness' sake, and yet she still knew next to nothing about him before his earldom had brought him crashing into her life. He knew everything about her—every detail of her shameful origins, her unwantedness, her yearning to belong—but had offered little detail in return, and she needed to learn the truth about the man she had wed.

'That sounds lovely, but there are other things I'd like to explore more.'

'Other things?'

Andrew glanced back at her over his shoulder, one eyebrow raised provocatively, and Emily felt herself blush.

'Not *that*. You know what I mean.'

He laughed again, although more ruefully than before. 'I'm to have no secrets? Is that it?'

A magpie flew close to the window and they watched it wheel away, a black and white blur against the sky. It wasn't much of a distraction but it seemed to help Andrew make up his mind, perhaps giving him the shortest of reprieves in which to marshal his thoughts.

'Very well. How about this…'

He turned away from the window, the early-morning sunshine throwing his silhouette into sharp relief. Outlined against the light, the breadth of his shoulders was more impressive than ever, and Emily couldn't even pretend to not stare as he came towards her and sat beside her on the bed.

'If you can find your way to the centre of the maze without my help, I'll tell you everything you want to know. Is that a deal?'

A small smile tugged at the corner of his mouth, a mouth now *definitely* close enough to kiss. If she just leaned forward a little more her arm would brush his, far more solid and muscular than her own, and on the end of that arm was a hand whose skill she wouldn't mind experiencing again…

The hand in question moved, held out towards her.

'I said, is that a deal?'

Before he could change his mind she pressed her palm to his, sealing their bargain with a firm shake. His strong fingers gripped hers and she had to bite back a breath at the current that crackled through her even at that contact—perfectly innocent, and yet the sudden intensity of his eyes making it feel anything but.

He let go of her hand, watching attentively as she tucked the bedclothes around herself more securely. His smile had grown somewhat strained, and she was mildly bemused at how swiftly he levered himself off the bed.

'If you'll excuse me, I'll leave you to get up.'

'Oh. Of course.' Disappointed at the idea of him exiting the room—taking his shoulders with him—she tried nonetheless for a casual nod. 'You have something important to do?'

'Not especially. It's just that if I stay here with you much longer there's a danger I might not let you get out of bed at all.'

As the hem of Emily's skirts whisked around yet another corner—one he was confident led to a dead end—Andrew wondered how much time he had left. The maze was large, but not huge, and despite her false starts they were drawing nearer to the centre, the clock counting down to the conversation he had hoped to postpone for another day.

He *could* have pursued the subject of her father while they were in their bedroom, he admitted to himself, as he waited for his wife to re-emerge from behind the hedge. But he'd deliberately let the moment slip. Emily had given him the perfect opportunity to warn her against building her hopes too high and he should have taken it, although he knew very well why he had not.

Sitting up in his bed she had looked like an angel, all rosy cheeks and tumbled hair, the early-morning light gilding her pale skin, and he hadn't wanted to ruin it with something as ugly as the truth. For today at least he had hoped to spare her that unhappiness, but she'd continued asking questions. He knew she wouldn't rest until he answered them, and posing the challenge of the maze was a final attempt to give himself more time in which to think.

'Am I going the right way, at least? Can you tell me that?'

She peered back at him, smiling at the shake of his head. From his position a few paces behind he could make any number of long, leisurely examinations of the subtle curve of her hips, and it made deciding what he was going to say much more difficult, each step she took a distraction he could have done without.

The air had taken on an autumnal freshness, but the sun was still bright and Andrew clenched his hand into a fist against the sudden temptation to stare. When the sunshine was in front of her—as it was at that moment—he could see through the thin fabric of Emily's cream gown, and the sight took him straight back to the night before, the image of her lying beneath him making his breath claw at his throat. It had been intense—the heat, how she'd curled around him and refused to let him go—and it had confirmed the suspicion that had been growing inside him almost from the first day they'd met.

She might have wed him as a means to an end…but for him, things now went far deeper.

She looked back at him again and he forced a grin, hoping it didn't look as tight as it felt. His feelings for her were blossoming, unfurling like a vine scaling the walls of a fortress, and yet soon he would have to cause her pain. Speaking about his past wasn't something he relished, but it was what it might lead to that really made him reluctant, more talk of fathers something he had little reason to desire.

'I think we must be close now.'

Emily lengthened her stride, the sound of her new silk slippers pattering faster. A curl had come loose from her chignon and it dangled teasingly down her back, inviting him to catch up with her and wind it around his finger in an imitation of her wedding band. Every time she moved her hand he saw it shining there, a tiny golden crown on her slender finger, and as she rounded another corner he tried not to revisit how he had kissed that very same hand so passionately only a few hours before.

*Focus. You have other things that need attending to.*

She was right, after all. The centre of the maze was only a few turns away, and he braced himself for the moment she'd discover it. When he'd first found his way through as a boy he'd been so proud of himself, doubtless as Emily would be too, and he could still remember how he'd gone running to tell Uncle Ephraim about his triumph.

The old Earl hadn't cared. His nephew's news had been a pointless interruption, and Andrew realised he was frowning as he recalled the pang of childish disappointment. He'd resolved long ago that when he had his own children he would celebrate every single achievement and he still felt the same, the prospect of having a family so much closer now Emily had entered his life.

'Is that it?' She pulled up short, looking directly ahead. 'Have I found the end?'

The winding hedges had straightened out and a clearing lay before them, partly visible beyond a metal arch set into a tall bank of greenery. There could be no mistaking it—certainly not for Andrew, who had already seen it once that morning—and in spite of his circling unease he couldn't help a spark of pleasure at Emily's smile.

'Well done. You got there far more quickly than I did the first time I tried.'

She darted ahead, ducking beneath the arch to enter the clearing, and he followed the loose curl still beckoning from between her shoulder blades. Gravel scrunched beneath their feet but he wasn't surprised when her slippers fell still again almost at once, knowing she wouldn't have expected what was now in front of her.

She spun round to look at him, eyes wide.

'Andrew! When did you do this?'

It had been time-consuming to make repeated trips from the Hall to the centre of the maze, each time carrying something with him, but her delight made the effort more than worthwhile. A glance over the top of her head showed the scene was just as he'd left it—a small table taken from the drawing room flanked by two chairs, laid with cakes and sandwiches sheltering under net cloches to keep out the flies. He couldn't take the credit for the cakes—for that he'd have to thank Huntingham's cook—but the sandwiches were his own work and he felt an absurd twinge of pride as he tried for a nonchalant shrug.

'This morning, while you were getting dressed. It takes an age for a lady to dress even with a maid helping her, so I hazarded a guess that without any servants you'd take twice as long.'

'You guessed correctly. What a wonderful surprise.'

Moving towards the table, Emily touched the vase of flowers set down in the middle of it, the petals stirring beneath her fingers. Andrew had picked them himself, and he was glad he'd bothered when he saw her face was alight, that alone something for which he would happily have gathered a whole field full of blooms.

There was quiet appreciation in it, her pleasure just as genuine for a simple bunch of flowers as for the most expensive gown, and it only confirmed his certainty that he had made the right decision in his choice of bride. When he'd had little money he'd had to grab any small joys he could find, and Emily's smile as she picked up one of the cloches to peep underneath told him she'd been much the same.

'This was so kind of you. How do you know how to do these things? First a tea tray, now this… How is it an Earl is so well domesticated?'

It was a real question, asked with real interest, and Andrew sighed internally as he readied himself.

'When I said I'd answer all your questions I hadn't expected them to start the moment you found the middle of the maze. Will you at least sit down first?'

He pulled out one of the chairs and Emily sat obligingly, although the interest in her eyes didn't dim for so much as a second. They roamed over the array of delicacies in front of her and, although Andrew's shoulders seemed to have tensed, he still enjoyed the puzzlement mixed with her curiosity.

Her reaction was understandable. Not many men would know how to make a luncheon, and still fewer Earls, and as he took his own seat he wondered where to begin.

'You wanted to know about my life before I came back to

Warwickshire. In part that explains why I know one end of a kitchen from the other.'

She leaned forward eagerly. 'I do want to know. I'd like to hear as much as you're willing to tell me.'

To buy himself a few extra seconds Andrew passed her a plate. On his own he arranged a few sandwiches and a generous slice of honey cake, although he seemed to have left his appetite back at the Hall. Emily took a carraway bun but he could tell her full attention was fixed on him, waiting with polite impatience for him to start.

'You remember my Uncle Ephraim.'

'I certainly do.'

'Of course. I suppose there's little chance you'd forget him.' Andrew raised a sardonic brow, wishing he hadn't started so clumsily. 'He was my father's older brother.'

At Emily's encouraging nod he went on, more hesitantly than he liked, but her unspoken reassurance drew him out almost against his will. 'My father was intended as his heir and so, beginning when they were just children, my uncle determined to wield as much control over him as possible. For the most part it worked. A younger son has little money of his own, and by withholding it Uncle Ephraim was able to keep my father in line...or, at least, until he met my mother.'

He paused to make himself take a bite of honey cake. Emily nibbled at the carraway bun, but he could tell she barely tasted it, too focused on him to be distracted by anything else.

'What happened when he met her?'

'My uncle tried to forbid the match. My mother was respectable, you see, but had no fortune, and that wasn't good enough for my uncle. My father, however, was determined, and no matter the objections he was set on making her his wife. Ephraim was furious. But, in the absence of anyone else to proclaim as his heir, there was nothing he could do, aside from being as unkind to her as possible, in the hope of driving her away. As my existence suggests, his attempts didn't work.'

He laughed shortly, but there was no real humour in it. What came next was his least favourite part. It was only Emily's intent gaze that made him inclined to tell it—not a secret, but still something he would rather not have voiced.

'When I was five years old my father died,' he pushed on, trying not to be swayed by her immediate murmur of sympathy. 'Of course, there was no chance of Uncle Ephraim stepping in to help my mother in her grief. He was content to leave us almost penniless and alone, my mother not having any family left after the death of her parents before I was even born. My uncle named me his heir, but that was as far as his interest in me went until I was a little older, when he began to think of trying to mould me in his image just as he had my father many years before.'

Emily shook her head, her eyes holding a world of compassion. There was still vivid interest, but pity outstripped anything else, the kind that from anyone else would have made his hackles raise; but his wife's was somehow much more appreciated.

'What happened after your uncle cut you and your mother off? Where did you go?'

'Up to Derbyshire. Houses were cheaper there and the little bit of money my mother could scrape together would stretch further.'

He sat back in his chair, briefly studying the clouds overhead. Aside from a couple of wisps the sky was clear, reaching out into the distance in a blue so bright it hurt his eyes, and he thought back to the times he'd gazed up at it as a child and wished things were different.

'My upbringing wasn't exactly what you'd expect for a boy in line for an earldom. My mother was able to somehow find the money to fund my education, but not for much else. We had no servants or any of the luxuries of the *ton*, even though by rights she was still Lady Gouldsmith...which is how I came to learn proper use of a kitchen.'

There was a pinch between Emily's sandy eyebrows. 'But... I don't understand. Without your uncle's assistance, how did you survive?'

'The same way as everyone else.'

A lone butterfly alighted on the vase and Andrew watched it daintily sip from one of the flowers, its tiny tongue like a straw. 'As soon as I was old enough, I found work. Tutoring, mostly, for local families that liked the idea of their sons being educated by a gentleman. It brought in enough money for us to live, although by that time I was a lost cause as regards to behaving like a proper Earl-to-be—much to the aggravation of my uncle, who you could argue bore the blame for it.'

He managed a smile. Not a particularly convincing one but the best he could do, although Emily didn't see it. She too was looking at the butterfly, but he had the impression she wasn't really taking it in, no doubt too busy unravelling his story.

'So that's what you meant. When we first met you said we had more in common than I might have assumed.'

'Just so. I believed—still believe—we're of a similar kind. We both know what it's like to struggle, to feel we don't fit in, and that was far more important in my choice of wife than money. There are some things it can't buy.'

For a moment she was quiet. Birds called among the hedges and a gentle breeze played with the hedges' leaves, but Emily didn't speak, whatever she was thinking hidden behind veiled eyes until at last she turned them on him.

'Thank you for telling me that. I understand it probably wasn't enjoyable.'

She looked at him with such tender understanding that anything else he might have intended to say was instantly forgotten, wiped away by the sweet empathy he hadn't known he'd craved. For years he'd balked at dwelling too long in the past, but she had a way of making him feel seen, perhaps briefly even glad he'd finally laid himself bare—but then she went on.

'We're alike in another way you're too kind to mention, however. We both had to grow up without our fathers, albeit for very different reasons, and I believe that too makes us more similar than an outsider looking in might first imagine.'

Andrew felt his stomach contract.

*Careful, now. This is what you knew was coming.*

It was the turn he'd predicted the conversation would take even as he'd hoped it wouldn't. Sympathy still radiated from Emily so strongly it was almost tangible, and he knew her remark was based in concern for him that did her credit. She imagined they shared another mutual pain, and in some ways she was right; although unbeknownst to her, *her* pain was only just beginning, whereas time had dulled the worst of his own.

'I meant what I said before.' He began carefully, feeling his way like someone walking on cracked ice. 'It's possible to overcome that loss. The ache will never quite go away, but you can soothe it in other ways and with other things.'

The faint crease reappeared between her brows. 'I understand that, although… Forgive me. I would never want to compare our situations or be insensitive to your very real loss, but I still have hope that I'll find him. Until I've exhausted every avenue I won't give up.'

She picked up the bun that had lain almost untouched on her plate and Andrew watched with growing unease as she brought it to her mouth.

He was going to have to be more obvious if he intended to make his point. Clearly she hadn't taken his veiled meaning, and he would have given anything not to press harder, only the desire to make her see sense insisting he go on.

'Even if there's a chance it won't bring you the happiness you expect?'

Emily hesitated, a carraway seed held daintily between finger and thumb. 'What do you mean?'

'Just as I say. The very last thing I want is for you to be hurt, either by your father or by building your expectations of him too high.'

The sapphire brightness of her eyes dimmed into confusion, but he couldn't let himself halt the charge. It was a conversation he'd been dreading, but now it was upon him he had to see it through whether he wanted to or not.

'Have you considered there might be a possibility, however small, that he wouldn't want to see you?'

The delight when she'd realised she'd solved the maze, her appreciation of his efforts to lay the table, her powerful compassion when he'd told her of his past unhappiness—every trace of those emotions vanished as she sat in front of him, hurt clouding where once she'd worn a smile he'd never wanted to forget. His aim had been to spare her upset, but looking at her now he knew he had only caused more and internally he cursed himself for his blunder, his attempts to help somehow managing to make things worse.

'He cares for me. I know he does.' Emily spoke quietly, although nobody could have missed her conviction. 'He wouldn't have paid for my schooling if he didn't. For some reason he was unable to keep me with him, and so he tried to do the next best thing, even if placing me with the Laycocks turned out to have been a mistake.'

'Emily—'

She cut him off with a single shake of her head and Andrew found he didn't have the heart to overrule her. She had such strength in her beliefs that it would have seemed cruel if he'd carried on trying to squash them, and yet he became aware of a growing ache in his chest as she sat stiffly in her chair, all her prior openness snapping shut like the jaws of a hunter's trap.

'I understand what you're saying, and I appreciate your concerns, but I'm certain I'm right. If I can find him I will, and I truly believe he'll be glad I did.'

The urgent desire to reach out for her gripped him, to take hold of her hand and press a kiss on the soft palm, but he knew it was too late. She was standing up and good manners dragged him to his feet likewise, although he wanted to catch her in his arms rather than bow with unhappy civility as she began to move away.

'Thank you for this morning, and all the effort you went to arranging luncheon. If you'll excuse me, however, I think I'll return to the house.'

'Of course.' He took a step towards her, one hand outstretched. 'Shall I escort you?'

The hurt in her eyes cut through him as she shook her head, subtly moving back out of his reach. She was trying to hide it, as always so attuned to the feelings of others, but he knew her too well to be blind to her pain, and the knowledge that he had caused it was a punishment like no other, only able to watch as she began walking away.

'No, no. Please, do finish eating. I'm sure I can find the way back by myself.'

## *Chapter Ten*

The music and laughter were far too loud but Andrew forced himself to keep up a polite smile as he moved through Admiral Strentham's ballroom, nodding whenever an acquaintance caught his eye, although it was Emily he was looking for among the glittering hordes. She'd disappeared soon after they had arrived and he knew she was avoiding him, an air of awkwardness hanging over them since his ham-fisted efforts to talk to her three days before.

He hadn't particularly wanted to come out this evening, much preferring to have stayed at home, attempting to cajole his wife into speaking to him without keeping her eyes trained on the ground. But the Admiral's invitation had been of many months' standing, and in the end he'd been left with little choice but to staple on a smile and hope Emily would spare him a friendly glance.

Not that he felt he deserved one, he acknowledged gloomily, bowing as Lady Fortescue and her daughter glided by. His attempt to talk sense to her had failed miserably and he could tell he'd cut close to the bone. It was little wonder she didn't seem to want to be in the same room as him. There had been no repeat of the heady passion of their wedding night and it was a torture to lie beside her at night, unable to touch her while memories of doing just that ran riot through his sleepless mind. He needed to apologise and he needed to do it soon…although the fact he still believed in what he'd said made an apology somewhat more complicated.

It was *how* he'd said it that he ought to beg pardon for, he thought, vaguely aware of being approached by a couple of gentlemen he recognised from his club. He'd hurt her feelings, and for that he reproached himself, but surely the message itself had been sound? His intention had been to save her from future pain, if he could, and if that meant upsetting her *now* perhaps that was the price that must be paid, although it was not an idea he liked and he realised he was frowning as the gentlemen now in front of him each offered an unsteady bow.

The two men straightened up and Andrew made sure to keep his face carefully blank. Neither was someone he would have sought out given the choice. He'd first met them years ago, on one of his ill-fated visits to Ephraim, and the condescending manner in which they had addressed him when he'd had little money still rankled now he had more than both of them put together. Standing with them was a waste of time he could have been using to look for Emily, but he had to exchange at least a few words, even if only to prove the impoverished upbringing that had once amused them hadn't left him with equally poor manners.

'Good evening, Sir Reginald, Mr Lewis.'

He managed to sound civil, or at least enough for Mr Lewis to clap him—with a touch too much familiarity—on the shoulder.

'Breamore. We've come to congratulate you, sir. On your very recent, very swift marriage.'

Sir Reginald nodded in agreement, his colour just as high as his associate's. The ruddy cheeks were those of a man who had already drunk a fair amount and probably intended more, no doubt accounting for the unexpected friendliness.

'Swift indeed,' the slightly swaying knight hiccupped. 'Not to say I'd have waited either. The new Countess is a very beautiful woman.'

'Yes. Easily the handsomest in the room, or perhaps even the neighbourhood. Small wonder you were in such a rush.'

The two men chuckled and Andrew felt himself bristle. Emily wouldn't enjoy being spoken of with such libidinous undertones, and he didn't appreciate it either, his protective instincts coming immediately to the fore.

'She is without question handsome, yes.' He tried to keep the dislike from his voice, although probably his unwanted companions were too deep in drink to notice either way. 'But she is also clever and kind. Fond of music, skilled in the pianoforte and well educated. There are many aspects to Lady Breamore than just a comely face, and I consider myself extremely fortunate to have found her.'

Mr Lewis peered up at him dully. 'Well…quite.'

He didn't sound entirely certain. Clearly in his view such virtues in a wife were less important than having a pretty face, and he seemed to forget all about them as soon as Andrew finished speaking, leaning forward again with intoxicated sincerity.

'But her hair, Breamore. That striking coppery gold. I was saying to Reginald that it reminds me of someone.'

Sir Reginald nodded so hard his watch danced on its chain. 'Yes, although we just can't place it. Has the Countess family hereabouts that we would be acquainted with? Nobody seems to know anything about her. It's as if she appeared out of thin air.'

Hidden by the high collar of his shirt, the muscles of Andrew's jaw tautened.

It had only been a matter of time before someone asked outright about her background. He owed the two overly intimate men nothing—nothing about Emily was any of their business, he thought coolly—but he knew the *ton* too well to think Lewis and Reginald were the only ones who had been wondering, drunk enough now to raise the subject that must have been on countless lips. Whatever he replied would spread like wildfire, passing from one ballroom gossip to another until every Society family had heard whatever answer he gave, and it occurred to him that his mother had been right.

*She said ages ago I'd need to guard Emily against the ton if they came sniffing for answers. At least this way I can try to influence what they believe.*

Affecting to consider for a moment, Andrew beckoned them closer.

'I'd only tell you gentlemen this on account of your attentions to me when I was a child. You remember, I think, when I used to come to visit my uncle?'

'Oh, yes. We always thought you such a promising young man.'

Either Sir Reginald had forgotten how scathing he had been about a shy boy's ill-fitting coat, or he imagined he was being cunning, but his falseness didn't make Andrew hesitate. The two men could be of use to Emily if he could just strike the right note, and he even went so far as to lay a friendly hand on Mr Lewis's back, drawing him closer against the ballroom's noise.

'I'll tell you this in confidence, then,' he murmured, glancing around as if worried about being overheard. 'My wife has no family to speak of. She lost her parents when she was very young and was instead raised in a genteel establishment by respectable guardians, the best, naturally, but of course not quite the same as family. She doesn't speak of it, for fear of seeming proud, but you can tell her quality just by looking—as I'm sure you've noticed.'

He was almost amused by Sir Reginald's immediate nod, accepting the fudged version of events without question. It wasn't a lie; she *had* been raised by respectable people in a school with the potential to be called genteel, although 'the best' might be stating the case a little too strongly. She had indeed lost her parents, however, one in death and the other through his choice to abandon his illegitimate child, and there was some satisfaction in hearing Emily praised now by the very same people who would have scorned her if they had known that truth.

Attempting earnest concern, Andrew looked from one inebriated gentleman to the other. 'That will remain strictly between us, I trust? My wife is a very private person. She wouldn't want to think she was being spoken of.'

Mr Lewis held a finger up to his lips. 'On our honour. We won't tell a soul.'

That was precisely what Andrew had wanted to hear. There was no way they would hold their tongues, and such an outrageous lie only proved it. By the time the Admiral's ball was over everyone would know the amended account of Emily's background but would be loath to mention it to her, and her acceptance by the *ton* would have become assured with no real effort at all.

'Thank you, gentlemen. I knew I could rely on you to keep your counsel.'

He bowed, moving away before they could rise from their own unsteady stoops. Talking of Emily made him want to find her all the more, and he redoubled his search, scanning the crowds but still catching no glimpse of her crown of autumnal curls. She should have been easy to spot and yet there was no sign of her, and his unease was just beginning to build when a voice from behind sent something skittering down his spine.

'Are you looking for someone?'

He turned, knowing there was only one person who could make the hair on his nape stand up with just five words.

'Not any longer.'

Emily stood at his elbow, a vision in ivory crape that fell around her like an angel's folded wings. Her hair was threaded with pearls and they gleamed when she moved, which was almost constantly, her head turning this way and that as if she'd rather look anywhere than directly at him. Part of him was simply glad to see her, relieved she hadn't slipped away while his back was turned, but a larger part cursed himself for having made her now so clearly ill at ease.

'I thought I hadn't seen you in some time. Where have you been hiding?'

'I wasn't hiding.' She looked down at her hands, carefully adjusting the silk fingers of her gloves. 'Your mother wanted to introduce me to some old acquaintances of hers. I've been speaking to them this past hour, until it was suggested I might want to return to you.'

She seemed on the brink of shooting him a glance, perhaps a swift flash of blue from beneath lowered lashes, but then she switched her attention to the dancers taking the floor and Andrew's stomach clenched.

He had to act. On their wedding day he could have sworn

she'd felt something for him, some emotion mirrored by his own heart, and when she'd lain beside him in the midnight heat of his bed he had known for sure. There was a connection there worth saving, worth tending like a sapling that might one day become a solid oak, and unless he found a way to make things right he might have ruined his marriage before it had truly begun.

The band had struck up again, accompanying a rousing quadrille, and under the pretence of making sure she could hear him he moved a cautious pace closer.

'Perhaps you weren't hiding, then—but you *have* been avoiding me.'

Emily kept her gaze trained on the dancers, but the edge of her cheek flushed a dangerously pretty pink. 'That's not the word I would use.'

'Is it not? When every time I've entered a room you've left it, and we've barely exchanged ten words since you left the maze?'

He saw the line of her jaw tighten and knew instinctively what she was thinking. Her mind had scrolled back to the same moment as his, that of three days before, when she had excused herself with unhappy courtesy, disappearing among the hedges before he could say anything more to sour the dream she'd cherished since she was a girl. Watching her hurry away had brought an anchor down over his heart and he could see she wanted to do the same again now, only his hand on her arm stopping her from fleeing all over again.

'If you were avoiding me, it's my fault.'

His chest tightened as she looked down at his hand but she didn't shake him off. She allowed him to keep it there, the first real contact they'd had in days, even that chaste touch coming as a relief.

'I realised as soon as I opened my mouth that I'd hurt you,' he continued, revelling in the warmth of her bare arm through the palm of his glove, 'and I wanted so much to tell you I'm sorry. Please believe that was never my intention. I'd meant to express concern, but—'

'Not here.'

At last she turned, and his pulse leapt to finally feel her eyes on him. 'I would like to listen to you, but not now. Not while we could be so easily overheard.'

She studied him for a moment, her cheekbones lit by that ready blush, and he was powerless but to agree.

'Of course. Whenever you'd prefer.'

The ballroom was still hot and noisy, but that didn't seem to matter as much as it had only a few minutes before. He had apologised, or at least begun to, and Emily had stayed to hear him out, and although she had resumed watching the dancers she seemed to have drawn a fraction closer to his side, making no attempt to move away even when he released her from his gentle grasp.

For a few steps they observed the couples without speaking. Emily seemed absorbed in the music and Andrew was content to bask in the pleasure of having her close to him, until she raised her voice above the scrape of violins.

'Do you dance? I've never asked.'

'I've been known to. Do you?'

'Whenever I can. I love music, as you know, although Miss Laycock would frown if we ever used it for something so trifling as enjoyment.'

Andrew nodded, a picture of her dancing springing forth immediately. It was something he'd like to experience for real rather than just imagining. She'd be graceful, her shoulders back and chin perfectly parallel with the ground, the skipping and twirling showing the supple lines of her figure to their very best advantage. It would be a sight to make every man in the room stare, himself among them, and he was only sorry it seemed unlikely he'd get the chance to see it.

'Did you intend to dance this evening?'

Emily hesitated. 'I would have liked to, but I think not. The only man I'd care to stand up with is you, but I understand that among the *ton* partnering with one's own husband is not the done thing.'

She didn't look up at him, which was probably for the best. His lips itched to curve upwards at being dubbed *the only man* and he thought it unwise to let her see, his position in her good graces still too precarious for comfort.

*Perhaps I haven't chased her away after all.*

The first glimmerings of an idea sparked at the back of his mind.

If Emily wanted to dance, but was too shy to partner with anyone else…

He glanced around. Nobody seemed to be watching them, and still concealing the beginnings of a smile he dipped his head closer to his wife's alluringly delicate ear.

'It's true the *ton* has their way of doing things. It's fortunate for us, then, that neither of us truly considers ourselves of their number.'

He felt her shiver, perhaps from the soft warmth of his breath on her neck, and he had to pause briefly to bring himself back under control. When she stirred with instinctive pleasure like that it reminded him of their wedding night, his hands and mouth roaming wherever they had wanted to, and he had to remind himself that he still had some way to go before she was likely to grant such an honour again.

'Come with me. I think you'll like what I have in mind.'

Emily could feel her heart beating all the way down to her silk dancing shoes as she followed Andrew through the crowds, still with no idea of where he was taking her. All she knew was that he had said to go with him, and she'd been quick to agree, being near him again a relief after the days of distant unhappiness since she'd hurried away from him in the maze.

At first it had seemed things were coming together, falling into place with an ease she'd realised afterwards she shouldn't have accepted so readily. He had finally opened up to her, telling her about his childhood and filling in the gaps she had wondered at since the first day they'd met, and the trouble he'd gone to with the table and flowers had touched her already receptive heart.

Armed with the knowledge he had been raised in genteel poverty—even forced into employment akin to that she had so narrowly escaped herself—she had made the mistake of thinking he had been right. Perhaps there were more similarities between them than she'd believed, the chasm between his world and hers maybe not so insurmountable after all…but then it had all fallen apart.

Clusters of well-dressed ladies and equally well-oiled gentlemen filled the room, curious stares tracking her progress among them, but Andrew didn't falter in his purposeful stride. He seemed to be heading towards the back of the ballroom. A set of tall double doors were propped open, leading out into the night beyond, and Emily made sure not to lag behind as he led her to them, her already thudding heart making an extra hard thump when he glanced over his shoulder to make sure she was still close by.

'Out here. The terrace.'

With the smallest trace of a smile he plunged into the darkness, his smart navy coat disappearing into the gloom. None of the revellers cluttering the doorway seemed sober enough to have noticed him leave, and so Emily followed suit, slipping between the curtains and taking a deep breath of cool air as she stepped onto the patio beyond.

Andrew was waiting for her a few paces from the door, a tall figure bleached by the moonlight. The terrace was empty apart from the two of them, and it was something of a surprise to find herself suddenly alone with him after the jostling clamour inside—although not an unpleasant one.

'This is better. It was suffocating in there.'

'Yes. Too loud to think clearly as well.'

The relentless babble of voices was indeed quieter, but the ability to think clearly was still slightly out of reach. Andrew's dark gaze was to blame for that. Fixed on her face, his eyes were two obsidian pools, almost the same midnight black as the sky stretching out overhead, and she wasn't sure whether it was his unwavering attention or the autumnal breeze that raised goosebumps on her skin. It was the same involuntary reaction to his presence she'd felt on their wedding night, and she tried not to let herself stray back to it, some last vestiges of what had occurred the day after still lingering.

He hadn't *meant* to hurt her, of that she was sure. There was some truth to his accusation she'd been avoiding him, but it hadn't been from pettiness or injured pride that she'd kept herself apart. Deep in the very darkest depths of her soul she held a fear, a secret worry that had haunted her since she was a little girl, and without knowing it Andrew had reached inside her and dragged it out into the light.

*There's a chance my father might not want to know me. Something I never dared admit to anyone, not least myself.*

It had been too painful to spend much time with him after he'd unwittingly voiced her worst nightmare, she thought now, watching the moonlight play across his sculpted face. Shame had overcome her: the mortification that he too imagined she might be rejected, unable to inspire any affection in her erstwhile papa—and perhaps, by extension, himself?

If Andrew doubted she could capture her father's heart, then wasn't there a chance he thought her incapable of securing *anyone's*, the growing feelings he inspired in her therefore unlikely to be returned? Because her feelings *were* growing and she couldn't deny it, widening and lengthening until soon they would encompass her entirely, and if it transpired that he thought her somehow unfit to be loved then her misery would be complete.

But she couldn't tell him that. To reveal the inner workings of her heart when she couldn't be sure how such a thing would be received was out of the question, and she rubbed her arms as she tried instead to turn her mind to more practical things.

'Why are we out here? If the ballroom was too warm, I fear this terrace isn't warm enough.'

In a puzzling reply, Andrew cupped a hand to his ear. 'Do you hear that?'

Emily stood very still. What was she supposed to be listening for? The night-time breeze whispered around her and a hum of voices came from the other side of the open terrace doors, but aside from that she could make out nothing but the merry din of the band.

'All I can hear is the music from inside.'

'Exactly.'

With an impressive flourish Andrew bowed, holding out his hand as he rose. 'You said you wanted to dance. Here on the terrace there's nobody to frown at us—if you'll do me the honour?'

Surprised, Emily looked from the outstretched hand to his

face, a slow warmth spreading through her at what she saw there. His countenance was in shadow now, whatever expression was on it hidden by the moon dipping behind a cloud, but even in the darkness there could be no disguising the intensity of his eyes. They watched her without wavering, and she was certain she saw relief when she placed her fingers into his palm.

At once he drew her to him, his arms around her as she'd longed for even during the self-imposed exile she'd thought so necessary. The band were playing a waltz, a new dance considered somewhat risqué given how closely the partners were required to twine together, and she had never been gladder to hear the soar of a cello that allowed her to sway in Andrew's hold.

One of his hands was on her back, pressing them almost chest to chest as they began to move in a smooth rise and fall. He stepped in perfect time with the music, surprisingly light-footed despite his height, but Emily barely had any attention to spare for something so irrelevant. Her hand was on his shoulder and she could feel the muscle beneath his coat, a constant undulation that lit sparks in her blood, and when his thumb moved in the tiniest caress, scant inches from her waist, she thought she might see stars.

They travelled and turned, the terrace their own private dance floor away from prying eyes. Andrew kept watch over her head in case they should be disturbed, but that didn't stop him from looking down at her every other step, the heat building low in her gut flaming higher when he pierced her with the smile she saw even in her dreams.

'Will this do?'

Her own lips had lifted without her even realising. 'It will indeed. I had no idea you were so graceful.'

'I can take little credit. A man can only move well if he has a good partner.'

He revolved them skilfully, Emily's heart slamming into her ribs when his leg brushed lightly against her skirts. She should have kept her chin elegantly raised, but somehow it insisted on dropping closer to his chest, her head almost resting against it as his hand on her back encouraged her ever nearer. In truth she would have been happy to stay like that for ever, cradled in his strong embrace with no one to whisper or stare, the unfortunate conversation that day in the maze fading into the background as Andrew's palm burned through her gown. He had tried to make amends and she knew it was genuine—but it seemed he had more to say, her nerves tingling as he spoke into her ear.

'Now that we won't be overheard… I truly am sorry for the misunderstanding between us. Causing you pain was never my intention.'

She lifted her head to peer up at him, the tingling growing more intense as she realised just how close she was to his mouth.

'I know that. I know you would never purposefully hurt me or anybody else.'

Almost imperceptibly she felt him relax, his shoulders dropping the smallest degree. She hadn't realised quite how tense he had been, and she wondered that her acceptance of his apology had been the key to his release, touched that he should care so deeply. Perhaps her good opinion was more important to him than she had assumed, a thought that made her glow warm, although something still stood in the way of the harmony she so earnestly wanted.

He didn't altogether agree with her quest to find her father. That much had been made clear, and it seemed unlikely they would come to terms that suited them both. While she understood his perspective, he didn't appear to comprehend hers, but if they were to move on he would have to meet her halfway.

Still looking up at him she tried to think how to explain, the knowledge that she was easily within reach of kissing him making it much more difficult.

'I know you meant to warn me, but still believe he'll be glad I found him. I *have to* believe that. Do you see?'

She could tell by his face that he didn't. His jaw had tightened again, his brows on the verge of drawing together, and she went on quickly before he could reply.

'You grew up knowing that you were loved. I did not. The only thing that kept me going through my loneliness was the idea of one day meeting my father, the one person in all the world I was convinced might care for me, and I clung to that hope throughout everything. At one time that belief was all I had and I can't abandon it now I'm so close to the end. Do you understand?'

Her words came in a rush, half to get them out without being interrupted and half because Andrew's hand was drifting lower. He cupped the small of her back and she realised she was tilting her body against his, the space between them now far narrower than was strictly polite, but apparently neither of them inclined to mind.

'I'm trying to.' Andrew's voice was delightfully low against her earlobe, more vibration than sound. 'If it's important to you then it's important to me, even if I don't fully follow your reasoning.'

He gazed down at her with such frank honesty she felt her cheeks kindle, only realising when he settled both hands on her waist that they had stopped moving. The music had finished and she hadn't even noticed, too bound up in his sweet words and even sweeter grip to care about anything else, and when he lightly brushed his thumbs over her lower ribs she almost crumpled to the paved ground.

In the moonlight he was handsomer than ever. His eyes held hers and it wasn't in her power to look away, black locked onto blue in a connection that awakened every nerve. 'But he isn't the only one who could care for you. Just so you know. There's someone else who thinks very highly of you indeed, and he isn't very far away.'

With heart-stopping gentleness he brought her towards him, encouraging her closer until the thin crape of her bodice was pressed to his shirt. Without thinking her hands went to his shoulders, sliding together so she could lace her fingers together behind his neck, and the touch of his lips was worth every moment of the unhappiness she'd felt for the past three days.

It wasn't a kiss to set fire to the air around them, as on their wedding night. This was slower, softer, holding a different kind of passion from before, but no less powerful for its quietness. When they first wed there had been urgency, finally able to act on the desire that had overwhelmed them both, but now there was something more in the unhurried meeting of their lips, and in the tiny part of her not yet given over to bliss, Emily knew Andrew felt it too.

There was a deeper meaning to the way he kissed her now, the terrace and the noise of the ball beyond it paling into insignificance with the movement of his mouth. He had admitted he cared for her and, with every ragged breath, Emily told him the same thing in reply—and if a shadow from the doorway hadn't fallen over them, she thought she might just have uttered three words that would surely have changed their marriage for ever.

'Breamore? Is that you?'

Leaning away from her Andrew uttered a curse, although he didn't surrender her completely as a man weaved his way towards them, evidently a little worse for wear. For her part Emily could hardly see, her head swimming with pleasure and the honey-sweetness of Andrew's confession, and she knew her curtsey was somewhat unsteady when Mr Lewis offered her an equally untidy bow.

'Good evening, my lady. The Admiral sent me to find you. He wants to toast you as our neighbourhood's new first lady. Shall I tell him you'll come in?'

Even in the darkness she could see his smirk. She had a horrible suspicion he had just seen more than he ought to, although the sensation of Andrew's hand sitting unseen on the base of her spine gave her the courage to lift her chin.

'You may. I shall be along directly.'

Her determined dignity seemed to do the trick. Mr Lewis's grin faded and he bowed more respectfully, staggering back to the doors and vanishing with only a faint scent of port left behind.

Immediately she turned to her husband. 'Do you think he saw us?'

Andrew shrugged. His hand traced circles against her now, tempting her to shudder with feral enjoyment that had no place at a respectable ball. His eyes were on the door Mr Lewis had just disappeared through, but when he bent to murmur into her ear Emily knew all his attention—and more—was fixed on her.

'To be honest, I don't much care if he did. Shall we go in? The sooner they toast you, the sooner we can leave—and I think we have more making up to do.'

# *Chapter Eleven*

The days turned into weeks, the changing colour of the leaves on the Huntingham estate keeping track of how much time had passed since Emily had taken up residence. As autumn wore on she found herself feeling more and more at home in her new role as Countess, much to her surprise, although her growing contentment brought problems of its own.

Every day her feelings for her husband grew a little deeper while, with aggravating irony, her reluctance to tell him so developed at much the same rate.

Quite when she had fallen in love with him she wasn't sure, she thought as she examined the milliner's window display, noting the pallor of her reflection in the glass. It had happened so gradually that she'd mistaken it first for mere attraction until finally realising—once it was far too late—that there was no way back. With every kind word and thoughtful gesture Andrew had won her heart, now so firmly his it seemed impossible she would ever be free, and the knowledge frightened her right through to her core.

There was a particularly interesting bonnet in the window and she pretended to study it as she tried to quiet the tumultuous voices of various trains of thought all vying for her attention. Andrew had business with his lawyer in Leamington and she'd gone with him, thinking a stroll around the various boutiques would help distract her from the constant push and pull of her mind, but so far nothing had succeeded.

All she'd managed to do was wonder if he would prefer her in a pink gown she'd seen or the matching blue, whether he'd choose a white parasol or a cream to accompany her walking dress—and what he'd say if she confessed that she loved him, a conversation she'd rehearsed in her head so many times she could imagine it word for word.

*Andrew, I have something to tell you...*

*Andrew, I have something to say...*

Belatedly she realised the milliner's assistant was watching her from the other side of the window. From the girl's expression it seemed she was worried Lady Breamore had lost her wits, and it dawned on Emily that staring vacantly into space without appearing to see what was before her was *not* proper conduct for a Countess. Hurriedly she moved away. Andrew took up so much of her consciousness now it seemed she couldn't escape even in window-shopping, although she knew that no matter how much she thought about it her situation remained the same.

She couldn't tell him. There was now too much at stake. In a cruel paradox, the more she came to care for him the less she could admit it, her heart ripe to be broken if Andrew's response wasn't the one she longed for. He had affection for her and certainly desire, and since the Admiral's ball she had begun to suspect he might feel the same—but the risk was too great, baring her soul to him a step she couldn't undo. If it turned out she was wrong it would plunge them into awkwardness they might never overcome, the fact they had wed out of convenience seeming less crucial now but still not one she'd forgotten. It would be far safer to wait, biding her time until he spoke first, and until then she would just have to try harder to keep herself in check.

'Not, of course, that he makes it easy,' she muttered as she walked, reflecting that talking to oneself probably wasn't any more acceptable than slack-jawed gawking, but carrying on all the same. 'If there was ever someone more capable of making a woman fall in love I'm sure I don't want to meet him.'

Out of the corner of her eye she saw a man touch his hat to

her and she responded with an automatic smile, followed just as automatically by the same thought as always. Precious few of the *ton* who now treated her with such civility would have behaved the same when she was plain Miss Townsend, unwanted semi-orphan with a made-up name, and for what felt like the thousandth time she scanned the street for any oddly familiar stranger, more from habit than any real hope.

She'd moved among Society for months, admired and respected wherever she went now that she bore Andrew's name, but the one person she wanted to meet still hadn't crossed her path. Either her father had fallen off the face of the earth or she'd been mistaken, perhaps blundering down the wrong path for almost the entirety of her life, and her disappointment weighed heavily on her spirits when combined with her uncertainty as to the secret workings of Andrew's heart.

Feeling somewhat under a dark cloud she checked her dainty gold watch, one of the gifts with which Andrew had filled her trousseau weeks before. He would be at least another hour at his lawyer's office and she hesitated, trying to decide what to do. There was a coffee house at the end of the street that smelled extremely enticing but she wasn't sure whether an Earl's wife was supposed to frequent such places, making a mental note to ask Eleanor next time she came to tea. In a way there were more restrictions on an upper-class lady than her lower counterpart, she mused, not for the first time, and she was just about to turn to wander slowly back the way she'd come when a loud noise from behind made her start.

A carriage had come bowling down the high street, moving far too quickly for a road with so many pedestrians, and the bellow of the coachman for people to stand aside sent Emily reeling back. The horses clattered past her at a tremendous pace, so close to the pavement that she could smell their sweat as they rushed by, and indignantly she looked up to see which gentleman thought himself so important that his haste was worth risking others' lives.

She only caught the most fleeting of glimpses as the carriage hurtled around the corner, a figure at the window little more than a pale blur—but even that fraction of a second, less than a single blink, was enough to steal every last ounce of her strength.

She stood rooted to the spot, staring after the carriage even after it disappeared from view. All around her other shoppers frowned and grumbled, irritated or startled by the coach's dangerous approach, but Emily barely heard them. Her heart was too loud and her breathing too fast, and when an urgent order came from her brain to her legs it took her a moment to force them into action.

The first step felt like she was wading through treacle, but when she hit her stride she found she was running, her skirts flying out behind her as she dashed for the corner. Heads turned to follow her, some mildly disapproving and others curious as to why a Countess might be moving so inelegantly fast, although she couldn't possibly slow down. There wasn't a second to waste—if she let the carriage get too far ahead she might lose it and the man inside, that single snatched peek at him sending a skewer through the very centre of her chest.

A coat of arms was painted below the window he had peered out of, the crest she *knew* she had seen a smudged version of before, although it was the man himself that had helped her make the connection. His hair was a striking copper-gold, still vibrant despite approaching middle age, and the sidelong shape of his nose was one she knew very well indeed. It reminded her of one she'd seen countless times before, able to look at it whenever she chose…

As long as she stood in front of a mirror.

Her lungs ached with each gasping breath of cool autumn air but she kept throwing herself forward, her slippered feet hardly touching the pavement. A respectable young lady didn't run, and the unfamiliar effort of it hurt her throat, a stitch burning into her side as she flung herself round the streetcorner, almost colliding with a couple walking the other way. A wheezed apology was all she could manage and she knew they'd turned to stare after her as she hurried away, the curls coming down beneath her bonnet the same colour as those of her quarry.

The street ahead was just as busy as the one she'd left and her stomach turned over when she saw the carriage caught behind another, brought almost to a standstill on the narrow road. The driver was straining up from his seat in an attempt to see what was causing the problem, and Emily fell back into the doorway of a butcher's shop as the coachman cast an aggravated eye behind him, his impatience at being forced to a crawl obvious indeed. What his passenger thought of the delay she had no way of knowing, although she was glad their predicament gave her the chance to catch her breath.

She closed her eyes, leaning against the closed door as she tried to wrest back control. Her heart was racing and, despite the cold wind, her forehead was damp beneath the lace edge of her cap. She'd acted on instinct, dragged along by a voice that wasn't her own, but now the first urgency had passed reality came trickling back like water on the brink of causing a flood.

*Who is he? And why do I feel I know him, despite never having seen him before?*

The answer was obvious; and yet she didn't dare acknowledge it, pressing her back against the door so hard she felt the handle bruise her spine. The possibility wouldn't be deterred, however, circling round again so there was no hope of ignoring it, and when she opened her eyes the gleaming black hulk of the carriage suddenly seemed one of the most spellbinding things she'd ever seen.

Tentatively she slipped from the doorway, cautiously following as the coach trundled slowly along. No matter how the fine pair of matched horses tossed their heads they couldn't move any quicker, and Emily had more than enough time to gain ground, twitching the brim of her bonnet lower as she tailed behind.

All her attention was on the window, or, more precisely, the scant gap between two almost fully drawn curtains where she had seen the occupant's face. There was no sign of him now and a sense of unease began to filter up through the layers of her excitement and shock, a vague apprehension that she had somehow made a mistake.

*I need to see him again. I need to be sure.*

The carriage in front had begun to speed up and Emily realised her stride was lengthening to keep pace. In desperation she looked around, hoping some serendipitous event might present itself, and at the very same moment her fervent prayers were met with a decided answer.

The impatient coachman shouted for a young lad selling fruit to mind out for the wheels—at which the curtains were pushed aside and a man appeared briefly behind the narrow slice of glass.

Emily's legs failed her.

She'd meant to keep after her prey no matter what, but the face at the window made following any further impossible. It was another fleeting thing, lasting no longer than the first, but the second blow to her windpipe convinced her beyond all doubt.

The coach was drawing away from her, gaining speed as it careened down the road, and she watched it go with eyes suddenly clouded by tears. The final detail she caught before she was blinded completely was the coat of arms painted proudly on the door, a distinctive image that imprinted itself into her mind as firmly and indelibly as a blacksmith's brand.

*I wonder what Andrew will say when I tell him.*

In a daze she turned to totter back to the high street, hardly aware of where she was placing her feet. Probably she made an interesting spectacle, with her hair half tumbled down and mud spattered on the back of her skirts, although that didn't seem to matter much now. There was only one thing on her mind and it brought a smile to her face, tears still beading her lashes but happiness bubbling up all the same, and at that moment seeing her husband was all she wanted.

*I wonder what he will say when I tell him I've found my father at last.*

Descending the steps of Lambeth & Sons Solicitors, Andrew looked around for Emily. She'd agreed to meet him at half past the hour but evidently some shop or other had delayed her, and he found himself pleased rather than annoyed that she was nowhere to be seen. It had taken all his powers of persuasion to convince her that his money was now hers to spend as she wished and it was a joy to see her quiet pleasure at a new pair of stockings or penny bouquet, inexpensive trifles that brought her as much delight as a new barouche would to many of the other ladies of his acquaintance.

In most other ways she was a natural Countess, elegant and dignified as if she'd been born into the title, but the disinterestedness he'd liked so much before they wed was still very much in evidence, and he supposed there was little chance it would change now.

Reaching the bustling street, he peered left and right, wondering from which direction she would appear. There was a fashionable dressmaker across the road that seemed a likely candidate for a distraction, as did a confectionary shop a little further down, and he was just weighing up whether he had time to slip inside for a twist of barley sugar—one of the only indulgences he'd been able to afford as a boy, and still secretly enjoyed even as a grown man—when a flicker of red cloak caught at the corner of his eye.

With the same leap of his heart that always accompanied any glimpse of his wife he turned towards her, ready to tease her for being late, but then his stomach dropped down to his boots.

His first thought, hot and raging, was that she'd been attacked. Her usually beautiful, piled-up hair streamed from beneath her bonnet as she stumbled towards him, somehow pulled loose from its pins, and her wide eyes glistened with unshed tears. One or two had already escaped to leave tracks down her flushed cheeks, and he blazed with the sudden need to know who had caused them, hardly aware that he was moving as he strode to meet her.

'Emily? What's happened? What's wrong?'

He took her hands, feeling at once that they were shaking as though she was gripped by a fever. She was pale aside from a crimson blotch over each cheekbone, and it crossed his mind that she might be about to faint, quickly drawing her to him to thread a steadying arm around her waist. Even the thrill of holding her against him couldn't replace his urgency to know who he needed to hunt down and thrash, his blood beginning to burn that someone had dared cause her distress, but his anger segued into confusion when she shook her head.

'Nothing's wrong. I think, finally, everything might be right.'

She peeped up at him from beneath the brim of her bonnet, her head resting against his shoulder, and his bewilderment climbed up another ten notches. The tears she'd been holding back were falling freely now, but she was smiling unrestrainedly, and the combination of opposing emotions were more than he could immediately understand.

'I see...'

Carefully, not unlike how a doctor might treat someone having recently sustained a blow to the head, he guided her away from the middle of the pavement, depositing her against Lambeth & Sons' railing. It was a busy afternoon and plenty of passers-by cast inquisitive glances at a crying woman and her brooding companion, although it seemed Andrew's expression was enough to prevent any of them from thinking to interfere.

'You need to sit down. Let me call for the carriage, then you can explain exactly what's going on.'

Giving her no time to argue he crossed to the roadside. His carriage waited a few shops away and he signalled the driver to come closer, returning to Emily's side when the horses began to move.

'Here. Let me help you.'

The carriage pulled up alongside and Andrew half lifted her into it, the perplexing fight between happiness and tears still waging its war on her face. She all but collapsed into her seat and he felt obliged to sit close beside her, always glad of an excuse to be near, but still at a loss as to her current state of mind.

When the carriage jerked forward, carrying them the first few yards towards home, he gently took her hand.

'So? What's happened to make you so...troubled?'

It wasn't quite the right word, but it was the best he could do. In truth he had no idea how else to describe her and it wasn't a surprise when she shook her head again, the loose splendour of her hair shifting over her shoulder as she moved.

'I'm not troubled. In fact, I don't think I'll ever feel troubled again.'

At his frown her smile widened. How she managed to look so beautiful with her eyes raw and skin mottled he didn't know, although the sight transported him abruptly back to the day he'd found her in the forest, on the first occasion he'd been privileged enough to see her unvarnished feelings. *Then* there had been no half-concealed joy in her face, only resignation and despair, and the memory of it would have driven him to take her in his arms if it hadn't been so obvious she had more to say.

'I couldn't wait to tell you but now I'm not sure I know how. I suppose the best way is to just come out with it, but...'

She looked down at her hands. One of them still lay in his keeping and, in spite of every other distraction, he felt a spark when she tightened her fingers around his, even the slightest touch enough to bring him under her control.

'I found him,' she murmured, her voice wavering with suppressed emotion. 'As much as I've ever been of anything in my life, I'm certain I've found my father.'

There was a flash of hydrangea-blue as she glanced at him, eager to see his reaction, but Andrew felt as though he had been turned to stone.

'Your father?'

Emily's nod was so enthusiastic he might have feared for her neck if he'd had any attention to spare. Instead every fibre was consumed by sudden dread, and it was all he could do not let his instant dismay come flooding into his face.

She'd found him at last? Could it be true?

And if it was...how long would it be before she wished she hadn't?

The carriage rattled over a bridge, the horses snorting loudly as wood rang hollow beneath their hooves, but nothing could divert his focus.

'When? Where?'

'In a carriage, speeding down the high street.' She spoke more strongly now, allowing her elation to shine through. 'I caught only the swiftest glimpse but I'm willing to wager everything I own that it was him.'

Emily leaned towards him, alight with hope that plunged a knife into his heart. 'His hair was identical to mine, both in colour and curl, and his nose might have been my very own. He was exactly the right age and the coat of arms painted on the door of his carriage was the same I saw on my papers, the imprint left when his signet ring got covered in ink.'

With every word the gleam in her eye had grown brighter, although it dimmed a fraction as she looked up at him and he realised his countenance was at risk of betraying his concern.

'I can see you doubt me. If you had seen him yourself, however, I'm confident you would not.'

The faintest touch of disappointment blunted the edge of her joy, and inwardly Andrew cursed himself for causing it. He was caught on a tightrope, trapped between dampening her excitement or encouraging it, knowing that she would end up unhappy either way.

He had to do something, however. He couldn't sit idly by while she careened so close to the edge, and cautiously he squeezed her hand, hoping he could find the words that had been so elusive in the maze.

'It isn't that I doubt you. I just think one glance seems a fragile foundation to base your hopes on. The last thing I would want for you, above anything else, is to have the pain of finding them dashed.'

Her head came up, her faded smile coming once again to the fore.

'They won't be. I have every intention of seeing him again to make doubly sure.'

'How do you intend to do that?'

'The coat of arms wasn't smudged this time. I saw it clearly. Two lions, two swans and a set of crossed swords, quartered on a background of yellow and red. Do you know it?'

Eagerly she watched him, not noticing when the carriage hit a bump that made the whole thing bounce on its axis. Nothing was of interest to her except following the thread of discovery, and he saw there was no hope of escape, drawn into her quest whether he liked it or not.

'Yes. I know it. As a boy I was very interested in heraldry. Every crest I ever saw I committed to memory, although I never dreamed such useless knowledge would one day have value.'

He tried to smile, attempting to muster something that might mirror the glow on her face, but his mouth didn't want to oblige.

Of its own volition his mind spun back over twenty years, clicking to a halt on some rainy day he could only half recall. The thing he remembered clearly was gazing up at a coat of arms affixed to the tack of an enormous horse, which blew and stamped as Papa spoke to the rider seated high up on its back. The man's face was lost to the mists of time, but the shield-shaped plate was as clear as ever, swimming in front of him now as if he'd seen it mere hours before.

'That particular coat of arms belongs to an old and noble family. The current bearer left to live abroad many years ago but it seems he must have returned.'

Emily nodded jerkily, appearing to be holding her breath. 'And his name…? What is his name?'

A creeping coldness spread through him as if he'd swallowed a bellyful of ice. Once he gave her that final piece of the puzzle there would be nothing standing between her and having her dreams ground into dust. It was the key that would allow her to unlock the truth and he had no choice but to give it to her, knowing with crystal certainty that she wouldn't rest until he did. Everything in him recoiled from it, wanting to turn away—but her eyes were too wide and full of anticipation, and they made it impossible for him to disobey.

'Lord Wagstaff. Lord Cedric Raleigh Wagstaff.'

Her slender hand, which he had no intention of letting go of, trembled against his palm. Her shoulders slumped and for one alarming moment he feared she would slide off her seat, all strength seeming to leave her as her lips parted in a breathless gasp.

'Lord Wagstaff? That's his name?'

Andrew nodded, the tendons in his neck hard as iron bars. 'Yes. He has a small estate just outside Warwick. I'd heard his father died just before Uncle Ephraim did. He must have returned to take whatever inheritance was left to him if you saw him in town.'

Falteringly Emily loosened the fastening of her cloak, giving him a glimpse of opaline throat. In the dip between her collarbones he could see her pulse fluttering in much the same way it did when he kissed her by candlelight, although now wasn't the moment to revisit such infinitely more agreeable times.

Her hair was still half loose around her shoulders and carefully she gathered it to one side of her neck, her hand quaking all the while. She appeared to be trying to compose herself and Andrew waited, the deep thud of a warning drum loud in his ears.

At last she took a shuddering breath, exhaling slowly. 'I've learned at least *some* caution. I won't appear on his doorstep uninvited as I did with yours. But how can I bring about a meeting? There must be some way for us to be introduced…'

Her fair brows twitched together. In the sunlight streaming through the carriage windows they were almost translucent, but he still saw how they shot up when she was struck by an idea.

'Lady Merton's garden party! It's Saturday next. Do you think Lord Wagstaff will have been invited?'

'Perhaps. I couldn't say.'

'I think he must. Such an important figure in Society is sure to be included.'

She gripped his hand harder, so sweetly delighted he was tempted to lift her fingers to his lips, despite his mouth feeling too stiff to deliver anything close to a kiss.

'I can scarce believe it. After all this time…'

Her free hand was pressed to her bodice, doubtless to steady the wild leaping of her heart. It must have been flinging itself about like a bird in a cage, although when she turned in her seat to properly study his face she seemed to have seized back at least some control.

'You *are* pleased…? You don't seem it.'

'I am. Of course I am.'

The lie lay heavy on his tongue. It was bitter, more like a mouthful of bile than words, and he had to force himself not to grimace as it fell from his lips. 'If you're delighted, I'm sure I am too. Your happiness means more to me than anything else.'

That at least was true, he thought as he watched Emily's smile regain all its previous strength. Her happiness *was* the most important thing to him, growing in significance over the weeks and months until he could think of nothing that concerned him more. From his first sight of her in Huntingham Hall's parlour in her shabby dress and downcast face she had intrigued him, a fellow adventurer looking for a place to belong, and somewhere along the way from would-be governess to Countess he had fallen in love with her.

She leaned against him, gazing out of the window with that lovely curve still shaping her lips, and he slid his arm around her, a lump rising in his throat as she nestled closer. She trusted him now, he was certain of it, and perhaps her feelings matched his own, something unspoken between them that would carry on growing with each passing year. Surely there was no need to put into words what she inspired in him, so obvious even a simpleton would have realised the truth? Because Emily was no fool, in spite of her wildly misplaced naivety, and as the coach carried them homeward Andrew wondered if it was *he* who might be wrong.

Was there a chance—slim, but maybe not completely non-existent—that Wagstaff would indeed be pleased to meet his daughter again after so many years…?

# *Chapter Twelve*

Emily's hands were shaking so much she could hardly tie the ribbons on her mask, the curling feather attached to the topmost edge waving with every tremble of her fingers. For the entirety of the past week she'd ached for the moment she'd get to wear it, but now the time had come she felt like she was struggling to breathe.

She glanced again into the mirror, seeing herself lingering in Huntingham's grand entrance hall. Night had fallen beyond the front door. If she didn't hurry they would be late, a snub sure to be noticed by their hostess, and yet…

'Do you need some help?'

Eleanor appeared from the drawing room, resplendent in a gown of midnight blue with her own mask pushed up into her hair. She would pull it down once they arrived at Lady Merton's house, but for now Emily could see her mother-in-law's expression clearly and her heart sank as she recognised the same unease that had been on Andrew's face for the past week.

With some effort she forced the realisation aside. 'Yes please. I can't seem to remember how knots work.'

Lady Gouldsmith came up behind her in a rustle of expensive skirts, and Emily watched as her reflection's mask was tied into place, hiding the determined set of her mouth.

Andrew might have been harbouring some reservations, just as his mother was, but she wouldn't be changing her mind. Her whole life had been leading up to this evening and she had to see it through, every unanswered question she'd ever had now ringing like a deafening cacophony of bells. The one person who could throw some light into the darkness would be there tonight, and nothing would stop her from speaking to him, even if she had to walk to Lady Merton's party in her bare feet.

There was no danger of that, however. The carriage stood waiting at the bottom of Huntingham's steps and the time to set out came closer as Eleanor gave the ribbons at the back of Emily's head a final tweak.

'You look wonderful. It seems a shame to cover such a pretty gown with a cloak. Quite what she's thinking, having a garden party at night…in autumn…'

Lady Gouldsmith shook her head at their hostess's irrationality. It was a fair observation. The cold night air made cloaks not just necessary but essential, and Emily readjusted the one that hung around her in soft folds. It had a cowl she could draw over her head and she raised it now, the hood hiding her distinctive hair beneath a swathe of shimmering ivory. Combined with the mask she was unrecognisable, an anonymous stranger gazing back at her in the mirror, and she wasn't quite sure why she felt a sudden chill skitter down her spine.

Trying to ignore it she smiled. 'I'm glad you're coming too. Andrew has been so quiet of late. Even when we're in the same room it's as if he isn't really there.'

Eleanor possessed excellent manners, but she also wasn't afraid to speak her mind. 'He's worried about you,' she replied shortly, firmly brushing a speck of lint from Emily's shoulder. 'As am I. If I thought you'd listen I'd try to persuade you not to do what you intend this evening—but as I know you won't, I'll save my breath.'

Somewhat stung, Emily opened her mouth to respond—or to defend herself? She wasn't quite sure—but the sound of boots made her close it again as Andrew stepped into the hall.

He looked from his mother to his wife and she found herself

momentarily distracted from the whirl of excitement and apprehension swooping through her innards.

In the evening shadows his eyes seemed darker than ever, or perhaps it was the deep navy of his coat that made them so richly obsidian, his hair likewise almost black in the candlelit hall. Every trace of stubble was gone from his jaw, the subtle cleft in his chin more prominent in the best possible way, and despite having seen him every day now for months she still felt herself stir when he raised one quizzical eyebrow.

'Is everything all right?'

'Of course.' Eleanor stepped in before Emily could stumble onto an answer. 'I was just helping Emily with her mask.'

She drew back as her son came forwards, although Emily thought she caught one last concerned glance before Lady Gouldsmith turned away. If Andrew saw it likewise he didn't remark on it, instead stopping so close she could smell the warm scent of his cologne.

'You look beautiful. From what I can see of you, that is.'

He smiled, slightly more tautly than she would have preferred, and she saw his mother was correct. One glimpse of those stiff lips told her he was ill at ease and she was glad of her mask to hide how her forehead gathered into a frown.

Was he really *that* perturbed? He'd had a full week to voice his misgivings and hadn't uttered a word, either against or in favour of what she had planned, and she had assumed he had accepted it at last. She knew he hadn't always grasped the importance of what she was doing, but surely now he understood, perhaps uncertain but at least not planning to stand in her way—although even if he'd wanted to, the time for an intervention had passed.

'Shall we go?' With resolute cheerfulness she turned around, looking directly at him rather than his mirror image. 'I imagine it would be considered extremely rude if we were late.'

'It certainly would.'

He stood aside so she could see past him to the front door where Eleanor stood waiting. She had pulled her mask down and Emily felt another of those unwelcome shivers at the smooth, blank face that gazed back at her, a strange thrill of the uncanny that made her apprehension suddenly surge upwards.

'Ladies first. After you.'

Even with so many other things demanding her attention, Emily couldn't help but stare at the wonders before her.

As Eleanor had hinted, most of the *ton* had thought Lady Merton half mad to hold a party outside at night, but in truth it was a triumph of hostessing, and more than one lady was heard to wish she had thought of it first.

The guests bypassed the house completely, welcomed in through a side entrance that led directly into the sprawling back garden where strings of paper lanterns were festooned from every available tree. Torches guttered in elaborate holders staked into the ground, so many that the night-time chill was eliminated almost entirely, although great piles of shawls and blankets were available to anyone who might be even the slightest bit cold. In the middle of the vast lawn a bandstand had been erected, bedecked with flowers picked from her famous hothouse, with an area nearby as a makeshift dance floor on the carefully levelled turf. At every turn there were candles and vines twined around statues, gazebos made from metal wrought as fine as filigree, and a rumour was fast spreading that there were to be fireworks after the main event of a real pineapple had been cut and served to the crowds of astounded guests.

'This is… Have you ever seen anything like this?'

'No.' Andrew was peering incredulously up at a man on stilts, whose job seemed to be distributing glasses of champagne to anyone who came near him. 'Even by *ton* standards this is something else.'

The band had struck up and a few couples were already forming up to dance as Emily took Andrew's arm, his mother drifting away to speak to some acquaintance she had recognised despite her disguise. The sea of blank faces was mildly discomfiting and, as they moved further into the crowd, Emily was again glad of her own mask. When she'd first stepped into the garden amazement fleetingly managed to overshadow everything else, but now her breathless anticipation resurfaced and she had to will her fingers not to cling too tightly onto her husband's sleeve.

Together they made slow progress through the chattering throng, stopping occasionally to return a nod or curtsey to some faceless acquaintance. The masks made it difficult to tell one person from another, although her mind raced too fast to wonder if she had sailed past anyone she knew, her gold-ringed eyes darting this way and that in search of the only person whose identity she was truly interested in uncovering.

'I can't tell who's who. With their faces covered everyone looks the same.'

Anxiety began to trickle in. Rising up onto her tiptoes, she scanned the crowds around her for some flash of the tell-tale copper-blonde hair she'd glimpsed at the window of Lord Wagstaff's carriage. Wherever she looked porcelain facades gazed back at her, unnerving with their dark eye holes that lent them a faintly sinister aspect, while bright snatches of coloured gowns peeping from beneath cloaks were like slices of daylight in the gloom.

The smell of woodsmoke and roasting meat hung in the air, interspersed by the occasional scent of roses so at odds with the time of year, and from every direction came a din of music and laughter and voices that rose and fell without end. If she had wanted to feel as though she was at a carnival she would have enjoyed herself immensely. But in her current state the tumult of sounds and smells and strange visuals was dizzying, pulling her in too many directions at once, and she felt her chest begin to grow tight.

*How am I to recognise him? Someone I caught only a glimpse of and is now hidden in plain sight?*

Andrew's arm shifted slightly beneath her fingers and hurriedly she loosened what she realised was a biting grip, although a glance up at him gave no indication as to whether her accidental pinching had hurt. Just like everyone else his face was covered. His mask was painted navy, perfectly matched to his coat, and it did a frustratingly good job of hiding his expression. The only clue she could glean as to how he was feeling was in the stiffness of his shoulders, as ever able to draw her attention despite everything else clamouring for it, although for once even their charms couldn't distract her for long.

Pressing a hand she wished was more calming to her chest, she took another sweeping survey of the revellers spread out across the darkened lawn. Expensive coats gleamed in the torchlight but no one man stood out among them, the hair peeping from beneath every hat either brown or blonde or grey. For a few of them it was impossible to tell the colour, and with the feeling she was clutching at straws she turned back to Andrew.

'Do you know how tall Lord Wagstaff is? Even that small hint might be of some use.'

'I'm afraid not. I haven't seen him since I was a very young boy.'

His voice was noncommittal, its vagueness fanning the embers of her frustration.

Couldn't he at least *try* to be of more help? He couldn't have failed to see she was on tenterhooks, turning left and right like a weathervane as she searched through the darkness, and yet he stood unmoving beside her as if his boots were nailed to the grass. It was on the tip of her tongue to ask him to be more proactive, perhaps using his impressive height to see over the tops of people's heads—but then Lady Merton glided past them, her hands held out towards a guest standing half hidden beneath a nearby tree, and all at once Emily wondered how she hadn't seen him before.

The world around her grew dim as she watched Lady Merton take the man's hand and pull him out from the shadows, the moonlight glancing off the carved ivory of his mask. It concealed his face, of course, and his hat hid almost the rest of his head; but his sideburns were exposed, grown long in the latest fashion, and the colour of them made it impossible for Emily to see anything else.

A bright, unmistakable copper-gold.

'Emily? Are you unwell? You're trembling.'

She heard Andrew speaking to her but it was as if he was on the other side of a closed door. He seemed far away, or perhaps it was her that had been transported, time and distance meaning nothing as she stood and stared.

If he said she was trembling then she believed him, although she wasn't aware of any unsteadiness in her hands. In truth she felt the exact opposite, suddenly certain instead of unsure, any doubts falling away like a tree shedding its leaves. Lady Merton and her friend were too far away for Emily to hear them but sight alone was enough, a quiet amazement stealing over her as Andrew bent down to catch her reply.

'It's him. Over there.'

She barely managed a croak, her throat immediately dry. Under her numb fingertips she thought she felt Andrew's forearm tense but it barely registered, her attention fastened on the man she was now so convinced she had seen somewhere before.

'That's Lord Wagstaff. I'm positive that's who I saw in Leamington, looking out of his carriage window.'

The tremor that had so alarmed Andrew grew in intensity, Emily at last registering the weakness in her limbs. It would soon be a struggle to walk and a frantic fear washed over her that she might be about to collapse, allowing the moment to slip through her fingers as she lay insensible on the ground. She had to approach him before her nerves could stop her in her tracks, and without truly realising it she found she'd taken the first step.

But there wasn't a second.

At once she spun back to Andrew, wildly impatient when he didn't move. Her hand still lay in the crook of his arm and he held on to it firmly, forcing her to wait or risk straining her wrist.

'What's the matter?' She stared up at him, trying to contain the temptation to get behind him and push. 'This is what we've been waiting for! Please come with me, I need you to introduce us.'

Again she stepped away from him, certain that this time he would oblige, but again his immovable arm held her back.

'I can't. Forgive me, but I can't have any part in this.'

She wheeled to face him, unable to grasp what she had heard. The music was loud and the voices all around them were raised, and it would have been easy for her to have mistaken him if the eyes behind his mask hadn't been filled with such anguish that any response died on her lips.

He looked down at her, the terrible sadness in his eyes sending a fist of ice into her chest. 'Please reconsider. I've held my tongue out of respect for your feelings, but now I *must* speak. If you do this you *will* be hurt, and you *will* regret it, and I would much rather you spared yourself the pain.'

'But…' Confused, Emily faltered, suddenly wishing she could see his face rather than expressionless porcelain. The unhappiness in his eyes and voice cut into her, and her first instinct was to draw closer against him, only the bewilderment of his abrupt change of heart holding her back. 'I thought you understood now. I thought you knew what this meant to me. Why are you saying this again, when everything is just about to fall into place?'

Incomprehension held her almost unmoving, but the swiftest glance over her shoulder showed Lord Wagstaff still near the tree. Caught between the burning need to run to him and the desire for Andrew to explain himself she swayed, the unsteadiness in her legs ramping up its efforts to bring her to the ground.

Frustration clawed at her, hot and almost angry as she waited for Andrew to speak. Hadn't they talked about this already? Hadn't she told him in no uncertain terms why she had to carry on? She hated that he was so clearly worried, the knowledge cutting deep, but couldn't he try harder to understand? She was on the brink of gaining the love she'd always wanted, and the ache inside her that had first taken root when she was a child came again to make her feel as though she was being eaten alive.

Andrew tried to bring her closer, gently increasing the pressure on her hand, but she didn't move. If she took a step towards him her nerveless legs might not let her come back again, although the longing to lay her head against the front of his shirt was strong when she saw the unfeigned tenderness in his eyes.

'I can't support you doing something to hurt yourself. Don't you see? You think you need to find your father so you finally have someone who loves you, but I—I want to tell you—'

There was a crashing of broken glass.

Instinctively Lady Merton's guests turned as one to see the stilt-walker sprawled on the ground, surrounded by the shattered remains of a great many champagne glasses. It seemed something had caused him to lose his balance and there was a whirl of activity as their hostess sprang into action, calling for servants to clear up the mess and a doctor to see to the injured man. Her guests gathered to get a better view, even the band ceasing to play as attention shifted to the scene of the accident, and in the commotion Emily saw her chance.

Even Andrew was momentarily distracted, and a moment was all she needed to extract her hand, slipping away from him before he could say a word to stop her. A flicker of guilt accompanied her as she wove through the crowd, alongside a powerful curiosity as to how he would have finished the sentence he left hanging in mid-air, but her heart was pounding so hard she could barely hear herself think. Lord Wagstaff was still by the tree and with Lady Merton gone to take command he was now alone, and there was nothing to stop her as she bore down on him, every step an effort but sheer force of will driving her on.

He was attempting to see the face of his pocket watch when she reached him, tilting it so it might catch the light of a nearby torch, although when he heard her approach he snapped it shut.

'Good evening.'

His bow was slightly hesitant, as Emily might have noticed if she hadn't been wrestling to control her breath. It came fast and shallow and she knew she sounded strangled when she replied, her curtsey more of an untidy bob than a Countess's regal sweep.

'Good evening, sir.'

She rose unsteadily, her heart trying to punch a hole through her ribs. Lord Wagstaff peered at her—his eyes green in place of her blue, but perhaps a similar shape beneath his mask?—but didn't say anything more, doubtless wondering why a strange woman had come charging over to him without a word of introduction. He shifted uneasily, clasping his hands behind his back and Emily thought she might have to do the same. The urge to fling herself into his arms was overpowering, and she was only just able to hold it back, squeezing her hands into fists so tightly her nails bit into her palms.

*My father. I'm talking to my father.*

A surge of dizziness swelled and to her horror she felt herself sway, her vision filled with sudden lights. Under other circumstances she would have leaned on Andrew for support, but he was on the other side of the crowd, his attempt to follow her blocked by the army of servants who had descended to surround the stilt-walker, and so there was no one except Lord Wagstaff to lurch forward to steady her when the garden around her began to spin.

He wasn't as tall as Andrew, but his hands were almost as strong, and a streak of lightning lanced through her as she felt him take hold of her arm. Up close the giveaway shade of his sideburns was more vivid than ever, and she nearly choked to spy a reddish curl peeping from beneath his hat, containing a thread of grey but still identical to her own. She couldn't see his face and yet she had all the proof she needed, the shock when he touched her surely an instinctive reaction to having found the truth at last, and as he propped her against the tree she was glad to have something to hold her up.

There could be no denying it. Nobody could look at him and disagree he was the man who had signed her over to the Laycocks, the mysterious lord whose name she had longed to discover for almost twenty years. By some miracle she had found him, at last on the cusp of finding the love she had craved for so long, and she had to bite her tongue to stop happy tears from prickling at her eyes.

'Thank you, sir. I'm not sure what came over me.'

She tried to smile, remembering too late that he wouldn't be able to see it behind her golden mask, but she realised he wouldn't have noticed it even if her countenance had been exposed. He was looking at the top of her head rather than her face, and for a split second she wondered why before a cold breeze around her ears answered the question.

Somehow when she'd stumbled her hood must have been knocked back. Her hair was no longer covered by her cowl and the soft pile of curls had seized Lord Wagstaff's unwavering attention, his gaze fixed on them as if he was powerless to drag it away.

He made an odd movement, checking some reflex, but then he turned his head away, muttering to himself as he fumbled with the ties at the back of his mask.

'This wretched thing… Perhaps I can't see properly…'

Emily froze, watching mutely as he pulled the mask away from his face. At first she couldn't see it clearly, his head still turned away—but then he looked directly at her and she had to cling to the tree or risk sliding to the ground.

'Have we met before, ma'am?'

Lord Wagstaff's expression was guarded—wary, even, but Emily couldn't see it. The shape of his nose was of far more interest, so similar to her own, and she was certain there was a likeness in the sandy arch of his eyebrows. It wasn't quite like looking into a mirror, but there were too many shades of familiarity to be a coincidence, and her voice shook with emotion too strong to be contained.

'I think so. It was many years ago, but I believe we have.'

Her arm felt as though it was made of paper, but she just about managed to raise it. Lord Wagstaff followed the movement without blinking, seeming to have turned into a statue as she reached for the ribbons on the back of her own mask and carefully, tremblingly, untied it from her face.

She lifted it free…and Lord Wagstaff's reaction was immediate.

He stared at her, his mouth falling open, and even in the moonlight she saw he'd blanched bone white. His eyes darted from her hair to her face to her shaking hands, taking in every inch of her with wordless shock, but then he reeled back, stumbling away as if she was a snake about to strike.

'No. Forgive me—no.'

He held up both hands to fend her off and Emily faltered in the act of reaching for him, her arms dropping loosely to her sides. Confusion and dismay roared up all around her, snatching away the exhilarated wonder of mere seconds before, and she could only watch as he moved further and further away, his face as white as the ivory of the mask he had let fall onto the grass.

'Wait. I think there's been some mistake—'

She tried to follow but he shook his head. It wasn't an angry gesture, more imploring, desperate, and she staggered to a halt as he turned away, almost running from her now in his haste to escape.

'Wait! Please!'

Lord Wagstaff didn't look back. He reached the edge of the crowd and began to push his way through, willing to risk such rudeness to put distance between them, and in her mounting bewilderment she heard her voice crack as she called out far more loudly than she should have.

'But—you're my father!'

He didn't stop. But the conversations of those around her most certainly did.

Every head turned in her direction, every face still hidden behind a mask lighting up with the scent of scandal now drifting in the air. At first there was silence...but then the muttering began, a low buzz that Emily barely heard above the blood rushing in her ears.

She stood staring at the gap in the crowd through which he had disappeared, feeling the eyes trained on her as if each was a needle digging into her skin. A tiny kernel of pain had started to unfurl inside her, somewhere dark and so deep down she hadn't realised it was there, and it grew larger and more agonising as her sluggish mind caught up with the reality of what she had just done.

She had found her father, who'd had no desire to be discovered, and with the very same act she had revealed the truth to the *ton*.

Falteringly she looked around the sea of empty faces, seeking the only one that could bring her comfort—but the next moment she was hit with another flare of pain that almost made her double over. She wanted Andrew, the husband in whose arms she had come to feel so safe, but the agony in her gut flashed again to remind her she shouldn't wish for him any longer.

If her own father didn't love her, as she had managed to delude herself that he would, instead fleeing from her while all Society watched, what hope was there that Andrew could ever return the feelings that had grown in the once barren ground of her lonely heart?

It was a fact that hit her squarely in the chest, knocking the wind from her as she huddled into her cloak, wishing it could shield her from the empty-eyed stares. The cruel irony was that she had never wanted him more and yet she had no right to look for him, the proof she was unlovable laid out for all to see. She should have listened to his warnings instead of clinging stubbornly onto her futile hopes, she saw now with perfect clarity; but there was no way of turning back the clock, and with one last blind glance at the whispering crowd she put her head down and began to stumble towards the gate that led out of the garden, wishing she still wore her mask to hide the tears pouring down her cheeks.

The crowd was too thick for Andrew to reach her but over the tops of too many heads he saw how Emily's face crumpled before she hurried away, his heart shattering as the first tear glinted in the moonlight. All around him word of what had just happened was spreading, details already being embellished until by morning the truth would no doubt be barely recognisable and the ice in his belly turned to fire as he ripped the mask from his face.

'I hear Lady Breamore's name on many lips, but is there anyone who has anything to say to me directly?'

He managed—barely—to keep his voice steady, although his expression must have given him away. Nobody met his eye, the mutters petering out to leave behind a taut silence, and he felt the grimmest of contempt for the hypocrisy surrounding him on all sides.

*While they thought her a highborn lady they couldn't bow and curtsey low enough, but now...*

She might be a Lord's daughter, but her illegitimacy cast her in a very different light, as the murmurs showed. Rumours and counter-rumours would abound now as to her mother and other mysteries, and there was no hope of stopping them, although everything in him wanted to try. Unhappiness rose in his gullet, bitter at the back of his throat, and with every blink he saw the image of Emily's grief as she'd tried to run from her shame.

'Perhaps it could be remembered that my wife has treated every one of you with nothing but respect since she came to Huntingham.' He raised his voice so it carried on the still night air, giving every gossip the opportunity to hear him. 'The true value of a person lies in their actions and nature, not the accident of their birth—a fact that cuts both ways, from the poorest orphan all the way up to the Regent himself.'

The hushed muttering started up again at such an inflammatory declaration, but he had no desire to listen. Somewhere out in the darkness Emily was all alone, her soul in tatters and her dreams torn apart before her very eyes, and without a further word he turned on his heel and began to stride away, pausing only to offer an apologetic bow to Lady Merton as he passed.

'Please forgive me for making a scene at your party. I hope you understand.'

She gave him an appraising look, but then she smiled, the movement clear even behind her mask.

'A man must defend his wife, my lord. You'll hear no censure from me.'

With another civil nod Andrew moved away, heading towards the gate Emily had fled through. Out of the corner of his eye he saw his mother approaching it likewise, her mask now pushed up off her face, and he recognised the same pained determination in her countenance as he imagined was on his own. His chest felt as though it was in a vice, every breath a battle, although he had no thought to spare for his own feelings when Emily's had been so completely destroyed.

*I knew that this would happen... But I would have given anything in the world to have been wrong.*

## Chapter Thirteen

The breakfast tray on top of the dresser lay untouched. By now the tea must have been stone cold and the toast hard and dry, but Emily didn't stray from beside the window, staring out as a new day slowly came to life around her.

The sun was up now, casting a deceptively temperate light over everything it touched, although no such warmth bloomed in the icy hollow of her chest.

From somewhere in the hall she heard a clock strike. She'd been standing there without moving for over an hour, she realised dimly, only just able to recall how the servant who had crept in to make up the fire had been startled to find her already out of bed. Sleeping had been out of the question—the look on her father's face as he'd backed away from her had seen to that, his horror so vivid even a child would have understood it, and it thrust a knife between her ribs every time she closed her eyes.

What felt like a lifetime's worth of pain and misery had kept her company all night, from the moment she'd run from Lady Merton's garden until faint birdsong signalled the approach of dawn, but it wasn't only Lord Wagstaff's reaction that had laced her blood with frost.

Andrew had been kind to her afterwards, when he'd handed

her into the carriage and whisked her back to Huntingham without a word—but she knew the damage was done.

The place beneath her bodice where her heart should have been felt curiously empty. For the past twenty years it had held hope, a stubborn little flame that had refused to be extinguished, but now there was nothing but sorrow as deep as the ocean. In one night she had snuffed out that spark, not only regarding her father but her husband as well, and the knowledge that Andrew must be lamenting the day he'd met her was the worst feeling of all.

She raised a hand to her cheek, surprised to find it was dry at last. Perhaps she had no more tears left, finally knowing for certain that her husband would never return her love having made her cry more than she'd realised a woman possibly could. She had brought shame on him, every member of the *ton* now aware how far beneath himself he had wed, and he'd seen with his own eyes the rejection that illustrated she was unable to be cherished. If she had any sense she'd hide herself away before she could drag his name even further through the mud and she meant to start her penance that very day, keeping her distance from him so that even the sight of her wouldn't cause him further regret.

*I should have listened. If I had, perhaps...*

Slowly she sat down on the window ledge, barely registering the cold glass against her shoulder. There was no point in 'ifs'. 'If' she hadn't confronted her father, 'if' she had chosen to do things differently—these were all paths she hadn't taken and now she never would, her only choice to lie in the bed that she had made. Lord Wagstaff didn't want to know her and she had to accept it, just as she had to accept the fact she would spend the rest of her life without knowing the joy of being loved, and if the prospect made her want to weep then she would make sure to do so only in the silent seclusion of her room.

Because of her pride and foolishness, in believing a lie of her own making, she deserved nothing else.

Her stomach gave a groan but the idea of filling it brought nausea rushing to the fore. Even the thought of eating was more than she could stand, and she closed her eyes until the sickening plunge of her innards settled. She hadn't touched a morsel since luncheon the day before, too excited to manage even a mouthful at dinner, and now she might never have an appetite again. Not even Lady Merton's fabled pineapple could have tempted her, the thought of it bringing forth yet more pictures from the night before, and she wrapped her arms around herself as she tipped back her head and prayed for the strength to withstand the pain.

There was a knock at the door.

'My lady?'

The voice of her maid came as a relief as well as a crushing disappointment. For an instant she'd imagined it might be Andrew, and a longing to see him seized hold of her before she could stop it, the desire to feel his arms around her so intense she almost gasped aloud. He had spent the night in one of the guestrooms and the bed had felt far too big without him, although that was no longer any of her concern. If she was to withdraw from him—as he no doubt now wanted—she shouldn't let herself think of the former passion they had found together or the way he had held her as she slept, and with shame blazing a trail from her throat down into her belly she made herself stand up.

'Yes, Mary. Come in.'

The door opened and the maid appeared, hesitating on the threshold when she saw her mistress already dressed.

'You're up, my lady. But are you unwell? You look pale.'

Summoning a smile was impossible, but Emily tried at least to hide the strain in her face as she shook her head. 'I had trouble sleeping, that's all. I'm a little tired.'

The maid gave her a doubtful glance but didn't press any further, too well-trained to pry, and turned her attention instead to tidying the bottles and brushes on the dressing table. Evidently she hadn't yet heard the lurid tale of what had happened in Lady Merton's garden. But she would, along with the rest of Huntingham's servants, and Emily's innards twisted again to think she soon wouldn't be able to escape the whispers even in her own home.

'You haven't even looked at your breakfast, ma'am.' Mary

picked up the tray, eyebrows raised in restrained curiosity. 'Are you sure you're not unwell?'

'Quite sure. I just don't find myself very hungry this morning. If you wouldn't mind, it can go back to the kitchen.'

'Of course, ma'am.'

With a neat bob the maid crossed back to the door, the sound of it closing behind her feeling more like the clanging of a prison gate, and once again Emily found herself alone.

Moving back to the window she leaned forward until her forehead touched the glass, the chill of it matching the ice in her veins as she stared blindly out at the grounds below.

Was Andrew somewhere in the house, perhaps doing something similar? Or had he gone out, unable to stand being within the same four walls as the wife who had rewarded his gamble in wedding her with a mountain of shame?

She screwed her eyes shut but it didn't help ward off the hiss in her ear, the sharp little voice set on compounding her misery. There was no hope of ignoring it and she realised she was pressing her knuckles against the windowsill, the wood hard and cold against her skin.

*I can't do this to him. I can't let this go too far.*

If it was just herself that had been damaged by her actions the previous night she could have borne it, but she could not bear pulling others down with her. Her father would be subjected to mutters now, the same as Lady Gouldsmith, whose only crime was always having shown kindness to one in dire need of it. Was it fair to repay her now with notoriety, to be known among the *ton* as the woman whose daughter-in-law was nothing but an unclaimed indiscretion? It was a poor return for everything Eleanor had done…and as for Andrew…

It was just as well she had no tears left. The thought of him dragged so low would have made her cry if she'd been able to, the image of his kind, handsome face a torture Emily could barely endure.

Wonderful, sweet, thoughtful Andrew—who she should never have thought, even for so much as a moment, could ever truly be hers.

He deserved the world, not the ridicule she knew was certain to follow. People would stare now, for reasons other than his status and pleasing countenance, and to avoid exposing him to those intrusive gazes she would have done anything.

She stood up slowly, bracing herself against the windowsill. The room around her swam slightly, either from her not having eaten for so long or the sudden rush of grim determination that swept over her, and she breathed deeply as she waited for her head to stop spinning.

She couldn't erase the past. Nothing could undo all the mistakes she'd made, in her haste and desperation taking one wrong step after another until she had tripped and taken those she cared about down with her, but she could at least try to prevent any further damage. Shame and rejection followed her like a plague, and only by removing the source could those she'd come to love ever, in time, regain the respect she had caused them to lose.

The mirror on top of her dressing table gleamed in the morning sunshine and she made herself look into it, meeting her reflection's cool blue eyes.

Mary was right—she *was* pale, her face taut as if stretched too tightly over the bone beneath, purple shadows betraying her sleepless night. Her ghostly twin gazed steadily back at her and she watched its lips part, hearing the crack in her own voice when she spoke her decision out loud.

'There's only one thing to do, and I should do it now.'

With bleak resolve she crossed the room, stopping before the armoire in which her beautiful gowns hung in a silken parade. Somewhere beneath them was the small trunk she'd brought with her from Miss Laycock's school, pushed to the very back so only the battered leather handle showed, and with her mouth set in a tight line she bent down to pull it out.

Despite the chill wind Andrew had almost broken a sweat by the time he strode back up the Hall's front drive, his head down as he threw himself forward. Going for a walk had been supposed to help him make sense of the situation, but it had been an utter failure, his thoughts in just as much of a whirl now as before he'd set out.

He'd yet to see Emily that morning. She'd fled into their

bedroom the moment they had returned from the party and he hadn't thought it prudent to follow, giving her space even if everything in him had instead yearned to take her in his arms. Her white, anguished face was imprinted upon his heart and it made him grimace to recall how she'd looked in the moonlight, all hope and happiness drained from her as she'd watched her father turn his back and run.

'What do I say to her? How am I to proceed?'

The greyhound trotting at his side had no answer. It seemed he would have to decide on his own, and his frown was ferocious as he took the steps two at a time and pushed open Huntingham's heavy front door.

With the uncanny intuition of all good servants the butler materialised immediately, his hand already out to take his master's hat. 'Good morning my lord. Did you have a pleasant walk?'

'Not especially, but thank you for asking.'

Shrugging off his coat Andrew shot the butler a glance, seeing the other man's face was impassive as ever. Either he wasn't yet acquainted with the gossip currently spreading through Warwickshire or he was too professional to hint at it, and Andrew tried to smooth out the worse of his scowl.

'Is her ladyship down yet?'

There was the briefest of hesitations that reflected well on the butler's grasp of a sensitive subject. 'No, sir. The Countess is still upstairs. Mary enquired after her health and gathered Lady Breamore is tired after a poor night's sleep.'

'I see.'

Andrew's stomach contracted. Past eleven o'clock, and Emily still kept to their room? It confirmed his fears that a new morning had not brought better spirits. His spine felt rigid as he gave the butler a nod and made for the stairs, cursing Lord *damnation* Wagstaff with every upward step.

What kind of man could look his own daughter in the face, he thought savagely as he climbed, and just turn away, cutting her off as if she was a stranger rather than his child? It was the outcome he'd always predicted, but to have seen it play out in front of him was cruel beyond imagining. Emily had tended to the little ray of hope inside herself for years, feeding it and keeping it alive throughout the entirety of her sad childhood, then as a lonely young woman, and at the very moment she had dreamed of her father had pinched it out to leave her in the dark. It was harsh and callous and the memory of it made Andrew curl his hands into fists, sorrow and anger curdling together in a mixture more bitter than anything he'd felt before.

On the upper landing he paused to try to regain his composure. Getting so agitated would be of no help and he still had no idea how to begin. His ire with her father clouded his mind, causing any soft words he might have grasped at to evade him, and he wondered if he ought to seek his mother's advice, before dismissing the idea just as quickly as it had appeared.

*No. This is between me and my wife.*

Her happiness was his responsibility, and besides, bringing someone else in would only add to her distress. She had already been humiliated in front of half the *ton* and he couldn't allow her to feel any more exposed, even if it was just his mother and not one of the gossips that had so delighted in the unhappy scene. How he and Emily went about working through the new strain on their marriage was nobody's business but their own and he had to remind himself to drop his shoulders as he approached their bedroom door, knocking gently on the polished wood and listening hard for any movement on the other side.

'Emily. Are you there?'

There was silence.

He knocked again. 'I believe you can hear me. Will you come out? I'd like to talk to you.'

This time he caught a faint sound from within, the slight creaking of a floorboard, and then the iron bar over his chest pressed down harder when he heard her speak.

'Please. It's best for both of us if you just leave me be.'

The quiet pain in her voice sliced through him, going right to the space she occupied in his heart. 'I disagree. If you come out—'

'No.' She cut across him far more abruptly than she ever had before. By the sound of it she was standing very close to the door, perhaps even leaning against it, and he would have given almost anything to magic it away so she might fall into his arms.

'You've already been so kind to me and I threw it back in your face. You saw what happened last night. I don't deserve your consideration and that was the proof.'

Andrew felt his face harden into a mask as stiff as the one he'd worn the night before. 'You don't deserve…?'

He couldn't finish the sentence, too dismayed to find the words. Was that really what she thought? Why she wouldn't leave the room? He'd imagined she was hurt, wounded by rejection but not that Lord Wagstaff's rebuff had made her question her very value, and he leaned urgently closer to the door.

'Because of your father? You'd take the actions of one stupid man as proof you're unworthy of being treated well, of compassion, of being—'

He clamped his mouth shut, leaving the last word unsaid. It wasn't the time to unleash it, not when she was so grief-stricken and confused, but it echoed through his head nevertheless and he had to bite his tongue to stop it from spilling out.

*Loved. You were going to say loved.*

He'd almost said it in Lady Merton's garden, a split second before the stilt-walker's accident had interrupted him, and it was just as true now as it had been then. To him Emily was worthy of being loved and he was the one who loved her, a truth he had no desire to deny. It hadn't been his initial reason for marrying her, and there was a chance she didn't feel the same, but as he stood with his hand flat against the door, pressing his palm to the wood as if he could push through it, he swore he would confess all the first moment he could.

There was another silence. Now there was no sound at all from the bedroom. No squeak of floorboards or faint rustling of skirts, and it took all of his willpower not to seize the door handle. She was clearly determined to be alone and he had no wish to force his presence on her, although he couldn't stop himself from trying one more time.

'This isn't right. You can't stay in there for ever.'

'I know. I know that very well.'

Something in her voice stirred the hairs on the backs of his arms. It wasn't quite resignation—more like the bleakest resolve, and any reply he might have made died in his mouth.

There seemed little hope of her changing her mind and to stand guard outside her door wouldn't help. When she came out—as she'd have to, eventually—he'd speak with her properly, but until then there was frustratingly little he could do. The crux of the matter was Lord Wagstaff, damn his eyes, and the damage he had done to his daughter's sense of self, and Andrew was just about to lean wearily against the wall when an idea took him by the throat.

Perhaps her father would be more open to knowing her if he actually *knew* her?

He straightened up cautiously, allowing the notion time to unfold.

There was never a second chance at making a first impression. Lord Wagstaff had fled before Emily had been able to show him all the qualities that had made Andrew fall in love with her, but what if those qualities were set before him now? Surely he couldn't spurn his daughter once he knew of her kindness, her sweet nature and the pleasure she took in music, all attributes that would make any father proud?

*What frightened him off was being confronted so publicly.* Andrew followed the thread of his thought, careful not to let it slip away. *But what if I could reach him in a more subtle manner?*

He glanced at the door. It was still tight shut, giving no clue whether Emily was close behind it or on the other side of the room. Part of him hoped she would hear it when he softly laid his fingertips on the wood, as gently as he would have stroked her hair in happier times, and then he turned away, making for his study with new hope just beginning to rise.

Some hours later, however, his dogged optimism had begun to flag.

With a grunt he swept the latest attempt at a letter off his desk. It floated to the floor to join the other drafts abandoned there, some screwed into balls and a couple even torn in half, and Andrew watched it go with narrowed eyes.

'Why is this so cursedly difficult?'

His voice was loud in the empty room. The only other sound

was the crackle of the fire and he pushed back his chair to walk over to it, throwing his quill down as if it was to blame for his inability to express himself as he wished. Above the mantle the portrait of Uncle Ephraim glared down at him—the same one that had been in the parlour until he'd had it moved—and Andrew glowered back, meeting the cold, painted eyes without flinching.

'You needn't look at me like that. Do you think you'd be better at writing to him? You, who never cared about anyone this much in your entire life?'

His uncle's sneer didn't soften; but then, it never had while he was alive, either. It was men like him that made people like Emily feel so worthless, Andrew thought fiercely, with their rules as to who was acceptable and who wasn't, and he realised he was pacing as angrily as a lion in a cage as he tracked back and forth across the hearth rug.

How was he supposed to sum up all her good qualities in a letter, when a lifetime wasn't long enough to list them? That was the question he was struggling to answer, demonstrated by the mountain of half-finished drafts scattered across the study carpet.

With a sigh he raked a hand through his hair, the cogs in his head working relentlessly. Was she still in their room? Had she decided to come out now he was no longer outside the door? For his part he was determined not to leave the study until he had committed enough to paper to change Lord Wagstaff's mind, although that now seemed more of an undertaking than he'd thought. Her agony was as real as if from a physical wound, and he couldn't let her go on suffering, his pacing increasing as he tried to force his brain to work harder.

He stopped in mid-stride.

It was no use. It wouldn't matter how long he spent with a quill in his hand. His feelings for Emily were too deep now to be contained by any piece of paper and it would be a waste of time to keep trying, especially when there was a far more direct way of telling Lord Wagstaff exactly what he would be missing.

It was what he should have done from the very beginning, and Andrew shook his head at his foolishness as he went to the study door, throwing it open and hurrying down the landing towards the stairs. Her father might have run away in public, with the eyes of the *ton* fixed on him as he'd fled, but a private visit would be different. In his own territory Lord Wagstaff would be less evasive, perhaps more inclined to listen—and at the very least he couldn't escape, even if Andrew had to follow him from room to room to make himself heard.

Outside the air was crisp but the speed with which he walked to the stable yard kept him from feeling any kind of chill. Constance whinnied from over the top of her stall door at his approach, and he remembered how he had lifted Emily up onto her back all those months ago, a wry smile twisting his mouth as he opened the stall and led the horse out.

*If I'm successful perhaps we'll go riding again, only this time without the sprained ankle.*

He saddled her as quickly as he could, only glancing up when one of his grooms appeared, looking unnecessarily apologetic as he took off his cap.

'I'm sorry, my lord. I didn't know you wanted your horse made ready. If you step back I can do that for you.'

'I know you can.' Giving the girth a final check Andrew turned to the groom, the dry half-smile still in place. 'And I don't doubt that you'd do it very well. But sometimes a man has to do things for himself—whether he's an Earl or not.'

Without another word he swung himself up into the saddle and shook the reins, urging Constance into a smart trot that flowed smoothly into a canter, and he felt his determination rise as he left Huntingham Hall behind.

Standing at her window, half concealed behind a curtain for fear Andrew might look up, Emily's aching heart tore in two as she watched him ride away, knowing that it was the very last time she ever would.

# *Chapter Fourteen*

It felt like the longest wait of her life but evening finally came, bringing with it the moment she had both longed for and dreaded.

Emily looked around the flame-lit bedroom, the curtains now tightly drawn against the darkness outside. Everything was ready. Her small trunk was packed and her old cloak folded on top of it, alongside the tattered bonnet she hadn't worn in months, everything she'd owned before she came to Huntingham in that neat little pile and not a petticoat more. All the splendour Andrew had heaped upon her since they'd wed was to be left behind, every gown and necklace and even the silver hairbrushes on her dressing table, and only knowing without question that she was doing the right thing gave her the strength to cross to the door.

Slowly, taking care not to make any noise, she eased it open. There was nobody out on the landing, just as she'd hoped. All the servants would be in bed at this hour, and Andrew...

Pain lurched in the pit of her stomach and she grasped the edge of the doorframe until the first onslaught passed.

*Don't think of him.*

She straightened up, teeth pressed together so hard it made the muscles ache in her jaw. The stern voice in the back of her mind was right. If she allowed herself to picture his smile or the way his eyes creased when he laughed she might weaken, and she couldn't afford to lose her resolve, no matter how much everything in her yearned to unpack her trunk and pretend she had never intended to flee unseen into the night. The time was almost upon her, only one thing left to do before she slipped away, although the letter in her hand felt curiously heavy as she crept down the shadowy landing towards the half-open door of his study.

For one heartbeat she stopped to listen. Was there any danger he might still be inside? He'd spent hours in there earlier, or so her maid had told her when she'd come with another tray that had gone untouched, but then apparently he had gone out in something of a hurry and Emily had no way of knowing if he had returned. His comings and goings would very soon be none of her business, after all, and she gritted her teeth harder still on another wave of pain that tried to bring her to her knees.

Instead of crumpling, however, she willed herself forward. There would be plenty of time for grief once she'd left, when she would struggle to drag her trunk the five miles to Brigwell. If she stumbled on her way back to the school at least there would be no one around to see it, the long walk giving her time to think how best to persuade Miss Laycock to let her stay until she found a placement far enough away that she wouldn't expose her husband to whispers he didn't deserve.

Only a few months ago the prospect of exile had seemed so bleak she'd tried to seek out her father to avoid it. The irony that in doing so she had brought herself full circle was almost too cruel, now back where she'd started but leaving a trail of destruction in her wake.

The study was cold when she warily stepped inside. If there had been a fire in the grate it had long since burned out and the only light came from the full moon shining through the window, the curtains still open to the night beyond. The smell of tobacco smoke and leather from the books crammed onto every shelf laced the cool air, and she allowed herself to take one deep breath, trying to commit the scent of Andrew to memory. She would keep it locked inside her, hidden deep where nobody could take it away, and it would be the only thing that consoled her when missing him made her feel as though she would never be happy again.

*He will be, though, and that's what matters.*

She clung to that scant comfort as she slowly approached his desk, hardly noticing how her skirts rustled over various sheets of paper lying discarded on the floor.

Once she'd gone the *ton* would eventually move on to some other scandal, find some other poor soul to scrutinise beyond all endurance, and the humiliation she'd brought down on him would eventually be swept under the carpet. A man as rich and powerful as Andrew could obtain a divorce, the process difficult but not impossible for someone of his standing, and then he could marry again, the second time to a woman far more suited to being a Countess—who would never bring disgrace upon his name.

With a throat full of broken glass she walked around to the back of the desk. The chair was thrown aside as if Andrew had stood up abruptly, and she couldn't stop herself from tracing her fingers over the arm where his hand must have lain only hours before. With every second that passed her time at Huntingham Hall grew shorter, and the sorrow nesting inside her grew more intense, emotion almost choking her as she reached down to place her parting note on the pile of papers strewn across the green leather top.

A word scrawled on one of the crumpled sheets caught her eye.

She stilled, frozen in the act of retracting her hand. The myriad pieces of paper scattered on the desk were covered in Andrew's handwriting, some almost full while others contained just a few lines, but the one beneath her note was the shortest of all. The writing had been heavily crossed out but the text was still just about legible, and all the breath left her body as her wide eyes skittered over it in full.

*Sir,*

*Please allow me to begin by telling you how much I love and respect your daughter, Emily Elizabeth Townsend. While I understand...*

It went no further, ending in an ink blot that looked as though it had been made by an impatient dash of the writer's quill, although all her attention was fixed immovably on the twelfth word of the second line.

She stared at it, four little letters hardly visible in the moonlight. The paper they were scratched on shone silvery and the words a deep black, and she had the strangest feeling they were staring right back at her as she picked the letter up, only realising she'd dropped into Andrew's chair when she felt the wood pressing hard against her back.

'What…?'

Again and again she skimmed the three lines, not trusting the evidence of her own eyes. Repetition couldn't help her take in what she was reading, and it was only when the words began to blur that she saw her hand was shaking.

Her breathing had become faster, her heart working at wild speed. Surely he hadn't *meant* for his sentiments towards her to be interpreted romantically? Wasn't that why the words had been crossed out and the draft left unfinished? There was no sense to be made of Andrew writing such a letter to Lord Wagstaff, confessing feelings he hadn't even admitted to the person who had supposedly inspired them.

In her unhappiness she must have misunderstood, for one wonderful moment thinking that perhaps her love was returned rather than the mere civility he no doubt intended, and her bewildered, tentative hopes came crashing down around her once more.

She let the paper drop from nerveless fingers, suddenly too wearied by her idiocy to hold it a second longer.

'Why do you insist on torturing yourself? Why be so stupid when you know that couldn't possibly be right?'

The silent study had no answer. In the quiet of the night she might have been all alone in the world, and she braced herself to stand up, suddenly desperate to be gone from the place she no longer belonged—if she ever had.

By the time Andrew woke she intended to be back in Brigwell, saving him from a scene his impeccable good manners were sure to find unpleasant. Out of a misguided sense of duty he would try to persuade her to stay, and in her weakness she might agree, the prospect of never being in his arms again making it hard to get to her feet. Everywhere she looked the ghost of him lingered, in every corner of the study as well as on every inch of her skin, and she was about to run away from the spectres of lost joy when her skirts brushed something lying by her feet.

Instinctively she looked down. Another piece of paper was on the floor, this time tightly folded and without knowing exactly why she bent to pick it up. Perhaps it was just to hold something Andrew had held, for one last time bringing him a fraction closer, but as her hand closed around it she felt the hairs stir on the back of her neck.

With immense caution she glanced at the other half-formed letters spread over the desk. *One* badly worded draft could be misinterpreted...but could half a dozen? Or more, if she were to pick up all the ones lying in screwed-up balls on the floor? Probably to do so would just cause her even more disappointment, and yet she found herself unfolding the paper in her hand, holding it up to the window behind her so the moon could illuminate the scribble within.

*Sir,*

*Please excuse my writing to you. Such an imposition is rendered essential, however, by the love I bear for my wife, Miss Emily Elizabeth Townsend, as was...*

Lightning lanced through her entire body.

There it was again. The single most beautiful word she'd ever read—*love*—spelled out in Andrew's handwriting so clearly it might have been daylight outside rather than the middle of the lonely night. Once might be a mistake, but to write it twice was surely intentional, and gripped by sudden fervour she cast about for another discarded page, snatching it up as though she feared it might escape.

*Sir,*

*I hope you will not be distressed by this letter. I write only to recommend to you someone I love dearly, whom I believe would inspire similar sentiments in yourself if...*

Again the writing ended abruptly, but it was enough to send her folding back down into the chair.

The room seemed to reel around her as she sat, gazing mutely at the papers spread out in front of her. With each halted attempt at writing the picture became clearer, but she didn't dare look at it, afraid that doing so might make it disappear.

Like wildflowers in a meadow her hopes had begun to bloom, and yet it seemed impossible they wouldn't be cut down, the blade of cold reality surely waiting to slice through the tender stems. Her head knew it was dangerous to dream, but her heart refused to listen, pounding inside her as if challenging the rest of her to keep up, and she was too distracted to hear footsteps growing closer until the study door flew open so violently it banged against the wall behind.

'Don't go. For pity's sake, don't leave.'

Andrew was halfway across the room before she could blink, although her subconscious recognised him at once, a thrill spilling through her as she took in his sliver of bare chest and disordered hair. It looked as though he had just leaped out of bed, perhaps pausing only to pull on a pair of breeches beneath his half-open nightshirt, and judging by the rapid shortness of his breath he had run all the way. She wanted to jump up likewise, meeting him with the same passionate urgency that clearly held him in its grip, but her legs had turned to water and her head was spinning and it was all she could do not to fall off her chair.

He came directly towards her, not stopping his charge until the desk would let him go no further. 'I had to speak to you. I was going to wait until morning but I couldn't let you suffer even a minute longer, and when I saw our bedroom door open and all your belongings packed—'

He broke off, running both hands through his chaotic hair. He looked like a man on the brink, and in that moment Emily had never loved him more, all his calm and suavity fallen away to show the naked emotion within. He wasn't an Earl as he stood in front of her, clearly desperate for her to stay. He was just her husband and she was just his wife, and suddenly all the muttering *ton* in the world couldn't have convinced her that he didn't know his own mind.

With unsteady fingers she picked up the first letter, neither noticing nor caring that in her trembling it shook like a leaf. 'Did you mean this? Or should I say, these?'

She watched him glance down. In his haste it seemed he hadn't noticed what she was holding, and she saw his face change almost imperceptibly, the tight mask of dismay taking on an exasperated edge.

'Yes. Every word. The difficult part was finding the right ones, as I'm sure you've noticed.'

He tried to take the paper from her but she snatched it away, pressing it to where her heart leapt beneath the bodice of her old gown. 'The right words for what?'

'I thought that would be obvious.'

The darkness should have made it difficult to see what passed through his obsidian eyes, but somehow the fire in them burned bright enough to cut through the night. He looked down at her, slumped back in his chair hardly able to move, and the hopeless wonder of his smile was something she knew she'd never forget.

'To tell Lord Wagstaff that if he chose not to know my wife he would be missing out, of course—on the kindest, sweetest, most beautiful woman I ever met, who would take my heart with her if she left.'

Emily's lips parted but nothing came out. Everything she'd ever longed to hear hung in the air between them, and she couldn't seem to speak as he came around the desk and took her hand to raise her gently—but insistently—to her feet.

'I went to see him. I was certain that if I could just tell him about you, about the real person rather than whatever faded memory he might have had of you as a baby, he would change his mind. And it turns out, I was right.'

Andrew spoke quickly, earnestly, perhaps trying to explain before she pulled away, but she had no intention of the sort. His free hand had found its way to her waist, and the relief of his touch almost felled her, the only medicine that could have made the pain inside her vanish without trace. His grip was light but so safe she never wanted to move, and she felt herself sway at the warmth of it, cutting through the ice of her misery to leave only sunlight behind.

If Andrew had read the growing shift in her expression he didn't show it. He went on, determined that she hear what he had to say, and she was happy to listen so long as he didn't let go of her hand or relax the heated pressure of his palm.

'He wanted to come to see you anyway, and my visit assured him he would be welcome. Apparently he immediately regretted his conduct at Lady Merton's party but was too ashamed of himself to call to apologise, fearing that he had pushed you away for ever. If you'll allow it he'll come to call on us tomorrow...or should I say, today.'

Emily's breath stalled in her throat. The pure elation of being close to Andrew again when she'd thought she would never get another chance had caused her mind to spin with joy, but now she tried to focus on more than just the movement of his lips. If her pleasure-addled brain had understood him correctly he had been to see Lord Wagstaff, and even more astoundingly had discovered that her father might not have abandoned her after all—something she struggled to comprehend, a delicious flicker licking over her when she felt Andrew's hand tighten to keep her firmly upright.

'He wants to see me? Truly?'

'Yes. I believe that deep down he always did.'

Carefully, evidently aware that her legs were hardly working, he brought her nearer, his other hand releasing hers so he could tilt her head up to look directly into her eyes. 'It was shame that kept him from you all these years. He was persuaded not to marry your mother by the threat of disinheritance, and he bitterly regrets his weakness in choosing his fortune over her. Apparently you look so much like her he knew who you were the moment you removed your mask, and he was so overcome with grief and remorse that he lost his head and ran.'

'That's why he never came for me when I was a child? Because he thought…?'

His nod made ending her sentence unnecessary. 'He felt he was a sorry excuse for a man and that you were better off not knowing him. In a misguided attempt to have you brought up well he paid the Laycocks to take you in, leaving a considerable sum set by for your schooling and other expenses on the condition they never revealed his identity. He was very upset when he learned Miss Laycock told you the money had run out on your twenty-first birthday, by the way—apparently you should have been given a substantial sum he left for you when you came of age, but it seems the dear headmistress had other plans than to let you have what was legally yours.'

He gave another of those bewitching smiles, although behind it she sensed a mountain of concern that almost made her smile in reply. Everything she thought she knew about her father, her childhood and even her old guardians had been thrown into disarray, and it was hardly surprising he seemed uneasy about the effect of his words, his fingers soft against her cheek as if to comfort her was his only thought.

'So it wasn't me he was ashamed of. It was himself.'

She let her gaze wander over his downturned face, fresh heat kindling inside her as she ventured from his eyes to his mouth and lingered there, his lips so close now the smallest stretch would bring her up to meet them. She knew she ought to be elated by what she had learned about her father, as well as angry at Miss Laycock's greed, but somehow all she could truly concentrate on was the man in front of her and the question that had risen unbidden to the tip of her tongue.

'And what of you? Are you ashamed? Doesn't it bother you what the *ton* will think of me now, and what they're likely to say about you for marrying me?'

This time there was nothing uneasy about the upward tick of his mouth, and it sent an involuntary shiver through her from head to toe. 'Even if I knew every word in every language on earth it still wouldn't be enough to express how much I don't care. As I said before, we're not really part of that world. Now everyone knows the truth we have nothing to hide—and their whispers be damned.'

It was the only answer Emily needed to hear.

She leaned forward, her heart singing as she felt Andrew's arms wrap around her, holding her to the broad expanse of his chest. He lowered his head and she raised hers and they met in the middle, each seeking the other and a glittering cascade of happiness washed over her as his lips found hers and stole every last sigh of sorrow she'd expected to make.

Twining her arms around his neck she pulled him closer, revelling in the solid strength of his body pressed to hers. Through the open front of his shirt she thought she could feel his heart beating in time with her own, an intimate rhythm she never wanted a day to go by without hearing, and when he swept her off her feet it felt like the most natural thing in the world to lean against his shoulder and feel as though she'd come home at last.

'Did you know it's two o'clock in the morning?'

His voice against her ear made even her bones feel weak, deep and warm and full of promise, and she shrugged as she felt him begin to carry her towards the door.

'I thought it was late. Perhaps, as I'm no longer going anywhere else tonight, I ought to go back to bed.'

'May I escort you?'

'You may do much more than that.'

# *Epilogue*

*Two years later*

The bundle of blankets his mother placed in his arms was warm and soft, and Andrew's heart felt full to overflowing as he looked down at the crumpled face nestling among the folds. The baby's nose was like his but the sparse hair was a distinctive copper-gold and he didn't know when he'd last seen something so beautiful until he looked up, meeting Emily's eye as she lay exhausted but radiantly happy in the middle of their bed.

With her usual brisk tact Lady Gouldsmith left the room—although not before thoroughly plumping Emily's pillows and pouring her a fresh cup of tea—and with extreme care he shifted the precious load into the crook of one arm, freeing a hand to seek out Emily's, lying on the hurriedly changed sheets.

'He's got your hair.'

'And your nose.'

She smiled, squeezing his fingers far more gently now than she had at the peak of her pains. She looked shattered after her long ordeal, during which he had stubbornly refused to leave her side, but already some of the colour was returning to her cheeks, and her face as she gazed at her brand-new son was so astoundingly lovely that, for a moment, Andrew struggled to breathe.

Sitting in a chair beside the bed, cradling his child while he held his wife's hand, he had everything he'd ever wanted. Nothing could replace the loss of his father, but his mother had taken such joy in her daughter-in-law and Emily loved her now in turn, the relationship with her own papa likewise deepening as they grew to know each other.

People still muttered about her occasionally, throwing the odd lanced barb when she and Lord Wagstaff were seen out in public arm in arm, but the opinions of such narrow-minded individuals didn't matter. Since their unconventional marriage Andrew had gained a wife he loved and now a family, too, and so long as Emily was happy he couldn't care less about the mumbling of the *ton* or anyone else who might venture criticism where it didn't belong.

'What shall we name him?'

At the question Emily eased herself up a little higher against the pillows, wincing slightly as she moved. 'I thought you might like Matthew. For your father.'

He stroked her knuckles with his thumb, touched by her consideration. 'I would. Thank you. And for a middle name?'

She was busy adjusting the coverlet with her free hand but he could have sworn he caught a glimpse of a furtive smile. 'How about Ephraim?'

'Ephraim?' Surprised by such an unexpected suggestion he sat forward, quickly leaning back again when the movement caused the baby to stir. 'For my uncle? Why?'

Emily shrugged, the smile growing wider. 'If you think about it, it's because of him that we first met. If I hadn't come here looking for him, our paths would never have crossed and we wouldn't have found the happiness we have now.'

Andrew laughed, although he couldn't argue with her logic. 'He would hate that. The sentimentality of being credited with a love story? That would have put him in the foulest temper the world had ever seen.'

He laughed again and this time Emily joined in with the spiritedness he had adored watching grow over the past two years, no longer the shy young woman who had first appeared in the parlour of Huntingham Hall. She was confident now and he was glad of it, knowing herself to be worthy of love and to give it in return, and as he gazed down on the child they had made together he thought nothing could ever dampen their joy.

'Very well. Matthew Ephraim Gouldsmith it is. And here's hoping he grows to be more like his first namesake than his second.'

* * * * *

# The Scandalous Widow

Elizabeth Rolls

MILLS & BOON

**Elizabeth Rolls** lives in the Adelaide Hills of South Australia with her husband, two sons, several dogs and cats, and a number of chickens. She has a well-known love of tea and coffee, far too many books and an overgrown garden. Currently Elizabeth is wondering if she should train the dogs to put her sons' dishes in the dishwasher rather than continuing to ask the boys. She can be found on Facebook and readers are invited to contact her at books@elizabethrolls.com.

**Books by Elizabeth Rolls**

**Harlequin Historical**

*The Dutiful Rake*
*The Unruly Chaperon*
*The Chivalrous Rake*
*His Lady Mistress*
"The Prodigal Bride"
in *A Regency Invitation*
*A Compromised Lady*
*Lord Braybrook's Penniless Bride*
*A Princely Dilemma*
"Christmas Cinderella"
in *A Sprinkling of Christmas Magic*
*A Marriage of Equals*
*Lord Martin's Scandalous Bluestocking*

***Lords at the Altar***

*In Debt to the Earl*
*His Convenient Marchioness*

Visit the Author Profile page
at millsandboon.com.au for more titles.

## Author Note

Althea Hartleigh has resided in my head since she appeared as the dreaded Other Woman in *The Dutiful Rake* over twenty years ago. From her beginnings, she refused to conform to my expectations, and I have wanted to write her story for a very long time.

Going in, I found that although I knew her already, there were still mysteries. I knew her first marriage had been disastrous, but not why. I also needed to know what happened to her in the fictional years since *The Dutiful Rake*.

Being Althea, she hadn't waited to be rescued!

That she had written her way out of financial ruin surprised me. It has never been easy to do, now or then. While Jane Austen, sadly, made only about £600 from her books in her lifetime, there were women who made far more. One of these was Ann Radcliffe, who wrote *The Mysteries of Udolpho*. I have taken a path between these two, allowing Althea the financial success of Radcliffe, while staying closer to the style of Austen.

By the time Hugo appears to disrupt Althea's life, she doesn't need any man to rescue her. But even if she doesn't know it, she does need love, a family and a friend to depend on.

Tell you a secret? The pair of them sniped at each other for several pages before I realized Hugo was the hero! I thought he was just "the lawyer," but like Althea, he confounded me.

I hope you enjoy their story.

For Gabby & Anna.

This is for all the friendship and laughter
in the Hawks' Nest kitchen over so many years.
And huge thanks for letting me make you
ladies of "ill repute" in the last book!

# *Prologue*

*Early March*

Althea Hartleigh held the letter her manservant had handed her between thumb and forefinger and considered it carefully. Yes, that was her name and style, set out correctly in a neat, businesslike script. On the reverse—no need to look again, it was engraved on her memory—was the name, style and address of her brother's solicitor. No postmark.

'This was hand-delivered, John?'

She hadn't meant to sound snappish. The whiskery nose of her small scruffy terrier emerged from under her desk in hopes of a walk, but retreated immediately.

'Yes, ma'am. Chap's waiting in case you wish to send a reply.'

She hardly ever lost her temper now. There was so rarely anyone with whom to lose it. For the past several years she had deliberately lived her life free of familial entanglements and obligations. Who the hell needed them?

But now memory rose up, flooding through her in a scalding torrent—memories she preferred to forget. Everything she had lost, and decided she no longer needed or wanted, spilled over in a fury of hurt. Her fingers opened, and the letter fluttered into the fire. Satisfaction burned darkly as the letter flared. No doubt Frederick's solicitor, the hapless Mr Hugh Guthrie, was really a very nice old man. She knew he had delivered Frederick's last communiqué some years ago under duress, and she had felt sorry for his obvious discomfort, but if Frederick wished to speak to her, he could find the intestinal fortitude to face her.

'Ma'am? Is that your reply?'

She stared at the merrily burning letter a moment longer. The wax of the unbroken seal went up with a hiss. She clenched her fists, then forced them to relax, and reached for calm.

'You could say that.' Poor Mr Guthrie didn't deserve her venom. 'Please inform the messenger that, while I have no personal animus towards his master, my brother Frederick may burn in hell along with all his works for all I care.'

'Yes, my lady.'

As the door closed behind him, Althea reflected that she must have shocked John to his boots for him to fall back on calling her *my lady*. For a moment she wondered if burning the letter unread had been the best decision she could have made. She dismissed that. It was done now. Time to gather her thoughts. She sat back at her untidy desk, picked up her pen and dipped it in the ink. Back to work. This letter was important.

Ten minutes later she was still staring at a blank page, the thoughts she actually *wanted* ungathered. The ink upon the quill went dry as thoughts she very definitely didn't want churned through her.

*Damn.*

Words eluded her. She wished her thoughts would do likewise. Had she done the right thing?

'Too late if I haven't, Puck.'

A tail, attached to the dog beneath her desk, thumped.

'Damn.' Saying it aloud didn't help either.

She looked under the desk, met hopeful brown eyes. 'We'll walk down to the bookshop.'

She bent down and changed into her outdoor shoes, conveniently located under her desk.

The tail increased its activity and Puck, correctly interpreting the shoe change and the word *walk*, trotted over to the door where his leash hung. Althea rose. One of the many nice things about living alone was that no one cared if your bonnet and cloak hung on the back of the parlour door with the dog's leash, or that your outdoor shoes lived under your desk. It wasn't slovenly. It was *convenient*. Your shoes and cloak were exactly where you needed them if you decided on impulse to go out, and no one cared or fussed at you over it. She retrieved a pair of gloves from her desk drawer and drew them on. Her house, her home, her life and her choices. No one told you that, no, you might not have a dog under any circumstances. Having a dog and keeping a pair of gloves in the drawer of your desk might not be very important choices, but they were *her* choices.

Her finished library books were already on the hall table. Selbourne's Antiquarian Books a few streets away had a circulating library attached. By rights she should finish her letter before going for a walk. Instead she'd change her books and take some fresh air—well, as fresh as London air ever got—and settle her mind. She could negotiate better afterwards.

Her stomach was still knotted twenty minutes later when she pushed open the door of Selbourne's, despite the brisk walk. Why should she feel guilty about burning a letter from Frederick's solicitor? Whatever social crimes her not-so-beloved brother was laying at her door now, she didn't need to see them set out in his solicitor's elegant script.

Smiling at the proprietress as she rose from her desk, Althea asked, 'Have you anything suitable for mentally consigning uncongenial relatives to a place of great heat?'

Miss Selbourne, a lady some years older than herself, raised her brows as she took a dog biscuit from some fastness in her desk. 'I believe I can accommodate you with a nice translation of *The Divine Comedy*. Puck?'

The dog sat immediately, and Miss Selbourne tossed the biscuit to him. He snatched it from the air, trotted to the fireplace where Miss Selbourne's much larger, if equally scruffy dog opened a tolerant eye in greeting, and then Puck settled down to enjoy it.

Althea smiled, some of her restless irritation melting away. She liked this shop, and she liked its owner. She had no idea how Miss Selbourne, whose married name was Lady Martin

Lacy, managed to balance marriage, family and owning a business in practical terms, let alone the legal quagmire for a married woman running a business. Sometimes she wanted to ask, but that would require a greater intimacy than she was prepared to accept. Relationships, most of them, were too wretchedly complicated.

*One week later*

Hugo Guthrie spent as little time as possible hanging around inn yards. Especially on cold March days, and extra-especially the Bolt-in-Tun on Fleet Street. In his admittedly theoretical experience, inn yards were an excellent place to have your pockets picked whatever the weather. They were also excellent places to find a whore for the night. Often you could have both for the price of one, with your choice of whore slipping a little something extra into your drink and making off with your possessions. Including your clothes.

Or so he had been told. He was not interested in learning such things from his own experience.

The Bolt had a particularly well-earned reputation for drunken sprees and otherwise riotous gatherings. Again, this was second-hand knowledge.

With these dubious delights in mind, he kept close to the wall of the inn, making sure his wallet was secure along with his watch. For good measure he added a forbidding frown for any suspect female who thought to approach him.

It wouldn't do his reputation in the legal fraternity any good if his partner had to rescue him naked from some stew near the Bolt. He glanced at his watch for the umpteenth time—the stagecoach was now officially late.

Probably not unusual. Indeed, when he'd come down a couple of days ago, to ask the landlord what time the coach was due in from Hastings, he'd been told as much. But he hadn't dared risk being late. Not for this particular coach. So he'd arrived early, whiling away the first hour in the tap with a quiet pint of ale.

The pint a pleasant memory, he'd decided to wait in the yard despite the light drizzle. He stiffened as a respectable looking female sauntered in. It was possible she *was* as completely respectable as her garb implied. That she'd merely come to meet a relative off the stage...or it was possible that she was a brothelkeeper, looking not for clients, but for new girls. And, if the latter—he noted her speak briefly to a much younger, prettily dressed female—it was also likely she was keeping an eye on the current girls.

Men and horses came and went through the narrow tunnel leading out to Fleet Street. Two young bucks rode in a hired gig with a dappled cob between the shafts. Errand boys scurried in and out, doubtless with a sprinkling of pickpockets amongst them. A stray dog nosed about, but made off when an ostler threatened it with a broom. All sorts made their living around an inn.

He idly wondered, if he took all due precautions, it might be interesting to spend more time in places like this, watching the bustle from a safe distance. With his back firmly to the wall.

A small ginger cat strutted across the yard, a large rat dangling from its jaws, and disappeared into the stables. From the plush state of the cat's fur, Hugo surmised that the creature more than earned its keep. He pulled his cloak a little closer against the rain and the wind that whipped against it even in the sheltered yard. He'd wear his muffler if he did this again.

'Here she comes!'

The yell from a man by the gate heralded a clatter of hooves and rumble of wheels, magnified by the confines of the tunnel, as the stagecoach lumbered in.

Hugo stepped forward as soon as the vehicle drew to a halt, taking care to stay out of the way of the ostlers managing the four sturdy, sweating horses who looked as though they needed a feed and a rest.

The doors opened and passengers alighted. None of them, he saw at a glance, were the pair he was supposed to meet. Worry gnawed in his belly. What if they'd got off too early? What if—

'Sorry, guv. 'Scuse me.'

He turned, moving aside for the ostler. 'My apologies.'

'No problem. Just got to help this little lass down.'

*Little lass? Down?*

Hugo looked up at the dark-haired child, no more than eight, which the guard was helping down from the roof. Another girl, several years older, started to scramble after her. Her hood tumbled back to reveal a pale face and honey-gold curls.

'Now, hold on, missy.' The ostler set the little girl down and held up his hand for the older girl, who clutched a valise. As soon as she was down the girl hurried to the smaller child who clung to her hand.

Hugo didn't believe it. Didn't want to believe it. The bastard hadn't even paid for inside seats?

He swallowed. What the devil did he know of young girls? What was he supposed to say to them? Sometimes the obvious was best.

He cleared his throat. 'Miss Price? Miss Sarah Price?' He wondered at the croaky sound of his own voice.

The girl, her knuckles white on the valise, looked at him. The little girl, eyes reddened and swollen, shrank against her. Hugo's stomach knotted.

'Yes. Who…who are you?'

The defiance in her voice and lifted chin told him everything he didn't want to know. And everything Sarah Price didn't want him to know—that she was terrified.

'I'm Mr Guthrie, Mr Hugh Guthrie. Your father's lawyer. I'm here to meet you and your sister.' He smiled at the little girl, who practically disappeared into her sister's shadow. 'Did no one accompany you?'

Why was he even asking? The man who had refused to look after these children, had put them on the stagecoach in outside seats, wasn't going to waste a return fare on a servant to accompany them.

The older girl shook her head. Suspicious green eyes looked him up and down. 'How do we know you're who you say you are?'

Hugo took out the letter he'd been sent. It was the last thing he wanted to show the poor child, but he couldn't expect her to trust him without question. 'This was sent to me by your cousin, Mr Price-Babbington. Asking me to meet you today.'

Still the child hesitated. Beside her the smaller girl began to shiver.

'Sarah?' The voice was a mere whisper, as though the poor little scrap scarcely dared speak. 'Did he know Papa?'

Hugo tried again. 'Sarah, your sister—Kate, isn't it?—is cold. Why don't you come into the inn with me? I… I can secure a private parlour. Perhaps some dinner.'

The little girl looked hopeful. 'Dinner? Really? The driver shared his food with us, but we didn't have enough money at the last stage for anything.'

The rage Hugo had been tamping down since receiving Price-Babbington's instructions for these girls flared up all over again. Damn the bastard to hell and back. No. Not back. Price-Babbington could stay in hell where he belonged.

'Dinner, then.'

Sarah Price's expression still spat defiance. 'Are you taking us to the orphanage after that?'

He clenched his fists. 'No.'

He'd spent the last week tracking down as many members of their family as he possibly could. While he didn't hold out any hope for their father's estranged—not to mention impecunious and disgraced—sister, Lady Hartleigh, to take them in—apparently she hadn't even bothered to read his letter—there were plenty of other relatives who could. He'd hoped that by now one of those relatives would have replied in the affirmative.

The next words out of his mouth burned every bridge there had ever been. 'There won't be any orphanage.'

He'd write to the entire family again. They couldn't *not* respond, surely. Meanwhile, Hugo contemplated the wreck of his own neatly ordered world while he waited for them to do so.

# *Chapter One*

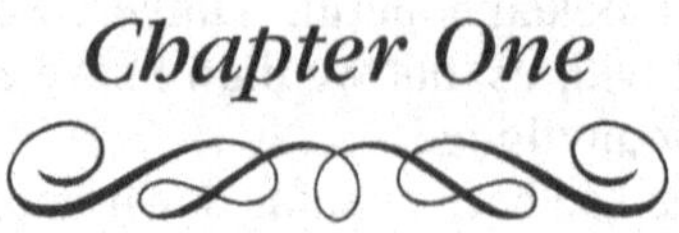

*Two weeks later*

Althea set her pen down, and sprinkled sand on her completed columns of figures with pardonable pride. After four years of hard work and stringent economy she was solvent and looked like she would remain so. She even had a nice little nest egg. Money, safely invested, that brought an income she could live on comfortably. Not extravagantly as she once had, but comfortably. She was safe. Well, as safe as she had ever been. Certainly safer than she had been during her marriage, let alone the first two years of her widowhood.

Because she'd made herself look at figures.

She *hated* figures. As a very small child she had got into trouble for praying to God to 'uninvent arithmetic' so she wouldn't have to do it. Nanny had thought it was funny and told the other servants so that it got back to her governess.

Miss Fairley had informed her small charge that she was both ignorant and irreligious. Extra sums for a month was the penance.

Althea stuck her tongue out at the defeated figures. She *loathed* doing the household accounts, but adults often had to do things that they hated and found boring, and do them properly. Responsible adults that was—those who wished to understand how much money they had to live on and thereby remain out of a debtors' prison. She might hate the household accounts, but she liked managing for herself and not being dependent on anyone.

Now that she had finished the thrice cursed accounts she could get back to the new people strolling around in her head. She needed to get them out of her head and onto paper so she could find out what they were going to do. At least she was reasonably sure that Miss Parker… Sarah? Sarah Parker? She liked that. It was a decently plain name. Nothing outlandish—no Esmeraldas, thank you very much—and she'd always liked the name Sarah. Hmm. Hopefully if she got Sarah onto the page a gentleman would show up to annoy her in due course. She pulled out a piece of paper and picked up a pencil.

This was another way she could be in charge. In theory at least, the people in her head did what she wanted them to do. In theory. The reality was that they were as stubborn and uncooperative as any other people.

*Sarah Parker...*

She could work with that for now. If it wasn't right she'd know soon enough, because Miss Parker would freeze solid on the page and decline to budge. Mr Annoying wouldn't show up either.

She stretched, wriggling her tight shoulders. Beneath her feet there was an instant upheaval and Puck's greyish, brownish nose poked out from under the desk. Hopeful brown eyes smiled up at her—she knew that under the desk a decidedly scrappy tail would be blurred. The flyaway ear twitched and the droopy one did its very best to stand up. It failed.

She rolled her shoulders and sighed. 'You're quite correct. It is time to go out. I've been at this desk far too long. We can discuss Miss Sarah and her potential swain on our walk.'

Head cocked to one side, Puck uttered a whine.

'I'll point out to you that it was raining until quite recently. And I was doing my accounts. Seeing how much it costs to feed you.'

Puck whined again, emphasised with a paw on her knee, and she grinned. 'Oh, very well. Leash. Where's your leash?'

The dog shot across the room, his tail a paean to the heavens, and grabbed his leash that hung from the doorknob. He trotted back, dropped it at her feet and sat expectantly.

Althea laughed outright as she stood up. 'Good boy. Give me a moment to change my shoes and—blast!'

The doorbell jangled loudly.

She wasn't expecting anyone. No one called much anyway, and the one person who might call unexpectedly at this hour—her friend, Lady Rutherford—was not currently in London. John would send the unwelcome caller away. He knew better than to admit anyone when she was dealing with the accounts.

She sat down again. Best not to go out into the front hall while John was lying through his teeth, telling whoever it was that she wasn't home.

The door opened and John came in. 'I'm sorry, ma'am. A gentleman to see you.'

She knew better than to think John would have accepted a bribe to make the attempt, but some gentlemen she knew could be unpleasantly insistent. 'I'm not at home, John. You may tell him I said so.' It had been a while since any gentlemen had thought it worth their while to call on her. She'd hoped they had given up.

John hesitated. 'Ah, it's that lawyer, my lady.'

She stared. 'A lawyer? Mr Brimley?'

John held out a salver with a card on it. 'The one who wrote to you, ma'am.'

She took the card in disbelief.

*Hugh Guthrie Esq*
*Guthrie & Randall Attorneys at Law.*
*Lincoln's Inn Fields.*

Not her own lawyer then, but her brother's lawyer. Her stomach twisted into icy knots as she read the name on the card. Hadn't her deliberately rude response to that letter a couple of weeks ago—or was it three weeks?—been sufficient? She remembered Mr Guthrie well enough, although the debacle of his last visit had hardly been *his* fault. He was a nice enough old man and he had only been doing his job. However—'I'm definitely not at home. Ever.'

John nodded awkwardly. 'The thing is, my lady—' He broke off.

'Oh, spit it out, John.' It wasn't his fault either.

'He's got two little girls with him.'

Had she misheard? 'Two *what*?'

'Little girls.' He elaborated. 'Well, one's not so very little. About twelve or so I'd guess. T'other's the little one. They look proper done up, my lady. Got caught in the rain, I daresay.'

She gritted her teeth. That was nothing to do with her. Only… what could Frederick's lawyer possibly want this time? And why had he brought two girls? She'd only find out by seeing him. It wasn't as if she could drop a whole lawyer, not to mention two young girls, into the fire.

'Very well. Show them in.' Whatever Mr Guthrie wanted, she'd settle this for once and for all. Her conscience delivered a solid, if unwelcome nudge on behalf of two damp, possibly cold children. 'And ask Mrs Cable to heat some milk. I suppose there is cake? And biscuits?' As a child she'd preferred biscuits to cake.

'Yes, my lady.' John bowed and removed himself.

Althea looked at Puck. 'Sorry.' The dog's tail drooped along with his whiskers. 'Burning the letter didn't work. I'll get this done and we'll go. Goodness knows why he'd want to see me again anyway. Surely you can only be disowned once?'

That had been…she frowned, calculated dates…six years ago.

Catching a glimpse of herself in the mirror, Althea cursed. Of course Frederick's solicitor had to call when she'd been doing her accounts, wasn't expecting visitors and had bundled her hair up all anyhow. With another curse, she snatched off the eyeglasses she used for reading and writing.

She looked around to make sure the room was tidy. Why give any ammunition for the family's view of her as an impecunious slut?

The room was tidy except for the overflowing bookcase. Not grand, but comfortable and clean. And hers.

She glanced at Puck. 'We'll see what he wants, then send him on his way. Maybe you could find a nice growl?'

Puck waved his tail agreeably, not looking in the least like a dog who could find a growl. Even a nice one.

The door opened.

'Mr Guthrie,' John announced.

Her breath jolted in. It wasn't the same Mr Guthrie. Not unless Time itself had reversed when she wasn't looking. This man was much younger. Although she thought there might be a resemblance in the tall, spare frame. Even in the neat, utterly respectable black suit.

The other Mr Guthrie must have been seventy at least. This one looked to be in his forties. Cool grey eyes skewered her from under heavy brows. Two girls—she assumed John was correct, and there were girls under those damp cloaks—trailed in behind him.

'Lady Hartleigh? Née Miss Althea Price?'

She stiffened at the icy tones that oozed disapproval—who the hell was he to look down his nose at her?—and donned the grand lady mask she rarely bothered with nowadays. 'The same. This is quite a surprise, Mr Guthrie. Either you have discovered the Fountain of Youth—and if so you might be so good as to furnish me with its direction—or it was some other Mr Hugh Guthrie who called upon me several years back.'

'My late father, ma'am.'

She hid the wince. 'Ah. My sincere condolences then.' Drat it! Now the fellow was looking at her as if she were a bedbug. Worse, she deserved it.

'Thank you, ma'am. I found your direction amongst his files.'

'You amaze me.' She had changed address since the previous Mr Guthrie's visit. Finally accepting that the mansion in fashionable Mayfair was far beyond her extremely limited income, she had moved to this far more modest house in Soho. Possibly one of the best decisions she had ever made.

He acknowledged that with a nod. 'I may say that it was no mean feat finding you.'

'I'm surprised you bothered. I hope Frederick is paying you handsomely.' She didn't bother to sweeten her voice.

'Papa is dead.' The taller of the two girls pushed back the hood of her cloak and lifted her chin.

Althea choked back a gasp.

It was as though she stared into the mirror of her childhood. Bright, honey-gold hair, a perfect—if she did say so herself—heart-shaped face and, most disconcerting of all, her own green eyes.

*Dead.* Frederick was dead? So that letter, the letter she had burned unread… Oh, *hell.*

'You're Frederick's daughter.' Who else could the child be, with the same hair and eyes she and Frederick had inherited from their mother?

'And Kate.' The girl put a protective arm around her sister.

'Kate.' She supposed she'd known there were two of them. Hadn't she? 'And you're…' She floundered, searching for the name. She didn't even know her nieces' names. And Frederick was *dead.* How was she supposed to feel about that? And what did it have to do with her? Frederick, dutifully followed by the rest of the family, had disowned her six years ago and made quite sure the entire world knew it.

'Sarah. I'm Sarah.' The green eyes were defiant.

*Sarah? Oh, damn.* Miss Sarah Parker's nascent literary existence flickered, guttered…

'Sarah.' At Guthrie's gentle but firm voice, some of the defiance ebbed, or at least was banked.

'Yes, sir.'

'May they sit down, Lady Hartleigh? It's been a difficult time for them.'

'What?' She pulled her scattered wits together. She had been living alone too long if she couldn't think to offer a seat to a pair of damp, exhausted children. 'Yes. Yes, of course. Come near the fire, girls, and take off those damp cloaks. Puck! In your bed.'

He was sniffing at the smaller girl's ankle with enthusiasm, but looked up with his *Must I?* expression.

The girl—Kate—looked up. 'Can we pet him? We like dogs. Only we weren't allowed to have one.'

Althea found a smile, even as memory reared up. 'If he isn't bothering you.'

She had never been allowed to have a dog either. Her father had disapproved of house dogs—*'women mollycoddling animals'*—and her husband had flatly refused her request. *'Have some revolting lapdog all over the house? Certainly not.'* She clenched her fist. She made her own decisions now and she had a dog. Then she returned her mind to the real problem: What were Frederick's daughters doing here?

Kate didn't bother with a chair. She dropped straight down on the hearth and Puck, viewing this as an invitation, got as much of himself as possible into her lap. Small arms closed about him, and the child buried her face in his rough coat.

Sarah stood, her expression uncertain.

'Sit down, Sarah.' Guthrie spoke again. Steady, reassuring. The sort of voice that could ease you into doing things you weren't entirely sure about.

Althea nodded. 'Yes. Please, sit down. John is bringing hot milk and cake. Or biscuits. Possibly both.' Good God! She was wittering. 'Mr Guthrie, I am at a loss as to why you have brought the girls here. Surely—'

'No one wants us. You probably don't either. Mr Guthrie's office clerk said you burned the letter he sent you.'

'Sarah.' The gentle reproof in Guthrie's voice had the girl—her *niece*—flushing scarlet.

'It's *true*!'

'But not a conversation you were supposed to be listening to, Sarah.'

Althea stared in shock at her elder niece. That might have been her own voice. Hard and cold, stating an unpalatable fact before someone could stuff it back down her throat.

'I'm sorry, sir. I didn't *mean* to listen. I just heard.'

'And if you do *just hear* something not meant for you, Sarah, then you do not blurt it out.'

'No, sir.'

Kate looked up as Puck licked her face. 'Mama died two years ago. And we couldn't live at Wellings any longer.'

Althea stared at them, a cold certainty growing in her. 'Your mother, too?' No, this couldn't possibly be happening… And why on earth hadn't Frederick remarried? If she knew anything about the man he had become, it was that he had been desperate to sire an heir.

Sarah sat down on a chair beside her sister. 'She won't care about that, Kate. Why should she? No one else does. And even if she did, you're telling it all backwards.'

Again that hard, bitter voice lashed at Althea.

The door opened and John came in with the maid, Milly, each bearing a tray.

Althea breathed a sigh of relief at the distraction. 'Thank you. John, the milk and cake—oh, and the biscuits for the young ladies. Milly, please set the tea tray on my desk.' She moved her account books out of the way.

'Does Puck like cake?'

Althea smiled, quelling the panic that threatened to explode. 'He does, but the cake is for you and your sister. Here.' She took several small, dry biscuits from her desk drawer. 'These are his.' She gave some to each girl. Kate took them eagerly, Sarah with a scowl.

Ignoring the scowl, Althea walked back to her desk and sat down. 'Please sit, Mr Guthrie.'

Guthrie seated himself.

'Milk, sir? Sugar?'

'Neither, thank you.'

Tea dispensed, the niceties dealt with—and her nieces occupied with Puck, hot milk and cake—Althea spoke very quietly. 'Why are you here, sir? And what did my niece mean by that extraordinary statement?'

'That no one wants them?' The lawyer sipped his tea. 'Precisely what she said. No one in either family will take them in. I wrote to everyone I could think of.' He shot her a cool glance over the teacup. 'Including yourself.'

Ignoring that last comment, she set her own cup down

sharply. That wasn't how things were supposed to work. 'Surely Frederick made provision for them, appointed a guardian?' The estate had been entailed on the nearest male heir. Since Frederick had died without a son that meant the estate had gone to their cousin Wilfrid. But he *must* have provided for his children… And the last thing he would have wanted was for *her* to take them in!

'Your brother named his heir—your cousin, Wilfrid Price-Babbington, as the girls' guardian. As Kate said, their mother died two years ago. Childbirth. You…ah…remember Price-Babbington?'

'I do.' Only too well. A boastful sort of boy, very full of his own self-consequence and always tale-bearing. Perhaps she was being uncharitable; people did grow up. Witness the change in Frederick from the adored brother of her childhood to the man who had—no, she wasn't going to think about what Frederick had done. But if Wilfrid had improved on her memories, why was her brother's solicitor here with her nieces?

Guthrie frowned. 'Lady Hartleigh, your brother died two months ago. Were you not aware?'

She favoured him with a glittering smile. 'Mr Guthrie, I am the family's skeleton. Very much *persona non grata.* They prefer me to rattle safely in my closet, and they certainly don't furnish me with the latest news.'

Disapproval wafted from him. 'Hardly the latest. You make no effort to stay in touch?'

She snorted, sharply aware of a little spurt of anger. Who was he to question her decision? 'If you found my old address in your father's files—and I truly am sorry he is dead, I liked him—then you probably found a copy of the letter, notarised no less, that my brother ordered him to deliver and read out to me. It was very explicit about *why* I was *persona non grata.*'

His mouth flattened. 'I did read that. In fact, I read it at the time.'

She sipped her tea. 'I'm sure you were enthralled.'

'Disgusted would be closer to the mark.'

She stiffened, but leaned back with her best supercilious smile. 'Really? Well, don't let me keep you.'

He glared at her. 'I meant that I was disgusted with your brother for sending such a letter. Especially that he used my father to deliver it. I'll withhold judgement on the rest. Lady Hartleigh, those children deserve better of us than this sniping.'

She clenched a fist, then drew a careful breath. 'You're right. My apologies. If Frederick named Wilfrid guardian, then why—'

'He refused to act and instructed me to enter the girls in *some charitable institution*.' He hesitated. 'Lady Hartleigh, if you didn't know your brother had died, then you can't know the circumstances. He had gambled away the bulk of his fortune.'

'Oh, good God! The idiot! Then—'

'What little was left he bequeathed to his heir. Along with a request that Price-Babbington take responsibility for the girls.'

'A *request*?' Althea didn't bother to hide the derision. 'Would that be a *gentleman's honour* sort of request?'

A small cynical smile curled his mouth. 'Precisely.'

She should show him out now. Every instinct screamed it. 'And how do you come into this, sir?'

'When Price-Babbington refused to act as guardian I wrote to the girls' other relatives. On their mother's side as well as your family. No one was prepared to take them.'

'So, they're homeless and penniless.' She let out a breath. Why the hell hadn't she refused to see him? 'When you say, *no one*—'

'I mean *no one*.' He was speaking softly, but lowered his voice further so that she had to lean forward. 'I have made enquiries. I did that before the girls reached London. Sarah is of an age where she will be accepted by the Adult Orphan Institution.'

Adult? She was a *child*!

'How frightfully charitable of them. And Kate?'

'She is not old enough. She may go to the Female Orphan Asylum at Lambeth.'

Althea gritted her teeth. 'I see. So why are you here?' She didn't need this. She didn't *want* this. She *liked* her life now. It was *her* life. The life she had built for herself. The one with no blasted family.

Only…they were children. Not the adults who had turned on her.

'The rest of your relatives replied in no uncertain terms declining to take the girls,' he said. 'Since your response was to consign your brother quite literally, I understand, to hell—'

She winced. He knew she'd burned the letter, then.

He went on. 'I suspected that you wouldn't read any other letter I might send you.' He shot her a cool glance. 'I thought it wiser to call on you myself.'

Althea gritted her teeth She was *not* going to bare her soul to this man and explain precisely *why* she'd burned that letter.

He spoke carefully. 'I thought after my father's last visit that your response was at least understandable.'

His forbearance positively grated on her. Althea grasped at what felt like the last straw of her patience. 'If you want me to write to their—my, *our* relations, I can assure you that—'

'They need a home, Lady Hartleigh. You're their nearest relation. Their aunt. The only person who hasn't given an outright refusal. They need you.'

'You want *me* to take them.'

'You're their only hope, Lady Hartleigh.' He scowled at her. 'And, despite that letter my father was forced to deliver, he said he thought you…had much to recommend you.'

Half an hour ago she had been so proud of her nest egg. That enormous—*hah!*—buffer of a few thousand pounds. She looked over to the fireplace where the girls drank their milk and munched on cake. Kate still sat on the floor with her arm around Puck, who leaned on her like a dog starved of all affection, and kept his focus on the cake.

Adding two young girls to her household, extra food, clothes, shoes—good Lord, they were growing, and they'd need a governess eventually—was impossible. It would stretch her budget to the limit and beyond. She couldn't do it. She wasn't *going* to do it.

As if her gaze were a tangible weight, Sarah looked up, her mouth a flat, hostile line, her eyes blazing with *don't care* defiance.

Althea knew that gaze, knew the hurt hiding behind it. She'd seen it in her own mirror often enough. Yet despite the defiance, Sarah leaned closer to the smaller girl, her hand creeping to her little sister's shoulder.

*They'll be separated. Alone.*

She might be used to being alone. Damn it, she *liked* being alone. She didn't want to be saddled with children. Not now. Refusal was the only sane response.

She reached out and rang the bell.

*Blast you, Frederick.*

John reappeared so fast she suspected he'd been waiting in the hall.

'Yes, my lady.'

'Please help Milly prepare the spare bedchamber for the young ladies.' Ignoring Guthrie's startled intake of breath, she looked straight at Sarah, and spoke the final words to nail her decision shut. 'They will be living with us now.'

Hugo felt he had due cause for wondering if he'd been catapulted into a different universe.

'You'll...you'll take them.' He'd have sworn she was going to refuse. That she was ringing to have them shown out.

Those green eyes narrowed, firing chips of ice.

'Yes, Mr Guthrie, I will.' Her voice matched the cold fury in her eyes. Who was that fury for? And on whom would it spill out? Should he leave the girls with her after all?

She turned back to the servant and her voice softened. 'Soup for the young ladies, too, please, John.'

Relief sighed out of him. Whoever was the focus of her icy rage it would not spill over the girls. Not if she could think of hot soup for a pair of frightened children and keep calling them *young ladies*.

He'd come here because… Why the devil *had* he come? Not because he had expected Lady Hartleigh—by all accounts self-absorbed and heedless, not to mention impecunious—to take Sarah and Kate. That letter from her brother, disowning her… it had been damning.

He shoved all that away. He'd come because Althea Hartleigh had been the girls' last chance, and there were things he needed to say to her, tell her. Only not in front of the girls. If she hadn't known about Frederick's death, then obviously she couldn't know the circumstances.

He had to get the girls out of the room. 'Ah, Sarah, perhaps you and Kate might like to look at your room? Take your valises up and unpack.' Please God, Lady Hartleigh would understand and back him up.

Sarah gave him a suspicious glance, and who could blame her? They had been kicked out of the only home they knew and all their relatives, except this one, had refused to take them in. For the last fortnight they had been living in two-roomed lodgings that, while perfectly adequate for a single man, were cramped for that man and two lively young girls. His landlady had been deeply unimpressed.

'What if we don't *want* to stay? What if Aunt Hartleigh doesn't like us? What if *we* don't like *her*?'

Kate tugged at her sister's hand. 'Don't, Sarah.' Her voice shook. 'Please! I don't want to go to an orphanage!'

'I'll wager you don't.' Lady Hartleigh's voice was brisk, matter of fact. 'I suggest you at least look at the room, Sarah. Which room did you have at home?'

'Home?'

'Yes. At Wellings Park. I grew up there, remember.'

'Oh. It…it was at the back. Two down from the schoolroom.'

'Ah. The big room. That was your father's when we were children.' She smiled at Kate. 'Did you have the little one next to the schoolroom?'

Kate bit her lip. 'Yes.'

'That was mine. I'm afraid you'll have to share here.'

Kate nodded. 'We don't mind. We've been sharing Mr Guthrie's bed.'

Hugo shut his eyes. *Oh, Lord!*

'Er… I've been sleeping on the sofa. My lodgings are only two rooms.'

Lady Hartleigh blinked. 'Most uncomfortable, I should think. The sofa, that is.'

His shoulders and neck agreed.

Lady Hartleigh turned to the girls. 'Take your things up and unpack. You have my word of honour that unless you request it, you will *not* be going to an orphanage.' She smiled at Kate. 'Take Puck along with you.'

Kate beamed. 'May we? Thank you. What sort of dog is he, Aunt Hartleigh?'

Hugo considered the scruffy rough-coated little creature, with its mismatched ears and bedraggled tail. *Good question.*

Puck's owner looked amused. 'One with a tail. In polite company we call him a terrier and leave it at that. And perhaps you might call me Aunt Althea. A little less stuffy and formal, I think. Off you go.'

Kate trotted out—happily enough, he thought—the dog at her heels.

Sarah lingered, her gaze hard and suspicious. 'Why?'

Hugo opened his mouth to reprove her, but shut it again. Best if they sorted it out. He wasn't going to be here to mediate, after all.

Lady Hartleigh met that direct gaze, seemed to consider her answer. 'How old are you, Sarah?'

'Nearly fourteen.'

Hugo cleared his throat, hid a grin. The child was a solid six months short of that.

Lady Hartleigh, despite flicking him a glance, appeared to accept the reply at face value.

She nodded. 'There's no mystery, Sarah. Quite simply, when the news gets out that you are living with me it will annoy the rest of the family greatly.'

Sarah looked at her uncertainly. 'Annoy them? You want to annoy them?'

'Good God, yes. Don't you?'

Hugo choked on a laugh.

'Kate's only *eight.*' Sarah bit her lip. 'I want to *kick* them!'

Lady Hartleigh nodded her approval. 'Very reasonable. For the moment, however, we shall content ourselves with annoying them. Now, go and unpack.'

# *Chapter Two*

Hugo took a deep breath, preparing to speak…

Lady Hartleigh rose abruptly and walked over to a side table. 'I believe I need something rather stronger than tea, before you tell me whatever it is you did not wish to say in front of Sarah and Kate. Brandy, sir?'

She had understood then. 'Yes, please. I understand this must be a shock to you.'

She shot him an amused glance as she picked up a decanter. 'Just a little. There I was, contemplating my most excellent household economy, and lo! I have two nieces to fit in.'

She poured two glasses of brandy.

'Will they be an imposition, ma'am?' Was he doing the right thing in leaving the girls with her? The house looked comfortable enough, the lady dressed plainly but with elegance, even if her glorious honied hair was a little dishevelled. He'd noted what he thought was an apron stuffed under a cushion. Had she been at some household task? He knew she was far from wealthy.

She frowned, passing him a glass. 'I don't like that word. At least not for children. My accounts, on the other hand, are always an imposition.'

'There is no money with them.' He hated saying it, but he

had to spell everything out clearly. He sipped the brandy. It was excellent.

She snorted. 'If there were, Mr Guthrie, one of their loving relatives would have snatched them up instantly.'

He blinked at this brutal summation. He strove for truth at all times, thinking of it as a clear flame—Lady Hartleigh wielded it like a burning sword.

'You don't think much of your relatives, do you?'

Her laugh was bitter. 'No, sir, I do not. And I can think of at least two members of my sister-in-law's family who could have provided a home for them. While as for Wilfrid—' her free hand balled into a fist '—best not to let me start on Wilfrid.'

He sipped his brandy again, enjoyed the fiery burn as much as the controlled blaze of her temper. 'There was a reason, beyond the lack of money, your family declined to take the girls. You haven't asked how your brother died.'

She sat down. 'No. I became distracted with the girls, but I assumed an illness, an accident perhaps?' She let out a breath. 'That's not it, is it? You'd better tell me.'

No gentle way to put it. 'He shot himself.'

Her glass rattled as she set it down. 'The gambling debts.'

Lord, she was quick. 'Yes.'

A careful pause. 'He really gambled *everything* away?' A bitter laugh. 'How ironic.'

He didn't understand. 'Ma'am?'

'My apologies.' She waved it away. 'I was speaking to myself. It's not relevant. Are you telling me that, apart from the lack of money, the family abandoned those children because of Frederick's suicide? They feared the taint?'

He nodded and sipped his brandy. 'Yes. Exactly the word they used. Several family members said they did not care to have "that" in their homes. It was covered up, fortunately—an accident as he was cleaning a pistol—but the family knows. Price-Babbington was particularly vocal on the matter. How he could not possibly have that "weakness"—that was how he put it—in his home, with his impressionable sons.'

Not an unusual response. An unvarnished verdict of suicide could see the victim's entire property sequestered by the law.

If the coroner were sympathetic enough not to want the family's property sequestered, the usual verdict of *suicide while of unsound mind* was still a disaster. In that case they might have the property, but they were tainted with the label of insanity.

Lady Hartleigh made a rude noise. 'Apparently Wilfrid hasn't looked in the mirror recently if he's worried about *weakness*. So he brought them up to London and left them for you to dispose of.'

'Not quite.' He deliberately kept his voice even, emotionless. 'He wrote to request that I make the arrangements to enter them in *"appropriate charitable institutions"* and informed me that they would be on the stagecoach a week later. I met them at the Bolt-in-Tun.' Even now he felt sick at the thought of what might have happened to the girls if he had not received the letter in time, if he had not met that stagecoach.

'Good God!'

Hugo watched, fascinated, as she brought herself under control. Those white knuckles slowly relaxing, the careful breaths. There was silence, as if she did not trust herself to speak further, but he had the impression that she knew as well as he what might have happened if he had not been there. Possibly even knew the Bolt's reputation.

'And you've been looking after them ever since.' She met his eyes. 'Thank you.'

The frank gratitude in her face made him squirm. 'No decent man could have done otherwise.'

Her mouth flattened. 'A pity Wilfrid does not comprehend that. Do the girls know how Frederick died? Please don't tell me one of them found him!'

'No, thank God. The servants did. They heard the shot in the library.'

She snorted. 'The very place a man would clean a pistol, of course. Why not somewhere logical like the gun room?' She shook her head. 'I'm glad for the girls' sakes that it was covered up and they don't know. You may rest assured I won't inform them. At least not until they are very much older.'

He breathed a sigh of relief. 'You'll still take them?'

Her brows lifted. 'Mr Guthrie, I am far from being the mercenary, cold-hearted bitch that letter made me out to be, thank you very much.'

He opened his mouth. Shut it again. Informing her that she might not be a—*that word*—but that she certainly had teeth, did not present itself as the course of wisdom.

'Obviously not.' A second thought occurred. One that gave him a very great deal of pleasure. 'Should you like me to write polite notes to your relatives? Apprising them that the girls are safe with you?'

Her brandy stopped an inch from her lips. 'How much will that cost me?' She cleared her throat. 'My accounts, you know. Which reminds me, you will be out of pocket already, so—'

'Stop right there.' He fought to suppress the flare of annoyance. She was only trying to be fair. 'I won't take a penny for helping those girls. And as for the letters, annoying your relatives will burden neither my pocket nor my conscience.'

She sipped her brandy as a smile glimmered, Titania plotting mischief. 'Full of unintelligible, lawyerly language?'

He kept a straight face. 'Not too unintelligible. We want them to understand they've been insulted.'

She raised her brows. 'Of course. Do be sure to stress my Christian charity, won't you? Especially to that insufferable prig Wilfrid!'

Apparently eyes really could dance. He found himself smiling in response. 'I thought you weren't going to start on him?'

She rubbed her nose. 'I did say that, didn't I? Oh, well. *Tant pis.*'

His pent-up laughter escaped. 'We'll consider the letters pro bono. Especially the letter to dear Wilfrid.'

Those elfin green eyes regarded him much as he thought Titania might have considered a mortal.

'You don't like Wilfrid either.'

He definitely wasn't going to start on Wilfrid. What he thought of Price-Babbington was beyond unprintable. Although he had a sneaking suspicion that Althea Hartleigh would only roar with laughter. 'Insufferable prig is the least of it!'

Laughter rippled. 'How very restrained of you, sir.'

He found himself laughing back into that dancing green, and

he had the distinct impression that she knew exactly the words he had refrained from using. Which, much to his surprise, did not shock or disgust him in the least.

Walking back alone through Soho Square an hour later, Hugo shook his head. He'd considered visiting Althea Hartleigh a waste of time. So much so that he nearly hadn't bothered.

Thank God he had.

The lady—and she *was* a lady, whatever her fool of a brother had thought—had been a surprise all round.

When the girls had come back down, Kate bubbling and Sarah subdued, she had provided them with soup and toast. She had been calm and matter of fact with them, allowing them to settle and have their meal. She hadn't bothered with overtures, hadn't gushed, hadn't assured them she was delighted to have them.

An intelligent female. Sarah would have repelled any overtures and disbelieved any reassurances.

He let out a breath as he walked down towards the cab stand outside St Anne's church. Sarah had asked when they would see him again and Lady Hartleigh had said nothing either for or against when he had explained, gently, that they had someone to take care of them now. They didn't need him.

Kate's mouth had wobbled.

Sarah's mouth had set like granite, and she'd given a sharp nod, addressing herself to her soup. Just one more person who had abandoned them.

He wanted to see the girls again. While his conscience had refused to allow him to dump them in orphanages, he had also become fond of them. His lodgings, although cramped, had been brighter and cheerier with their company.

*What would you have done if she had refused to take them?*

Hell's teeth! He confronted the truth he had refused to admit until Althea Hartleigh had shocked him witless—he would be looking for new lodgings, lodgings that could accommodate two young girls. He would have willingly moved back into a house very like the one he had left in his grief ten years ago.

*And what the hell would you have done with them? Schooling? Providing a dowry?*

While it hadn't happened yet, and he still couldn't imagine it, he might marry again one day. What would a wife think of a pair of orphans with no claim of kinship? The thought slid across his mind that a woman who would consider two orphaned girls an imposition—*I don't like that word...not for children*—was not a woman he would care to marry anyway.

Still, taking on the girls would have been difficult, if not downright impossible, and since when had he become so damned impulsive that he'd been prepared to keep them? Thank God Althea Hartleigh had confounded all his expectations and proven herself to have a heart.

How had his father described her? He remembered the old man coming back from that last visit, shaking his head over what he had described as a family spat turned vicious.

*'She was always a pretty child, not that I saw her often, but now? A walking, breathing temptation, my boy. Aphrodite and Helen rolled into one. But I think her brother is a fool for all that. I very much doubt she's the whore he's painted her.'*

The pater had been right about Frederick Price being a fool. And yes, Althea Hartleigh was...beautiful, without a doubt. Aphrodite? Perhaps. But still, Aphrodite never seemed to have much of a sense of humour. Titania was more like it, for his money. Wicked mischief glimmering in green eyes that could lure a mortal man to glorious, abject folly.

Easy to believe what Frederick Price's letter had claimed—that she'd had a blazingly indiscreet affair with the Earl of Rutherford. Not to mention several others prior to the Earl. The family had considered itself disgraced, and she might consider herself cast off. According to rumour, she had disappeared largely from society not long after the Earl's marriage. Yet, despite the fact that she was clearly living in reduced circumstances, away from the fashionable world she had married into, she had been the only one willing to take in a pair of orphans.

Perhaps Price had got it wrong, and had listened to unfounded gossip.

No. He didn't think so. Something about Lady Hartleigh told him that she probably *had* earned that reputation.

For being female? Because while he had made enquiries about her before his visit, he had found nothing that would have even raised an eyebrow had she been a man. Of course, the tale of her sins had been embellished with speculations on her deviousness, and her cunning plan to ensnare Rutherford into marriage.

Odd though. It was pretty universally known that she had run through all her money. A little circumspect investigation had garnered that information. But while she wasn't living in luxury, she was living very comfortably. He'd seen no sign that she was in dire financial straits, nor had his recent enquiries turned up any disgruntled tradesmen. It seemed Lady Hartleigh paid all her bills on time and lived within her income.

Still, he nearly hadn't gone to see her because of her very dubious reputation. And even when he had decided to call on her, he'd expected a beautiful harpy. Instead he'd found a charming siren. One who could probably lure an unwary man to his grave, watery or otherwise, let alone her bed. Or even a wary man.

He took a steadying breath.

Sirens were dangerous. And he was mixing his metaphors to boot. She wasn't a harpy, but she couldn't be both siren and Titania. Could she? Somehow the woman had repaired her finances, at least to some degree. And, if she *had* conducted a series of affairs with wealthy gentlemen, that was one way she could have done so.

That or her circumstances had never been quite as dire as they'd been painted. He hoped that he hadn't done the wrong thing in leaving the girls with her.

Either way, he would have to keep an eye on things from a discreet distance at least for a short time and pray she never realised. He was no Oberon, and he didn't fancy a pair of ass's ears, that—if Shakespeare were to be believed—was the fate of mortals who flirted with faeries.

Later that evening, her nieces safely in bed, and her dog missing in action—she suspected that Puck, having deserted her, might be curled up on Kate's feet—Althea stirred up the fire before settling down to her desk again.

She adjusted the lamp. Miss Sarah Parker was fictionally dead before she'd made it as far as the page. Having a Sarah in the house, as well as one instigating mayhem in her head, was just impossible. Far too confusing. She needed a new name for the wretched girl.

She jotted down name after name, finally underlining *Lydia.* Lydia Parker. The clock chimed ten. Althea ignored it. If she wanted to add to her capital, and thus her income—even more important now she had added two extra people to her household—she needed to get this book properly started.

Half an hour later Althea still only had Lydia. That was the problem with finishing the proofs of one book. Your ungrateful publisher immediately began badgering you for another. Which, she freely admitted, was better than being told never to darken their doorway again. But she still had to start the wretched thing.

This afternoon she'd had ideas aplenty rattling around in her imagination, distracting her from her accounts. With the explosion into her life of Sarah and Kate, every idea had fizzled out like so many damp firecrackers. Lydia. She had Lydia. A girl—no, a woman—of decided opinions. The hero unfortunately had yet to make an appearance on the stage of her imagination. Not even a name. Perhaps she should consider allowing Lydia to enjoy an existence of blessed singleness and have a cat instead of a husband?

'Or a dog.' She scowled. Leaving Lydia happily single at the end of the book, with a couple of cats or a dog for company, would not please her publisher. But really, the poor girl did not *need* to marry. She had a perfectly adequate fortune, enough interests to keep her occupied, and unless the right man for her turned up...

*Women find their highest purpose and joy in being a wife and mother.*

She snorted. How often had she heard that? But right now she had a character who appeared utterly uninterested in such things. Rather like herself.

*What would you do if the right man turned up for you?*

Althea scowled at her page of notes, refusing to contemplate a slightly ascetic face with heavy brows over direct grey eyes. She neither needed nor wanted a man, right or wrong. Men complicated everything. Especially since they always thought *they* were right. She nudged her mind back to creating complications for Lydia.

*You could take away her fortune. Or at least reduce it vastly.*

Then Lydia would be forced to consider marriage to save herself and her younger sister. *Younger sister?* Althea blinked at that revelation. Noted down *younger sister. Name?* Plenty of drama and conflict in that. Except she didn't want the wretched girl forced into marriage for those reasons alone. She needed a better story than that.

*Better not to think of Lydia as 'the wretched girl' if you don't want your readers to think of her like that!*

With a muttered curse, Althea dipped her pen in the ink and started scribbling in earnest. Sometimes you had to start writing and see what someone did when you let them loose on the page…

An hour later she had discovered Lydia's aversion to seed cake—*why?*—and one Sir Edwin Jamison had strolled into her head and out onto the page. Since he was sniffing around her younger sister, Sophie, Lydia had taken him in extreme dislike, which suited her creator perfectly. He didn't like cats either, and Lydia's cat had taken that as a challenge.

Sometime after the clock chimed midnight, Althea shuffled her pages together and locked them in her desk drawer. Her shoulders ached, and she covered a yawn. She hoped Sir Edwin had annoyed Lydia enough for one evening to have the words coming easily again tomorrow.

# *Chapter Three*

*Late April—*
*Lincoln's Inn Fields*

'Lady Hartleigh.' Hugo rose from the chair behind his desk. 'This is quite a surprise.'

He'd taken a full half minute to recover from the shock after his office clerk had told him she was there, requesting a moment of his time. Shock was one thing. The leap of his heart, the sheer delight bouncing through him at the sight of her, was positively frightening.

Had she somehow divined that he was having her watched? So far the reports had been completely benign. No gentlemen had called. At all. Her three servants thought the world of her, and she had only left the house for walks with the girls and the dog, to pay bills, or for very local social engagements, so innocent as to beggar belief.

*Her ladyship visited the circulating library at Selbourne's Antiquarian Books. A gentleman opened the door for her and the young ladies.*

That was as close to any sort of encounter with a gentleman as Althea Hartleigh had come.

*She bought flowers from a street seller.*

And that was the closest she had come to extravagance. She paid her bills either on receipt or on a monthly basis.

He pulled himself together, came around the desk and placed the visitor's chair for her. 'Will you be seated? I… I hope all is well with the girls? How do you go on?' Lord! What had happened to his lungs? And his brain—he was babbling for God's sake!

She sat, arranged her skirts. 'Oh, we're all well enough. They wished to come with me, but I thought it better not.'

His heart sank—all the delight at seeing her died as disappointment bit deep. 'You regret your impulse then?' He couldn't keep the chill from his voice, didn't even want to.

She looked up sharply. 'What? No, not in the least. I need to make a new will, Mr Guthrie.'

'Oh.' Commendable, responsible and utterly unexpected.

'As it stands, bar a couple of personal bequests, ensuring that my dog is looked after and annuities to my servants, everything goes to charity. Which is all very admirable, but not when I have family dependent on me.'

He sat down again. 'If you have a will, then you already have a solicitor. Why are you here?'

She smiled, an amused twinkle in her eyes. 'I did have a solicitor. He has taken a sudden fancy to grow roses.'

'I—he what?'

'Mr Brimley has retired. He has purchased a small villa at Richmond and intends to grow roses.'

'Ah. That would be Mr Harold Brimley.' He grinned. 'I believe *his* father retired to Reading to breed dogs. Spaniels, if I remember correctly.'

She stared at him. 'Are you serious? Spaniels?'

'Oh, yes. He was a contemporary of my grandfather's.'

'And what did *he* breed?'

'Grandfather? Books,' he said gravely, enjoying the tart humour in her voice. 'My father did the same. And birds. He liked watching birds.'

A peal of laughter escaped her. 'How very conventional.'

He grinned. 'I daresay I'll do the same one day. Books and birds. We're a boring lot, we Guthries.'

Still laughing, she said, 'Oh, I doubt that very much. Not the books and birds. The boring part. Now, about this will. I have given it some thought, and—'

'What about my colleague Mark Brimley?' He forced himself back to the matter at hand, and from the worrying delight that Althea Hartleigh did not consider him boring. The firm of Brimley, Brimley & Whittaker was still running, albeit minus one Brimley. He didn't like to think he might be poaching a client. Mark Brimley was more than competent to draw up a will. Although he could imagine him muttering over clauses to protect a dog.

She grimaced. 'Mr Brimley's son? If you must know, he didn't like my, er, thoughts. Or me for that matter.'

Ah. There was that, too. His undoubted competence aside, Mark Brimley was the sort to believe women shouldn't have thoughts at all. He would disapprove mightily of a woman like Althea Hartleigh.

He took a deep breath. 'Perhaps you might outline these thoughts?'

He listened, made careful notes, asked a couple of questions for clarification.

When she had finished, he set down his pencil carefully. 'The choice of trustees for something like this will be of the utmost importance. There isn't a great deal of money involved, but still.' How the deuce was she so beforehand with the world? 'Do you have anyone in mind? I should recommend three. Then if one dies or is unable to act, there is time to appoint another.'

She nodded. 'Yes. Two of the three I have already written to, and they have agreed.'

He picked up his pencil. 'And they are?'

'The Earl of Rutherford.'

His pencil hovered over the paper. 'Rutherford.'

'Yes. The countess is a friend of mine.'

He met her cool, clear gaze directly. 'You amaze me.'

Nothing in her faltered that he could observe. Instead an amused smile flickered. 'Mr Guthrie, if Meg Rutherford were to eschew the company of every woman in London that Rutherford bedded before he married her, she would lead a very solitary existence.'

Society gossip didn't come his way. But once he'd realised Althea Hartleigh was all that stood between the girls and an orphanage—barring his own insane and illogical impulses—he'd dug up every scrap of information he could on the lady and her previous affairs. And if everything he'd discovered about the earl were true, she had a fair point. Still.

'And the other?'

'Mr Jack Hamilton.'

He blinked. 'Hamilton? Member of the Commons, pushing for reform and the complete abolition of slavery? That Jack Hamilton? Is his wife also a "friend"?' Hamilton's name, as far as he knew, had never been linked with hers. Possibly he had missed something, but Hamilton appeared to have led a positively blameless existence. As had Rutherford since his marriage several years ago.

She smiled. 'She is, although Hamilton was never my lover. And she has agreed that, should something happen to me, she will take Puck.'

He always appreciated openness in a client, but this was—he struggled for the right word. There was no suggestion of boasting. Just a statement of fact.

Rutherford had been her lover. Hamilton had not. And his wife had agreed to take the dog.

He would have considered this attitude perfectly normal in a man, particularly an aristocrat. In a woman? Shameless.

And yet, she was not shameless. Not that she appeared to mind what he might think of her. She was speaking to him as an equal. He wasn't quite sure how he felt about that.

He frowned, looking over his notes. 'I should tell you that tying Kate and Sarah's money up so tightly in trusts will make most men think twice about marriage to them.'

'Good.' Gloved hands clenched to fists in her lap. 'A woman should not be dependent on her husband *doing the right thing.*' He blinked at the viciously soft tone as she went on. 'If they are to marry, I want them to be safe.'

*As I was not.*

She barely stopped herself saying it aloud.

And even with that left unsaid, she'd said too much. It was a gauntlet flung down. She didn't care. Better to know at once if she'd misjudged him. If he disapproved of her personally it didn't matter, as long as he was prepared to act for her. For the girls. All that mattered was getting her will and the trusts in place.

She said simply, 'A decent man should understand that. If he cannot, then a woman is better off without him.'

Guthrie raised his eyes from his notes. 'Is that what the younger Brimley choked on?'

She snorted. 'My unholy attitude to husbands? We didn't progress that far. Your learned colleague choked when we reached Rutherford as one of the trustees. His not so delicate remarks about *my* indelicacy got my back up.'

'Fancy that.' He made a few more notes. 'Right.' He looked up again. 'Who is the third trustee?'

Despite herself, she snorted out a laugh. 'You don't disapprove?'

He raised his eyebrows. 'Of what? Your affair with Rutherford? It's none of my business. Of protecting Sarah and Kate from—' he scowled—'fools like their father, not to mention the insufferable prig who tossed them to the wolves? That you made provision for your dog? No. Now, stop distracting me. Who is your choice for the third trustee?'

'You.'

*'Me?'* He looked as shocked as if she'd tipped a bucket of water over him. 'You want *me* to act as trustee?'

'Yes, of course.'

'*Of course?* Damn it, Lady Hartleigh, how the hell do you know you can trust me?'

'Althea.'

'What?'

'My name. You must know it's Althea.' Amusement at his stunned expression—the dropped jaw and slightly wild eyes—danced in her. Who knew solicitors could be so very charming? 'I think if you've progressed to swearing at me, you can use my Christian name.'

She continued as he stared at her. 'As for how I know I can trust you? You brought the girls to me. Instead of entering them in orphanages, you tried to find them a home while you gave them your bed and slept on the sofa.' She took a deep breath. 'You kept them safe. That's how.'

There was more she could have said. Things she had only discovered just now. His calm acceptance of her as...as a *person*, as someone with flaws and foibles, but who didn't need to be lectured like a child on the perceived folly of her previous choices. Her initial instinct had been spurred by his kindness and care for the girls. He had looked after them from the start—she could trust that he would continue to do so.

And she did not believe that, had she refused to take the girls in, he would have dumped them in those orphanages.

'Lady Hartleigh—?'

'Althea.'

He grimaced. 'Althea. There is something else that puzzles me. I have to say I am more than a little surprised at how...beforehand you are with the world. I was under the impression that your own inheritance was gone and that your husband left you very badly off.'

She stiffened her spine. 'Correct.' They were going there, were they?

'Then you found a way to repair your finances.'

His tone remained even, uninflected. But she could *hear* the questions seething underneath. Like a swan gliding on still water while the feet must paddle madly underneath. Two could play at that game. 'Also correct.'

'Are you able to tell me *how*?'

'No. At least, I don't choose to do so. Beyond telling you that I found something to sell. And *not* myself.'

'That's...good to know.'

The slight hesitation made her wonder if his mind had gone precisely there. And that stung, but she didn't dare tell him the truth. If news of her authorship got out it was perfectly possible that her reputation, deserved or otherwise, would destroy sales of any future books. It was doubly important now that she had the girls to provide for. It wasn't that she didn't trust *him*, but secrets were safer the fewer people who knew about them.

What was the saying? *Three may keep a secret if two of them be dead.*

'Do you need to know in order to act for me? I can assure you that I have done nothing illegal nor immoral to alleviate my finances.' And why the devil was she feeling so hurt and angry that he might believe she had whored herself to survive? You had to care about someone for their opinion of you to hurt. And she'd been close enough to disaster that she wouldn't have judged any woman forced into that choice.

Keeping her voice light, she said, 'Do I understand you would rather not act? Or be on Christian name terms with me?'

His mouth opened. Shut again. Then—'Hugh. Hugo.' He leaned forward, held out his hand across the desk. 'And… I apologise for my unseemly and disrespectful suspicions.'

She took his hand, felt the reassuring grip of strong fingers, wondered at the flicker of awareness that shot through her along with a wave of relief. *Good Lord!*

She managed a smile, despite the speeding of her heart, her leaping pulse. 'Delighted to meet you, Hugo.'

Over the following hour they thrashed out the details. Or most of them.

He'd never drawn up anything quite this stringent, and said so. 'I'll need to ask a few questions of my partner before you sign anything. He's had more experience with this sort of trust than I have.'

She nodded. 'Good. Thank you.'

'You don't mind?'

'That you can admit when you are unsure, and be willing to ask for advice? Of course not. I'd mind if you made a mull of this. In fact, I'd come back to haunt you.'

Laughter welled up. 'You'd make an interesting ghost. Very well, I'll ask my questions, get these documents drafted and have them sent over to you.'

She fiddled with her reticule.

'Something more?' He hadn't thought she was capable of uncertainty.

'I mentioned that the girls wished to come with me this morning.'

Her gaze was firmly in her lap. Was Titania ever shy?

'You did.'

'I hoped perhaps you might deliver the documents yourself. If you have time?' She looked up and, to his disbelief, there was the faintest tinge of colour staining her cheeks. 'We—the girls, that is—would like very much to see you. Even when you don't have documents to deliver.'

Something in him leapt. 'You would not object if I visited them occasionally?'

She shook her head. 'No. If not for you, Sarah and Kate would have disappeared into orphanages without me ever being aware of their fate. And, the thing is, they took a liking to you over and above that. They…they would like to see you from time to time. I believe it would reassure them. And if you are to be one of their trustees it would not be at all inappropriate.'

He nodded slowly, thinking. At least, he hoped he was thinking, because he didn't give a damn about appropriate. 'Then perhaps you might care to meet me at Gunter's with the girls on Saturday afternoon. They will enjoy ice creams while we sip tea.'

She raised her brows. 'Sip tea? You may please yourself, of course, but I assure you I will enjoy an ice at least as much as the girls.'

He grinned at the return of confidence. 'I will enjoy an ice myself.'

A few moments after Lady Hartleigh's departure, Hugo's senior partner strolled in. A portly gentlemen some fifteen years older than Hugo's forty-two, Jacob Randall exuded good nature and a sort of guileless benevolence that was deceptive in the extreme.

'That's set hearts aflutter in the office. Your new client tipped Jem a sixpence for opening the door for her, and it appears her smile has slain even that confirmed old bachelor Blainey.' Jacob sat down, stretched out his legs and crossed them. 'I was going to talk about the idea of taking on another partner next year, but your recent visitor seems a far more interesting topic.'

The bright blue eyes gleamed with curiosity.

Hugo nudged his notes across the desk. 'Possibly. You tell me.'

Jacob read them through, his eyes widening as he read. 'That's something to get your teeth into all right and tight.' He looked at Hugo hopefully. 'May I stick my nose in?'

Hugo grinned. 'By all means. I was intending to consult you. This isn't quite my area, you know.'

Jacob snorted. 'The hell it isn't. I'm sticking my nose in because tying money up like this is just plain fun, not because I think you can't handle it.' He reached for a pencil. 'Right. The first thing you need to consider—'

They scribbled notes, argued points of law and generally enjoyed themselves until the silence from the outer office and the clock chiming six brought them back to reality.

Jacob winced. 'I need to go home now, or I'll be late for dinner. Again. And Alice will claim justifiable homicide.' He gave Hugo a hopeful smile. 'Care to come home with me?'

'And be justifiably murdered when we talk law over dinner?'

Jacob grinned comfortably. 'We'll leave the law here.'

Hugo very much doubted that. They never did, and Alice nearly always told them to stop. 'I'll come, and thank you very much.' Alice Randall was a kindly woman who never seemed to mind an extra and unexpected guest at her dinner table. And what else did he have to do this evening? He would otherwise read his book over his dinner in the tavern and then retire to his very empty lodgings.

Jacob clapped him on the back. 'Good. You've been a little out of sorts recently. You should get out more.'

Hugo tidied away his papers. 'Then no doubt you'll be delighted to know that I'm taking three females to Gunter's Tea Rooms for ices on Saturday afternoon.'

Jacob stared. 'Three? You dog! Nothing like making up for lost time, I always say.'

'Since I'm entertaining my new client and her nieces I thought to take the expense out of petty cash.'

Althea, Sarah and Kate walked from Soho to Berkeley Square on Saturday afternoon. Puck trotted beside them, Kate holding his leash. The child chattered brightly, full of questions about everything and everyone she saw.

Useful, because it took Althea's mind off the ordeal ahead. She had controlled her instinctive recoil when Hugo Guthrie suggested taking them to Gunter's, but oh, good Lord!

Gunter's Tea Shop in Berkeley Square. Where all society liked to be seen. Where she would probably be cut dead by people she had once considered friends. Her stomach executed an ungainly roll, but she made herself respond to Kate's excited questions. The child gasped as they walked into Berkeley Square. So many grand houses! Did Aunt Althea know people who lived here? She did. And what about that grand lady waving at them? Did Aunt Althea know her?

Aunt Althea did, and waved back to the Countess of Rutherford, who was descending the steps of the Earl and Countess of Jersey's house, accompanied by her husband. She had not realised that the Rutherfords had returned to town.

'Lady Rutherford. A friend of mine.' She had said nothing so far to the girls about the arrangements she was making. No doubt Meg would call very soon, quite possibly accompanied by Rutherford to discuss the trusteeship.

'She looks nice,' said Kate.

Althea glanced down with a smile. 'She is. Very nice. They both are.'

And right now she wouldn't have minded in the least if they were walking into Gunter's with her.

Althea stiffened her spine, ignoring the squirming in her stomach. Did it matter if people cut her? She wasn't going to see *them*. She was taking her nieces for a treat with the man who had cared enough to ensure they had a home.

'Come along, girls. Gunter's is over there.' She pointed to the east side of the square. 'We mustn't keep Mr Guthrie waiting.'

Sarah's steps faltered. She had been very quiet on the way

from Soho, although to be fair, her little sister had chattered enough for both of them. But this was different.

For the first week after arriving in Althea's life, Sarah had been full of sulky silences. She did as she was asked, completing her lessons, eating her meals mechanically even as she glowered. Then she had seemed to settle. She spoke voluntarily, laughed and commented on a favoured dish. She seemed to enjoy the lessons Althea gave them. French, mathematics, history. She had arranged music lessons for them with the daughter of a friend in Compton Street not far from Selbourne's Books.

Althea had relaxed. Kate was easy to manage, a delight, affectionate and eager to please. Sarah, she thought, was a great deal like herself. Cynical, suspicious and far less willing to accept things at face value. She liked Sarah very much indeed.

But after Althea's visit to Lincoln's Inn, Sarah had retreated into herself again. She was not rude, far from it. She couldn't even be said to sulk, going through her days with an almost painful obedience. She was, Althea thought, plain miserable.

Last night the child had crept down to the parlour long after midnight. Althea had heard the creak of the stairs as she was readying herself for bed and gone out to look. Following her down quietly, she had heard muffled sobs from behind the door and yet she had hesitated to walk in and ask what was wrong. Surely the child deserved some privacy? If Sarah wished to confide, then she would… What did *she* know about young girls and their needs? Plus, she was tired. Her writing now had to be done in the very early mornings before the girls woke up, or in the evenings after they were in bed. Sometimes she excused herself from their daily walk and sent them with John to squeeze out a few more pages.

Perhaps she could mention Sarah's unhappiness to Mr Guthrie? Or Sarah might confide in him herself if she were given a chance. Walking into Gunter's and seeing Hugo Guthrie rising from his seat, Althea admitted that she had been a complete coward.

She was going to have to confront Sarah with or without his help.

# Chapter Four

From his seat inside Gunter's, Hugo saw them cross the street and his heart—stupid organ!—leapt. Lord, if Alice Randall knew about that he'd never hear the end of it from Jacob. They'd both chuckled over his *assignation* the other night. And now Lady Hartleigh was laughing at something Kate was saying, the child almost dancing as she chattered, and his heart was dancing right along with her. The dog trotted beside them, ridiculous tail waving, and he smiled. God only knew what had gone into the creature's ancestry, but it had a tail to wag and that seemed to be enough for his mistress.

Then he saw Sarah's face. Utterly blank. Something wrong there. And Althea—were those shadows under her eyes? She looked as though she were not getting enough sleep. He rose as they entered the shop.

'Ladies.'

Kate bounced forward. 'Good afternoon, Mr Guthrie. Are we really to have ices? I've never had one! Do you have them all the time?'

He laughed. 'I don't have them very often, no. So it's a treat all round. Good day, Sarah.'

'Sir.'

She sat down as he imagined one might sit in a tumbril. If there were seats in a tumbril. Perhaps not.

Hugo turned to Althea with raised brows.

She shook her head very slightly. 'Good day, Mr Guthrie. I hope we are not late?'

He grinned. 'Not at all. I believe ladies arrive neither late nor early, but when they are meant to arrive.'

A ripple of laughter.

'Very tactful. I must remember that.' Althea sat down with a swish of her skirts.

The tea room was full, but he had secured a table by dint of arriving very early and enjoying two cups of coffee while he waited.

Carriages were lined up all along the square under the trees, and waitstaff dashed back and forth with orders so that, if ladies wished, they might enjoy their ices in the privacy and comfort of their carriages.

In order to get business out of the way he handed Althea the drafted documents, safely sealed. 'You will wish to examine those. If you are satisfied, I can have them ready for signing next Saturday.'

She nodded. 'Thank you. This will take a great deal off my mind.'

'Do you wish to look at them now?'

She smiled. 'No, Mr Guthrie. That can wait. Let us examine the menu. It's years since I've been here.'

Even looking at the menu and discussing with Kate the merits of vanilla versus strawberry or even toasted almond, Hugo noticed the way people, particularly the ladies, were reacting to Althea.

It was obvious that many of them knew her. Startled glances when she walked in turned swiftly to sneers and backs turned. Not one person came up to greet her. Fleeting glances, followed by whispered conversations. That annoyed him, but it was the so-called gentleman who eyed her as if assessing a likely filly, trying to catch her gaze, that had his metaphorical hackles rising. He suspected that it was only his own presence that kept the fellow at bay.

With Kate and Sarah hotly debating their choices, he leaned over, speaking softly. 'Lady Hartleigh—Althea, I had not thought that this might be awkward for you. Would you rather—'

'Miss out on an ice cream? Absolutely not.' She gave him a glittering smile. 'Think what a public service I am doing, sir. They have something to talk about for a change.'

Several heads turned sharply, and he hid a grin. She'd said it loudly enough to be heard.

He reached out and gripped her gloved hand. 'Well done.'

Utter stillness as she raised her eyes to his face. And yes, there were shadows under her eyes. His hand tightened on hers. Her eyes, those fairy-green eyes, widened. His heart quickened as her fingers returned his clasp. Had he lost his mind? What was he thinking to behave in such a familiar fashion? She was his client, a titled lady, not a woman he could—

'Althea! How nice to see you here!'

Hugo looked up with Althea at the lovely, musical voice. A tall woman and even taller gentleman stood there smiling. The lady's eyes of deep blue grey held pleasure, and her hand was extended to Althea. Hugo forced himself to release her.

Althea rose to shake the woman's hand. 'I had no idea you were returned from the country. May I present my solicitor? This is Mr Guthrie, Lady Rutherford. Mr Guthrie, the Earl and Countess of Rutherford.'

Hugo rose to shake hands, and Lady Rutherford's smile deepened. 'A pleasure, sir. And these must be your nieces, Althea. Rutherford read your letters to me. Don't get up, girls. We don't mean to intrude.'

As his countess chatted to Althea, Rutherford stepped a little closer to Hugo. 'I understand we have some business to conduct, Guthrie.'

'We do, my lord.' For the life of him he couldn't keep the chill out of his voice as he rose.

Rutherford raised his eyebrows. 'Should I call at your offices? Or is it easier for you to call at our home in Berkeley Square? I would like to see those documents before Lady Hartleigh signs anything.'

'Oh?' Again he couldn't help the chill.

Rutherford grimaced. 'Yes.' He studied Hugo for a moment and seemed to reach a conclusion. 'Let's put it this way, Guthrie.' He shot a glance at the ladies and lowered his voice. 'Althea Hartleigh has been appallingly treated by too many men. Myself not least of them. This is one way to make amends. Are the documents ready?'

'They are.' Hugo considered a moment. He had an extra set of the drafted documents. Rutherford's house would be a great deal more private than the office. 'When is a convenient time for me to call on you, my lord?'

Rutherford took out his card case and a pencil, scrawled a brief note on the back of a visiting card, and handed it to him. 'Tomorrow afternoon? Any time after five o'clock. Give that to my butler.'

Hugo tucked the card in his pocket. 'Very well, my lord.'

Rutherford nodded. 'Thank you. I'll say this. I'm glad to see that she has found someone to look after her interests. Good day to you, Guthrie. We won't impose ourselves on your party.'

He was as good as his word, gathering up his countess and taking his leave without the least appearance of any snub. Indeed, the countess's suggestion that Althea should 'bring your nieces to stay with us this summer' was seconded by Rutherford immediately.

Althea smiled, said that was very kind, but gave no indication of acceptance or refusal.

Why had he wanted to hear her decline? Did he want to reassure himself she was not wearing the willow for the earl? It was none of his business either way.

Still puzzling over it, he smiled at the girls. 'Have you made your choices?'

They had. At the countess's recommendation Kate had decided on raspberry and chocolate, Sarah thought toasted almond and vanilla. Althea, perhaps not surprisingly, had chosen ginger ice cream.

Althea wasn't quite sure what to think when Hugo insisted on walking back to Soho with them. On the one hand it looked very peculiar. On the other hand it meant she could walk home without the complication of telling any importunate gentleman to go to hell in front of the girls. She had noticed the interest of Mr Mainwaring in Gunter's.

Not even the brief interlude with Meg and Rutherford had sufficed to quell the leers he sent her way.

For most of the way the two girls walked on ahead with Puck. Sarah had brightened over the ice creams and pot of tea they had shared with Hugo. Kate had wrinkled her nose at tea and asked if she might have lemonade.

Sarah dropped back to walk with them as they turned into Wardour Street. 'May I…may I speak to you, Aunt Althea? Privately?' She cast an apologetic look at Hugo. 'It will take only a moment, sir, and it's the only way Kate won't hear. I've told her I want to ask about more arithmetic lessons.'

Althea choked back a laugh at the expression on his face.

He patted her shoulder. 'Of course. I'll walk on and distract her.' He lengthened his stride and left them together.

Althea said nothing. Best to wait, let Sarah speak when she was ready.

'I'm… I'm sorry!' Sarah blurted out, the threat of tears in her shaking voice.

Without further hesitation, Althea put an arm about her shoulders. 'Oh? What have you done that I don't know about?'

'I… I didn't trust you.' Her voice shook. 'When you went to see Mr Guthrie the other day and wouldn't take us, I thought… I thought—' She hung her head.

Althea could have kicked herself. She tightened her arm. 'You thought I went to tell him I didn't want you after all.' Hugo had thought the same for a moment. 'Has this anything to do with your visit to the parlour last night?'

'You knew?'

Althea nodded.

'I… I didn't want to frighten Kate, but—' Sarah broke off, dragged in a breath. 'I knew I was going to cry and if she woke up she'd want to know what was wrong, so I sneaked out. I thought that—'

'That I was going to hand you over after lulling your suspicions with ice cream?'

She could have kicked herself again. If she'd had the courage and compassion to walk into her own parlour last night and *ask* the child what was wrong—or even days ago when she had noticed Sarah's change in behaviour.

Sarah looked up, her eyes damp. 'I thought you might not bother with the ice creams.'

Althea hugged her close. 'It's all right, Sarah. It's my fault. I should have told you what I was about. And I should have asked you what was wrong.'

She had not wanted to alarm the girls by raising the spectre of yet another death—her own—turning their world topsy turvy all over again. Perhaps that had been the right decision for Kate. Apparently not for Sarah.

She held up the folder of documents. 'I went to see Mr Guthrie to have him make a new will for me, and to ensure that if something happened to me you and Kate would be safe and provided for. These are the drafts.'

Sarah stared at her. 'You mean a last will and testament?'

'Yes. And I have appointed trustees to look after you. Guardians. Mr Guthrie is one of them. Lord Rutherford is another. So you're both safe. You don't have to worry about landing in an orphanage ever again.'

Sarah stopped dead. 'You did that for us? You asked an *earl* to be our guardian? And Mr Guthrie?'

'Yes, and—'

The hug smothered her. Sarah flung her arms around her and clung. Slowly Althea's arms closed about her niece. When last had anyone held her, hugged her like this? She couldn't remember. Her throat closed on an aching lump.

Finally Sarah let go. 'I… I don't know how to thank you.' A tear slipped down her cheek.

Althea patted her cheek, brushing the tear away and praying that the heat pressing behind her own eyes wouldn't spill over. 'I think you just did. Let's catch up with Mr Guthrie and Kate, before she comes back to find out what maggot you've got in your head that you'd ask for more arithmetic.'

'You aren't going to tell her?'

Althea shook her head. 'You asked to speak to me privately. So no. It's between us, unless you choose otherwise.'

Sarah let out an audible breath. 'You can give me more arithmetic if it helps. I should have asked you, shouldn't I? But it felt like if I asked, I'd *make* it happen.'

Althea considered. 'I can understand why you didn't. I wasn't raised to question adults either. But yes, in future if something is worrying you, tell me. And—' she fixed Sarah with a stern glare '—I fail to see why I should come up with an extra arithmetic lesson that I will then have to correct!'

They caught up with Kate and Hugo as they drew level with Gifford's Music Emporium and something slid into Althea's mind. Above the shop there was a small concert hall—she had been planning to attend a concert there next Saturday evening.

'Are you enjoying your music lessons, Sarah?'

Sarah turned a careful gaze on her. 'I *am* enjoying them.' She sounded as though that surprised her. 'Miss Barclay is nice, too.'

Althea laughed. 'So would you enjoy attending a concert with me? This is not extra arithmetic.'

'Oh.' Sarah giggled. 'I might.' She tugged at the end of her little sister's plait. 'Kate would. She used to slip off and play for fun at home, not because our governess Miss Burford said we had to practise.'

'I *like* music,' Kate said. 'It makes me feel happy when I play.'

Althea gestured to Gifford's. 'There's a concert upstairs next Saturday. Would you like to go?' It wasn't only the music. She had avoided most social entanglements for years, but now she had the girls to think of. Living like a particularly reclusive hermit was no longer an option. Even if her stomach turned over at the thought, she was going to have to rejoin society.

Kate stared. '*Can* we? I mean, are children allowed?'

'If you promise to be very still and quiet. And I have a further suggestion to make. I'll explain over supper.'

Hugo left them very properly at the door. He walked away perhaps even more bemused than the first time he had left this house. Whatever had been bothering Sarah enough to risk extra sums was clearly resolved. He rather thought a few tears might have been shed, but she was radiant as he left, teasing her little sister as the door closed behind them.

And Althea? Her eyes remained shadowed and tired, but after that little *tête-à-tête* with Sarah, something seemed to have lifted from her mind. Apparently by interfering, and becoming personally involved, something Jacob had warned him against, he had done the right thing.

Later that evening as he ate dinner at the inn near his lodgings, he wondered idly what suggestion Althea might be making to the girls. He suspected that supper in the Soho Square house was not nearly as peaceful as his solitary meal. Oh, there were diners at the other tables, including a group of half-sprung young gentlemen who were becoming very boisterous over their steaks and tankards. But Hugo had long ago cultivated the ability to remove himself mentally from his physical surroundings.

A good book at dinner, the newspapers at breakfast, and he could banish a near riot from his mental space. Only sometimes he looked up from his book and tankard of ale, and wondered if life was sliding past while he sat in his usual corner. Regulars might stop briefly to speak, but for the most part he maintained a slight distance—people had accepted that.

He stared at his pint. It hadn't always been this way. Once upon a time he had gone home for dinner, had gone home to a house that held everything of joy, all the potential and expectations of a nascent family. And it had all ended in screams of agony followed by a shattering finality of silence, all the potential and expectations snuffed out when his Louisa died in childbirth. All his joy extinguished, and grief an endless ache in his heart.

That joyful home seemed as unreal as a fairy tale. He had left it in the past years ago, and had achieved a measure of contentment. Jacob's wife Alice, thank God, had given up producing possible brides for him, as had the wives of other friends. He was comfortable enough as he was. The even tenor of his life suited him. Calm, logical and steady. One day he would retire to the villa by the river at Petersham, which his father had left him and where his Aunt Sue currently resided. He'd breed books. He might have a dog, too. A companion for walks along the river looking for birds to note in the journal he and his father had kept.

He frowned at the ale. Was it possible he had allowed his life to become regimented? Or even deliberately cultivated a certain boredom?

He shrugged off the thought. Tomorrow he would be calling on an earl. A glimpse into that world would be a rarified treat for him. None of the firm's clients were aristocratic. His partner and his father before him had preferred to confine their dealings to the upper gentry.

His father's reasoning had been succinct. *'They pay their bills.'*

The following Monday morning Hugo looked curiously at the two notes proffered by his clerk. 'What have we here, Timms?' More surprises? He was still getting over the shock of being invited to dine with the Earl and Countess of Rutherford the previous evening. And the further surprise, despite his reluctance, of liking the earl very much.

There was something to be said for a man who so clearly loved his wife and showed it in a dozen tiny ways. Hugo suspected the man didn't even realise. He shoved away the ache in his own memories and returned his attention to his clerk.

Timms grinned. 'Chap—footman, I'd say, although he's not wearing livery—says you need to read this one first.' He handed over a missive with Hugo's name set out in large, careful script. Hugo couldn't help smiling as he noted the single, very small splotch of ink marring the penmanship. He thought he knew who had written that…

'Very well. And the other?'

Timms handed it over. Hugo's hand shook, and he fancied that a subtle faery scent clung to the paper, that the blob of wax sealing it, once broken, might release an irreversible enchantment. The handwriting, also setting out his name and style, was as lovely and feminine as Althea herself.

Devil take it, what was wrong with him?

'Is the footman waiting for a reply?'

'He said if you wished to reply at once he could wait. Up to you, sir.'

He nodded slowly. 'Ask him to wait.'

He broke open the first note. Read the contents and stared. The concert Althea had mentioned to the girls. An invitation from Sarah and Kate to attend with them. To thank him for the ices and everything else he had done for them. At once open, and utterly prim. He found himself swallowing a lump as he remembered the tiny, doomed daughter who had lain in his arms for that one short day before joining her mother in the silence of death.

Lucy, he had had her baptised, summoning the priest urgently when the doctor and midwife had warned him the baby was unlikely to survive. To him Lucy had been a gift. Given—and swiftly, cruelly taken away.

He tucked the letter safely away in the small drawer where he kept notes from his father. What the hell had the rest of their family been thinking that they would have let Kate and Sarah be swallowed up by orphanages?

He opened Althea's note. A simple confirmation of the invitation. A suggestion that he might care to come to the house early and escort them to the concert after partaking of refreshments…

*Which should give me sufficient time to sign all the copies of the various documents, assuming the final copies are ready. I had a note from Rutherford this morning that you and he had gone over them and he thought they were more than adequate to protect Sarah and Kate's interests. If this does not suit you, please say so.*

There was no question that he wanted to see her again. And it wasn't because she was beautiful, or he hoped it wasn't. He had called off the watch he had set on the house in Soho Square first thing that morning. He couldn't settle it with his conscience to spy on her any longer. Either he trusted her with the girls, or he didn't. And if he didn't, then he should never have left them with her in the first place.

The woman who had changed her will, set up trusts at some expense to herself and persuaded two powerful men to protect her nieces, should it ever be necessary, was a woman he could admire.

Admiration was not a problem.

Staring at the note, he thought he knew exactly what advice Jacob would give him. After dinner the other night Jacob had walked him to the door.

*'Ragging on you aside, I'm a little concerned about this outing with Lady Hartleigh and her nieces, Hugo. No good can come of too close an association with a client. You know that as well as I do. Cannot this meeting take place in the offices? A little more formally?'*

This? Accepting an invitation to a concert? Saying that the girls had invited him would have Jacob's eyebrows disappearing into his fast-receding hair. Damn it. His own father would be frowning over it.

It would be easier if he had never met her.

But he *had* met her. The problem was that he *liked* her. Of course it behoved him to maintain a relationship with the girls, since he was about to become one of their trustees. But still, some part of him wondered what he was getting himself into pursuing a—pursuing a *what*? Relationship? Friendship?

*If this does not suit you...*

It suited him only too well, because the real problem was that he desired her. And possibly not just desired her.

Ten years. He had been alone for ten years, and in that time, while he had occasionally felt a mild interest in a woman, it had been precisely that. Mild. Yes, he had liked women. He *did* like women. But the thought of pursuing any relationship had not interested him.

He had loved Louisa. He loved her still, and the tiny daughter he had held so briefly. He had assumed that part of his life was over. Once he had wondered if he might love again one day, but in ten years it hadn't happened.

And now he had discovered in himself a burning desire for a client, coupled with that nagging undercurrent of *feeling*. A woman with a dubious past, and one moreover to whose nieces he stood, he supposed, as a sort of father figure. A future guardian, should something happen to their aunt.

Surely a sensible man could ignore that fierce attraction and pursue a disinterested friendship with a woman, couldn't he? They had a common interest in the girls' welfare, and—who was he trying to convince? He wasn't at all interested in being disinterested. Or sensible.

And yet. They were from different worlds. His family had been solidly middle class, professional. Althea had been born into the upper gentry and had married into the aristocracy. She might have withdrawn from that gilded circle due to her straitened finances, but she still had friends within that world. It had been clear last night that, while Rutherford himself might maintain a discreet distance, both he and the countess considered Althea Hartleigh a close friend.

It was also clear that if she ever chose to step back into aristocratic circles, they would help her. And there was a puzzle. For some reason, and he didn't think it was guilt, the countess insisted on maintaining a friendship with Althea.

Last night they had dined in Rutherford's library. Something, he understood, the pair of them did routinely when they were alone or had family with them. Friendly, intimate. The conversation had been mostly about the girls and the arrangements that were in place for them.

Lady Rutherford was thinking further ahead. Potentially to marriage. She was prepared to bring them out, give them a season.

*'If that is what they and Althea want. A London season, or somewhere else if Althea thinks it more appropriate.'*

He let out a breath. Where could he possibly fit into that scenario? He was comfortably off, yes. More than comfortably off. But he did not delude himself that he would be welcomed into aristocratic company, except in a very private capacity. And it seemed to him that Althea had no desire to step back into the world of the aristocracy. She maintained those friendships, but refused to use them to her own advantage. What if she wished to use them to ensure good marriages for Sarah and Kate? That would be another matter altogether.

He knew what Jacob would advise. He knew what his own father would have advised. But he didn't even know what *he* wanted yet. Except that he wanted to keep on seeing Althea. And the girls. Those wants were each independent of the other. And somehow he had to maintain a professional relationship with all of them, when he wasn't feeling even remotely professional about Althea Hartleigh.

He blew out a frustrated breath. It ought to be simple enough. If ever his personal feelings for Althea and his professional judgement came into conflict, he had to err on the side of being professional. That was the logical and rational thing to do.

Escorting a woman and her nieces to a concert was hardly a breach of professional conduct.

He picked up his pen, dipped it in the ink pot and penned his acceptance to Sarah and Kate's invitation. Then he folded Althea's letter up and slipped it into the inner breast pocket of his coat.

# Chapter Five

Althea wondered if anyone had ever looked forward to one of Mr Gifford's concerts with quite so much anticipation. The girls had been in a buzz of excitement all week about this evening's concert. She glanced at the shining heads, bent over their schoolbooks, and then at the clock. Ten minutes and she'd be sending them upstairs to change their shoes and put on coats for their walk with John and Puck.

She cast a disgusted glance out of the window. In the middle of the square, King Charles II sneered down at the flower bed beneath him, despite the bright, sunny day. No walk for her. Since they had the concert this evening, she needed to work this afternoon. Not that she had explained any of that to Sarah and Kate. The fewer people who knew how she augmented her income, the better.

Not even her newfound friends could know—Kit Selbourne at the bookshop and Psyché Barclay who ran the tea and coffee shop, the Phoenix Rising. To her surprise, the moment she had dropped her self-imposed reserve, she had discovered them to be friendly and willing to take her into their tight little circle. She had known of their connections to the world she had left behind. It had never occurred to her that they might have deliberately put that world behind them, too.

In approaching Kit for advice on where to find a music teacher, and perhaps some sort of governess or tutor for the girls, she had discovered an odd world where people simply *were*. No one cared that Psyché was Black, or that Kit used her own name rather than her aristocratic husband's to run her business. No one even cared that she, Althea, had been ostracised by society after conducting an affair with the Earl of Rutherford.

And they knew. When, at the first friendly invitation, she had dropped the information at Kit Selbourne's feet rather like a bomb, Kit had shrugged.

*'Yes. We're aware of all that. And that no one, least of all his countess, is drumming Rutherford out of society.'* A small smile. *'It would be another matter if you attempted to seduce one of* our *husbands.'*

*'Or they attempted to seduce me?'* Despite society's prejudice, it was not always the woman's fault.

The smile had taken on a glint. *'Oh, we'd slice the idiot up for the dog's dinner in that case.'*

And just like that she had friends again. A social circle, who, between the demands of their work and families, visited each other and closed around each other when help was needed.

Psyché's daughter taught the girls music, and the tutor who taught Kit's boys took Sarah for Latin and mathematics. And in between it all there was somehow time for cups of tea and an occasional supper.

Odd, though. Now, when she had so many restrictions on her time, it was as though she worked better, despite being so tired from working late into the evening last night. Rather than staring out the window daydreaming this afternoon, having the deadline of the girls' return focused her mind most wonderfully.

Her mind already sliding into the next scene—wherein Miss Lydia Parker was spoiling to give Sir Edwin the set down of his life—Althea cursed silently as she heard the doorbell.

The girls looked up.

'Are you expecting someone, Aunt Althea?'

'No.' Both Kit and Psyché would be working. 'John will see who it is.' And hopefully send them away.

A wonderful thing having a servant you could depend upon

to distinguish between welcome and unwelcome visitors, and get rid of the unwanted ones without a fuss.

The door opened and John came in with the salver kept for receiving visiting cards. His expression was apologetic as he extended it to her.

Althea picked up the card with foreboding. Read it.

'Did you happen to notice the sky, John?'

He looked at her enquiringly. 'The sky, ma'am?'

'Yes. You know. Up there.' She pointed upwards. 'Blue stuff, or grey as the case maybe. Was it all still up there? Or are there bits of it littered about the square?'

He grinned. 'Far as I noticed it was all up where it's supposed to be, ma'am.'

'Hmm. Perhaps it will fall down later. Show my aunt in—no. Wait.'

She turned to the avidly watching girls. 'You may go upstairs and get ready for your walk.' She absolutely did not need to expose her nieces to the nosiness of Miss Elinor Price, whose reputation in the family hovered between that of Basilisk and Gorgon.

Sarah tilted her head questioningly and Althea sighed. Best to be open with her. 'My great-aunt, Miss Elinor Price.'

Kate looked impressed. 'So she's sort of like our *great*-great-aunt? Is she frightfully old?'

'Frightfully. I'm surprised she's still alive. Now off you go.'

John cleared his throat. 'Ah, Miss Price said she'd like to see the young ladies—'

'What I said, my good man, was that I'd see Frederick's brats, too. And I'm still alive, Althea, because the devil won't have me.'

Althea met her aunt's hard, bright glare with an affable smile, as her affronted relative stalked into the room.

'I've always suspected that the devil had a great deal of good sense about him. Do come in, Aunt—since you are in already. Thank you, John.'

The servant retreated as Elinor Price advanced, leaning heavily on her stick.

'If someone told you *this* was an eligible address, Althea, they lied.' Elinor glanced around, her expression scornful. 'And what the devil is *that*?'

Puck had emerged from under the desk.

'A dog, Aunt Elinor. *My* dog.'

Elinor subjected Puck to a gimlet-eyed stare. 'If you say so.'

Althea shrugged, beyond caring how rude it was. 'I do. And as for the address, I was assured that it was far enough out of the way that no one would bother calling on me here. But as you say, they lied. Apart from your carriage, Elinor, what brings you here?'

After Hartleigh's death, Elinor had been very quick to join the rest of the family in blaming her for the parlous state of her finances, and condemning her supposed lack of morals.

'Going to ask me to sit down?'

Althea eyed her thoughtfully. For all the old lady's belligerence she struck Althea as frail, and a quick mental calculation told her that Elinor must be verging on ninety by now. 'Very well. Do sit down, Elinor. To what do I owe the honour of this visit?'

The old woman sat, glared. 'An impertinent letter from some solicitor! I came to see if it was true. That you'd taken in Frederick's daughters.'

Althea's temper slipped a notch. 'As you see. They are living with me now.'

'Why?'

'Is it any business of yours?'

'Hoping for some money with them, were you? You ran through your own fortune fast enough, didn't you? After you ran through Hartleigh's!' She thumped the stick on the ground.

The hell she had. 'I had no idea you had such a taste for unfounded gossip, Elinor.'

A snort greeted that. 'Unfounded? Hah!'

A little more temper slipped its restraints. 'Did no one mention the ten thousand pounds' worth of gambling debts that Hartleigh's executors saw fit to pay out?'

Audible gasps came from Sarah and Kate.

Elinor Price gripped the top of her cane harder. 'Fustian! He gambled no more than was genteel! Frederick told me that.'

Elinor had always thought the sun shone brighter when Frederick rose from a chair. The temptation to set her right, to tell her the truth about what Frederick and Hartleigh had done, burned inside Althea, but she quenched it. Sarah and Kate were right there.

Instead, Althea took a death grip on her temper and shook her head with a pitying smile 'You really ought to get out more, Elinor. Someone might tell you the truth.'

However, it wasn't going to be her. At least, not all of it.

Mentally editing, she said, 'Ten thousand pounds was the figure, which I think you'll agree was a little more than can be considered genteel.' Fury scorched through her. 'And that was after he had persuaded my trustees to release the bulk of *my* fortune at various times to pay off earlier gaming debts.' And for other *expenses* that, if possible, had stung even more.

She took a sharp breath. This was verging on the subjects Sarah and Kate definitely did not need to know about.

'So.' She favoured Elinor with a brilliant smile. 'May I offer you a cup of tea, Aunt Elinor? Since the truth doesn't sit comfortably with you?'

Elinor heaved to her feet. 'Why, you impertinent baggage! How dare—?'

'She's *not*!'

Sarah was up, too, fists clenched and her face red.

Althea turned. 'Sarah, sit down, sweetheart.' For the life of her she couldn't bring herself to reprove the child.

'No! She's being horrid to you, and you were the only one who'd take us in after Papa died and Cousin Wilfrid said we couldn't stay. Even though you haven't got nearly as much money as some of our other relatives!' She turned on Elinor. 'Like you! I know you were on Mr Guthrie's list. And you're as rich as Midas! So go away!'

'Charming!' Elinor glared at Sarah. 'Do you imagine she took you without there being something in it for her, child? I've no doubt your cousin Wilfrid gave her something for taking you off his hands.'

Sarah snorted. 'I don't think so. Since we were going to orphanages otherwise! He didn't even give us enough money to buy our dinner on the way to London. What would *you* know about it anyway? No wonder the devil doesn't want you! You'd put him out of a job!'

'Orphanages? *Frederick's* daughters? What nonsense is this?'

Seeing Elinor's jaw drop, and not entirely convinced the old lady couldn't throw actual lightning bolts or at least spit venom, Althea stepped between them. 'There you have it, Elinor. Good day to you. I'll see you out. Sarah, dear,' she turned to the child, 'ring for John. A pot of tea for me—' tempting to lace it with brandy! '—cake and milk for you and Kate before your walk. You may give Puck a biscuit.'

She strode to the door, opened it. 'After you, Elinor.'

'Kicking me out, are you?'

'Well spotted.'

She shut the door behind them with something perilously close to a bang and stalked to the front door.

Elinor looked at her, scowling. 'You think I can't and won't ask questions? Find out the truth?'

'Have at it, Elinor. With my blessing. But think about *who* you ask. And whatever you find out, do not bring it back here to distress my girls.'

The old lady snorted. 'Don't think I don't know who your principal trustee was after your father died, girl! And what did that chit mean, that Wilfrid wouldn't let them stay? He was supposed to be their guardian. What was he thinking giving them over to *you*? And what was all that nonsense about orphanages?'

Althea opened the front door. 'Elinor, mind your own business. If you came to assure yourself that Frederick's daughters are safe, you may rest assured they are as safe as I can make them, and that's no thanks to either their father or Wilfrid. Good day to you. Happy gossiping. But please, don't bring what you find back here to those girls!' She softened her voice. 'Whatever you do, please don't do that. They don't deserve it.'

A footman hurried across the pavement towards them from Elinor's waiting carriage.

The old lady's scowl deepened as she waved the footman off. 'That letter. From the solicitor telling me they were with you. First thing I knew about Frederick's girls being homeless.'

Althea snorted, and realised that she sounded for all the world like Elinor herself. 'Mr Guthrie assured me he had contacted all the other possible relations before coming to me. I had assumed you were on his list. Sarah certainly seems to think so.'

The thin old mouth flattened. 'Apparently I was. Servants didn't tell me because I've been ill. Doctor had me near buried. So there's that.'

Althea softened a little. 'Oh. I'm sorry you've been unwell, Aunt.'

The old lady gave a sniff. 'I daresay. I'll get to the bottom of this. Don't think I won't.' She beckoned to her footman. 'I'll bid you good day.'

Althea watched as the footman handed the old lady down the steps and into the carriage.

Elinor put down the window and leaned out. 'That girl's got a nasty tongue in her head. The same as you always had.'

Althea inclined her head. 'Thank you, Elinor.'

Impossible to know if the answering snort betokened amusement or irritation. With Elinor it could have been either, or both at once. As the vehicle rattled off Althea closed the front door behind her and leaned back on it. If Elinor poked around there was every likelihood she'd stir up a veritable hornets' nest. She took a deep breath, hoping she could send the girls out for their walk without too many questions.

Something had upset Althea. Hugo had noticed almost immediately on arriving at the house. On the surface she appeared her usual self during their light meal. Bright, cheerful, a little cynical—although never the latter with the girls. But there was *something.* A little more reserve perhaps. She had been a little short with him, her brow furrowed, although she had relaxed during the concert, clearly enjoying the music. The quartet was excellent, starting with Mozart, then Haydn and finishing with Beethoven.

Sarah, unsurprisingly, had fidgeted a little. Kate, to his amazement, had sat enthralled, leaning forward in her seat in utter silence. At the gathering for refreshments, she was still very quiet, her eyes dreamy.

'You enjoyed the concert, Kate?' He passed her a small plate with cake on it.

She nodded. 'I'm going to practise the piano more.'

Hugo blinked. 'Practise? Where do you do that?' He hadn't noticed any sort of instrument, let alone a piano at the house.

Kate smiled. 'Miss Barclay teaches me, and I am allowed to go to their house to practise. Mrs Barclay runs the Phoenix. It used to be a coffee house for gentlemen, but now anyone can go. We have tea there after changing our library books.'

He had been introduced to Miss Barclay, the daughter of Mr and Mrs William Barclay. He had met them before the concert. Mrs Barclay was the owner and proprietor of the Phoenix Rising. He wasn't quite sure how that had come about, but the teashop had been one of the establishments that had provided a great deal of information about Althea's household. Barclay, he understood, was employed as a steward for the Marquess of Huntercombe.

The mix of guests was interesting to say the least. Mrs Barclay, a tall, elegant Black woman, was not the only female business owner present. There was also Miss Selbourne who, confusingly, was also Lady Martin Lacy, married to the youngest son of the Duke of Keswick. She ran Selbourne's Antiquarian Books across the road from the Phoenix. He wasn't entirely sure if he should call her Miss Selbourne or Lady Martin. She answered to both with seeming equanimity.

'Did you enjoy it, Mr Guthrie?'

He smiled at Kate. 'Very much. Although I wondered if I had offended your aunt.'

She scowled, bit into her cake. 'I think she's still cross about Great-Great-Aunt Price.'

Hugo realised too late that he shouldn't have raised such a topic with the child. 'Oh. Well, never mind.' Great-Great-Aunt Price, he assumed, must be Miss Elinor Price.

'She called before our walk and said the horridest things to Aunt Althea. And then Sarah said rude things to *her* and Aunt Althea kicked her out.'

Fascinated despite himself, he asked, 'Kicked who out? Not Sarah, surely?'

Kate swallowed. 'Kicked Great-Aunt Price out, I mean. Then we had cake and milk and went for our walk.'

'Was it a nice walk?' A desperate attempt to change the subject if ever there was one.

'Oh, yes. But Aunt Althea was still out of sorts when we came home. She came with us after all. And I think she was going to work, but Aunt Price annoyed her so much she said she needed to clear her head instead.'

What work? Her accounts? Needlework? But why would Kate say *going to work*?

He tried again to change the subject. 'Why don't we speak to Miss Barclay and her mother about extra practice for you?'

Kate's smile glowed. 'Can we? I don't think they'll mind, but I have to *ask*, not expect.'

Relieved, he nodded. 'Of course. Come along.' He'd confess and apologise to Althea for his accidental prying later.

# Chapter Six

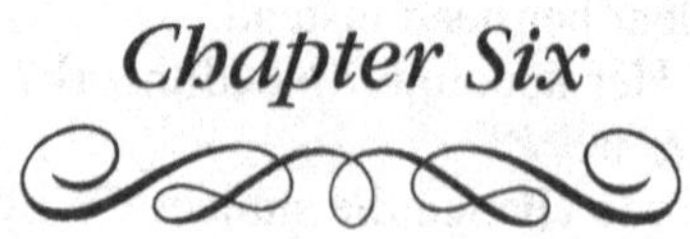

'I owe you an apology.'

The girls were walking ahead a little and he had offered Althea his arm. He liked the feel of her hand resting there. Clear through her evening gloves, the layers of his shirt and coat, it burned like a brand. His heart beat that little bit harder in response. And somehow at the same time it felt right. Comfortable. As if it were exactly where it was meant to be. In the same way that the whole evening had felt right.

She gave him a sideways smile that kicked his heartbeat up yet another notch. 'Whatever for?'

He caught at his scattered thoughts. 'I…er…understand you had an unwelcome visitor today.'

Her fingers tightened sharply on his arm, then eased.

'Oh. That.' She wrinkled her nose. 'Not exactly a visitor. And not entirely unwelcome. She didn't stay long enough for either.'

Hugo had the impression she was choosing her words carefully.

'My great-aunt. She disapproves of me. How did you… Ah, Kate.'

'Yes, hence the apology. I didn't mean to pump her. Exactly. I thought perhaps *I* had offended you.'

'You? How?'

'I had no idea. Stupidly, I mentioned it to Kate. She told me all about Miss Price. Is it Sarah's rudeness that annoyed you?'

Her soft chuckle reassured him a little. 'No. Not at all. Elinor infuriated me. She received your letter of course and came to see for herself. Apparently it was the first she knew of the business. She said she had been unwell, but she does like to poke her nose into anything she considers family business. I shouldn't have permitted her to set my back up. Sarah reacted to that.'

'She's very loyal.'

Althea smiled. 'Yes. I'm not sure what I've done to deserve her partisanship though.'

'Giving them a home, perhaps?'

She waved that away. 'Little enough.'

He begged to differ. What she had done was life changing for those girls. And he still did not understand where her money came from.

Althea Hartleigh had been left the most impecunious of widows. Her own fortune had been dissipated. And, given that dissipation, how had she learned to manage her now straitened finances?

She had turned her financial affairs over to him and, looking through her accounts, he had seen there were occasional lump sums being paid to her. At irregular times, and in increasing amounts. Over the past few years those sums came to around six thousand pounds, much of which she had invested safely in government funds.

His first assumption, that she had sold some jewellery, he now doubted. Surely if she had decided to sell jewellery she would have done it all at once? Unless she had concluded that she would get better prices if she did it bit by bit. And from all he could see Althea hadn't been *forced* to the sale of anything. Her accounts had been in order when each of those sums had appeared. Except for the very first payment, five years ago, the money had not been used to keep her above hatches, to pay off debts or to keep her household running. Significantly, she had told him what that first payment had been for—the sale of her very expensive mansion in Mayfair. After that, the unexplained money was invested, adding to her financial security, and she lived off the income of her investments, not the payments themselves.

He knew she lived frugally. Only the one manservant, her cook/housekeeper and the maid. No horse or carriage. She walked most places, or very occasionally took a hackney. Her gowns were elegant, but far from modish or expensive, and she didn't have many as far as he could tell. She didn't entertain—no dinner parties or card parties. She had a limited circle of friends and accepted occasional invitations to dine.

It still niggled at him that she might have an extraordinarily discreet lover. One who managed never to be seen? Surely no one was that discreet? Further than that, he knew beyond doubt that she would not conduct herself in that way with the girls in the house. If it had been just the one payment, it might have been a single payment from a former lover.

Rutherford, perhaps. But apart from the sale of her Mayfair house, the first of those unexplained payments had been over a year after Rutherford's marriage and the end of their affair. And the payments had continued, the most recent a few months ago. He didn't see Rutherford doing that or, for that matter, Althea accepting.

Besides, she had told him straight out that she had found something to sell apart from herself. He knew her well enough to know that not only was she *not* lying about this, but that she wouldn't lie to him. Logically, if she'd wanted to lie, selling jewellery was the obvious one. He would have believed it.

But when he had first met Althea, he had not noticed dark shadows under her eyes. He'd noticed them when she called at his chambers, as if she were not getting enough sleep, and they were only becoming deeper.

And Kate had said *work*.

It was none of his business unless she chose to tell him. And he didn't care to look too closely at the reasons he was determined not to believe she had a lover.

They had reached the house, and for the first time in years Althea was unsure of what to do with a man. She could invite him in, offer him tea or coffee. Slightly improper, but who cared? She was a widow, not a marriageable young lady. No one was going to worry about her reputation, and she was perfectly sure he wasn't going to make a nuisance of himself.

On the other hand, *his* reputation might suffer if he was thought to be consorting with a notorious widow.

When in doubt, ask.

'Will it sink your reputation straight into the gutter if I invite you in for tea or coffee?'

He gave her a sideways glance. 'A mere invitation won't sink me. Even accepting your invitation—if that was an invitation and not a hypothetical query—won't render me damaged goods. It's what might accompany the tea and coffee that could be construed as damaging.'

She snorted out a laugh. 'Ginger biscuits?'

'I think my virtue is safe then,' he said gravely. 'Except possibly for indulging in the sin of gluttony, I see little danger in ginger biscuits.'

To her surprise he took the key from her and opened the door, gesturing them in.

'After you.'

Kate gave Hugo her most innocent yet impish smile. 'Are you coming in, sir? I'm not in the least tired. Are we having biscuits?'

Before he could step into the trap, Althea fixed Kate with a mild look. 'It's so far past your bedtime, you'll probably need early bed tomorrow night if you don't hurry. Or even an afternoon nap instead of a walk.'

Kate pouted, but Sarah gave her a poke in the back. 'Don't be a brat, Kate. It's after ten. You heard the church bell walking home as clearly as I did. Come on.'

For an instant, Althea wondered if Kate would argue, but she gave a sigh instead. 'Oh, very well. Goodnight, Aunt. Goodnight, sir. Thank you for the concert. It was lovely.'

'You're very welcome.' Althea bent to kiss her. 'Milly will bring up your milk and biscuits. Make sure you clean your teeth properly.'

Sarah kissed her. 'We will. Goodnight.' She dropped Hugo a little curtsy. 'Goodnight, sir.'

John popped into the hall. 'Tea, ma'am?'

'Yes, please. And milk and biscuits upstairs for the young ladies.'

The parlour fire had nearly gone out and Hugo, seeing her bend to stir it up and add coals, nudged her aside.

'May I?'

'Thank you.'

Oddly, it didn't seem as if he were suggesting she couldn't do it, it was more offering to do something for her. Because he wanted to, because he could. She sat down with a little sigh. She needed to work for another hour this evening. Perhaps she shouldn't have invited him in. But it was so nice to sit down and let someone else stir up the fire for a change. She refused to call a servant every time something needed doing. And that would not be the same as watching Hugo add coals to the fire, simply because he wanted to do it for her.

A little warning voice sounded. *Don't start wanting a man to do things for you. For any reason.*

She pushed it away. This was friendship, kindness. She had made herself forget how pleasant it could be to have friends you saw regularly, who could be part of your life.

'Should I sign those papers now?'

He looked up with a frown. 'Absolutely not. You should read them over first, check them against the drafts you and Rutherford approved.'

She knew he was right. And she wanted to see him again…

*Are you mad? What are you doing?*

'Very well. I'll do that tomorrow and bring them to your office. Leave them with your clerk. Or…' She hesitated, unsure of herself.

He sat down opposite her, nodded slowly. 'You could do that. Or…?'

'Or you might like to come to supper next Friday night.' Hurriedly, she added, 'I have asked the Barclays and Lord Martin and Kit if they would like to come. And their families.'

He looked surprised. 'That's unusual for you.'

She stared. 'Is it?' How the hell did he know that?

He flushed. 'I mean, I had the impression you preferred to avoid society.' He shifted in his seat. 'That you didn't accept invitations or issue them.'

She thought about that. 'True. But they're not "society" precisely. They're friends. I think.'

She thought a little more, watching him. Was the chair uncomfortable? She had never found it so, but he was shifting in it rather… He might have correctly divined her preference to keep largely to herself, but how had he known something so specific, that she rarely issued invitations?

Irritation stirred, then fury uncoiled, hissing, raising its head. 'You've been watching me.'

His cheeks, even the tips of his ears, burned. If she hadn't been so annoyed it would have been endearing.

'I'm sorry.'

Most of her rising anger dissipated at that simple apology. No attempt at evasion. Not even an attempt at justification. She forced herself to think a little further.

'The girls.' He knew her reputation. Perhaps even suspected how close she had been to a different solution for her lack of funds. 'You wanted to be sure they were safe, that I really was a fit and proper person to have charge of them.'

It stung. More than a little. But she had to admit, she had probably earned a little scrutiny from a man who only wanted to protect those children. They had already been put through hell.

She scowled, then forced out the words that had to be said. 'Thank you.'

He looked stunned. *'Thank you?'* Now *he* looked annoyed. 'For what? Insulting you comprehensively?'

The rest of her anger vanished as if it had never been. 'For caring enough about the girls to risk insulting me. For being someone I can trust, always, to have their best interests at heart.'

'If it matters, I withdrew the watch after you called at my office.'

'Oh?' The blush was endearing, and that he still looked ashamed.

'I reasoned that a woman so determined on protecting the girls from the world in general, and men in particular, would hardly behave in a way likely to cause them harm.' That faint smile flickered. 'Your own logic really. I like it.'

At that moment, a slight scratch at the door heralded John with the tea tray. Althea took the reprieve and busied herself pouring tea, as she attempted to bring her thoughts under some semblance of control.

She handed Hugo his cup and a biscuit, as something far more disturbing than anger flickered inside her. A growing interest in a man who liked a woman as a logical, rational being? Rather than a pretty doll to be admired for her beauty, a prize to make other men envious of your luck in possessing her?

She *knew* such men existed. She was neither stupid nor unobservant, and she had seen those relationships for herself.

But for her? She sipped her tea.

Very few men ever seemed to look past her beauty. She knew she was beautiful. There was no point in pretending otherwise, and from her sixteenth year she had considered it a penance. Other girls had either viewed her as competition in the quest for a wealthy husband, or attached themselves to her in the hopes that proximity would bring them to the attention of men. The mothers of those girls had murmured little slights—that it was a shame her eyes were that odd shade of green, or that she thought far too much of herself.

The men had courted her for her beauty and fortune. Not one of them had been interested in Althea Price. The girl who actually enjoyed playing the piano. The girl who covered page after page in a carefully hidden journal with her imaginings.

'Those thoughts are going to be worth a great deal more than a penny.' He set down his cup and the half-eaten biscuit.

She blinked. 'My apologies. I don't think I have ever received a nicer compliment.'

Hugo stared at her. Was every other man in London blind? He started to say so, but thought a little further.

*A nicer compliment.*

He didn't think he had ever seen a lovelier woman. He would be lying if he pretended not to see it, not to appreciate it. But her beauty wasn't why he liked her. He picked up his cup again, absent-mindedly dipped his biscuit in it. How many people bothered to look past that lovely façade? How many of them saw the woman he saw?

He thought Rutherford did. Belatedly. And the countess saw her. The people he had met tonight? Barclay, Lord Martin and their wives? Who did they see when they looked at Althea Hartleigh?

Ah. She had invited them to supper next Friday. She would not have invited them into her home if she were not comfortable with them. And from all he had learned of her, she had never done so before. Which meant…

'You have lived here, what? Five years? And you have only recently become friends with the Barclays and Lacy and his wife.'

She gave him a wry smile. 'And how do you know that?'

'Because this is the first time you have ever invited people to supper as far as I can make out.'

She sighed. 'My reputation. When I moved here…let's say I was raw. Tired of people cutting me, gossiping about me. I decided to keep myself to myself, and the hell with the rest of the world. I wasn't going to give anyone an excuse to accuse me of casting lascivious eyes on her husband, or whatever other nonsense they could invent.'

He could understand that, hiding away to lick your wounds. Hadn't he done much the same, moving back into lodgings that didn't constantly remind him of everything he had lost?

'And the girls changed that.' They had changed things for him, too.

She laughed. 'You really do know me.' Dipping her own biscuit, she said, 'All very well for me to adopt the habits of a medieval anchorite, but that is no life for children.' She ate the biscuit and sipped her tea. 'They need to be educated. They need to know people. How can they navigate the world if they do not live in it?'

He nodded. 'So you took the risk and emerged from your cell to meet your neighbours.'

'I suppose so.' She smiled. 'Not much of a risk, as it turned out. I always liked them, and it turned out they knew all about me and didn't care in the least.'

Others, he knew, had cared. The people in Gunter's tea shop, whispering and sneering behind their hands. Some of them, no doubt, had once called Althea their friend. The so-called gentleman whose greedy eyes had slithered all over her. He could imagine the sort of compliments that type would offer, and thanked God that Althea was intelligent enough to discount such dross.

'Supper,' he said. 'I would like that very much. However.'

She raised her brows. 'However? That sounds as though there is a caveat coming.'

'Not a caveat precisely,' he said. 'But before I accept, and you cannot rescind your invitation—'

Laughter rippled. 'Don't wager too much on that, Hugo.'

He smiled. 'In the interests of honesty and full disclosure, I should tell you that you are beautiful. Possibly the most beautiful woman I have ever seen. I would have to be blind and six months dead not to notice that.'

'You do seem to be breathing.'

'And plan to keep doing so.' He smiled at her. 'Your beauty is a distraction though. People don't see past it, I suppose.'

She stared. Shook her head slowly. 'They see beautiful, destructive Lady Hartleigh who made a play for an earl, failed and retired from society ruined and humiliated.'

He scowled. 'Is that how you saw yourself?'

She shrugged. 'It's true enough.'

'The hell it is. I see a woman who tried to extricate herself from an impossible situation not of her own making, in the only way she could.'

He leaned forward and gripped her hands. 'Do not tell me that those women who cut your acquaintance and gossiped behind their hands at Gunter's would not have done exactly the same.' How had she put it once? 'Were you truly the—and I quote—mercenary bitch people like to see, you would hardly have retained Rutherford's friendship and respect, let alone gained that of Lady Rutherford.'

* * *

She could hardly breathe—her heart tripped. He still held her hands, at once steely and gentle, as if he sheltered her from everything, yet would release her in an instant should she wish it.

She did not wish it. What she wanted—

He raised first one, then the other hand to his lips and brushed a kiss over her fingers.

The world tilted and whirled around her as her pulse leapt and fizzed like the fine champagne she had once enjoyed. In the past five years her pulse had not so much as flickered over a man. Oh, she had seen plenty of men she considered attractive, but that had been a theoretical thing. She had merely observed their attractiveness. She had not felt any tug of interest, and considered it far less of a loss in her life than champagne.

This was a great deal more than a tug. What she wanted was insane, impossible and far more dangerous than anything else she had ever wanted in her life.

For a moment she stared at her fingers where his mouth had touched, wondering that her hands looked much the same. Slowly she raised her eyes and found his waiting.

So serious that deep, peaceful grey. Well, usually peaceful. Now they were not peaceful at all. A storm lurked in the depths. A storm she could call or banish.

Her breathing hitched. 'Hugo?'

He leaned forward, still holding her hands, but stopped a heartbeat away.

Her choice. Call or banish.

She leaned forward the last heartbeat and their lips met.

Not the storm, not yet. It was there, but this kiss was gentle, sweet. Almost shy. There was no demand as their mouths moved together. Desire was there, but banked. There to be stirred up should one of them choose it, but this was lovely. A courtship in and of itself. This was a kiss she had never known before. She was not sure she had known it existed.

Someone deepened the kiss. Perhaps it was both of them. Mouths opened, tongues quested and touched. Someone sighed in pleasure and another sigh answered. And still the desire remained simmering, dancing in the wings, waiting for the storm.

She was ready to call it.

* * *

Somewhere a bell chimed. And kept chiming.

Hugo forced himself to break the kiss, and felt as though something had ripped inside him. Her lips clung now, and he didn't want to stop kissing her. But the damn clock reminded him that, like Cinderella, he couldn't stay for the entire night.

She sat back a little, her eyes questioning, *wanting*, and his resolve wavered. Those faerie eyes were a little dazed, her lips soft from their kisses. Temptation, he realised, was the absence of all thought. He forced himself to sit up and think. *His* reputation could remove itself to hell and back, but if he remained here kissing Althea, it would not stop with kisses. And that would do very real damage to her reputation.

His lungs were tight and he had an aching erection. They had kissed and held hands, and he was burning for her.

*Slow down. This is not something to gulp.*

He summoned a smile. 'I'd look a fool running down your front steps with one shoe, wouldn't I?'

She frowned. 'One—oh!' Something of her wicked smile dawned. 'You'd make an odd sort of Cinderella.'

He touched her cheek, felt her quiver. 'We aren't going to rush into this, Princess Charming.'

'Rush into what?'

He let out a breath. 'I suppose when we know that we might move a little faster.' He rose. 'I should leave. Before I do something irreparably stupid.'

She saw him out. He didn't risk kissing her again, but waited on the step to hear the key turn and the bolts shoot home. There were moments when doing something irreparably stupid—like banging on her door and asking to come back in—seemed like an excellent idea.

# Chapter Seven

In Althea's former life, the supper parties she held had been formal, elegant affairs. Silks and satins had rustled, the food and wine had been of the finest, and the musical entertainment had been sophisticated. None of the guests would have dreamed of arriving with a bottle of wine or a pie to add to the table, and no one would have brought a fiddle to play.

Those formal, elegant affairs had been worked out and planned down to the last lobster patty. Champagne had flowed, and the bill afterwards had been eyewatering. In addition, Althea had been obliged to send invitations to a great many people she *knew* disliked her, and would gossip the next day about who *hadn't* attended. Even if the supposed absentee had been there visibly enjoying him or herself.

She never had a chance to converse with the people she really wanted to, because Hartleigh had insisted that she be seen with the *right* people. And then, while she pinned a false smile to her face, he lost money in the card room.

Once, when he had criticised her poor household management skills in general, and the bill for a recent supper party in particular, she had suggested that using the music room for dancing rather than cards would be cheaper. She had kept to her room for three days until the mark of his slap faded.

An unusual loss of temper on his part. Mostly he remembered to hit her where the bruises wouldn't show.

In short? She loathed everything about supper parties.

Attending a supper at Selbourne's Books a few weeks ago had given her an entirely fresh perspective. Supper parties, when you only invited people you actually wished to spend time with, could be a great deal of fun. Children and dogs—and one cat—gave a certain measure of unpredictability, but that only added to the fun.

Her own supper party ran along similar lines. A hearty soup, full of meat, vegetables and barley was set out in her rarely used dining parlour, along with a ham, a large pat of butter, freshly baked bread, fruit, a decent cheese and two apple pies. There was not a lobster patty in sight, and champagne had been conspicuous by its absence.

The company was refreshingly informal. Miss Barclay brought her fiddle to play after supper. Kit Selbourne and Lord Martin's sons—fifteen and seventeen—bore Kate and Sarah off to the parlour to play cards.

'It's quite safe.' Kit smiled reassuringly at Althea. 'We don't even permit them to gamble for pins from my sewing box.'

'A good thing, too.' Lord Martin grinned at his wife. 'For all the use those pins get, they must be nearly rusted away.'

'I hear you're sewing your own buttons on now, Lacy.' Will Barclay helped himself to more cheese and poured a glass of wine for his wife.

Althea laughed along with the rest and wondered where this sort of party had been all her life. She had friends, people who liked her for herself, and hosted a party because of that. Not for whatever social cachet they might gain. And Hugo had come. He had, without ever overstepping, acted almost as a host, helping her to ensure that everyone enjoyed themselves. She wished... She put that wish, the wish brought into being with that kiss a week ago, away. It was not possible. For so many reasons, nothing was possible between them but friendship. And in the end, that friendship would be longer lived than an affair anyway.

'It's our turn next,' Psyché Barclay said at the end of the evening as they gathered up their belongings. 'Perhaps in three weeks?' She smiled at Althea. 'Bring the girls. And Puck.' She turned to Hugo with another smile. 'You should come, too, Mr Guthrie. I know Martin and Will want to pick your brains about the law. I'll let Althea know.'

Althea rose. 'I'll see you out.' And when she came back, after the girls had gone up to bed, she would have to tell Hugo what she had decided, and apologise for leading him to believe something other than friendship had been possible.

Hugo considered that friendly, almost casual invitation as Althea saw her other guests out. Courtesy of Althea, he'd stumbled into a new circle of friends.

'Did you enjoy it, Mr Guthrie?' Kate barely smothered a yawn.

He smiled. 'I did. So much so that I'm nearly as ready for my bed as you are.'

Her eyes widened. 'Oh, I'm not tired!' This time the yawn escaped entirely.

'Well, if you aren't, I am.' Althea came back into the parlour. They had all ended up in there with coffee and tea, with anyone under twenty consigned to sitting on the floor.

'I'm going up,' Sarah announced. 'Goodnight, sir. Come along, Kate. No one wants to carry you up when you fall asleep in that chair.'

Kate sighed. 'Goodnight, Aunt. Thank you for letting me stay up. Goodnight, sir.'

She trailed out after Sarah, covering another yawn, and the door closed behind them.

All evening he had waited for this moment, when he could have Althea all to himself and speak to her privately. It had been a revelation seeing her like this, with the neighbours she had only approached to give the girls as normal a life as she could.

His parents had held similar family suppers through his boyhood. Friends and neighbours gathering on a Saturday evening to talk and often dance. As had happened this evening, the younger people had gone off to play games. Later they had joined in the dancing. He smiled to himself. He had kissed a girl for the first time at one of those parties, and fallen in love with Louisa.

Even after they had married, he and Louisa had gone to his parents' supper parties.

With Louisa's death everything had changed. The supper parties had stopped while they were in mourning, and it had been easier to withdraw a little. Otherwise he had to contend with his friends' endless sympathy, and later, their gentle attempts at matchmaking. He hadn't been interested.

He'd found a solace moving back into his parents' house, and then removing to bachelor lodgings when his father retired and they moved to Petersham. He'd achieved a balance, a steadiness that he had been unwilling to disturb for a conveniently comfortable marriage. He had loved Louisa deeply and irrevocably. He had never been able to imagine loving another, nor did he wish to offer a woman the insult of being a consolation prize.

But now he smiled at Althea, and she smiled back. Damned if he could say what it was that drew him to her. Oh, she was beautiful. And sharp-tongued, waspish and fiercely independent.

He was going to kiss her again.

She flung up her hand, and took a step back. 'No.'

She had thought about that kiss all week. Thought about more than the kiss. Curse it, she had fantasised about having an affair with Hugo. And in a week of thinking, and fantasising, she had forced herself to confront reality. Over the course of a sleepless night—last night—she had decided that it wasn't going to happen.

He stopped, a faint frown creasing his brow. 'No? To what are you saying *no*?'

'No, you can't stay.'

His brow cleared. 'Of course not. I was going to kiss you goodnight.'

He took another step, smiling, and her resolve shook. She wanted his kiss as much as her next breath.

'No. I've been thinking. We can't do this. We mustn't.'

'Kiss?'

Did he have to be so ridiculously appealing? She let out a shaky breath. 'Have an affair.'

His eyes widened. 'An affair. Right.'

No. It would be wrong. Oh, not for her, but—

He sat down on the sofa.

'What are you doing?' He should be leaving. Annoyed, but leaving.

'I'm sitting down for this conversation.'

'What conversation?'

'The one we're having instead of kissing each other goodnight.'

Why couldn't he behave like a normal man and try to kiss her anyway? Then she could be angry and kick him out. Instead he was being logical and rational about it. Which meant *she* had to be logical and rational, too.

She took a deep breath. 'It's not that I don't *want* to kiss you…' Even though she worried that it would end up being a great deal more than a goodnight kiss. 'Or even have an affair with you. But…'

'What?'

Oh, Lord, she was making a mull of this!

He shook his head. 'Now I'm completely confused. Are you saying that you *do* want to kiss me, and eventually, at some point, have an affair with me?'

She nodded. 'Yes. I would like that. But we can't. It's not possible. So we shouldn't be making everything harder with goodnight kisses.'

'Very well.' He took off his glasses, polished them on a pristine handkerchief. 'Would you care to tell me what brought you to this conclusion?'

Trying to order her thoughts, Althea sat down herself. 'I'm not sure where to start.'

'Anywhere will do.' There was a decidedly snippy tone in his voice.

She glared at him. 'We're friends.' Doubt struck. 'Aren't we?'

His smile came. 'Yes. We are. Is that in the credit or debit column?'

'Both,' she admitted. 'The thing is, if we had an affair, we might not be friends after it ended.'

'Then you envision our hypothetical affair having an end?'

She refrained from snorting. 'Hugo, affairs *always* end. That's part of the definition of an affair, it's finite. I don't think it's a good idea to risk our friendship on something finite.'

'Anything else?'

'The girls.' Even if she had been prepared to risk their friendship, she couldn't risk the girls.

'Go on.'

He was going to make her spell it out?

'Hugo, you know what the world is like. If we have an affair, inevitably people will know. It would damage their reputations.' He said nothing and she rushed on. 'It's ridiculous, and unfair, but I have to contend with the world as it is for their sakes.'

'Ah.' He nodded. 'That, at least, is a valid reason for not risking an affair.' He set his tea aside, rose and walked across to her.

'What are you doing?'

'Guess.' He reached down, took her hands, and brought her unresisting to her feet.

'This is not at all a good idea.'

He smiled and her resolve cracked. 'Probably not. I'm full of all sorts of bad ideas these days. You're an appalling influence. But you're forgetting one thing.'

Just one? With his mouth barely a breath from hers, his strength and scent enclosing her, she was in danger of forgetting her own name. Despite her misgivings—the ones she was struggling to remember—her foolish arms were around him.

If it couldn't be an affair, could it be tonight? One night, nothing more, and afterwards pretend it had never happened? Or at least act as if it had not. She wasn't that forgetful. Which reminded her…

'What am I forgetting?'

'I suppose it's not exactly forgetting. More like misinterpreting.' His mouth brushed hers. 'I don't want an affair.'

And his mouth was on hers, or hers was on his. A meeting of equal desires, with no pretence of coyness. She gave and took, pleasure upon pleasure, a dance of tongues, beating hearts and mingled breaths.

The fire glowed, illuminating his face in flickering shadows as they drew apart slowly, and Althea strove to gather her scrambled wits. Oh, God. It was worse than she'd thought. She was falling—

No. She mustn't even *think* that.

She swallowed. 'If you don't want an affair, then seducing me into—'

He stopped her mouth with another brief kiss. Then, 'Althea, you idiot, I want to *court* you, not seduce you!'

For a moment her wits continued to scramble. 'Court—seduce—*court me*?'

His eyes remained steady on hers. 'Yes.'

'No!' She blurted it out. 'I mean, you can't.'

He went very still. 'You'd have an affair with me, if not for the girls, but you refuse, categorically, even to consider the possibility of marrying me?'

'Yes, no. I mean, it's not you, it's—'

'Me? There's something about me that renders me suitable for an affair, but unthinkable as a husband?'

Oh, God, she'd insulted him, and she was going to destroy their friendship anyway. Panic tumbled around inside her, tying knots in her belly as she fought for the words she needed. 'It's marriage, Hugo, not you. It's marriage and what it means for a woman that I don't want.'

Hugo stared at her. How in Hades had he not foreseen this difficulty? He was a lawyer, for pity's sake. He knew the law as it pertained to married women. They could not own property unless it was tied up in trust. They could not sign a contract, or make a will, without their husband's consent. They had no right to guardianship of their own children. The list went on, offset by the protection a husband was honour-bound to provide.

But honour could not be legally enforced. He already knew that Althea's first marriage had somehow left her ruined financially, as well as socially. She had firsthand experience of how marriage could leave a woman exposed. Vulnerable.

And he knew the usual arguments. Women were not capable of managing their financial affairs. They were too flighty, too emotional. Their intellects were unsuited for anything beyond the domestic sphere, and should they attempt it they would destroy all that was nurturing and maternal within them. In short, they would be unnatural.

He let out a breath. 'I cannot say that you are entirely wrong. But.'

She looked utterly miserable, and that tore at him. 'I'm sorry, Hugo.'

'You haven't heard my but.'

A smile flickered. 'Continue then.'

'Courtship goes both ways. We continue our friendship, but with marriage as a possibility. I will say nothing more on the subject until you give me leave.'

'Until I give you leave?' She stared. 'But what if—'

'You never trust me enough to risk it?'

Because that's what it came down to. Trust. He suspected if she didn't care for him enough to marry him, she would have said so outright.

'That's my risk, isn't it?' He took her hand, felt it tremble in his. 'We don't need to discuss it until you wish to. Until you've had time to think it through. And we remain friends.'

'Have you considered my reputation?' She drew her hand away. 'What it might do to your career?'

'Yes.' He honestly didn't care. He would be financially secure even if he stopped work immediately.

She frowned. 'Then you must know my reputation could ruin you. I can't believe you would risk that!'

'I did think of it,' he told her. 'And I decided that I didn't much care.'

He rose. 'I'll bid you goodnight, sweetheart. Trust me. I've thought it through. I honestly can't think of anything that would make me regret asking you to marry me.'

# *Chapter Eight*

The following Monday morning Hugo saw several clients and, after the last of them took his leave, began drafting a will. His attention on the will, he ignored the bell on the outer door of the offices. He had no further appointments, so it was none of his concern.

A moment later Timms appeared at the open door.

'A Miss Price to see you, sir?'

Hugo frowned at the clerk. *Sarah?* What on earth—

'An elderly lady, sir,' said Timms. 'With Mr James Montague.'

'Montague…?'

'Am I to be kept waiting all day?'

Hugo rose instinctively at the acerbic tones. 'Thank you, Timms. Close the door please.' He came forward. 'Miss Elinor Price, I presume?' He nodded to Montague, an older solicitor he knew by sight and reputation. 'Sir.'

The old lady glared at him as the clerk made his escape and shut the door. 'The same. You, my good man, have some explaining to do!'

Montague coughed. 'Miss Price, as I said, it would be best to permit me to—'

He broke off under the force of the lady's steely glare and Hugo knew a fellow feeling for the chap.

Clearing his throat, he gestured to chairs. 'Please be seated, Miss Price, Montague.' And braced himself.

Half an hour later, Hugo felt as though he had been trampled by a team of plough horses. Miss Elinor Price was a force to be reckoned with. She had accepted his flat refusal to discuss Althea's private business with either herself or Montague, but he had confirmed the truth of what she'd pried out of several relatives about Frederick's death. And Wilfrid Price-Babbington's refusal to act as guardian, or provide for the girls.

She sat in silence for a moment. 'Mr Guthrie, what would you have done had my niece *not* given those girls a home?'

'What do you imagine I would have done?' he parried. 'I had my instructions.'

A smile flickered. 'So you did. I do not believe you are the man to abandon those children to an orphanage. Not if you went to the effort to write to their relations and seek out my niece.'

'Two orphanages,' he said, avoiding the challenge. 'The difference in their ages meant they would not remain together.'

Her eyes narrowed. 'Tell me, Mr Guthrie, are you married? And no, it is absolutely none of my business.'

Montague made a sort of choking sound.

'No, it's not,' Hugo said steadily. 'I am a widower. No children.'

'Miss Price, really. All this is most unnecessary. I feel—'

She waved Montague to silence. 'Very well, Mr Guthrie. You have declined to discuss Althea's private business with me—very right, too, on reflection—but since you acted for my great-nephew, Frederick, may I assume you are aware that he cast his sister off?'

He nodded slowly. 'I am aware.'

'Have you read the letter he sent her, and chose to circulate within our family?'

'I have.' He couldn't keep his voice quite uninflected.

'One of his accusations was that she had squandered her inheritance.'

'All the more reason—' Again Montague quailed in the face of his client's gorgon stare.

Hugo wondered where this was leading, and in truth he had no idea what had happened to Althea's fortune. 'I cannot discuss Lady Hartleigh's finances with you, Miss Price. Not in any particular.'

She let out a frustrated sound. 'No. Of course not. Do you consider her a frivolous individual? Incapable of teaching those girls to manage their own affairs?'

He had to admire her tactics. 'No, Miss Price. I do not. While Lady Hartleigh certainly has a frivolous side, she is more than capable of teaching those girls to manage. I think perhaps it will not be improper to assure you that she has given this careful thought. She has made arrangements to ensure their ongoing safety and well-being should something happen to her. And it will *not* involve orphanages or going into service.'

Miss Price pursed her lips. 'Has she now? Thank you, Mr Guthrie. I'll take up no more of your time.' She rose and held out her hand. 'Good day to you, sir. Thank you. I know how to act now.'

Hugo shook her hand. 'Good day, Miss Price. Thank you for your understanding.'

Amusement flickered in her eyes, not unlike her great-niece. 'I believe I have understood a great deal, Mr Guthrie. And *you* may believe that I consider Wilfrid Price-Babbington's actions reprehensible. Far beyond anything I could possibly condone.' She let out a breath. 'Come, Montague. I have affairs to put in place. We will return to your offices immediately.'

With a final nod she stalked from the office. Montague, with an annoyed look at Hugo, hurried after her.

Hugo sat back in his desk chair as the door shut behind them. He closed his eyes and swore fluently. Then checked himself. No. That wasn't fair. This was precisely why his father had always advised against any personal involvement with a client.

*'Under no circumstances whatsoever, my boy. I've seen it happen. Leads to nothing but confusion and a devilish mess to sort out.'*

He was pained to have to admit his father's percipience, but if his suspicion was correct it would put paid to any courtship of Althea, even if she wished it.

Elinor Price had discovered that Wilfrid Price-Babbington had refused to act as guardian to Kate and Sarah. He had inherited their father's estate and thrown them out as paupers. Hugo suspected that, unless Montague managed to talk her out of it, the old lady was about to change her will. Which would make the girls heiresses.

He drummed his fingers on the desk.

He couldn't possibly tell Althea any of this. It was no more than speculation, and although Miss Price was not a client, he was still bound by confidentiality. And without Althea knowing, as the girls' guardian, that they might stand to inherit something from Miss Price, he could not under any circumstances court her.

If she accepted an offer of marriage it would, at the very least, make him the girls' co-guardian. It would create the devil of a mess, and might even cause Althea to wonder about his motives for offering marriage. For an intelligent and beautiful woman, she seemed absolutely blind as to *why* a man might want to marry her rather than have an affair with her.

He was damned if he was going to hurt her, any more than the world had already done so, by putting further self-doubt in her mind and heart.

And if Miss Price did leave the girls substantial sums of money, their marriage prospects went from possibly respectable to limitless. Especially with the Earl and Countess of Rutherford behind them.

Hugo swallowed. There was nothing he could do but remain Althea's friend and adviser, and wait.

Unsurprisingly Jacob strolled in a few minutes later. 'What the devil brings Montague here with a client?'

Hugo explained.

His gaze firmly on the top of the window, Jacob said, 'I believe you do not need me to spell out your only course of conduct in this situation.'

There was absolutely no hint of question there. It might not have been what Hugo had been envisaging when he assured himself that, in a clash of personal feeling and professional conduct, the latter must take precedence.

Still… 'I think, Jacob, that I may continue to supervise the girls' well-being and maintain a polite, professional connection with Lady Hartleigh. I believe we can be friends, without it tipping over into anything…improper.'

Jacob nodded slowly. 'Friends, yes. Very *platonic* friends. If you can do that, there is no problem. Like you, I cannot approve of the situation those girls were left in, and if Miss Price does alter her will it changes their lives materially. Keeping an eye on things is perfectly appropriate, and naturally two children will feel far more secure in their own home rather than these offices. But—*platonic*.'

Hugo nodded. 'I need to leave for the afternoon, Jacob. I have a couple of things to see to.'

Jacob eyed him narrowly. 'Things that involve Lady Hartleigh?'

'Yes.' He wanted to tell Jacob—his partner and one of his oldest friends—to go to hell.

Jacob frowned. 'Obviously you cannot tell her any of this. It would be highly improper. So—'

'It's a private matter, Jacob.' Hugo gritted his teeth. 'I can say no more than that.'

Jacob cursed fluently. 'Don't tell me you've already offered the woman marriage?'

'No.' Not quite. Hugo began tidying his desk. What the hell was he going to say to Althea?

*Three nights ago I intimated that I was interested in asking you to marry me. Spoke too soon? I'm not interested after all? Something came up?*

'Thank God for that. Very well. I'll see you in the morning.'

He was still wondering what he could say as he rang the doorbell of Althea's house. He could offer no explanation. Unless Miss Price chose to tell Althea that she was changing her will, he could not give so much as—

'Why, Mr Guthrie, sir.' The maid opened the door. 'I'll let

the mistress know you're here. The young ladies have this minute gone for their walk with John. Let me take your hat and gloves, sir.'

'Thank you.' He handed them over and waited.

The maid set the hat and gloves down on a hall table, and opened the parlour door.

''Tis Mr Guthrie, ma'am.'

He'd noticed that Althea's staff never seemed to call her *my lady*. What did that say about her marriage, that she did not even care to use her title?

The maid turned, smiling. 'She'll see you, sir. Go right in.'

Althea was seated at her desk, a large notebook closed in front of her.

'Hugo.' She rose. 'How nice to—' She broke off, searching his face. 'Is something wrong?'

He swallowed. 'Not wrong exactly. Althea, when I spoke with you on Friday night, about…about—'

'Courting me?' She sat down again, her face composed.

'Yes. That. I—' *Should not have spoken?*

'You've changed your mind.' A light, calm voice, as though she commented on the weather.

'What? No. That is, I… I can't court you, but—' He floundered. 'It's not that I've changed my mind. It's a…a professional thing.'

She nodded slowly. 'I see. I did tell you that you needed to consider my reputation. Since you are here in the middle of a workday, I suppose your partner has concerns.'

'No. I mean, he does, but it's not about *you*. Exactly. It's a professional situation.'

'And will that professional situation change?'

'It…yes. But I have no idea when that might be, no control over it. And…' He forced the words out. 'I cannot ask you to wait under the circumstances. There can be no understanding between us. You…you must consider yourself a free agent.'

Her green eyes were carefully blank, her face betrayed nothing. 'Understood, sir. I never consider myself anything else.'

That clipped, cool voice said everything.

His heart cracked. 'Althea—I'm sorry. I can offer no explanation, no excuse.'

She rose. 'None is required, sir. After some considerable thought in the last couple of days, I am convinced that I would very much prefer to remain single anyway. Good day to you. I assume you will not wish me to apprise you of the date for Mrs Barclay's supper party?'

He hesitated. It might be better, safer, not to see her, but—

'Did we not agree to remain friends?'

'We did.'

'Then, if you wish to send me a note about the date, I would be happy to attend.'

'Very well, sir. Good day.'

Althea remained utterly still until she heard the front door close behind him. Then she leaned back in her chair and closed her eyes. It would be nice if closing your eyes closed off memories. The memory of his kiss, of his face as he corrected her assumption that he wanted an affair.

*Althea, you idiot, I want to court you, not seduce you!*

She couldn't blame his partner for having concerns. She'd raised them herself. But she wished—oh, how she wished—that Hugo had said nothing last Friday. She swallowed as the heat behind her eyes spilled over.

For two days she had been thinking, wondering if she dared try again. Perhaps it was better that Hugo had come to his senses. She had been perfectly content living by herself, managing for herself, in the past few years.

And yet these stupid tears slid down her cheeks. She didn't *need* marriage.

A few more tears spilled.

She might not need marriage, but apparently she had wanted it, with Hugo, more than she had cared to admit.

*I am convinced that I would very much prefer to remain single anyway.*

At least she could still tell a believable lie.

# Chapter Nine

Hugo was more than slightly surprised to receive a note from Althea about the Barclays' supper party. He had fully expected her not to send one.

At supper, he took advantage of a brief private moment to say as much, under cover of applause for Miss Barclay's playing.

'Whyever would I not, sir?'

He tried not to let that polite *sir* sting. 'I thought you would prefer not to see me.'

Her eyes remained steady on his. 'It's not about me, though, is it? The girls wish to see you.'

'But you do not.' She was pale, and the circles under her eyes were still there. He wanted to ask what had caused them, but he had no right to ask her anything that encroached on the personal.

She bit her lip. 'As you see, remaining friends is a great deal more difficult in practice than it looks on paper.'

He reached for her hand. The quickest, lightest clasp. 'Perhaps we need to try harder.'

She sighed. 'Perhaps we do. I'll let you know about the next supper party, sir.' She gave him a ghost of her old smile.

'And perhaps you and the girls might come for a walk with me on Sunday after church, if the weather permits.'

She nodded slowly. 'They would enjoy that. Oh, look! Miss Barclay is getting Kate up to play.' Delight and pride beamed in her smile.

Sunday walks and informal supper parties. Slowly they reset their friendship, as Hugo accepted that Althea had retreated to a more distant friendliness. She did not always join the Sunday walks. Sometimes he just took the girls and Puck.

Even so, Hugo enjoyed the parties, especially the company of Will Barclay and Lord Martin Lacy. Lord Martin was about his own age and they struck up an unexpected friendship.

Lord Martin was startlingly down to earth. Especially for the youngest son of a duke. From everything Hugo had ever heard about the younger sons of the aristocracy, they were usually wild to a fault and had no idea of the value of money.

Lord Martin admitted as much.

*'Comes of being raised in a luxury that we can't maintain once we leave home.'*

Apparently he and Miss Selbourne had found a way of life that suited them both, which rarely involved society gatherings. Lord Martin, he knew, had a government job, but he spoke of that very rarely.

Spring leafed out and flowered, and London heated as May slid into June. Hugo's office baked in the growing warmth. Another month and he'd be taking his summer holiday at Petersham in the house his father had retired to.

His mother's sister, Sylvia—his Aunt Sue—lived there now. He wished, deeply, that he was looking forward to his summer holiday as much as he usually did. Long walks out along the river, watching for birds, noting them in the latest volume of the journal his father had started. Rambles in Richmond Park and quiet evenings reading aloud to Aunt Sue while she sewed or knitted, or—increasingly as she aged—dozed in her chair.

This year he kept thinking of Althea and the girls remaining in London as the city sweltered its way towards July. And those dark circles deepening under Althea's eyes.

Hugo took the note his clerk handed him, and his very humdrum day—drafting a will, writing a letter to another client and advising on a trust—brightened considerably. Sarah's handwriting. Now, what was so urgent that it couldn't await the planned supper in Soho Square this Friday night?

He broke the seal, smiling…

*Dear Mr Guthrie,*
*Aunt Althea has asked me to let you know that we cannot have our supper on Friday night this week. Kate has chicken pox.*

*Aunt Althea says she—Kate—is not terribly unwell, but very headachy, itchy because of the spots and grumpy with it. I have tried sitting with her because I had it years ago, but she won't mind me at all—Kate, that is—so Aunt Althea is sitting with her much of the time to see that she does not scratch at her blisters. Aunt Althea says this might make them scar or go nasty.*

*Aunt Althea asks me to say how very sorry she is, and that she hopes you will understand.*
*Your Affectionate Friend,*
*Sarah Price*

Hugo let out a breath. At least Sarah had already had chicken pox, so was unlikely to catch it again. Most children did catch it at some point. Sometimes it was serious. He remembered his own mother and Aunt Sue, nursing *him* in turns. How old had he been? Nine? Ten? They had told him he was lucky to have it then and not when he was older. In adults, they'd said, it was often very nasty indeed. He hadn't cared. He'd felt quite sick enough, thanks very much, and there had been blisters in some very sensitive places, too. He squirmed remembering his mother dabbing calamine lotion on them. He suspected that he'd been a perfect little pest.

At times he'd been so desperate to scratch that only his mother's or aunt's presence had stopped him. And Althea was doing that alone. Even if Kate's illness were not serious, it was still exhausting.

He stared into space, drumming his fingers on the desk. Independence, of course, was a good thing. He valued his own independence, respected it in others. Then there was friendship…

Before he could overthink the situation, he pulled a fresh piece of paper towards him and dipped his pen…

*My very dear Sarah...*

The doorbell penetrated Althea's intermittent dozing with its insistent clang—why had she ever thought this was a comfortable chair?—but she ignored it. Kate was asleep, her fever somewhat reduced, but Althea had no doubt that if she left the room the child would be awake and scratching in minutes. Seconds, probably. Whoever was at the door, she didn't care.

She sank back into her doze, sore shoulders, aching neck and all, and hoped she could have a good night's sleep again soon.

Hearing the squeak of the doorknob she spoke softly without opening her eyes. 'She's asleep, Sarah. Her fever is down and she's not quite so itchy. I think the calamine is helping. Tell whoever it is to go away.'

'I'm very glad to hear it. But I'm not going away.'

Her eyes snapped open at that deep voice, and she shot out of the chair. Good God! Her oldest gown and she hadn't even bothered with stays this morning.

'Hugo.' She kept her voice as soft as his. 'What…what are you doing here?' What day was it? It couldn't be Friday already. Could it? Besides… Her mind cleared a little. 'Did you not receive Sarah's note?'

'I did of course. It occurred to me that you could use some assistance.'

'Assistance?'

'Yes. It's what friends do for each other.' He eyed her. 'Why don't you go and have a proper sleep, in an actual bed?'

'Kate—she might wake up, and—'

'I promise she will mind me just as well as she does you. I won't let her scratch her spots.'

'But what if you catch it?'

'I've had it. Off you go.' He made a shooing motion as he came towards her. 'Begone!'

She thought about narrowing her eyes at him. She ought to resent being shooed, and *begone*—as if she were some demon to be banished. But she was too grateful, and the kindness in his eyes disarmed her in the gentlest way. Besides, she didn't have enough energy left to narrow her eyes properly.

'Would you…would you like coffee?'

He brushed a strand of hair back from her brow, tucked it away. The light touch left her breathless.

'Sarah is bringing some up. Go and sleep. You need it.'

Did she look that bad?

'Yes, you do. Off you go.'

But his fingers remained lightly circling her temple. She wanted nothing more than to stay right where she was for ever, absorbing that soothing touch. How nice to lean on someone for a change.

And not simply anyone. *Him.*

For a moment.

As if he had read her heart, his arms came slowly around her. Offering, inviting only. There was no compulsion, just the invitation. And she accepted, stepping closer, allowing her head to rest against that steady shoulder, feeling his arms close in comfort, support. Friendship.

A moment. A moment's rest and kindness. That was all it could be. After that initial misstep, they had established a friendship, one she valued deeply. Friends did not demand of each other. Nor did they risk spoiling a friendship by asking for more. Not when someone had clearly stated that there could be no more.

He released her as she gathered herself to step back.

'Go and sleep, Althea.'

She didn't bother removing her gown and fell asleep almost before her head touched the pillow. Waking slightly puzzled to find herself in any bed at all, let alone her own, she had to think for a moment…

'Oh, Lord!'

She rolled over to look at the clock on the chimney piece, sat bold upright as the relationship of hands and numbers coalesced into meaning, and scrambled out of bed still blinking sleep from her eyes.

Over two hours, closer to three, she had left Hugo nursing a sick child. A quick glance told her that her gown was rumpled past shaking out. She got out of it, draped it over a chair and found a fresh one, along with a set of stays she could do up at the front without assistance. Her hair was a disaster and probably needed washing, but she brushed it out vigorously, twisting it up into a knot anchored with an army of pins.

Her mirror informed her in no uncertain terms that she looked far from her best. Then she rolled her eyes at her reflection, and hurried out of the room. Of all men, she did not have to worry what Hugo thought of her.

He was her friend who had come to help. He didn't care what she looked like. Still, a woman had her pride.

She opened the door to the girls' room, hoping Hugo had been given something to read, and that if Kate had woken up—

The room was dark and empty. She had told Kate that *if* she was a good girl and slept, and her fever did not return, she might come downstairs for a while that evening…

Her lamp illuminated a note on the pillow.

*Fever not returned. Downstairs having supper.*
*H*

Her heart light, Althea hurried out of the room.

The parlour door opened to admit Althea and Hugo looked up sharply. She smiled at him. He noted the colour in her cheeks as Puck got up from his basket and trotted across to greet her. She bent to pat the dog. She'd looked so tired and worn down, her eyes heavy and shadowed.

She didn't look so very much better now, but at least she didn't look as though a puff of wind might bowl her over.

He nudged Kate, nestled beside him on the sofa, half-asleep. 'Look who's woken up, sweetheart.'

'Aunt Althea!' Only a little croaky, the child sat up. 'Mr Guthrie said you were awfully tired and he sent you to bed. I slept and I'm not feverish still, so he carried me down and we had supper.' She wrinkled her nose. 'I had broth. Again. And Sarah put the lotion on my spots first. There are less of them now, I think.'

'Fewer.' Althea came across to them and leaned down to kiss Kate on the brow. 'If you can count them, it's fewer. But that's very good.'

Sarah stood up. 'Come and sit down, Aunt. I'll fetch you a bowl of soup. It's being kept warm for you in the kitchen.' She hurried out, stopping to hug Althea.

Hugo watched as Althea sat down and the dog sat himself on her feet with a contented sigh.

She smiled at him again, and his heart shook a little, remembering that moment she had leaned on him, the feel of her in his arms.

'Thank you, sir.'

Comfort. She had needed comfort. And professional ethics still made anything beyond friendship out of the question. 'You look much better.'

She grimaced. 'Then judging by what I saw in the mirror just now I must have looked an absolute fright!'

'You did rather.' He shut his eyes briefly. 'My apologies. That didn't quite come out as I meant. Here.' He poured a glass of wine that he had brought. 'Have this while I get my foot out of my mouth.'

She accepted the glass with narrowed eyes. 'Hag-ridden, was I?'

He grinned. The most beautiful woman he had ever seen was referring to herself as *hag-ridden*? 'Completely.'

Kate giggled. 'I think he's teasing, Aunt Althea. You could *never* look hag-ridden!'

Her fairy smile dawned, and his heart stuttered as Althea reached out to touch Kate's cheek lightly.

'Ah. Is that it? Thank you, Kate.' She shot him a gimlet stare. 'We shan't have to wash his blood out of the rug after all.'

Laughing outright, he raised his glass to her.

# *Chapter Ten*

Four days later Kate, although still tiring easily and retaining a fair number of fading blisters, was on the path to recovery. Children could be amazingly resilient, thought Hugo, as he strolled through Soho with Althea in the early evening. But the child was still wan and crotchety.

Summer now beat down on London in full force. He knew most of the aristocracy, including Althea's friends the Rutherfords, had left the city for their country estates. Parliament had risen and would not sit again until the autumn session.

The day had been relentlessly hot and stuffy. Kate had not wished to go out and Sarah had shaken her head listlessly when asked if she wished to accompany them.

*'No, thank you. I'll stay with Kate.'*

He couldn't wonder at it. The city was stuffy and exhausting. They needed to be out of London, too. As did Althea. She was heavy-eyed and pale still, as though she were not sleeping.

'Have you thought of taking the girls out of London?'

Althea sighed. 'Yes. Meg Rutherford wrote, suggesting I bring them both down to stay when Kate is strong enough to travel, and I would, but...'

'But?'

'She will have a houseful of guests, several of whom will

*not* take kindly to my presence. For the girls I would deal with that, but the distance is considerable.'

'How far is it?'

'Three days' travel. That's the other problem.' She smiled. 'I'm beforehand enough with the world to go on the mail, but the thought! Kate in the coach for three days! And back again.'

'What about Petersham?'

'Petersham?' She stared up at him. 'You mean the village?'

'Yes. My father retired there.'

'To breed books?'

He laughed. 'You remember that? Exactly. My mother's sister lives there now. I always go out to spend a few weeks with her in the summer and at Christmas. Why not come with me? Or—' he thought about it '—go ahead? I can't go down for another three weeks, and I can promise you that Aunt Sue will be delighted to have company in the meantime.'

She didn't answer immediately, and he forbore to press, content strolling with her in the fading light of the summer's day, imagining walking with her beside the Thames in the evening light, watching the last of the sun burn the far reaches of the river. If he took her there with the girls, would she see how it could be? Life with a family?

He caught himself up mentally. Althea and the girls had created their own family. He, for all his success, was the one who needed them.

He frowned a little. It shouldn't be about *need*, should it? *Need* was one of those slippery words. He might want Althea and the girls in his life, but it shouldn't tip over into *neediness*. That put a weight of obligation on the object of need.

Besides, there was still the matter of Miss Price's will. He hadn't thought of a way around that hurdle. If the old lady had told Althea what she intended, then it wouldn't matter. But, as Althea's solicitor, and since she hadn't discussed it with him, he had to assume that Miss Price was one of those people who preferred to keep the contents of their last will and testament a deep secret. Having seen some of the rows that could explode over the anticipated contents of a will, he couldn't blame her.

He could not imagine anything nastier in one's declining

years than being pestered, or worse fawned over, by a set of relatives pretending to care about you when all they wanted was a slice of the fiscal pie. Or for that matter the best pie dish.

'Would we not be very much in your aunt's way? In your way?'

Her question brought him out of his ponderings. He smiled. 'I should say not. Aunt Sue enjoys company, but she is a little frail now at eighty. She doesn't like to go out much. But she will still fleece you at a game of picquet!'

'And what about Puck?'

He nodded. 'More than welcome. Aunt Sue had a very elderly pug that died a couple of years ago. She loves dogs but says she won't have another because she doesn't want to put the responsibility on me if the dog outlived her. She still has a cat. Spudge can take care of himself, believe me.'

'*Spudge*? Why Spudge?'

He'd often wondered himself. 'I have no idea. So, now that you know the family's darkest secret—a cat called Spudge—will you come?'

She laughed. 'If that's your darkest secret I don't think much of it. Yes. Yes, please. The girls need this far too much for me to stand on pride.'

They had turned and were walking back towards Soho Square. Glancing at Althea, Hugo thought she needed to get out of London at least as much as the girls. Was it his imagination, or had her steps slowed? Was she leaning more heavily on his arm? He doubted it was a good time to inform her that she looked nearly as washed out as little Kate.

She rubbed at one temple.

'A headache?'

'Not really.' She lowered her hand. 'Well, a little one. I slept badly. It's the stuffy weather. I'm sure a pot of tea will help.'

*Two days later*

Hugo looked at the note his clerk handed him with a stab of foreboding. Sarah's handwriting again. He broke the seal, opened it and swore as he read it.

'Is the servant who delivered this still here?'

'Yes, sir. Said he'd been asked to wait for a reply.'

'Tell him it's coming.'

He wrote swiftly. He had appointments this afternoon… 'What's on my slate for tomorrow, Timms?'

'Ah…' The clerk frowned. 'Mr Ellison at two o'clock. There's a deal of paperwork for you, too, sir.'

'Get that together for me, if you would. I'll take it with me to work on. I'll be in for Ellison's appointment but not before. Reschedule any other appointments for the following two days.'

Althea couldn't remember ever being this ill. Too hot, too cold, too damn *everything*, and especially too itchy. Someone had put mittens on her hands. Althea surfaced to the sound of voices. Sarah's shaking, frightened tones, and Hugo's deeper, reassuring tones.

'Did she tell you that she'd never had it, Sarah?'

'No. She wouldn't let the servants help nurse Kate, though, because none of them had.'

'Very well. Bring up more barley water for your aunt, coffee for me, and don't worry. She'll be perfectly all right once this fever breaks. I'll look after her for now. You go and sleep. You can spell me in the morning.'

The voices anchored her. She was in her own room after all, not some strange dreamworld where nothing made sense. She drifted back into the tossing sea of bizarre dreams, insensibly reassured that she would eventually come back to shore.

For three days Hugo sat with Althea, at first wondering if he had lied to Sarah and Kate about her being perfectly all right. Even the doctor, who had called twice, looked grave.

'A very nasty case.' He shook his head. 'Often worse in adults, but this is the worst I've ever seen. Are you a relative of Lady Hartleigh's, sir?'

Hugo shook his head. 'Family friend and lawyer. Her elder niece called on me for help.'

Doctor Harvey frowned. 'I can arrange for a nurse if you wish. Not quite the thing, is it? I mean, a man nursing a lady.'

'Doctor, I think we're beyond impropriety. Lady Hartleigh is perfectly safe with me and her elder niece is managing anything too personal.' Such as dabbing calamine lotion in sensitive spots, or persuading Althea to do it herself. He removed himself from the room at those moments.

He doubted Sarah had physically grown in the past few days, but it seemed as if she had suddenly leapt from childhood to womanhood. She looked exhausted, but she was bearing up under the strain, and stepping in to make household decisions that Althea would normally have made. And Kate was minding what Sarah said without argument—doing her lessons, even going to her music lessons again. Sarah had encouraged that wholeheartedly.

*'Best to keep her busy.'*

He could only agree with Sarah on that.

When the doctor left the second time, Hugo sank back into his chair. He'd barely left it in the past few days, except when Sarah sat with Althea to let him get some sleep on the very small sofa.

Althea woke properly to a dim light. Everything ached, but not in that hideous burning way. More like the memory of aches really. Turning her head on the pillow she saw Hugo, in his shirt sleeves, head tilted back, eyes closed, in the same chair she'd used when nursing Kate. Someone had hauled it back from the girls' room. Faint snores told her that he was sound asleep. Had he read to her? She thought he had. *Pride and Prejudice*. Even if she did occasionally want to kick Mr Darcy, she liked that one. Maybe because she had wanted to kick Darcy. In the end he gave himself a solid boot and that did the trick.

She assessed herself. Headache completely gone, although she felt washed out and as limp as wilted spinach. Itching almost gone. She wondered what would happen if she attempted to get up and use the commode. There were vague memories of Sarah or Mrs Cable helping her onto it. Not Hugo. That was something. Unless she'd forgotten?

Thinking hard, she brought up memories of him helping her to sit up, holding cups of barley water to her lips, spooning broth into her and, yes, reading to her… But no memory of him helping her to the commode. She wasn't going to ask. If she couldn't remember it, then it hadn't happened.

The light from the lamp was too dim to read the time on the clock, but the quality of silence, inside and out, suggested that it was the middle of the night. She *really* needed that commode. It was only a few steps away…

She pushed back the bedclothes and Hugo's eyes snapped open.

'You're awake.' He rose, stretching. 'How are you feeling?'

*Desperate* was the word that came to mind. 'Better.'

He touched her brow lightly and his smile dawned. 'The fever's broken. Good. Would you like something to drink?'

She shook her head. 'Er, no. Not until—' How was she supposed to say this politely? 'Ah, if you could leave the room for a moment?' To prove that she *could*, she sat up. Wondered if she was going to collapse straight back down again. Regardless… 'I need to—you *know*.'

'Leave the—oh.'

'Yes, oh.'

'Compromise?' He came to the bedside. 'I'll help you over there, *then* leave the room. You call me when you're ready to get back to bed.'

*That* was a compromise? Althea thought about it, but her body was telling her very loudly that she didn't have much time for an argument. Nor did she have the strength. 'Oh, very well. If you insist.'

She ignored his grin, and the nasty little voice in her head that suggested she was being rather ungracious. She swung her legs over the edge of the bed and the world made an alarming swerve. Hugo's hand was there immediately, steadying her.

Drat it! She could stand up without—her feet touched the floor and her knees wobbled. Maybe she did need help.

Swallowing humiliation at her weakness, she muttered, 'Thank you,' and concentrated on making it safely to the commode with his arm around her waist.

She braced, gripping the back of the commode tightly as he stepped back. 'I'll…be all right now.' She hoped.

He nodded. 'I'll be outside the door. Call if you need me.' His head tipped to one side, his mouth a little wry. 'I mean that, Althea. Call me.'

She stared. 'I—yes. Thank you, Hugo. For…for everything.'

He leaned forward and his lips touched her brow. 'You're very welcome.'

It took another three days before Hugo would permit her to walk downstairs without assistance. And even then he hovered. When she wanted to snap, she reminded herself that the first time he had permitted her downstairs he'd carried her. She also had to remind herself that she'd fallen asleep on the sofa, her broth barely swallowed.

The doctor had pronounced himself satisfied with her recovery. 'As nasty a case as I've ever seen, Lady Hartleigh. You're very lucky to have had such a skilled and devoted nurse.' He shook his head. 'Otherwise. Well.'

She reminded herself of that, too, when she wanted to snap. And instead asked for help back upstairs and took a nap.

Hugo had returned to work, but he still called every day late in the afternoon, remaining for supper. Mrs Cable had discovered all his favourite dishes and added them to her repertoire. Kate had been cajoled and outright teased into trying green beans and discovered that they wouldn't kill her after all.

Althea was touched that the friendships she had made over those Friday night suppers had blossomed. Kit Selbourne and Psyché Barclay had each called several times since she had left her sickroom—Kit with an armload of books.

'I hear from Kate that you are off to Petersham to visit Mr Guthrie's aunt when you are feeling more the thing.' Kit set the books on the desk. 'I thought you might enjoy some of these to take with you.' Smiling, she added, 'When you come back from your holiday, we'll have you all to supper again.' A faint twinkle came into her eye. 'Mr Guthrie, too.'

Althea felt a slow burn on her cheeks. 'It's not like that.'

'Isn't it?' The twinkle remained.

'We're friends. Just friends.'

'Oh. That stage. I liked that stage. The next stage is even better, though.'

She knew better, but— 'The next stage?'

Kit grinned. 'The part where you seduce him.'

Althea nearly swallowed her tea the wrong way. 'Where I seduce *him*?'

Kit wrinkled her nose. 'If you wait for him to seduce you, you'll wait a very long time if I'm any judge. He's like Martin—too beastly honourable.'

Extrapolating, Althea said, '*You* seduced Lord Martin?'

'Only into bed,' said Kit with a cheerful lack of shame. 'I'll admit that he seduced me into marriage. Marriage was very low on my list of priorities at the time.'

'It's nowhere on my list at all,' said Althea. Or it shouldn't be. Nor was having an affair supposed to be on her list. It hadn't been for years, even before the girls arrived to complicate things. Men were a complication in and of themselves, and she had enjoyed being free of expectations or demands. But here she was, still wishing she could have an affair with Hugo.

Kit smiled. 'Ah. Enjoy your time at Petersham. We'll look forward to seeing you rested and back to health when you return.'

# *Chapter Eleven*

They arrived late on a golden afternoon, to the quiet house down from the Petersham Road. It sat on a rutted lane leading down to the river. The carriage Hugo had insisted on hiring for them drew up to the front door with a clatter of hooves and wheels on the gravel drive. Sarah and Kate scrambled down immediately, followed by Puck, his tail wagging madly.

*'It's not far to the river from the house. The girls will love it. Richmond Park is close as well.'*

Althea descended much more slowly from the carriage, steadying herself on the doorframe. Then Sarah was there, offering a hand. She took it, forcing a smile. 'Thank you, Sarah.'

Sarah's smile bloomed. 'Mr Guthrie said we had to be sure to look after you.'

Althea reminded herself that she had been very ill. The girls, according to Hugo, had been terrified that she might die. She had to remember that. But she hated it, simply *hated* it, that she still felt so utterly feeble at times. Especially if she didn't have a nap in the afternoon. Not that she had exactly missed her nap today. She had no recollection of anything between the Knightsbridge tollgate and Kate bouncing on the carriage seat as she announced their arrival.

Kate and Puck had reached the front door, which opened

to reveal a plump, motherly looking female. 'Now, I daresay you'll be Miss Kate?'

Kate nodded. 'Yes. Are you Mr Guthrie's aunt?'

The woman laughed. 'No, my dear. I'm Mrs Farley the housekeeper.' She bent down to hold out a hand to Puck. 'And who might this fine fellow be?'

'This is Puck.' Kate gestured to Althea. 'And this is my Aunt Althea and my sister.'

Althea reached the porch. 'Good day. I am Lady Hartleigh. Mrs Farley, I think you said?'

The woman dropped a small curtsy. 'Yes, my lady. Come in. I've sent for one of the men to bring your bags in. Miss Browne is in the drawing room. She said to send in tea as soon as you've arrived.'

Miss Browne, Hugo's Aunt Sue, proved to be a kindly, if acid-tongued lady. She took an immediate liking to Puck, who viewed the enormous cat on the back of her chair with awed fascination as they drank tea.

'You'll try it once, my boy,' Miss Browne told the dog. She smiled at the girls. 'Once Spudge has demonstrated that he's in charge they'll be fine.'

Kate swallowed a mouthful of cake. 'Why is he called Spudge?'

Miss Browne reached back to scratch the cat's chin. 'Originally I called him Smudge, because of his blotchy markings. But he was quite a pudgy kitten. Possibly because he developed a talent for sneaking into the pantry, and he's also a very good mouser. So I found myself calling him Pudge rather more often than not, and then one day I muddled them up. I meant to say, *You're such a pudge, Smudge.* But what came out was: You're such a spudge!'

Althea laughed. 'So that's his name. Girls, if you've eaten enough, you should say thank you to Miss Browne and we should see to our unpacking.'

Miss Browne waved that aside. 'Oh, pish. Nice to see two gels who can eat a decent meal. Now, after being cooped up in that carriage for a couple of hours, I'm thinking, Lady Hartleigh, that they might like to walk down to the river with the dog. One of the maids will be happy enough to go with them if you are not feeling up to it.'

Althea hesitated. She *wasn't* feeling up to it. But—

'You're tired, Aunt Althea,' said Kate. 'And Mr Guthrie did say we should look after you. We'll tell you all about it when we come back, and then you can come with us tomorrow.'

'Sensible girl.' Miss Browne nodded approval. 'Your aunt may give me her arm for a turn about the garden. Off you go and change your shoes. Ask Mrs Farley for some scraps for the swans.'

'And don't let Puck chase the swans,' Althea warned them. 'The King would be most annoyed if Puck hurt one of his swans!'

As the door closed behind the girls and Puck, Miss Browne snorted. 'If that good-for-nothing on the throne takes the least interest in the well-being of any creature besides himself it's news to me!'

That began a halcyon week of sunny days and balmy evenings. Shuttlecock racquets and birdies were found for the girls, and no one cared in the least how much noise they made. Rambles by the river each morning, and sometimes in the late afternoon, left Althea tired, but feeling that it was a good sort of tired. Not the dragging weariness she had felt in the immediate aftermath of her illness, but a feeling of tired limbs that had taken a decent amount of exercise.

And, very unexpectedly, she found a good friend in Miss Browne.

'Call me Aunt Sue, dear,' said the old lady as they sat in the shade after a slow turn about the lawn. 'It's Sylvia really, but Hugo couldn't say that as a small boy, and after a while everyone called me Aunt Sue. It will be nice to see him tomorrow. He would have come sooner but he had work to do.'

Althea grimaced. 'That might be my fault. He spent a great deal of time with us when Kate was ill, and then even more when I caught it.'

Sue smiled at her. 'I can't tell you how pleased I was when

he asked if you and the girls might visit. As if he needed to ask! It's his house, after all.'

Althea laughed. 'Pleased to be invaded by two young girls and a dog?'

Sue patted her hand. 'It's been a very long time since Hugo took the slightest interest in any woman. Not since Louisa died.'

'His wife?' She had known Hugo was a widower. And she had suspected that his wife's death had shattered him.

Sue nodded, her eyes sad. 'Yes. Childbirth. And the baby, too. Poor little mite barely lived a day. After that he moved back into his parents' house, then lodgings, and buried himself in his work. When he mentioned the girls in his letters…' She patted Althea's hand. 'He grieved for that little baby girl as deeply as for poor Louisa, I believe.'

Althea could easily believe that. In the early days of her marriage, when she had fully expected and wanted to become a mother, every month that her courses arrived had been a grief in itself. And when finally the truth had become obvious, not only to her but to society, that it would never happen and that the fault lay in herself…

She pushed those thoughts away. She had ceased to mourn the loss of that potential long ago, even learned to be grateful that an innocent child hadn't been dragged into the disaster of her marriage. Hugo had not had even that miniscule comfort.

'Well. That's all ten years ago.' Sue gave a sigh. 'I think it's been good for him, that he was able to help your girls find a home with you.'

By Wednesday afternoon Hugo had his papers and files almost in order. He had a list of the few things he had left to do the following day and on Friday morning, before he drove out to Petersham. Usually he hired a horse and rode. There was already a horse and small closed carriage out there. But this time, with guests, he thought having a gig might be useful.

Timms knocked on the door jamb. 'Mr Montague to see you, sir.'

Hugo glanced at the clock. He had an appointment in half an hour. Time enough.

'Show him straight in, Timms.'

Hugo rose as Montague stalked in. 'Good afternoon, sir. Please be seated. Timms, the door. Thank you.' The door closed as Hugo settled himself behind the desk. 'How may I assist you, sir?'

Montague assumed a smug, not to say sneering, expression. 'I have some news that you may find pertinent, Guthrie. I have no idea how you or possibly your *client*, if we are to consider her as such, worked on a poor, frail old woman, but I think you should know that wiser counsel prevailed, and Miss Price has not altered her will.'

His father's voice sounded in his head.

*'Never reply spontaneously in legal matters, boy. Always, even if you know the answer, give the impression of thinking about it first. Especially if your temper is involved.'*

Excellent advice—his temper was boiling at the implication that Althea was something other than his client, something illicit and nefarious. For good measure he steepled his fingers and nodded thoughtfully, while he lowered the temperature to a simmer.

'How interesting, sir. Useful information indeed, although I'm surprised you're telling me. After all, I might think to *prevail* upon Miss Price again.'

Montague smirked. 'Given the state of her health, it is no longer possible for her to do so. And even if it were, how you might get past those dedicated to her interests I cannot imagine.'

'How you imagine I did so in the first place, when that meeting in this very office is the only time I have met her, I am not sure. Nor how my client may be supposed to have done so, when Miss Price's visit to Lady Hartleigh's home was the first and only time they had met in several years.'

Montague stiffened in his seat. 'Are you denying that you made such an attempt?'

'Categorically.' No hesitation this time. Montague had crossed a line here. 'You are accusing me of highly unethical behaviour, sir, with no evidence whatsoever. If you have discussed the matter further with Miss Price, I cannot imagine what brings you here to tell me so. It should be a matter of confidence between the lady and yourself.'

'Why you impudent pup!' Montague was half out of his chair. 'Are you telling me how to conduct my business?'

'I'm telling you that Miss Price's final will and testament is no business of mine, yet you have chosen to make it so. She came to me for information, which I provided, as far as I could without breaching my own client's confidentiality. How Miss Price acted on that information was completely up to her.'

Montague made a rude sound. 'Don't play games, Guthrie. No doubt your client was counting on that money and—'

'Why? Did you tell her?'

'*I?* Tell that woman—'

'Because I didn't.' Temper spilling over now, Hugo spoke straight across the older man. 'It would have been mere speculation, and subject to change if Miss Price changed her mind. As, apparently, she did. Moreover, the contents of an individual's will are for them to divulge if they so choose.'

Montague's mouth set hard. 'I believe it is of the first importance to the ongoing security of the Price family for that money to remain safely in the family.'

'And I will remind you that those two girls are members of the Price family and, in justice, should have been entitled to some of that money. Their father failed to provide for them, Price-Babbington threw them out. If Miss Price was prepared to do something to redress that injustice, then she came to that decision without any advice from me, beyond what information you heard me give her. It seems, Montague, that the only person to influence her was yourself. Do you by any chance also act for Wilfrid Price-Babbington?'

A shot in the dark, but the man's darkly flushed face, and unwitting shift in his seat, told Hugo he'd hit the bullseye.

'How dare you, sir!'

Hugo shrugged. 'Your ethics are your own concern, sir. In truth, you've solved a dilemma for me in coming here. Your purpose, as far as I can tell, was to boast and put me in my place. Instead you've done me a favour.'

Montague stared. 'A favour? Done you a favour?'

Hugo grinned now. 'Not at all your intention, I'm sure, but I'll thank you anyway. Good day, sir. I have another appointment in a few minutes for which I must prepare.'

Hugo rose, strode to the door and opened it, to find Jacob, hand raised, about to knock. He strolled in. 'Ah. Montague. I thought I recognised your voice. To what do we owe the honour of another visit?'

Montague glared. 'I came to inform Guthrie here that my client Miss Price saw the value of my advice and decided against altering her will at the urging of, shall we say, *importunate* family members!'

Jacob nodded. 'I see.' He frowned. 'No, actually. I don't. I cannot conceive what business it is of mine or Guthrie's what dispositions—Miss Price, did you say?—chose to make in her will. But you may trust to our, er, discretion—I do like that word—that we shall keep this little lapse of yours *entre nous*.'

Montague, with no other choice, left with his nose in the air.

Hugo shut the door behind him and leaned on it. Anger still simmered. What Montague had done, dissuading Miss Price from leaving some money in trust for Kate and Sarah, was unconscionable. No doubt he'd make quite sure Price-Babbington knew who'd buttered that piece of bread for him, and pocket a very nice reward for his trouble.

Jacob let out a relieved breath. 'What the devil was the idiot thinking to come here boasting about that to you? Was he challenging you to attempt to change Miss Price's mind again?'

'No chance of that. It sounds as though she's dying.' And even if she weren't, attempting to influence her to change her will against her own lawyer's advice was out of the question.

'Pity.' Jacob scowled, a ludicrous expression on his normally cheery face. 'If ever a man deserved to be taken down several pegs, it's Montague. Damned idiot.'

Hugo went back to tidying his papers. 'It doesn't matter now, Jacob. It's done. And, as I told him, he's really done me a favour.'

Jacob sat down. 'I take it your friendship with Lady Hartleigh is about to become un-platonic?'

Hugo nodded. 'If she will have me.' He was not at all sure that she would consider him a fair exchange for her independence.

*'I am convinced that I would very much prefer to remain single anyway.'*

Since there was no longer the prospect of the girls inheriting any part of Miss Price's considerable fortune, then he was free to court Althea. She might or might not accept him. That was up to her. He might end up with a pair of ass's ears, but it was worth the risk.

# Chapter Twelve

Hugo arrived at the Petersham house in the afternoon, the sort of golden summer's afternoon that made him think he spent entirely too much time indoors. Occasionally he thought about retiring and moving out here permanently, but he enjoyed his work. Even enjoyed the bustle of London most of the time. Perhaps if he kept a horse, or even a gig, which he could easily afford, he could come out more frequently.

Since he had the horse and gig this time, if he needed to go into his office there was no delay. Plus, the cob seemed very quiet—he might give the girls some driving lessons. His mind had been considering all manner of activities for days.

Would Aunt Sue mind if he visited more frequently? She would tell him not to be ridiculous. That it was his house, and he might be there whenever he pleased. Which was true enough, but he was very conscious that it was *her* home. Still, she was older now, and she could not live for ever, although she would not appreciate a reminder. He should spend more time with her while he had the chance.

Life was far from fair to most people, he thought, as he steadied the cob for the turn into the shady lane running down to the river. You could double that when it came to women. Sue had never married, but she had cared for her ageing parents until they died. In return, Hugo's grandfather had left her a pittance on which to survive. The old man had assumed that she would live with her married sister or some other family member as a poor relation. All the money had been left to his son and grandsons.

His own father had ensured Sue's welfare by leaving her a little more money, and asking Hugo to allow her to live in the house for the rest of her life. She was safe, but the more he thought about it, the less fair he considered it. Forbidden to earn a living, unless they became governesses or paid companions, women of his class were forced to rely on the generosity and kindness of their male relations.

This had been brought home to him by the plight of the girls when their father failed to provide for them. He had been on the verge of writing to Sue about them, when he had looked again at the appalling letter his father had been forced to deliver to Althea all those years ago.

Sometimes he thought about asking her *why* Frederick Price had turned on her like that. And then he told himself it was none of his business.

Turning into the drive, he put all thought of Price out of his head. He was on holiday, and for once he had something like a family with whom to enjoy it.

A few moments later, having handed the cob and gig to the gardener cum outdoor man, Hugo strolled through the house to the rear parlour that looked out over the garden. Sue, Mrs Farley had informed him, was taking a nap.

*'Not as young as she was, Mr Hugo. Not but what the young ladies have brightened things up. Teaching them chess in the evenings, she is.'*

He stepped out through the open French doors, onto the terrace, and viewed a scene of surprisingly silent action. Bare legged, shoes discarded and their skirts hiked up with their sashes, Kate and Sarah were playing at battledore and shuttlecock. Punctuated only by panting and the occasional gasp and stifled giggle, they were utterly focused on keeping the shuttlecock aloft. They didn't even see him as it flew back and forth between them. He could see Sarah's fierce concentration as she batted it back to her sister, and noted that Kate, despite her smaller size, was holding her own.

Eventually Sarah missed a shot and the shuttlecock hit the ground. A groan burst from her, but Kate was jumping up and down, practically crowing, albeit quietly.

'Were you counting, Sarah? *Fifty*! It was fifty shots that time!' Dancing in a circle, she saw him. 'Mr Guthrie!' Her voice lifted as she ran to him.

He swung her up laughing.

'Did you see, Mr Guthrie?' Her voice had lowered again. 'Aunt Sue found the racquets and birdies for us and we've been practising. She's having her rest.'

He set her down with a smile. 'Is that why you were being so quiet?'

Sarah came up, holding her own racquet and the shuttlecock. 'Not entirely. Aunt Sue says she can sleep through anything and to make as much noise as we like, but...' She gestured with the racquet.

On the far side of the lawn, in the shade of an elm, a cane chaise longue was angled away from them.

'Aunt Althea brought her work out, but she's fallen asleep over it.'

Worry smote him. She'd been so ill... 'Is she still tiring easily?'

Sarah shook her head. 'Not so much. But we had a long walk by the river this morning.'

'Mrs Farley said she'd make us lemonade.' Kate tugged at his hand. 'Aunt Sue's lemon bush has lots of lemons. You can have some, too.'

After a glass of lemonade with the girls, and a reassurance that there had been plenty of lemons for marmalade as well, Hugo left the pair of them inside playing chess. Bearing a tray laden with a jug and two glasses, he crossed the lawn to the elm tree.

Her bonnet discarded beside her, Althea still slept with a shawl tucked around her. On the grass a notebook lay tumbled with a pencil. Smiling, he bent to retrieve it, and words caught his attention...

*'I cannot imagine what folly has led you to believe, sir, that I would be persuaded to accept an invitation to dance with you, let alone an offer of marriage!'*

For one horrified moment he thought he was reading Althea's private correspondence… Then—

*'My dear Miss Parker! Permit me to inform you that such an intemperate response to an offer of marriage is most unbecoming in a young lady!'*

*'No.'*

*'No?' Sir Edwin sounded as though he thought his ears might be deceiving him. 'What do you mean, no?'*

*'No, I decline to permit you to tell me ~~anything of the sort~~ such thing.' Lydia paused for thought. Best to be clear about such things. 'And, no, I do not desire to marry you, sir. Ever. Thank you.'*

It…it was a *story.* Althea was writing a *story.* A novel, in fact. His conscience woke up at this point and, burning with embarrassment at his transgression, Hugo closed the notebook, setting it and the pencil on the wrought iron table, along with the tray of lemonade.

It took some doing. He dearly wanted to know more about Miss Lydia Parker and her antipathy towards the hapless Sir Edwin. He wanted to know what had led up to the fellow's clearly unwelcome offer, and exactly why Lydia disliked him. For he had not a doubt that she disliked him intensely…

He couldn't even ask Althea to let him read it, because that would tell her immediately that he *had* been reading it. Without her permission. Was this something she did as a hobby? Some ladies painted in watercolours…others wrote poetry…

*'Aunt Althea brought her work out, but she's fallen asleep over it.'*

*Work?* He'd assumed Sarah had meant embroidery or some such thing. *Needle* work of some sort. Had Sarah meant work quite literally? And Kate had once said something about Althea's work… As in something one did to earn a living? Or was it merely a creative outlet for an intelligent woman?

Music drifted through her dreams. Music and warmth. She didn't want to wake up. Althea let herself float a little on the melody. Allowed herself to dream a little more. No one minded if you dreamed here, even if you dreamed of the forbidden, the warmth of strong arms and a tender embrace, a kiss that meant love rather than conquest—

A damp nose shoved into her hand brought her back to the waking world—a reminder that someone at least expected another walk. Scratching Puck's ears, Althea opened her eyes, and wondered if she were still dreaming.

Music still drifted through the French doors. Kate at the piano again. And beside her, reading, sat Hugo. That treacherous warmth and longing twined through her. Safer not to dream of him. But there he sat, bareheaded, even his coat discarded in the heat of the afternoon. Companionable. Reading while she slept. Not in the least romantic or passionate, but so comforting and easy. Perhaps, later in the book, there might be a moment like this for Lydia and—Good God!

She sat up, stomach knotted as she understood precisely where her unruly mind was leading her.

'Althea. Are you all right?' His hand, gentle and steadying on her shoulder.

'I…yes. I was dreaming. My notebook—' She'd been writing, and she'd dozed off. Where was it?

'Here. On the table.'

And there it was. Closed. The pencil beside it. 'Oh.' Had she put it there? What the devil did she say? 'My…er…diary.'

Blast it. Now she'd lied to him.

'Your diary.' The merest hint of a hesitation. 'Of course. Ah, should you like a glass of lemonade?'

She forced a smile, grateful for the change of subject, even as she wondered at that odd hesitation. 'Yes, please.' Oh, Lord. What did she say now? Had he seen? Realised that it wasn't a diary at all? 'Have you been here long?'

He poured her a glass and consulted his watch. 'Perhaps half an hour.'

'How rude of me to sleep through your arrival.' *Keep it light.*

'I was enjoying the music.' He topped up his own glass. 'Have you thought about buying a piano yourself? For Kate?'

'Yes.' Another change of subject. Her glance slid to the notebook. She didn't recall putting it on the table, but she pushed that aside and thought about pianos.

With the bulk of the money she made from her books she had added to her capital. It was safer that way. With the sale of this book, however, she could afford to set money aside to buy a pianoforte.

'Do you play?' Hugo asked.

She laughed, sipped her lemonade. 'Yes.' *All* young ladies learned to play and she had been no exception. Not that she had ever had Kate's talent, but she had enjoyed it, found it relaxing—when she wasn't expected to play as a sort of advertisement for how accomplished and ladylike she was. It was only after she was married that she had fully understood that. No one expected her to play after dinner any longer—that was the province of unmarried girls. Instead she had played privately, for herself, but music had been one of the luxuries she had given up when she first moved to Soho.

Then every penny had been counted twice and polished thrice before it was spent. The importance of balancing the household budget had outweighed her love of music. Back then she had asked herself *Is it necessary?* every time she had to make a purchase. She had known the fear of having bailiffs at the door, and every month she balanced her books to a penny. Even now she hesitated to spend money on anything but essentials.

But listening to Kate fumble a passage, go back and correct it, play it over and over until she was satisfied, as Miss Barclay had taught her—Althea tossed all that to the winds. She was not going to end up in the Fleet Prison for debt if she bought a pianoforte.

Hugo rose. 'I should go in and see if my aunt is up from her rest. I'll leave you in peace, Althea.'

* * *

Over supper Althea's suspicion that something was bothering Hugo deepened. He seemed awkward, unwilling to meet her eye.

She waited for a chance to speak privately with him, but Kate and Sarah were eager to tell him all about their adventures. And he was more than happy to be told—she would have known if he were faking it.

What would he have done had she refused to take the girls in? Watching them over the supper table, she knew the answer. He would have adopted them himself. Hugo would never have abandoned them. He hadn't been able to do it when they arrived in London, but had housed them and protected them. Therefore he would never have done it after he had come to know them, and, she thought, love them.

As she did.

After supper Althea listened as Kate's description of a bird she had seen that morning sent Hugo to the top of the bookcase. He brought back a pair of books on birds.

'Let's see...' He paged through the first volume. 'Ah. Here we are. Red-tailed kite. What do you think?'

Kate leaned over the book. 'I think...maybe. Can we look tomorrow? Would you mind?'

He smiled. 'I wouldn't mind at all. My father used to know all the birds you'd see around here. These are his books. We often used to walk along the river, seeing how many different birds we could spot. His journals are here, too. You might enjoy looking through those, too.'

Seeing the small dark head bent over the book with Hugo, Althea knew envy. Her own father had never spent time with her. Always it had been Frederick, the son, the *heir*, who was the focus of Papa's interest. She had been her mother's business. But Mama had died when she was ten, and she had been left to the servants and her governess. Papa had mostly ignored her.

Until she was fifteen and there had been her godfather's death, and her sudden change in status from respectably dowered daughter to heiress.

Then Papa had finally noticed her.

He had been furious. She swallowed. Better not to think of all that. At the time she had scarcely dared say a word lest Papa turn on her.

*'Oh, so the fine lady, the heiress, has something to say, does she? Pah! Giving yourself airs won't catch you a husband, girl.'*

Had he ever called her anything but 'girl' after that? She didn't think so. He had never sat helping her to identify the birds she had seen on her morning walk. And, if he thought she had seen a red-tailed kite, he would have gone looking for it with a gun.

Soon enough Kate's ill-disguised yawns raised the spectre of bedtime. To Althea's amusement there was no protest this evening. Hugo had promised to help her spot birds the following morning… 'But you need a good night's sleep so your mind and eyes are sharp.'

Kate got up. 'Yes, sir.'

She came over to Althea. 'Goodnight, Aunt Allie.'

Althea held out her arms for the hug. 'Goodnight, sweetheart. Sleep tight.'

Kate hugged her hard, whispered, 'Do you think Mr Guthrie would mind if I called him Uncle Hugo?'

Althea kissed her temple. 'Why don't you ask?'

Kate's eyes widened. 'But—'

'He won't mind you asking.' She knew that as surely as she knew her own name.

Kate took a deep breath. 'Mr Guthrie? Sir?'

He smiled. 'Yes? Whatever it is, ask away.'

'Would you mind… Would it be all right if I called you Uncle Hugo?'

For a moment he stared, and Althea wondered if she had been wrong, if she should have sounded him out first.

But then, his voice oddly constricted, he said, 'I should be honoured, Kate.'

Althea caught Sarah's gaze, nodded slightly.

Her voice a little gruff, Sarah said, 'Would you…would you like a game of chess? Uncle Hugo?'

She saw, clear in the dancing glow of the fire and lamplight, the naked pain in his eyes, mingled with…acceptance? Resignation?

An odd smile twisted his mouth. 'I…yes. Very much.'

A faint snore came from the corner.

Kate nudged Althea. 'Aunt Sue is asleep. Shall you take her up?'

But Hugo was already on his feet. 'I'll take her up. Set up the board, Sarah, and we'll play when I come back down.'

# *Chapter Thirteen*

'Shall we walk towards the sunset or the moon?'

They had reached the end of the lane. The river murmured ahead of them, and soft light danced on its hurrying surface. To the west the embers of sunset still flamed. In the east the moon rose over London. Further upstream at Teddington the tide had turned and was hurrying back toward the sea.

'We can have both.' Althea bent to release Puck. 'If we walk west now the moon will still be there to light us home.'

She shut her eyes and cursed silently as she straightened.

'Very wise.' He offered his arm, and against all her better judgement she placed her hand on it. Walked with him along the darkening, singing river toward Richmond. A faint splash near the bank told her something had gone into the water. Or perhaps it was a trout.

*Home.* Why had she called it that? *Back to the house* would be accurate. But in the past week she had felt so at ease, so comfortable, that it was easy to think of River Lane House as home. Easy, and dangerous.

Her hand on his arm felt at home, too. That was even more dangerous. Waking up to find him beside her this afternoon—why had her heart skipped a beat? More than one beat if she were honest. Safer, much safer, if she lied to herself about that. But lying was the problem.

She had lied to him. Lied directly this afternoon, but she had been lying by omission since they met. Once it had not mattered, or she had told herself that it did not. But somehow, against all the odds, they had become friends.

He had come when she needed help, and had very possibly saved her life. At all events he had nursed her through a horrible illness, opened his home to her, and she had repaid him with a lie. You didn't lie to friends. You might keep your private business to yourself, but you didn't lie. Not to friends.

If he disapproved of how she had rescued herself from debt, then so be it. She knew what some in society murmured—that she had dug herself out of debt by taking lovers. If she didn't care about that, why should she mind if Hugo disapproved of her writing?

She didn't care to look too closely at the answer. It cut too close to something she had determined upon years ago—never to allow herself to care what a man thought of her ever again.

'I have to apologise.'

'I need to apologise.'

They both stopped, stared at each other. Then, by mutual consent, they walked on. And somehow Hugo's free hand covered hers on his arm—a dangerous, comforting weight.

'Ladies first seems a little self-serving,' he said.

Despite the thumping of her heart and the knots squirming in her belly, she choked out a laugh. Then, before she could change her mind—'I lied to you.'

'Ah.' His hand tightened a little.

'About the diary.' How to explain? Where to start?

'You do know it was none of my business, Althea?'

'Yes, but—'

'First, will you tell me *what* Sir Edwin did to earn such a set down from Lydia? She's clearly furious with him.'

Althea tried to collect her thoughts. Lydia had dealt Sir Edwin three set-downs so far. She'd been writing his first proposal of marriage, though, and—

*He'd read it.*

A chill shook her, despite the warmth of the evening.

'Are you cold? Shall we turn back?'

His immediate concern banished the chill.

'No.' It was far too late for that. She could tell him it was a hobby, something to pass the time. And it had been that. Once.

Ahead of them a pale shadow drifted silently from the trees. Her breath caught. A barn owl on the hunt. 'We'd better not mention that to Kate. She'll slip out to see for herself.'

She felt a quiet laugh shake through him. And in their shared amusement, their mutual awe at the silent ghostly flight, the last chance of prevarication died.

'He offered marriage to her younger sister first.'

Hugo let out a crack of laughter. 'What a tactless clodpoll! What on earth possessed him to do that?'

Althea blinked. He'd spoken of Edwin Jamison exactly as he might on hearing of the folly of an acquaintance, someone *real.*

'It's a little complicated,' she said carefully. 'That's only his first proposal. He'll get it right in the end.'

'What? Lydia is going to forgive him for that stunning lapse of good sense and marry him?' He spoke of Lydia as a real person, too.

'Eventually. Once he learns his lesson.' She smiled a little. 'And once she learns that people, and the world, are not quite as cut and dried as she would like them to be.'

He chuckled. 'She's not perfect then?'

'Of course not. Who is?'

'No one. I don't suppose you'd let me read the rest?'

From her silence, the tightening of her fingers on his arm, he decided he'd gone too far.

'You...you could read it, as it is. Or... I could give you one of the first copies.'

'First copies?'

'Yes. When it is published.'

He took a deep breath. 'You're hoping to publish it?' Oh, lord. Publication was a risky business, especially for a woman. She would likely be expected to take all the financial risk, and—

He took another breath. Best someone explained it to her...

*Did she ask for your advice? Do you know her to be intelligent? Competent?*

'How do you go about it?' he asked instead.

They walked on in the velvet dusk, wrapped in the murmur of the moonlit river, a blackbird singing nearby. He always liked hearing a blackbird sing in the moonlight. And Althea remained silent.

Yet he did not believe she was ignoring the question or annoyed. Just…thinking.

Eventually she said, 'It's hard to know where to start.'

He understood that. Where did anything truly begin? When had he fallen in love with Althea? From the very first? When she had asked him to draw up her will? Five minutes ago? Or perhaps he was going to keep falling in love with her for the rest of his life.

'When Hartleigh died he left the devil's own mess. Mortgaged estates, half the family jewels turned out to be paste when his cousin and heir tried to sell some of them. He also left a pile of gaming debts. His friend and executor considered paying those far more important than working tradesmen.' Disgust sounded clear in her voice.

'What about providing for the widow?'

'Me? Provide for a barren widow?'

*Barren?* He set that aside. None of his business.

'I was probably below the tradesmen.' Now a little amusement slid through her voice. 'Anyway, once the dust settled, there was very little left for me.'

He knew from his father that she had inherited a fortune from her godfather, but very possibly that had gone to Hartleigh. It wouldn't be unusual, unless her family had seen to it that her money was very carefully tied up in trust.

She went on. 'My world had turned upside down. During my year of mourning I simply clung to the wreckage. The one thing I did own was the London house where we lived. It had been my godfather's, and it was mine absolutely. A separate trust. Even I couldn't sell it without consent.'

'So you stayed there.'

'I thought I had no other choice,' she said quietly. 'I was, although I didn't quite realise it at the time, in desperate straits. I had very little income, a house I couldn't afford to run or maintain, and no one to advise me. Reluctantly, I came up with the plan of marrying again.'

'Plan?' *Reluctantly?*

A bitter laugh. 'Oh, yes. It was definitely a plan. It wasn't what I wanted, but I saw no other way out of the trap I was in. I fully intended to marry Rutherford.'

'For money.' He had no right to judge, but he hated that she had been forced to that.

She shrugged. 'For money, status. For safety. We were involved in an affair, and he was kind enough in a distant sort of way. We both thought we would suit.'

Now a hint of laughter, genuine affectionate laughter, came into her voice. 'Fortunately for Rutherford he met Meg, and she thawed him out beautifully.'

'But not so fortunate for you.' Despite his liking for the man, he couldn't keep the anger from his voice. 'Did you enter into the relationship believing he meant marriage?' And how often did that happen? Wealthy nobleman embarks on an affair, holding out the lure of marriage, then meets a beautiful, younger woman, and drops his lover faster than—

'No, no!' She was still laughing. 'It wasn't like that at all. Don't blame Rutherford. Marriage was mentioned *after* we became involved.'

'And then he discovered how little you had?'

She patted his hand. 'Stand down, Hugo. If money had mattered he would not have married Meg. She had even less than I did. Stop looking for a villain and let me tell this story!' She was silent for a while as they walked. 'Sorry. I'm editing a little. There are things I cannot tell you, that are not mine to tell.' Another pause. 'Let us say, through sheer luck, I was able to help Meg out of a horrible situation.'

'I daresay Rutherford was grateful.'

She grimaced. 'Embarrassingly so. I did very little, and it wasn't at all heroic. The thing was that Meg decided she didn't care that I had once been her husband's mistress, and—well, we became friends. She insisted on it.'

'Rutherford did not object?'

'No. *I* objected, but Meg wouldn't listen.'

He could believe it. The countess's quiet loveliness cloaked a spine of pure steel.

'Where does this fit with your writing?'

'I'm getting to that. I sold the house in Mayfair.' Another silence. 'I found out a little about the trust my godfather had set up and I… I persuaded the trustees that I couldn't afford it. I couldn't afford to go about in society either, so I sold the house and moved to Soho, which provided me with a little capital. A smaller, cheaper house, far less expensive to run, and away from all the gossip. Frederick had written that letter, which somehow was seen by the entire world, so I was very much persona non grata with society anyway.'

'What about Rutherford and his countess?' Couldn't they have helped her face down the gossip?

She shook her head. 'I wanted their friendship, not their protection. And I was tired of society. When Meg tried to invite me to anything but a very private dinner, I declined.'

'So you wrote a novel?'

'Not exactly. Should we turn back now?'

'When you've finished your story.'

'Very well. Where was I? Oh, yes. I'd always written, you see. Poetry, too, when I was a girl. But Hartleigh never knew. No one did except my father. He tore up most of a story once, saying writing by a female was a waste of time. After that I hid it from everyone.'

He wanted to drag her father out of the grave and then pummel him back into it.

'It was my…escape, I suppose,' she continued. 'Private and freeing. Especially after I married. By the time I accepted the reality of my situation and moved to Soho, I had six novels more or less completed.'

He blinked. *Six?* 'And you had never tried to publish one?'

She shook her head. 'You're a lawyer. You know better than that. How should I have gone about it? During my marriage it was impossible. Hartleigh would not have helped. He would have been mortified that his *wife* was doing such a thing, and as a married woman I couldn't have signed a contract without his permission. Even if he had permitted it, the money I earned would have gone to him. But after his death it was different. Before that, publishing my stories never occurred to me. They were just for me.'

'Your escape,' he recalled.

'Yes. But now I needed money. I knew Meg enjoyed novels. She'd loved a book called *Pride and Prejudice*, which I had also read and enjoyed. So I asked her to read one of mine. Swore her to secrecy, and made her promise to tell me the truth.'

'Would she have?'

'If she hadn't, Rutherford would have.' Althea chuckled. 'She showed it to him, without telling him where it had come from, and asked his opinion.'

He caught his breath. '*They* helped you get it published?'

'Yes. Rutherford approached the publisher, negotiated, and it earned me one hundred and fifty pounds.'

Even now he felt the little bounce of delight in her step.

'I'd never been so proud of anything in my life.'

For a moment he couldn't speak. Pride in her achievement swelled in him. Finding herself in a mess, she had somehow dug herself out of a hole. Ahead of them a shadow whisked across the path away from the river and under a hedge. A fox. He registered that, hoping the chickens were safely secured for the night.

'And the other books?'

'Rutherford negotiated the second sale. That earned quite a bit more, because the first book sold out, and made a profit. Then he advised me as I negotiated the next sale. I wanted to be able to do it myself, and he agreed that it was better that way.'

'And since?'

'This is my second novel since publishing the first six. I did have to look at the early ones again. Revise them. Bring them up to date.'

'Up to date? You mean, the fashions?'

She laughed. 'There's that. But more the writing style. My earliest started life as an epistolary novel. Very old-fashioned. I had to rewrite that one completely.'

He stopped, turned to face her and held her hands lightly in his. 'You turned everything around for yourself.'

'I was lucky. And I didn't do it alone.' She tried to tug her hands away, but he held fast. 'I had—'

'Althea, you wrote the books. They sold.' He gave her a little shake. 'Taking advice on the business side of it was the sensible thing to do. Like you took my legal advice on setting up trusts for the girls.' He shook his head. 'That doesn't make you less independent. And you said you learned to negotiate for yourself.'

'You don't disapprove?'

He stared. 'What? No. Of course not.'

'Many would, you know.' She shrugged. 'Women, *ladies*, are not supposed to pursue anything intellectual, and many still think novels are rubbishing things that corrupt girls' minds.'

He laughed. 'Yes, I know. I don't happen to agree, but possibly my mind has been hopelessly corrupted already.'

She sighed. 'I thought my life was complete earlier this year. Oh, I'm nowhere near as rich as I once was, but I'm secure. I thought I had everything I could possibly want. Peace. Contentment. That financial security to assure my independence. Even some good friends.'

'All very fine things.'

'Yes.' Her laughter sounded odd. 'But then you arrived on my doorstep with the one thing I was missing, and didn't even know I wanted, let alone needed—a family. Thank you for that.'

He spent most of his life sitting in his office listening to clients, drafting wills, occasionally setting up trusts. Sometimes he wondered if he did any good at all. When he came to the end of his life, would one single person mourn him?

Except for Aunt Sue, for the past ten years he had not had the joy of family. In that, he and Althea were much the same. She had been dispossessed and reviled by her family. His had died.

And when he had met those girls off the stagecoach he had known he could never abandon them to orphanages. He had given Althea the family he had wanted. And now… Words hovered in his heart, longing to be spoken.

But they had to stay there. At least for now. She had confided in him as a friend—the suitor, the lover, must wait.

'What was the title of your first novel?' A much safer subject.

*'Barnabas Flowers; or, the Recalcitrant Suitor.'*

He stopped dead in his tracks. '*That* chucklehead?'

She gave him a sideways glance. 'You read it?'

'I wanted to kick his—' He broke off, did a quick mental edit. 'I wanted to kick his backside. Telling the woman to whom he was betrothed that love was for silly, immature girls?'

'You didn't like it then.'

He caught the flat, even tone. Grinned. 'I didn't say that. I said I thought Flowers needed a good, swift kick. And he got it, too, when Susanna cried off, saying she loved him too much to inflict him with a silly, immature bride.' He laughed out loud. 'And then she tried to match him up with her friend, who thought exactly the same way? Which he found cold and calculating.' He shook his head. 'You wrote that? I really didn't think he deserved her until nearly the end. You're sneaky like that. Showing the poor devil at his absolute worst, and then putting him through hell to mend it all.'

'Oh.' A moment's silence. 'You bought my book.'

He kept a straight face. 'Well, no. Sue gave it to me for Christmas.'

'Of course.'

He relented. 'But I did buy the next one. And the others.' He shook his head in disbelief. 'I thought you were selling your jewellery bit by bit to build up your capital.'

She laughed. 'I did that right at the start when I sold the Mayfair house. I had some pieces that had been my mother's, which Hartleigh hadn't been able to get his hands on. Rutherford helped with that, too, at Meg's suggestion. Jewellers are very good at offering extremely low prices in those circumstances.'

They had reached the bottom of the lane that led up to the house and on to the Petersham Road. On one side of the lane the woods clustered darkly, blocking the light of the rising moon.

He held her back a moment as they stepped into the shadows. 'Let your eyes adjust.'

They stood, enveloped in the balmy, velvet darkness. Neither had bothered with a hat or gloves. Who was going to see or care? The night breathed around them, faint rustlings in the woods attesting to the presence of some small creature.

'Hugo?'

*Yes, love?* He managed not to say that. 'Yes?'

'Thank you. For everything.'

He swallowed. 'That's a great deal.'

He felt her turn to him, saw the pale shadow of her face look up. 'It's true. The girls, and…everything. Your advice—'

'You paid for that,' he reminded her. She'd insisted on paying for his legal advice. Except the letters to her relatives. He'd held the line on that.

'You don't judge,' she said quietly. 'Ever. You know all the discreditable things about me, and you don't judge.'

'It's not—'

'Your business?' She shook her head and the faint light shimmered on her hair. 'It's more than that. You have given me your friendship, you came when I needed help. Thank you.'

'That's what friends are for.' He wanted more, so much more that he shouldn't ask for yet. He wanted to take her in his arms and… They needed time. She needed time. To see him as more than her friend, time to see what could grow between them, and time to trust that he would never use it to control and confine her.

Her hands slid into his and she rose on her toes. 'Thank you,' she whispered again, and touched her lips lightly to his.

Everything rose up in him, but somehow he found the strength only to return what she offered, to brush his lips over hers, and not take her into his arms. Slowly she stepped back and, the spell broken, they walked back up the lane through the velvet shadows to the house.

He could wait a little longer. He must wait.

# *Chapter Fourteen*

Althea had enjoyed the first week at Petersham with the girls and Aunt Sue. She had enjoyed feeling her strength return, no longer being exhausted and requiring a short stop when they reached the end of the lane. She enjoyed the simple routine of country life again. Of walking along the river each day, with Kate becoming more and more enamoured of the bird life around them.

The second week with Hugo there was something more.

At his suggestion she had finally told the girls her secret—that she was an author and that was how she established an income.

*They love you. Even Kate won't blurt it out when she knows it has to remain private between the three of you.*

And it was a relief to tell them. To no longer have to hide her work away when one of them entered the room was a relief in itself, and no longer having to work quite so late into the evening was a blessing. Kate had accepted it, and that it was something quite private that only they must know.

Sarah found the whole idea of writing a story fascinating.

*'You had to change a character's name because we came to live with you?'*

She had giggled over that, at the idea of a real Sarah being a complete distraction from the fictional Sarah.

More though, her interest went beyond the writing itself to how Althea managed the money. She was startled by the idea that, instead of using the money paid by the publisher as income, Althea invested it. And Althea used that curiosity to teach her a little about managing money, about knowing how much you had and how far it would go. The child—and she was nearing fourteen, no longer a little girl—had even asked if she might learn how the household accounts worked.

*'Because I'll have to do accounts like that one day, won't I?'*

Sarah was growing up, and it was joy itself to witness that blossoming.

Would she have told them without Hugo's prompting? She thought not. And she would have been wrong. Perhaps it was easier to know when to tell children things when you had brought them up from babyhood, been witness to all those changes in them.

And Hugo himself became part of the rhythm of their holiday life. He walked with them in the mornings, took one girl or squeezed both into the gig with him for a drive in the afternoons. Sarah, he said, was becoming quite adept at handling the placid horse he'd hired.

So much that she alone had not been able to give the girls. Already Kate was asking if they might come again next summer. If they were invited, of course. Even if they weren't, and Althea was shocked to realise how much she hoped they were, she would have to set money aside to take the girls into the country for a week or two next summer. She could afford to stay with them at an inn for a few days or even rent a small house.

She was thinking about this as she relaxed in the shade a week after Hugo had arrived. He had taken both girls out in the gig. A squeeze, but they managed somehow.

She smiled, thinking of Hugo's comment as he helped Kate in. 'We'll need a bigger gig if you keep growing like this.'

Her intention had been to work, but the drowsy warmth of the summer afternoon was seductive. The notebook and pencil were on the table beside her, untouched. Aunt Sue had gone upstairs for her rest, and the golden afternoon, the soft breeze and the green embrace of the elm were a lullaby.

She dreamed.

She knew it was a dream, but it seemed so real. The house and garden were as they were. But she was not alone. Her eyes were closed, but she knew Hugo sat beside her reading. She knew that he loved her. There was no need for words. She simply knew. In the same way that she knew that this was how it was supposed to be. Them. Together. But would he still be there if she opened her eyes…?

Hugo was there, sitting beside her reading, as she opened her eyes. It felt right. As if he and she were both exactly where they were meant to be. Together. He looked up, as if her gaze had touched him, and smiled.

Her breath caught at the unguarded expression in his eyes. As if he were looking at everything he wanted in the world.

Her world lurched dangerously. 'Hugo? You're back?'

He leaned forward and murmured. 'Yes. I'm here.'

As if he meant not just here now, but always. As he had been in the dream. Was that it? Was that what he wanted?

Her?

And could she give him that and retain herself?

'Mrs Farley made lemonade while we were out!' Kate's bright voice shattered the spell. 'She made enough for all of us.'

Aunt Sue seemed to think they should come back sooner than next summer. 'You should come for Christmas as well as next summer,' she said that evening, her knitting needles flying. 'It will be lovely to have young voices in the house, not only dear Hugo and myself. Kate might join the carol singers. She has a pretty voice to go with her talent on the piano.'

'I'm going to buy one for her,' Althea admitted. Kate had already gone up to bed, and Hugo and Sarah were having their nightly game of chess. 'I haven't mentioned it to her yet. I thought a surprise when we get home. But I have already written to Mr Gifford at the music shop, and to her teacher for advice.'

Hugo looked up from the chess and smiled. He said nothing, but his smile turned her heart inside out and upside down, as it had done this afternoon. She wished there was someone she could ask for advice on what to do about Hugo. His smile deepened and her foolish heart danced a slow waltz against her ribs.

'Check!' Sarah managed to control the glee in her voice a little, but not by much.

'The deuce you are.' Hugo looked back at the board. 'Let me see.'

The two heads bent over the board again, and Althea looked away to find Aunt Sue smiling a small, wise smile over her knitting needles.

The evening walk had become *their* time. Each evening after supper, after a game of chess with Sarah, after Kate's piano playing, when the girls were in bed, and he took Aunt Sue upstairs with the old cat winding about their ankles. After he came back down.

Althea waited for him in the front hall, Puck bouncing around her in excitement at the prospect of this night-time adventure. Tonight should have been no different.

But this afternoon there had been that moment when his control had cracked for a second and she had seen. Seen what he tried to hide. And he had seen the returned yearning. And again this evening before Sarah, taking advantage of his distraction, had mopped the chessboard with him.

They walked largely in silence as they often did. He carried a lantern tonight, since the half-moon had not yet made its appearance. The dog, released from his leash, ranged ahead of them, occasionally dashing back to reassure himself that his humans were safe and still coming along behind him.

'So, a piano for Kate?' He broke the companionable silence as they turned for home.

'Yes. She enjoys the piano here so much. She practises at least once a day, and I enjoy listening in the evenings. I might play again myself.' She smiled a little. 'It's not just for Kate. But I need to think of something Sarah would enjoy as much. Not that she's jealous. It seems fair.'

He liked that she thought that way. Not of alleviating jealousy, but of fairness. 'I've noticed Spudge doesn't make you sneeze.'

'No. Cats don't. What made you say that?'

'She wants a kitten.'

'Sarah? How do you know that?'

'She slips Spudge bits from her plate all the time. You don't sit next to her at supper.'

A choked laugh. 'Well. That's easy. And since Puck is now used to Spudge, I suppose he would adjust to a kitten. Thank you.'

'My pleasure.'

They walked on until they reached the lane, the dark tunnel of trees and the shadows of the wood. It was as though the lantern cradled them in a little world of light, holding back the shadows. Even at night the air was cooler under the trees—a gentle benediction.

Puck, caring nothing for benedictions gentle or otherwise, stiffened at a rustle and squeak in the woods and dashed off to investigate.

Hugo felt Althea turn to call him back, but he placed his fingers against her lips. 'Give him a moment. He never goes far and we're not in a hurry.' He could speak to her now, tell her what he felt, and ask her to think, to consider…

He took a deep breath. 'Althea, would you—?

Somehow she was much closer than he had realised, and her mouth was even closer. Then there was no distance at all. The lightest, merest brush of a kiss. A feather could not have touched him with more care, nor a burning brand have set him alight more completely. All the things he had been going to say before he touched her dissolved in the dusky shadows—his arms closed slowly about her.

He didn't rush, didn't grab her and haul her to him. She could have stepped back. Her choice. She did not. Instead, with the softest of sighs, she stepped into him and together they deepened the kiss. In the velvet shadows and lantern light there was nothing but the silken mating of mouths, the match of their bodies, and the mingling of sighs and breath.

He'd stepped back a week ago, wondering if he had misinterpreted. And if he had, *what* he had misinterpreted. Had he been wrong in thinking that kiss had signalled desire? Or was he insane to have stepped back, rejecting her?

Now she'd kissed him again. He knew her well enough to know that if she didn't want something he'd be the first to know.

So he gave himself without reservation to the kiss and to her. Soon he would want more than the kiss, would want to touch, to explore, but for now this was enough, and not enough. More was there, a fragile waiting and beckoning, but it was not now. *Now* was this tender, dreaming kiss in a world of shadows and banked longing. Then he could speak. Not rush her, give her time to think about his offer, his feelings.

*'Six nights.'*

It took a moment for the words, breathed against his lips, to penetrate his hazed mind, another moment for their meaning to register, and for him to understand what she was saying, offering, there in the perfumed night.

She returned to London in a week, and she was offering to be his lover for these last six nights. Six nights when he wanted a lifetime. And that was the one reason he couldn't give her. If she was offering six nights, the offer of a lifetime might send her running.

Weeks ago he had spoken. Spoken and been forced to back away from what he wanted. He could explain that to her now… Ask her to marry him as he had wanted to do.

There were other reasons they shouldn't do this. One in particular. One he thought she would accept as rational, even when everything in him screamed that this once he should toss rationality into the river.

'Althea, the risk. If I were to get you with child, then—'

In his arms she stiffened. 'I'm barren.'

He remembered she'd said that once, referring to herself bitterly as *a barren widow.* There had been pain then, too.

He held her closer. 'You say that, sweetheart, but—'

'In eight years of marriage I never quickened.' Calm, resigned. 'And in that time Hartleigh sired two illegitimate children that I know of.'

His heart broke for her. What could he say to that? To the quiet pain in her voice that spoke of tears long since shed. Seeing the way she had responded to Sarah and Kate, he did not doubt that she would have loved any children she had been granted.

'I'm sorry.' He pressed a kiss to her temple.

She let out a shuddering breath. 'Any regret is over long ago. But you need not worry about an unwanted—'

'A child, any child, would *not* be unwanted.' He heard the sharpness, his own deeply buried pain, in his voice.

'Hugo?'

He swallowed. 'You knew that I was married, that Louisa—my wife—died.' Ten years later, even as he was falling in love again, that pain seared, still roughened his voice.

'Yes.'

'She died in childbirth. Our daughter survived her by a day.'

They walked on for a moment, hand in hand, by mutual tacit consent. Althea had no words. There were some things, some hurts, for which words were a mockery, worse than useless. She had known this, too. But hearing him speak of it, she knew the grief, the pain, the loss that would never quite go away.

She stopped, turned into him and put her arms around him. Held him as his arms came around her. What could she say? There could be no comfort for such a loss. Her heartbreak each month had been for a child she had hoped for. Hugo had held the fulfilment of hope in his arms and lost it. She could only hold him and thereby tell him that he was not alone.

*I wish I could give you what you want.*

And she did wish it. But she couldn't say it. An empty wish at best. One she was safe from ever having to make good on.

After a while they walked on again, still hand in hand.

They were nearly at the gates before he spoke.

'Let me put it this way.' His words were precise, careful. 'Hypothetically. *If* you were not barren, *if* you conceived, would you accept an offer of marriage?'

What choice would she have? The difficulties and disadvantages, social and legal, faced by an illegitimate child were enormous. She could not inflict that on an innocent any more than he could. And the damage to her own already shaky reputation would harm Sarah and Kate.

She let out a breath. 'Yes.'

'You said once that you never wished to be married again. Would you hate it?'

Would she? Once she could have answered categorically *yes*. But she was no longer the same person, and she honestly did not know any more. And marriage to Hugo? That was another question altogether.

'I would not wish to give up my writing. Nor would I wish to stop publishing.' And God only knew how they'd squirm around the legal issues.

'Of course not.'

Another shaky breath. A man who didn't mind that his hypothetical wife might have a life and pursuits that were completely her own and not melded to *his* life, *his* pursuits? 'Then marriage to you would be…' *Wonderful, glorious, joyful…* 'Acceptable.' Hurriedly she added, 'Hypothetically speaking.'

'Well.' They turned in at the gate. 'Don't drown me in enthusiasm.'

'I… I didn't mean…' Oh, damn! Why did this have to be so difficult?

*Because this time it matters.*

Afterwards would matter. They had to remain friends, not just because of the girls, but because she couldn't bear to lose him as a friend. He mattered too much to risk that.

'You are having second thoughts,' he said.

*Third and fourth thoughts, for that matter.*

With him of all men, she must be honest. 'Can we do this and remain friends? And what about that professional situation?'

He halted her short of the front door. 'Answer me this. Why have you made this offer here, when you rightly stepped back from it in London? This wanting, on both our parts—it's not a new thing.'

Her breath caught. 'Because here we may be private. In London we cannot have that privacy. No matter how careful, how discreet. And I will not harm the girls with a scandal.'

He bent to her, pressed a kiss to her temple. 'Then you have answered your own question. We both understand the limitations of what can and cannot be. So yes, we can remain friends.'

She nodded slowly. He was right. They understood each other.

'There is one other caveat I must make.' They had reached the door as he spoke. 'You already mentioned harm to the girls. That, for me, comes under the same heading as an unexpected pregnancy—harm to an innocent.'

He opened the door as she digested that. 'You would offer marriage if there were to be a scandal.'

'Yes. Under those circumstances no professional situation would stop me. And I would expect you to accept it.' He closed the door behind them, locked and bolted it. 'Those are my terms. Half an hour.'

'Half an hour?' She swung off her cloak and he took it from her to hang by the door.

'Yes. For you to think. If you cannot accept those terms, lock your door and I will understand that to be your answer.'

She lifted her chin. 'Half an hour for us *both* to think. You may decide the risk is too great.'

A soft laugh broke from him. 'My risk? Finding myself obliged to marry a beautiful, fascinating woman? Dangerous indeed.'

She scowled at him. 'What about your professional reputation?'

He grinned, quite insufferably. 'My profession? I'm a lawyer, not a monk, love.'

She swallowed, desperate to focus on the important issue. Not the casual endearment that should *not* have speared her to the heart. 'And what do you imagine your partner, your other clients, might think about your marriage to a female bearing my reputation?'

He nodded slowly. 'I think it would not bother my partner. As for my clients? It's none of their business.'

'And if they made it their business?'

He shrugged. 'I am fairly comfortable. I own this house. I have a sufficient sum invested that I could retire quite happily.

I enjoy my work and I prefer to be busy, but I would not starve should my clients desert me *en masse*.' He kissed her lightly. 'As you say, that's my risk. Think about your own. My risk is for me to assess.'

# *Chapter Fifteen*

Hugo walked Althea to her door. 'Half an hour.'

He went to his own room at the far end of the upper corridor, considering his options for what the well-dressed lawyer might wear to an assignation in his own home. Certainly not his dinner attire. If anyone saw him still in his evening clothes in the middle of the night, especially dishevelled, there would be absolutely no doubt about where he'd been. He could change ready for tomorrow morning, but the same thing applied. It would raise questions.

Best if he changed into his nightshirt and a dressing gown. It was his house. Even with guests it was not unduly outrageous for him to wander about the upper corridor like that. Besides, he didn't dare stay the entire night with Althea. Much as he wanted marriage, it must be her choice. He couldn't trap her that way. If anyone saw him, he could say he'd heard a noise, wondered about an intruder…

*Every night for six nights?*

He'd worry about that when he had to.

He glanced at his watch. Twenty minutes. God help him, he was hard already. He already knew he was going to her room despite the risk. And the risk she had raised for him was not the one that terrified him.

There were times when risks were necessary. He knew that. His reputation?

He tossed his waistcoat and cravat over a chair. A moment later his shirt followed them. He didn't mind the risk to his reputation.

He risked his heart. Again. If he wanted her, then he had to accept that risk. He had already had his heart broken into a thousand pieces. Somehow, over the years since Louisa's death, it had reassembled itself. It wasn't quite the same heart it had been. Some of the pieces were different. Others seemed to be in different places. Perhaps it wasn't supposed to be the same. The problem was that it could be broken again.

The risk to Althea was the destruction of the life she had built for herself, the loss of her independence. He had told her not to weigh his risks in her decision, but he couldn't help weighing hers. She had built that world for much the same reason he had buried himself in his work—to protect herself. Her heart had not been broken as his had been, but she had been hurt, damaged somehow, by her marriage.

In an odd way he thought she had not been damaged by the affair with Rutherford. Somehow they had remained on friendly terms without any whiff of either holding a torch for the other. Rutherford's countess clearly loved Althea, and would have done far more than Althea would permit to help her.

He stepped out of his trousers, folded them neatly and put them away. She had weighed the risk to herself and her carefully constructed life. If she deemed that risk unacceptable then her door would be locked, and he would be in for a highly unpleasant night of frustrated desire.

He might also have to accept that winning Althea was beyond him. He wasn't sure which would be worse. Having her and then losing her, or never having her at all. It would be far more logical to remain in his own room and leave things as they were. Unconsummated.

Safe.

His gaze went to the little portrait of his father hanging by the door. One always thought of one's parents as staid arbiters of good sense and propriety. And yet he had heard a few stories about his father from his youth. Old friends who chuckled over their port and memories. And something his father had once said to him…

*'The things I regret for the most part are the things I didn't do.'*

Carrying a candle, he padded barefoot down the corridor to the big corner room he had insisted that Althea should have. It had been his parents' room and the one he usually used. He had told Aunt Sue not to mention that. Sneaky of him. One way or another he had wanted Althea in *his* bed. Even if he didn't share it with her. It was the principal of the thing.

He hesitated before reaching for the doorknob. All the what ifs in the world hung on this. Screwing himself to the sticking point he gripped the knob, and…

It turned. The door opened, and, the what ifs answered, all risks accepted, he stepped inside.

She was already in bed, a lamp burning on the bedside table. Seeing that he blew out his candle and set it on the little table beside the door, which held a bowl of Aunt Sue's potpourri. Rose and lavender scented the room, but he thought he could already smell the soap she used, the sweet fragrance of her hair.

Everything in him yearned towards her.

She smiled in the lamplit shadows. 'We did not change our minds.'

'No.' How could he have pretended even for a moment that this was anything as logical as a decision? Something he could choose, or not choose.

It simply *was.*

And he had absolutely no idea how to conduct himself. It wasn't *his* bed, even if he owned it and frequently slept in it. Tonight it was her bed. Did he climb in with her? Or should he wait for an invitation?

His breath caught and his blood hammered as Althea pushed back the bedclothes and slipped out of bed. She stood, slim and straight in those lamplit shadows, her simple nightgown falling to her ankles, her glorious honey-gold hair in a loose braid over one shoulder.

For how long had he wanted to see it loose? He wanted to unravel the braid, unravel *her*, and bury his hands and face in the silken gleam of her hair. He reached for control as she came to him, bare feet silent on the wooden floor. Desire was a slow burn in his veins, but he held back, hesitant.

It had been so long—if he reached for her he might explode, and he wanted to savour, explore, to *love* her, not just have her. There might be a time for that, but it wasn't this time.

And now she stood before him and he dared not move, in case—

'Hugo?' Her voice stroked his senses, he felt it deep inside. '*Are* you changing your mind? Is this not what you want after all?'

Her uncertainty undid him. 'I'm terrified,' he confessed.

Her lips parted, he thought in shock. 'Of *me*?'

She stepped back, but he caught her hands, drew her to him. 'Of dragging you to the floor and ravishing you there.'

'Oh.' That wicked faerie smile beckoned him straight to perdition. 'That sounds promising.'

He choked out a laugh. 'Promising?'

'Mmm…' She came a little closer. 'We should try that sometime.' *They should?* 'But for now…' She rose on her toes, still holding his hands, until her mouth was a whisper from his. 'Kiss me,' she breathed.

His heart pounding, he brushed his mouth across hers, then rested his forehead against hers. 'What if we end up on the floor, not sometime but this time?'

The soft, sultry laugh matched the wickedness of her smile. 'It's your floor, Hugo. I'll go on top.'

Her mouth returned to his and they took mutual pleasure, mutual delight in the deepening intimacy. Mouths mated, at once urgent and tender. Tongues touching, sliding in a dance of discovery, her taste a heady elixir, her arms an eagerness about him.

He learned her body through the veil of her nightgown, and thanked God for his own nightshirt as well as hers, because her touch, even muted by the linen, threatened to destroy him. And she was all graceful curves, warm secret hollows that promised every earthly delight. His hungry mouth found the beat of her heart there in the curve below her jaw. He joyed in the speeding dance under soft, fragrant skin, the trembling catch of her breath.

The ribbon securing her braid gave at a single tug, and at long last he slid his fingers into the twining silk, loving the cool fire of it slipping between them. It tumbled over her shoulders, sweetly alive, curling around his fingers, tempting and luring.

He buried his fingers in her hair, kissing, just kissing, as her careful fingers undid the button closing the neck of his nightshirt, and loosened the laces. He shuddered at the first touch of her lips to his bared throat, unwinding the tight coil of his control.

*'Althea?'* Something had happened to his voice, roughening and deepening it.

*She* had happened to his voice, his life, his heart.

'Yes. Please.'

He hadn't even been able to think what he needed to ask, but she understood, placing his fingers on the first of the ribbons that held her nightgown closed. A gentle tug and the bow was undone, along with more of his control.

More unlacing, and more of the dainty bows fell victim to desire, until he nudged the nightgown to bare one shoulder. He kissed his way along the grace of her collarbone to the curve of her throat. Warm skin, trembling breath, his name a soft gasp.

*'Hugo, please.'*

Beyond words, he swept her up into his arms.

Shock slammed through Althea as her feet left the ground and she found herself being carried naked to the bed. She felt small, dainty and utterly vulnerable in every way. What had she been thinking to allow this, to suggest it?

'Are you…are you ravishing me?'

He lowered her to the bed and discarded his nightshirt in one swift move. Her breath burned in her lungs as he leaned over her, braced on his hands either side of her, so that their noses touched.

'What do you think?' His voice, rough and gravelly, brushed over her nerves. He reached out and turned down the lamp.

She gave him the truth, there in the enveloping dark. 'I'm not.'

'Good,' he murmured. 'Thinking…' A nibbling kiss along her jaw stole her breath, had her tilting her head back in a wordless plea for more. He gave it and she moaned. 'Where were we? Yes. Thinking. Very useful for work…' He nipped her ear and her body shot fire straight to her centre. He licked where he'd nipped and she melted. 'But right now…'

He joined her on the bed, gathered her into his arms, and there was another searing shock as warm skin met warm skin.

'Right now?' she murmured against his throat. She had wondered if she would even remember what she was supposed to do in bed.

A rumble of laughter. 'I thought you'd have stopped my mouth by now.'

She found it with her own and did exactly that. She didn't need to remember anything. With Hugo it was at once new and deeply familiar.

He was everything she wanted, and everything she feared. The one man who could make her want something more than the quiet, contented life she had carved for herself out of the ruins of the old.

And then it was too late. Too late for anything but this fierceness of mouths and bodies burning. His weight, hard and male, pressing her deeply into the mattress, the salt taste of his throat. Fires lit everywhere under her skin, dancing along her nerves where he touched her, and everywhere she wanted him to touch her.

He seemed to know, finding all those places, learning them, learning her. Discovering what she liked, even as she remembered. And yet it was not as she remembered at all. There was pleasure, yes. She remembered that. But had it ever been like this? Wanting to return pleasure as much as she wanted it for herself. Not in fair exchange, but because hearing his soft groan as she stroked his flank was a delight in itself. She slid lower and found him hard and ready for her. More than ready, she knew, as he cursed softly. She stroked, curious, loved that she could make him shudder. Knowing it made her ache, there where she wanted him most of all.

'Witch.' He murmured it against her lips, and gently, carefully moved her hand. 'If you keep doing that it will all be over.'

Shock rippled through her as he captured her other hand, trapped them over her head in a gentle grasp. She stared up at him, wriggled, tested that grip. It held.

'Hugo?'

He kissed her deeply. 'You just say *no.*'

*You just—* She didn't want to say *no.*

She wanted, needed, it to be now. Five minutes ago. Every breath, every tender touch, raked fire through her. But he held her safely, held her back from what she wanted.

His free hand, his lips, quested over her mouth and breasts, drifting lower over her quivering belly. And then those careful, shaking fingers were finally at her core. Tender, curious, learning her inside and out, slick in her sudden wild need.

*Now, surely now...oh, please!*

'Soon, love.'

And she knew she had spoken, begged. But yet he held back, pinning her to the bed with a powerful thigh flung over hers, holding her open to his touch, stroking shock after shock through her so that all the fiery tension built and built. And at last, at last he rose over her, came to where she needed him to be.

Soft, wet, Hugo's world stilled, contracted to this place they occupied in space and time, his body pressing into hers, her body both giver and receiver. She gave a startled cry at his entrance. His heart threatened to burst as he forced himself to stop, barely inside her.

'Sweetheart?' It was all he could manage, fighting the demand of his body, as he saw her closed eyes and trembling lips. It had been a long time for her, if he was hurting her—

Her eyes opened, dazed, her breath coming in gasps. *'Yes.'*

She shifted under him, and all control shattered. He plunged deep, taking her next cry with his mouth, and she moved with him, as frantic, as wild as he. He knew, he could feel when her body leapt to peak, broke with him into a shattering beyond oblivion.

He thought he could happily lie right there for several eternities, cradled on her soft body slicked with his and her own sweat.

'I think you just ravished me.'

He raised his head, with some effort, at the slightly slurred murmur. 'I think we ravished each other.'

Her silent laughter shook through him. 'I think you're right.'

He was probably squashing her and made to get off, but her arms tightened.

'You're not at all—' a yawn '—too heavy.'

He smiled in the darkness. 'I will be if I fall asleep on you.' He eased to one side, disengaging from her lax body, to settle half over her, their legs entwined. Utterly sated and relaxed, he drifted, felt himself sinking, and vaguely hoped he didn't snore…

That jolted him back to reality. He didn't dare fall asleep in her bed.

'I can't stay.' He felt Althea stiffen, realising too late how it sounded, and he wanted to swear. 'Althea, love, if I'm caught in your bed—'

'I know.' She sighed. 'We're trapped.'

That couldn't stand.

He levered up on his elbow to look down at her. At his lover, warm and rumpled from their loving, her lips soft and damp from their kisses. 'It's not a trap for me, sweetheart. And there's nothing I'd like more than to spend tonight with you.'

*And all the tonights for the rest of my life.*

He couldn't say that. Not yet. Instead, he stroked a damp curl back from her brow. 'I want to wake with you in the dawn and love you again, but by then the servants will be awake.'

A gentle finger traced the line of his jaw. 'I know, but you can stay a little longer.'

He could stay a little longer. Settling back down with her,

he drew her close. She snuggled against him with a contented little sigh.

After a while she murmured drowsily, 'This is nice. Lying here, holding each other. I had no idea.'

He rubbed his cheek against her hair. That her marriage had not been happy, he knew. But that she had never known this simple joy, of lying in a lover's arms after making love, told him exactly how lacking that marriage had been in affection. Not untypical of aristocratic marriages, though, with husbands visiting their wives' rooms only to bed them, and then leaving.

He wanted to give her all the intimacy and affection she had been starved of, that she hadn't even realised she was missing. And he was so close to falling asleep with her in his arms that he needed to leave immediately.

A soft sigh and the heaviness of her limbs against him told him she was close to sleep herself.

'Althea?'

There was no answer. He pressed a kiss to her temple. She'd had that at least. Now she knew the pleasure of falling asleep in a lover's arms. Very carefully he set about disentangling himself from her sleep-weighted arms. A sleepy protesting murmur, but she didn't wake fully.

Tenderly he pulled the covers up around her shoulders. She gave a contented little huff and snuggled in. Relying on the faint moonlight, he located his nightshirt and dressing gown and donned them.

Safely clad, he bent over his sleeping lover and brushed a kiss to her brow. 'Sleep well, my darling.'

He opened the door a mere crack and peered out, letting his eyes adjust to the darkness of the corridor. Absolute silence. He opened the door further and slipped out, shutting it quietly behind him.

Five more nights. And five days. All the time he had left of her holiday to convince her that, together, they could have everything. Everything he'd thought lost to him for ever, and everything she'd never known she could have.

* * *

Waking to the chorus of birdsong in the soft darkness before dawn, Althea reached for him. And sighed, remembering. They had agreed they could not have this joy. And it would have been joy. Below, she could hear the faint sounds of the servants, the bang of the kitchen door, quiet voices.

Hugo had been a great deal more careful and responsible than she had. She didn't remember him leaving. The last thing she remembered was lying in his arms, her head on his shoulder, their legs entangled. Just lying together, sated and sleepy. She closed her eyes to bring back the intimacy, the tenderness.

*I had no idea.*

Her eyes shot open. Had she actually said that to Hugo? She thought she had.

Restless, she sat up. She supposed her bed was no emptier than it usually was, but somehow it *felt* empty, lacking.

*Taking a lover will do that.*

She shoved the nasty, cynical little thought away, along with the bedclothes. She had not *taken a lover.* She and Hugo had taken each other. For six nights. And she was terrified that after these nights her bed would feel empty for the rest of her life.

# Chapter Sixteen

Hugo knew what happiness was. He knew what joy was. There had been happiness and joy in his life before. In fact, Hugo admitted to himself, he had learned to be perfectly content, and even happy again in his life, before he met Althea.

Summer holidays, and the Christmas holiday, had always been special times out of his deliberately busy life. Times when he could come out here to the Petersham house, sometimes for several weeks at a time to be lazy, to read, walk by the river, watch birds, spend time with Aunt Sue, and generally do whatever he liked, when he liked. He could sleep in if he liked, drink his morning coffee in the garden, and just be. It was as close as he could get to the carefree summers of his boyhood.

This year had been different. If he'd wanted to sleep in, there would have been no opportunity. Not with leaving Althea's bed before dawn to avoid the servants, and tossing and turning in his own bed for an hour or so in order to make sure it looked slept in. Then the girls rose early and there was always something to be doing.

Kate was working her way through Aunt Sue's music and his father's bird journals. The child had started a list—two lists. Birds she had already seen, and birds she wanted to see. Sarah was spending a good deal of time poring over the chess board.

She was determined to excel. Apart from that she had taken to spending time in the kitchen, learning Mrs Farley's recipes.

*If I learn how to manage the house, I can do it for Aunt Althea—that would save her time. Then she can write more if she wants to.*

And then there was Althea herself. She wrote openly now, not bothering to hide what she was doing from them, although she didn't allow anyone to read it.

*'It's not ready. I'm still scribbling. You can read more when I've tidied it up.'*

He wasn't sure how he could go back to his London life as it had been without Althea. And yet he had not found the way to tell her what he wanted. She seemed perfectly content with things as they were.

Each night he went to her, and they made love. For that was what it was. He wasn't merely a man bedding a willing and beautiful woman. It wasn't mere bedsport. It was Althea and Hugo making love to each other. And each night she fell asleep in his arms, and he left her with increasing reluctance.

He wanted to sleep with her. Literally. He wanted to fall asleep with her. And not only that, he wanted to wake up in the dawn to make love with her again. Without caring if the servants or anyone else knew he was in her bed. Or that she was in his bed.

He'd thought of a way around it. Not completely around it, but enough. Maybe. It meant he had to buy a new, very expensive, watch.

All his life, unnecessary expense had been something to avoid. It was cold? Don an extra layer. Put a rug over your knees before heaping extra coals on the fire, even if you could afford the coals. Waste not, want not. He already had a perfectly good, functional watch. One, moreover, that he was very fond of. It had been his grandfather's watch and had been passed down to him through his father. He had one day hoped that he would give it to a son.

That last was irrelevant. The point was that he had a watch that kept time perfectly. He ought not to be thinking of buying another watch. Except he was. Because there was something his watch did not do that he needed it to do.

Two more nights. He had two more nights with Althea before she and the girls returned to London.

He announced his intended trip into Richmond over breakfast. 'I have something I need to do. Is there anything I may collect for you, Aunt Sue? Althea?'

Aunt Sue pursed her lips. 'You might buy some nice cakes for tea, dear boy. And strawberries. I think the foxes have been eating ours.'

He grinned. 'Cakes and strawberries. Anything else?'

'May I come with you, Uncle Hugo?'

He looked at Kate in consternation. Half of him—curse it, *all* of him—was more than happy to take her, but—

'We were going to walk back towards London as far as Ham House, Kate.' Sarah looked puzzled. The previous evening they had discussed very seriously the thrill of seeing Ham House again. Althea had admitted to a slight acquaintance with the owners, and that made it even more of an excitement. Even viewing it from the river gate.

Kate stuck her nose in the air. 'I should like to go to Richmond with Uncle Hugo if it won't bother him.'

Althea looked at him. 'What does Uncle Hugo say?'

He sipped his tea. 'That I would enjoy the company.'

Richmond was an easy drive along the main road. Leaving the horse and gig at the inn, Hugo strolled through the centre of the town, Kate chattering brightly and holding his hand.

'Where are we going, Uncle Hugo?'

He steered her into a narrow lane that led through to Richmond Green. The shop he wanted was a few doors down. 'Right here.' He opened the door for her. 'In you go.'

She looked around. 'It's a jeweller's shop. Oh!' Her eyes widened. 'Are you going to buy Aunt Althea a ring?'

'What?' *Oh, Lord.* 'Ah…no. Not right now, Kate. I need a new watch.'

'Oh.' She frowned. 'Is something wrong with the old one?

I'm sure they could mend it. Aunt Althea's clock stopped, and a man came to the house and made it work again.'

'No. It's working perfectly. I, er, need a spare watch.' He nodded to the woman who came out of the back room.

'Good morning, sir.' Then she smiled. 'Why, it's you, Mr Guthrie! How nice to see you again. And how is Miss Browne? I was hearing she had visitors apart from yourself.' She looked at Kate. 'Would this be one?'

'It would. Miss Kate Price, Mrs Henderson. And Miss Browne is very well. No need to ask how you go on.' He smiled. 'You look famously.'

Mrs Henderson fussed with her cuffs and blushed. 'Thank you, Mr Guthrie. How may we help you today?'

Hugo explained what he needed.

She nodded. 'Of course, sir. This way.'

Half an hour later he walked out with Kate, the dazed owner of a very expensive striking watch, guaranteed to sound on the hour, when you activated the mechanism. Just the hours. He had gently but firmly rejected the notion of a watch that would also strike the quarters. Life, he had noticed, seemed to move a great deal faster than it had when he was a boy longing for the end of the school term. He didn't need to be reminded of every passing quarter hour.

Fortunately, Kate had lost interest very quickly and made friends with the black and white shop cat, who was more than happy to be petted. Her distraction was complete when Mrs Henderson found a small, carved wooden brooch in the form of a bird, which she gave to Kate. This had Hugo, not wishing Sarah to be left out, selecting a small silver rose brooch. Mrs Henderson wrapped it with the watch. Kate already had the wooden bird pinned to her bodice.

Walking back towards the inn, Kate gave a little jig, swinging their hands. 'We mustn't forget the cake and strawberries. I'm glad you bought Sarah the rose, but should we find something for Aunt Althea and Aunt Sue?'

He laughed. 'Good point. Since you and Sarah have your brooches, I'd better find something for our aunts.'

Remembering that Althea had enjoyed her ginger ice cream

at Gunter's, he chose a jar of crystallised ginger for her. For Aunt Sue he bought pretty handkerchiefs and a new cap with bright pink ribbons.

When Kate looked a little puzzled over the handkerchiefs he chuckled. 'Aunt Sue would be the first to tell you she has more than enough *stuff*, as she calls it. But she does like pretty handkerchiefs, and she loves pink.'

Kate nodded slowly. 'Is it like when I told Mrs Henderson I liked watching the birds and she found the brooch for me? And she told me she had enough things to give something away.'

'Exactly like that. And your aunt likes ginger, and the jar is pretty afterwards. She can keep something else in it.'

'Because she's not as old as Aunt Sue, so she doesn't have as much stuff.' Kate nodded.

Hugo hid a smile. 'Something like that. Come along, and we'll find the cake and strawberries.'

Althea saw the little wooden brooch on Kate's bodice, and her heart tumbled helplessly. 'That's very pretty, Kate.'

Kate jigged. 'When Mrs Henderson, the shop lady, asked what I liked, I said birds, and she found this. And Sarah has—'

'Perhaps, Kate, love, you could let me present Sarah's gift first?' Hugo said mildly. He reached into his pocket and brought out a small parcel, which he handed to Sarah.

She stared. 'You bought me a present. Thank you.'

'A very little one.'

And Althea's heart misbehaved again as she watched Sarah unwrap a little box and take out the silver rose.

'Kate liked the bird and we thought, because you pick roses for the breakfast table, that you might like this.'

The girl looked up, eyes shining. 'It's beautiful. Thank you, Uncle Hugo.' She pinned it on at once, went to him and hugged him hard. 'I love it.'

Kate jigged up and down. 'Are you going to…'

This time she shut up with a mere look.

Looking slightly shame-faced, Hugo offered Aunt Sue a small parcel. 'I promise it's not *stuff*, Aunt Sue.'

She laughed. 'It feels like *stuff*, but never mind. If an old lady can't accept a gift from a handsome young man, even her nephew, then who? Thank you, my dear.'

Opening it, she smiled. 'Not *stuff* after all. Thank you very much, Hugo. My favourite colour, too. And what pretty handkerchiefs!'

Then he turned to Althea, and her heart stuttered. 'What? You didn't.'

He raised his eyebrows. 'And exactly what do you think Aunt Sue would say if I'd brought home gifts for her and the girls and forgotten you?'

'It would have been nasty, and quite pointed, I assure you.' Aunt Sue carefully unpinned the cap she had put on that morning. 'My sister and I brought him up better than that. And even dear Hugh, this one's papa, always brought me a little something when he bought Cecily a gift. Which was often.' She pinned on the new cap. 'How does that look, girls?'

Hugo smiled at Althea, and leaned close as he gave her the parcel. 'I remembered your preference in ice cream.'

Small, yet heavy. She resisted the urge to shake it. He couldn't possibly have brought home ice cream from Richmond. As a child she had always ripped the wrappings off presents, now her fingers trembled a little as she carefully undid the ribbon and removed the paper.

'Oh.' All these months and he'd remembered she had chosen ginger ice cream. For that matter she often had ginger biscuits. Mrs Cable knew she liked them. And he'd remembered. The little ginger jar turned misty. For goodness' sake! She was not going to turn into a watering pot over a jar of ginger!

'Thank you.' She had to push the words past a lump in her throat. She didn't remember a present that had ever moved her more.

'There's cake, too,' Kate announced. 'It's ginger cake.'

After supper they all settled in the parlour with the doors open to a glorious evening. Birds still sang as the shadows lengthened.

Kate sat down at the piano and, instead of riffling through the music as she usually did, opened the piece on top of the pile.

'Aunt Sue asked me to learn this one for her this afternoon. She said she used to play it.'

Hugo looked at his aunt curiously.

She smiled. 'I think you'll remember it.'

Kate struck up a waltz. And he did remember it. Aunt Sue playing it, on this very instrument, on a summer evening a few years ago. And his father, well into his seventies at the time, laughing and asking Mama to dance. They had danced here in the parlour as if they were in their twenties again. He'd been more than a little surprised that either of them had known the steps.

They had both been gone before the next summer, yet it was as if they were still here somehow, dancing and loving.

He rose, went to Althea. 'May I have this dance, ma'am?'

Words proved impossible. Althea placed her hand in his, felt his fingers tighten briefly on hers—it felt as if he held her heart. Careful, gentle and utterly dependable. What had she done?

She rose and he took her into the dance. She had danced in some of the grandest ballrooms in London once. Danced with dukes and earls, been sought after as a supper partner for her cursed beauty. As if she were some sort of prize. Hartleigh had married her for it—that and her money. Yet none of those grand rooms or wealthy aristocratic partners had meant as much as this waltz in a parlour, the tune from an elderly, battered piano, played by a small girl, winding its way around her heart.

The room wasn't huge, but there was space enough if they danced in small circles and he held her close. And he did. So close that her body, attuned to his over the last few nights, hummed with delight.

*What have you done?*

She smiled up into his eyes, deep grey eyes that smiled back, and couldn't bring herself to care. Only two more nights, but she'd had this. If it hurt for the rest of her life, she'd had two glorious weeks with him, and this last week when he'd come to her each night had been the loveliest week of her life.

*Two more nights.*

They would make them nights to remember for a lifetime.

* * *

Hugo slipped down the hall to Althea's room shortly after midnight. He should have come earlier, but he had hesitated, even after the house had fallen silent and the servants were abed. That dance had shaken him to the depths of his being. How could they continue this for even one more night without him speaking what cried out in his heart?

They needed to talk. And he needed to know what to say. Or perhaps not what to say, but how to say it. So now it was after midnight and he reached for the door handle, half expecting her to be in bed and sound asleep…

A single candle stood on the chimneypiece. Althea, standing by the open window, turned as he came in and shut the door. Consciously, he turned the key. He hated that. Hated the secrecy that felt as though he were somehow ashamed of this, what they did, but it was the only way he could protect Althea from being forced into choosing a path he was still not sure she wanted.

They needed to talk.

'I'm sorry. I've kept you waiting.'

She shook her head. 'It's all right. I was thinking.'

'Thinking?' About the same things he was thinking of?

'We have only tonight and tomorrow.'

His breath caught. 'Althea, we need to talk. We—'

'Yes. Later though?'

Her hand went to the sash of her robe. One tug and it was undone. And he was undone with it. Her gaze held his, not challenging but steady, a half-smile dancing in her eyes. A shrug of her shoulders and the robe slid to the floor.

Leaving her naked.

His blood hammered and the rest of the world blurred. His breath came in hard—like something else—and stayed there.

'Shocked, sir?'

He couldn't think enough for shocked. That velvet voice, all teasing seduction, stroked every nerve.

'You are…utterly—'

Now her gaze did turn challenging. 'Not beautiful, I hope.'

No. She *was* beautiful. That spoke for itself, not requiring words.

'Wicked.' He shook his head. 'Beautifully, wonderfully wicked.'

Her laughter danced. 'I think I like that, being wicked. For you.' She came to him, a pale sylph in the candlelight and shifting shadows.

*Just for me?*

She smiled. 'I intend to be more wicked yet.'

Hugo reached for her, drew her close, one hand on the sweet curve of her bottom. 'And if I wish to be wicked as well?' He nibbled along the line of her jaw, felt the jolt of her breath, her pulse speeding under his lips.

Althea stood on tiptoe, her arms lifting to wind about his neck. 'We can be wicked together.'

*Together.*

He wanted that more than his next breath. To spend the rest of his life with this woman—loving her, being driven to distraction by her independence, loving her all the more for it.

But her mouth was right there, warm and inviting. He accepted the invitation, tasted her deeply and was lost. He was never sure quite how they found the bed, but somehow they did, minus his nightshirt, and rolled together until she sat up, somehow straddling him.

The single candle on the chimneypiece danced light and shadows over her face. She smiled down at him. 'Wicked enough?'

'I'm not sure,' he murmured. 'Keep going.' She rose up, reaching between them to guide him to her entrance. He wanted to pull her down, possess her utterly. So soft, so wet… He held back, fighting for the control to allow her to set the pace. Slowly, slowly she took him into that wet heat, an endless possessive slide until she had all of him. Or he had all of her. Did it matter? They had each other and it was glorious.

She rocked a little and he reached up to cup one pale, lovely breast, stroked the tip, and felt her breath catch. Her hair tumbled forward around her face, framing it. *'Yes.'*

'More?' He lightened his touch, felt her quiver.

'More,' she breathed, moving on him. 'Much more.'

He gave her more, rocked under her, matching her slow rhythm, his hand on her hip only to anchor himself. Pressure built, his grip hardened as she finally, finally moved faster, until, with a smothered cry, she broke. Her head fell back as the storm caught her, and he watched in wonder as it swept across her, through her.

She collapsed onto him, trembling with the force of her release, and he caught her, held her trembling body close, as his own consummation stormed through him.

They lay, a tangle of limbs and pounding hearts, and he wondered if the world would ever—could ever right itself. He should speak now, tell her how he felt, what he wanted. For himself, for them.

'Althea, love.' The odd little sound she made told him that she was right on the cusp of sleep. Very gently he lifted her so that she lay warm and relaxed against his side. Wasn't it men who were supposed to fall asleep immediately?

'Althea?' A contented little sigh breathed out of her, and he smiled into the darkness. In the morning then. He would speak in the morning. Perhaps it was better to speak then, when they weren't dazed with lovemaking and half-asleep. He smiled again—fully asleep, in Althea's case.

Meanwhile, he would enjoy the sweet intimacy of actually sleeping with her. Carefully he reached out and set the striking mechanism on his expensive new watch. Praying it would do its job, Hugo settled Althea in his arms and closed his eyes.

# *Chapter Seventeen*

Althea jolted awake, wondering what had disturbed her, and realised that the pillow tickling her nose was Hugo's chest. What time was it? Something had made a noise. The servants? Why was he still here? She tried to sit up, but was held in place as his arm tightened.

'Hugo, wake up!' she whispered. 'We both fell asleep and—'

'My watch did its job and woke us.' He still sounded sleepy, but there was no mistaking the smugness in his voice.

'Your watch?'

'I bought one that strikes on the hour.'

She digested that. Watches were expensive at the best of times, and one that chimed on the hour… They weren't just *expensive*. 'That was what you bought at the jeweller? So that you could stay without risking—'

'So that I could sleep with you, yes.' He sat up and stretched. 'I wanted that more than I can say. We need to talk this morning, sweetheart. Not now. I can't risk falling asleep again. The servants will be up in another hour.'

He pushed back the bedclothes and got out of bed. She could hear him moving about in the dark, hear the small movements as he found his nightshirt and dressing gown. Then he was back at the bedside, tucking the bedding around her as he always did. Making her feel cherished and cared for.

*One more night.*

She could feel the heat pricking at her eyes and thanked God for the friendly darkness that had cradled their loving and now hid her tears. He bent, a darker shadow, to kiss her as he always did. Sometimes she wasn't quite awake when he left, but she always knew when he kissed her. Those kisses were going to have to last her for the rest of her life.

'I liked waking up with you, too,' he murmured. 'I'm looking forward to doing it again.'

*One more time. He'd bought a disgracefully expensive watch so he could sleep and wake up with her. Twice.*

Her lips clung to his, drawing out the kiss, drowning in the sweetness. Somehow she had to navigate her way back to their friendship, without him ever realising how much he'd come to mean to her.

He broke the kiss gently. 'Go back to sleep, sweetheart. I'll see you at breakfast.' Another swift kiss. 'We'll talk during our walk.' Then he was gone, a shadow moving quietly to the door, which opened and closed with the faintest of clicks.

Althea stared into the darkness and let the tears come. She wasn't sure what he wanted to talk about. Perhaps that they should continue their affair in London. And that she couldn't allow.

She didn't mind the risk to herself, but she couldn't allow the risk to the girls, or the risk to him, if a scandal ensued.

Like a fool she'd fallen in love. It wasn't the sleeping with him that had tipped her over that fatal edge. It was the living with him. He was easy to live with. He had his own habits and routines, but was more than happy to accommodate others. She found it endearing that he preferred tea first thing in the morning, but coffee later in the day, and a return to tea in the late afternoon.

He had brought some legal work down with him, and sequestered himself for a couple of hours each day after their morning walk. Now that she had told Kate and Sarah about her writing, she used those same two hours for her own work.

The girls either read, kept Aunt Sue company playing cards, or visited Mrs Farley in the kitchen. Kate had learned how to make lemonade. Sarah had learned how to bake Althea's favourite ginger biscuits.

*He had remembered her choice of ginger ice cream and brought her a jar of candied ginger.*

How could she have *not* fallen in love?

She had told herself that it was attraction, desire, that had made her want to start this affair. The truth was, she had already been in love. The affair itself had opened her eyes to that truth. That and his insistence on protecting her. She had been protecting herself for a long time. Both during and after her marriage. She was good at it. But oh, it was such relief to have someone who also thought her worth protecting, not because she might sully *his* good name, but because she was intrinsically important to him.

And simply because he was a good man. The antithesis of her husband, her brother and her cousin Wilfrid. None of whom had protected the women and children in their lives.

Hugo did. It was that simple. And he did it without making you feel useless or obligated or inferior. He made her feel that she mattered.

She rolled over, breathed the faint scent of Hugo on the sheets, on his pillow, and closed her eyes, hoping that she might dream of sleeping in his arms and waking the same way, of making love in the dawn.

Hugo had thought carefully about how he should raise the topic of marriage with Althea. He was still thinking about it over his eggs at breakfast. Aunt Sue generally breakfasted in her room, and the girls and Althea had yet to make an appearance, so his musings were uninterrupted.

*Tell her you love her first. Then explain about Miss Price's will.*

He topped up his teacup, considering. It was a very long time since he had told a woman he loved her. Hopefully things hadn't changed, but he was no longer a young man of twenty-five, who had fallen in love with a colleague's daughter.

*Telling her you love her is still the best way to start.*

First he had to get her alone. It wasn't the sort of thing a man wanted to blurt out in front of two young girls, especially when one of them already thought he should be giving her aunt a ring.

On their walk. The girls always ran ahead with the dog. Oh, one or the other of them came racing back from time to time, but mostly they could be assured of a reasonably private conversation. He glanced out the window. Sunshine poured from blue skies.

Perfect.

'Good morning, sir.' Sarah came in with a bunch of roses. She placed them in a waiting vase on the breakfast table. Something inside him bloomed at the thought of becoming used to that. To Sarah arranging a few flowers on the table each morning for years to come.

'Kate and Aunt Althea are just coming. They are still in the garden with Puck.' She helped herself to eggs and a piece of bread. 'Have you been to Paris, Uncle Hugo?'

'No. Why?'

'Aunt Althea has, and she says they have delicious pastries for breakfast each morning.' Sarah buttered her bread thoughtfully.

'The Scots like black pudding,' he offered. He did, too, for that matter.

Sarah screwed up her face. 'Ew! I'd rather try the pastries.'

'Practise your French,' he advised. 'Then you can tell them which ones you want.'

Sarah grinned and bit into the bread, as Kate trotted in, followed by Althea and the dog.

'Good morning.' Kate poured milk for herself and took it to her place. 'It's such a nice morning, we can walk for ages. Maybe all the way to Richmond and back through the park?'

Althea smiled as she sat down and poured tea. 'We'll see.'

He considered that possibility. If they did that, if Althea said yes, then he could stop at Henderson's again… They could choose a ring together.

A clatter of hooves on the drive distracted him from a vision of walking home across Richmond Park newly betrothed with Althea.

He returned his thoughts to the immediate issue. 'Can you really walk that far, Kate?' he asked.

She hunched a little. 'If we have a rest in Richmond I can. And maybe a rest on the way home?'

'I think we can—Mrs Farley.'

The housekeeper stood at the door, a letter in her hand. 'Messenger from London for you, Mr Hugo. He's waiting for an answer.'

*Something minor, please.*

Something he could scrawl an answer on the bottom and send back… He took the missive, broke the seal—Jacob's signet ring, not the firm's office seal. His heart sank. Not simple then, if Jacob had used his personal signet…

Opening it out, he scanned it. His stomach executed an ungainly roll. He read it again, slowly.

*How in Hades had that happened?*

He folded the letter carefully, placed it in his pocket. The last two weeks—the last week especially, and this morning in particular—all turned to ash in his heart.

*What have you done?*

'Hugo?' Althea's worried voice broke into the wasteland of his thoughts. 'Is it very bad news? Can I help?'

'What? No. I mean, it's not good news. I must return to London. Immediately.'

Dear God, the mess this would cause!

The outcry from the girls should have been heartening. Instead it tore at him. 'I'm sorry, girls. This is something…' He blew out a breath. 'Something I've made a mess of and now I have to mend.'

*If it can be mended.*

He rose, looked straight at Althea. 'I'm sorry. For…for everything.' He couldn't even explain now.

He saw her stiffen and cursed himself. Cursed all the things he couldn't say, both because the girls were there and because of his blasted ethics.

'Must you go immediately, sir?'

'I'm afraid so.' Beyond caring, he went to her, caught her

hand. 'I'll see you as soon as I can. But this is bad. And…it changes things.'

Her face went utterly blank. 'Of course, sir. I quite understand.'

No, she didn't. And, since he couldn't explain yet, he needed to shut up. Now. He was making everything worse.

The sun was as bright, the birdsong as lovely and the river as beautiful as it was every morning. And yet to Althea it might as well have been pouring with rain and smothered in a suitably gloomy fog.

How had she become so attuned to his presence that she missed it like a limb? After he'd slipped from her room that morning, she'd lain awake, wondering what it would be like to awaken in the dawn to find him still in her bed, and to make love in the blooming light. As she'd drifted between dreams and the waking world, it had seemed that it might be possible.

*'We'll talk after breakfast. On our walk.'*

She had allowed herself to believe that one day she would open her eyes and know what it was like to have him there, smiling at her in the light, or perhaps have him kiss her awake.

But now something had changed for him.

*You aren't going to find out. You had this brief interlude to enjoy yourself. With no obligations, no expectations. Don't spoil what you had by wishing for what you can't have. You set the rules yourself.*

She hadn't understood that she'd be breaking her own heart.

They turned back a little way before Richmond on their walk. Somehow no one wanted to stop for cakes without Hugo. Sarah had been very quiet, lost in her own thoughts, and Kate was dancing ahead as they approached the lane up to the house, hoping, Althea knew, to spot a squirrel in the woods there if she were very quiet. Sarah had stayed back to walk with Althea, and they had leashed Puck. Otherwise the odds of Kate seeing a squirrel were little to none. Puck's attitude towards squirrels was that they had been created especially for him to chase and, if out of reach, which they always were, to bark at.

Kate safely ahead, Sarah finally spoke. 'Do you think *I* could write a book one day?'

Althea smiled. So that was what she'd been mulling over.

'I have no idea. Nor will you until you try.'

'Is that what you did? Sat down to write a book?'

Althea laughed. 'When I was your age, I used to wish desperately that I had a sister.' She had been so lonely when Frederick went off to school. He had come back changed, far less willing to have a younger sister tag along behind him. And then there had been her inheritance, and his bitterness that he, the boy, the fêted heir, had been passed over for a mere female. It should have been *his* inheritance. Even the Pater—he had taken to referring to Papa as *'the Pater'* in that lordly way—said so.

She swallowed, pushing away the hurt. 'So I imagined a sister for myself, but because she lived somewhere else we had to write letters to each other. So of course, I had to make up a reason for her to live somewhere else.'

'Was she married?'

'Oh, goodness, no! That would have been far too ordinary. I imagined that she was travelling with her godmother so she could write to me about all her exciting—who is that?'

At the foot of their lane a small black carriage stood, a nondescript pair of bays facing up the hill towards the main road. One man stood beside it, another on the box. Kate was very close, and the man stepped forward to speak to her.

Instinct had Althea lengthening her stride. No doubt he was only asking directions, but—the man gripped Kate's arm.

'No!' Althea leapt into a run as the man dragged Kate towards the open carriage door.

Kate's screams ripped through her. She'd never make it. Her skirts wrapped around her legs—she hitched them up, not bothering to yell. There was no breath for it and no one else to hear.

The man nearly had Kate to the carriage, her childish struggles useless as he clapped a hand over her mouth to stop her screaming.

He let out a yell, lost his grip and Kate was free, bolting back down the path towards Althea, even as Puck charged past, barking furiously.

The man on the box yelled. 'Come on! You've lost her!'

Puck reached the would-be abductor, snarling, snapping at his ankles. The man kicked out, missed, then ran for the carriage, harried by the dog. He leapt for the open door and swung up into the carriage.

The driver whipped up the horses and the coach rattled off up the lane.

Reaching her, Kate flung herself, panting, into Althea's arms. 'He wanted me to get in the carriage! He asked where the nearest house was. I started to tell him, but he said I had to show him, and he grabbed me!'

Her own breath shuddering in and out, Althea held her close.

Sarah came up breathless as Puck returned, his tail wagging, hackles still bristled. She dropped to her knees. 'Good dog!'

Althea turned. 'You let him off.'

Sarah nodded. 'He was tugging on the leash, and I knew *we'd* never be fast enough.'

'I *bit* that man!' said Kate with relish. 'And he *yelled*. Then Puck came. He was going to bite him, too.'

Sarah nodded. 'Good idea, but you should probably clean your teeth.'

Hysterical laughter threatened to erupt from Althea. 'Are… are you all right, Kate?'

The child nodded, but she pressed close. 'Why did he want me to go with him?'

Althea could only think of one reason—the same one that had ensured Hugo met the stagecoach when the girls came to London. It wasn't a reason she was going to tell them.

Sarah frowned. 'Maybe he thinks we're rich? Sometimes rich people are abducted, and their families have to pay to get them back.'

Kate looked unconvinced. 'We're not rich though.'

'No.' Sarah straightened up from petting Puck. 'But he might have thought we were. Don't you think, Aunt Althea?'

'It's possible. That does happen.' Surely any kidnapper worth his hire would make sure the victim's family had enough money to make it worthwhile? If only Hugo hadn't returned to London. Today of all days.

She wanted to hurry the girls back to the house, tell him what had happened and know that he'd sort it—she drew a deep breath and set her jaw.

For whatever reason, Hugo had gone back to London. She could sort this out for herself. She'd been sorting things out for herself for the last six years. With varying success, admittedly, but in this instance she knew exactly what to do, and she didn't require a man to do it for her.

Gathering Kate close, she spoke with a confidence she was far from feeling. 'Back to the house now. We'll send a message to the local magistrate with one of the servants.' If someone was prowling the area, looking for girls to sell into brothels, the sooner the authorities knew the better.

The illogic of it niggled at her, though. Luring unprotected girls off a stagecoach was one thing. Evil, yes, but not particularly dangerous for the perpetrators. It happened. People wrung their hands and said how dreadful, but nothing much was done about it. Abducting obviously cared for young ladies, even if they weren't wealthy, was something else entirely. The sort of thing that would have people looking out for these men with blood in their eye. It was stupid.

The magistrate himself called in the early afternoon. He was inclined to dismiss the brothel theory.

Kate, clutching Sarah's hand, had described her would-be abductor, then been sent off for milk and cake while the magistrate conferred with Althea.

'Mistaken identity, Lady Hartleigh.' Sir William Banner steepled his fingers as he frowned over their story. 'As you say, you are not really wealthy enough to attract a serious ransom demand. However, there are families hereabouts who *are*. Some with young girls. We're a little far out of London for the brothels to be looking for prey, I believe. And, as you so rightly say, it's a very risky business for them. I think your niece was mistaken for someone else.'

Althea nodded slowly. 'That does make more sense. You will warn those families, then, Sir William?'

He smiled. 'You may be very sure of it, ma'am.' The magistrate rose. 'In fact, I will call on a couple of the nearer houses on my way home. Thank you for alerting us to this, Lady Hartleigh. Ah, you may be sure I will keep your name and your nieces' names out of this.'

She hadn't even thought of that. The last thing she needed was gossip. 'Thank you, sir. I appreciate it.'

'You are a friend of Miss Browne? I believe she has her nephew staying? I've met Guthrie a time or two. Excellent fellow.'

'Yes. Unfortunately he was obliged to return to London this morning. His partner sent a message requesting his presence. Otherwise he would have been walking with us.' That niggled at her. What were the odds—the very morning Hugo was not with them, someone would attempt to abduct Kate?

'Most unfortunate. I doubt those fellows would have dared try for the child in his presence. I suggest you keep your nieces close, Lady Hartleigh. Perhaps take a male servant when you walk out until Guthrie returns. Good day to you.'

# *Chapter Eighteen*

Hugo stared at Jacob Randall. 'I don't understand. You're saying that Althea Hartleigh's nieces *have* inherited money from old Miss Price? But Montague informed me that, in his words, *wiser council prevailed,* and Miss Price had not asked him to draw up a new will.' He paced around his office. 'You were there, damn it! You heard him.'

Jacob sipped his tea. 'I did. And that's perfectly true as far as it goes. Montague *didn't* draw up a new will for Miss Price. Robert Kentham, of Kentham & Hardbrace, drew it up.'

Hugo didn't know whether to laugh or swear. 'Have you spoken to Kentham?' He knew the man, a few years older than himself. Kentham was likeable and utterly trustworthy. He couldn't quite see the man poaching clients.

'He came in yesterday looking for you. That's why I sent for you. Apparently the lady named you as executor as well as trustee to the girls.'

'Montague must be apoplectic.' He could spare a moment for a little pleasure at that thought.

'He's not happy, no. He showed up yesterday, fortunately after Kentham left, breathing fire and brimstone and demanding your head on a pike, as it were.' Jacob didn't seem unduly perturbed by that. Then again, it wasn't *his* head being demanded. 'According to Kentham, Miss Price asked her neighbour to recommend a reputable lawyer—who turned out to be himself—wrote to him and requested that he call on her without announcing his profession. She sent him a visiting card with her signature scrawled on it. Then, after the will was drawn up, signed and witnessed, she made the neighbour promise to alert Kentham the moment she, er, shuffled off her mortal coil.'

Understanding flashed. 'She didn't trust Montague to draw up the will properly.'

Jacob nodded. 'She said as much to Kentham, although she also thought, even if Montague did draw it up, he might destroy it and pretend it never existed. As you divined, he also acts for the principal beneficiary of the previous will, Wilfrid Price-Babbington. Which—' he pursed his lips in mild disapproval '—does strike one as slightly poor form.'

'So Elinor Price found another lawyer to conduct her business, and let Montague think he'd won.' He had to admire the lady's tactics, even as he mentally cursed the mess this had left him in.

'That's it in a nutshell.' Jacob set his teacup down. 'Those two little girls you were supposed to consign to orphanages are now heiresses. And there's more.'

Suspicion bloomed. 'What more are we talking about now?'

Hugo listened to the *more* and thought that, if Montague ever realised the mess this left him in personally, the idiot might consider the loss of a slice of Price-Babbington's fortune worth it.

He groaned and buried his face in his hands.

Jacob frowned. 'Should have thought you'd be delighted at this outcome.' He rose from his chair. 'Come now, Hugo. There's no real question that you did anything at all dubious. Montague caused this mess by forcing his own client to go around him and use Kentham.' He snorted. 'If the way he bleated to me yesterday, about the folly of allowing women to manage their own money, is any indication of his manner with Miss Price, it's a wonder she left Price-Babbington so much as a groat. *I'd* have disinherited him entirely for the pleasure of knowing how much it would annoy Montague!'

Hugo straightened. 'You don't know the half of it. I've made a complete mull of this. I need to return to Petersham at once.'

Jacob shook his head. 'You can't. Montague and Kentham are both coming here tomorrow. I assured them you would be here.'

Now Hugo did swear.

Jacob raised his brows. 'Rather ripe for you, isn't it?'

Hugo didn't answer, considering the alternatives. He could send a messenger to Althea, but what good would that do? This was something he needed to explain in person. And she was returning to town tomorrow anyway. He'd have to call on her in Soho and tell her what had happened. All of it.

The sky wasn't going to collapse even more completely if he told her in London rather than Petersham.

Assuring Kate that she had been mistaken for someone else, someone wealthy, didn't convince the child that she wanted to go for a walk that afternoon.

*Not without Uncle Hugo.*

Even the suggestion of taking one of the male servants with them failed to get her through the front gate.

'You and Sarah go, Aunt Althea. I… I don't feel very well.'

Shock, Althea thought. The fierce bravado of biting the kidnapper and escaping had worn off, leaving the child scared and insecure. She even looked pale.

'Perhaps a sleep, Kate.' The child might feel better after a rest.

It spoke volumes for how shaken Kate was that she didn't argue against the prospect of an afternoon nap, and allowed herself to be tucked up and the curtains drawn.

She woke screaming from a nightmare.

Aunt Sue urged Althea to stay on with the girls. 'Hugo won't mind at all, dear.'

But Althea held firm. 'I'll take them back to London in the morning as we planned, Aunt Sue.'

Aunt Sue sighed. 'If you think it for the best, dear. I'll keep an ear out and write to you when those men have been caught. It won't take long. They sound most inefficient. And Kate gave Sir William a very good description of the man she bit.' She leaned over and patted Althea's hand. 'Then you can bring them back for another visit later in the year. Come for Christmas, as I suggested. Kate won't feel scared if Hugo is here, and when she knows that the fellow is in Newgate!'

Althea and the girls reached Soho by the middle of the next day. Kate was still pale and inclined to cling. The suggestion that they might send a note around to see if she could visit Miss Barclay for a piano lesson brightened her considerably.

'May I?' Then her face fell. 'But, what if that man—'

'He doesn't know where we live, Kate,' Sarah pointed out.

Still, Kate bit her lip as she unpacked her clothes.

'John and I will both walk around there with you,' Althea assured her. 'And we'll both come to fetch you.'

The note being duly sent, a reply came back that Miss Barclay would be delighted to see Kate for a lesson.

Althea walked back, missing the fresh air of the countryside, and reminded herself that she did like London. That she liked the bustle, even the noise, although perhaps not so much the smells. She wrinkled her nose at the persistent odour of overboiled cabbage, and all the refuse of a large city full of animals and humanity.

Reaching home, she discovered that Sarah had removed herself to the little garden behind the house and was doing a watercolour of a pot of flowers.

'For Uncle Hugo, to thank him for having us to stay,' Sarah explained when Althea walked out to check on her. 'And I thought to do another that he can take out to Aunt Sue when he visits again.'

With time to herself Althea settled down at her desk and started reading herself back into her neglected book. Two days away from the story and she had completely lost the flow. Frowning, she picked up a pencil to make notes on a sheet of paper. Half an hour later the clanging doorbell dragged her away from the belated discovery that Lydia hated seed cake because the seeds became stuck in her teeth. Puck's nose appeared hopefully from under the desk.

Althea's heart leapt. *Hugo?*

She squashed the thought instantly. If he called, he called. If he didn't, she was perfectly content to be as she was.

Blessedly single.

The door opened to admit John. 'Ah, there's—'

'Stand aside, man.' John was hustled aside by a blue-coated man Althea recognised for a Bow Street Runner. Two more followed him.

She rose politely. 'Good afternoon, Officer. Is something amiss? Is this about that business at Petersham? Have they caught the men?'

'Lady Hartleigh?'

His tone chilled her. 'Yes.'

'Lady Hartleigh, you are under arrest for abduction.'

Her jaw dropped. She felt it. Thought, let alone speech, was an impossibility.

'Aunt Althea, what do you—oh. I'm sorry.' Sarah stood in the doorway, sketchbook in hand. 'I didn't realise you had someone with you.'

The Runner turned. 'Miss Sarah Price?'

'Yes.' She gave the Runner a tentative smile. 'How do you do, sir?'

'Very well, thanking you, miss. Where's your sister?'

Sarah looked at Althea. 'Aunt—'

'Officer Derby. Bow Street, miss. We're here to get you back where you belong.'

Althea found her voice. 'What the devil are you talking about? *I* reported the attempted abduction of my younger niece at Petersham yesterday! My nieces belong with me.'

Derby strode forward. 'Not according to the magistrate, they don't.'

'*What?* Which magistrate?'

'You'll have to come along with me.' He glanced at his men. 'Marston, you stay with this young lady. Phipps, search the house for the other girl. The pair of you are to take them back to their guardian when you've found her.'

'Yes, sir.'

One man left the room and the other strode forward to set a hand on Sarah's shoulder.

'Aunt Althea isn't going anywhere with you!' Sarah shook off the officer's hand and ranged herself at Althea's side. 'She's our aunt! You should be looking for the men who tried to abduct my sister!'

'I don't know about that, miss, but I was warned you'd likely not understand.' Derby's voice was not unkind. 'The fact is you and your sister were abducted by your aunt. It's my job to get you back to your home.'

'Abducted by Aunt Althea? What are you talking about?' Sarah's voice rose.

Derby cleared his throat. 'Well, miss, *abducted* means—'

'My niece knows what it means.' Althea pressed a warning hand to Sarah's shoulder. 'She wants to know why you think they were abducted by me. There must be some confusion. I reported the attempted abduction of my younger niece to Sir William Banner in Petersham yesterday. And how dare you set your fellow to search my house?'

Derby's eyes narrowed. 'We've a warrant, ma'am. For your arrest and the recovery of the two girls. And it's not my place to explain your lies to the poor young lady. Her guardian will do all that. Now. You'll come along with me. Let's not have a fuss and make things worse for the lass.'

*Guardian?* Althea's mind started to move again. As far as she knew, there was only one other person who could legally claim to be the girls' guardian.

'Officer, if my cousin—'

Derby stepped forward, reaching for her, and Puck growled furiously, ranging himself in front of his mistress.

Derby stopped dead, his expression grim. 'Call him off, Lady Hartleigh. I like dogs, but I have to do my duty and the little chap deserves better.'

Althea's stomach churned. 'Puck. Sit. Enough.' She turned to Sarah. 'Hold his collar.'

'You aren't going with them?' Sarah clutched at Althea's hand, even as she bent to grip the dog's collar.

What choice did she have? She patted Sarah's hand. 'I'll have to.' She found a smile. 'Don't worry. I'll be back before you know it.'

'It must be a mistake! A...a silly joke someone is playing! No one else wanted us. Not even Cousin Wilfrid!'

The child's voice shook, ripping at Althea's assumed calm, but the mention of Wilfrid hardened her fear into resolve. 'And the easiest way to sort all this out will be for me to go with this officer and see what's what.' She turned to Derby. 'If you would permit me to walk out of the room without laying hands on me, that will ensure my niece keeps control of my dog. Or rather...' She turned to John. 'If you would be so kind as to carry that message...' She hesitated. The last thing she wanted to do was give away Kate's whereabouts. 'To Lady Martin. Take the dog with you, please.'

The flicker of John's eyelids suggested that he understood completely. 'Aye, ma'am. I'll do that.' He took Puck's leash from its hook and walked over to him, bending to attach it. He looked up. 'Should I take him to Mr Guthrie for safekeeping, ma'am?'

Her breath caught. 'Thank you. I can trust him to care for a dog.' Please God, let Hugo still be in London. 'Go now.'

Before the other officer came back without Kate.

Derby frowned. 'I don't know that's—'

'You have a warrant for me, sir. Not my servants. And certainly not for my dog.'

Derby backed down, scowling, and John left the room with a reluctant Puck. A moment later Althea heard the front door bang. She breathed a little more easily. Kate was safe. For now.

She turned to Sarah, bent close. 'Will you trust me?'

Sarah nodded. 'Kate?' she breathed.

'You have no idea where she is. Be brave.' She straightened up and spoke louder. 'I assume Cousin Wilfrid has thought the better of his decision not to act as guardian to you and Kate.' She caught the telltale flicker in Derby's expression. 'A shame he didn't think to write and tell me.'

Sarah's face turned even more mutinous. 'Then you could have written back that we don't want to live with *him*.'

Phipps strode back into the room. 'Sir, there's no sign of the other child. Housemaid and the cook said they had no idea where she might be.'

Althea caught her breath. Mrs Cable and Milly were lying. Deliberately lying for her. They knew exactly where Kate was.

Derby glared at Althea. 'Where is she?'

Althea lifted her chin, ignoring the fear twisting sick and cold in her belly. 'I'll discuss that with a magistrate. Shouldn't you get on with arresting me?'

Please God, she wasn't about to spend the night in Newgate. And please, please God, Hugo would be able to sort this out. Clearly Wilfrid had decided that he wanted the girls. Perhaps there had been gossip about his behaviour in throwing them out, but why go about it this way?

Derby's jaw hardened. 'Right. Phipps, Marston, you take the young lady we do have back to Mr Price-Babbington. I'll deliver our fine lady to Bow Street.'

Hugo strode into Bow Street Magistrates' Court late in the afternoon, his mind ice cold. He had a suspicion he knew exactly what was going on, and cursed himself for not seeing this possibility as soon as he'd known that Montague had been outfoxed by Elinor Price. If he'd sent a message out to Petersham explaining the situation, Althea would have remained there rather than returning to an ambush. He shoved that aside. What mattered now was getting her released.

*Please God, he wasn't going to find her in a cell!*

When he'd reached Soho Square to inform Althea that Elinor Price had died, he'd found the cook and housemaid in a state of panic.

*'Just marched her off, sir,'* Milly had sniffled. *'And they took Miss Sarah. Said she'd been abducted by the mistress!'*

*'My lady foxed them, though. Good an' proper.'* Mrs Cable had said it with pride leaking through the fear. *'Little Miss Kate was gone for her music lesson. My lady refused to say where she was, an' we played dumb. John was already gone to find you.'*

Hugo thought he knew what had happened. Price-Babbington, realising his mistake in throwing the girls out, had brought abduction charges against Althea to cover his own callousness. Hugo clenched his fists. He had to remind himself that the law was his best weapon, and he had to wield it with logic, not emotion.

At the magistrate's, at this hour, there was only a clerk still at his desk to raise his head as Hugo stalked in, Puck beside him. Upon reaching his chambers after leaving Soho, he'd found John and the dog waiting in his office. He had tried to leave Puck with his own office clerk, but Puck had howled piteously, scrabbling to follow him. In the end he'd given in and taken the dog with him.

Now the court clerk stared at the dog, then raised his eyes to Hugo's face. 'May I help you, sir?'

'I am looking for Lady Hartleigh. I hope—' he paused for effect '—I hope, as will her good friends, the Earl and Countess of Rutherford, and Lord and Lady Martin Lacy, that she is being looked after, and that she has not been subjected to any distress.' That was a large assumption, as the earl and countess were away in the country. Lady Martin, though—or perhaps it was Miss Selbourne, as she had been in the shop—had immediately sent a note to her husband when Hugo had gone to the bookshop to ask her where he might find Lacy.

To do the clerk credit, he looked as though titled gentlemen and their ladies were tossed about so regularly as to be inconsequential. In fact, he scowled. 'The lady is here, sir. I don't know that I have any authority to allow you to see her, though.'

Hugo kept his expression inscrutable. 'I will see her immediately, if you please. And Birnie, if he is here.' He had a nodding acquaintance with Sir Richard Birnie, the Chief Magistrate.

The scowl deepened. 'And who might you be, sir?'

'Guthrie, of Guthrie and Randall.' He gave the address in Lincoln's Inn. 'Lady Hartleigh is my client.'

The clerk nodded slowly. 'Right. Sir Richard's not here, sir. 'Twas on the authority of one of the other magistrates that we put the lady in his office with a Runner on the door. Being as how there was some concern that the cells might not be the best place.'

Inside him the knot of fear unclenched itself. *Thank God.* 'Very wise.'

'But I've no authority to allow the prisoner—'

'The *what*?' Hugo leaned forward, resting clenched fists on the desk. 'Let me be very clear, my good man. Arresting Lady Hartleigh was a mistake of some magnitude. I advise you not to compound it.'

The clerk swallowed. 'I'll fetch Mr Wilcox, the magistrate on duty. He'll know what should be done.'

Hugo nodded benignly. 'An excellent idea. But first you will conduct me to Lady Hartleigh.'

For a moment the air hummed with the clash of wills.

Hugo smiled. 'Come, my good man. Do you imagine that I am about to slip Lady Hartleigh out from under your nose? It can do no possible harm for me to see her, and may do those in charge of this institution a great deal of good with her friends.'

'Ah, yes, sir.' He rallied. 'Er, the dog—'

'Stays with me.'

Puck walked sedately at heel until they reached the door of Sir Richard Birnie's office. At which point, ignoring the Runner guarding the door, he lunged forward, snuffling and scrabbling at the door.

The Runner blinked at Puck, then looked at the clerk. 'Mr Sutherland?'

'Yes, yes.' Sutherland waved. 'Officer Derby, this is Lady Hartleigh's solicitor. I have said he may wait with the lady while I fetch Mr Wilcox.'

The Runner frowned. 'You're not armed, I hope, sir?'

Hugo snorted. 'Hardly. Nor is the dog. Don't worry. My intentions are to remain law abiding.'

*As long as possible.*

The Runner opened the door and Puck shot forward, barking, ripping his leash from Hugo's grasp.

# Chapter Nineteen

Althea shifted position in the chair yet again. It was not at all a comfortable chair, but there was a limit to how many times one could circumnavigate a magistrate's office. There was also a limit to how long one could sit still with nothing to do. A lengthy inspection had convinced her that the many books on the shelves, while doubtless interesting to a magistrate, were not at all the sort of thing she could contemplate poring over.

She froze at the faint commotion outside the door. Male voices, and…scratching? For the past three hours she had slowly sunk into herself, wondering exactly when someone would decide that she was a great deal less trouble in a cell, with whatever other prisoners they happened to have on hand.

Or in Newgate itself. Perhaps she could put in a plea for the Fleet if they decided she was destined for an actual prison.

She had pinned all her hopes on dealing directly with Sir Richard Birnie, with whom she had a very slight acquaintance, and persuading him to allow her to go home. Mr Wilcox, a very junior magistrate, had declined to acquiesce in this without Sir Richard's authority. Much against the advice of the office clerk and Timms, Wilcox had decided that she would remain in this office for the time being. No doubt that was a great deal better than a cell, but—

The door opened. Perhaps someone had made a decision—she stiffened her rapidly wilting spine and prepared to argue in favour of the less dangerous Fleet Prison.

Barking wildly, Puck hurled himself across the room and onto her lap, nearly oversetting the chair and herself with it. Dazed, Althea clutched the dog, submitting to having her face thoroughly licked, hearing the frantic whines. It was a moment before she managed to look past the dog and see who had followed him into the room.

*Hugo.*

Her throat closed on a choking lump, and she realised in horror that she was seeing him through a mist of tears. She would *not* cry. Not in front of Hugo, and not in front of the Runner who had arrested her, or the clerk who had wanted to lock her in a cell.

'You will accord us a few moments privacy, gentlemen.'

Had she ever heard Hugo speak with that air of cool command? As though he not only expected to be heeded, but the notion of not being obeyed wasn't to be considered.

It worked. Derby and the clerk frowned, but the door closed behind Hugo.

He stood there for a moment, and she struggled for words. A simple thank you. Anything.

'I—' Her throat closed, and a lump rose up. She dragged a breath past it to try again. But Hugo crossed the room, hauled her up out of the chair and had her in his arms in the space of that despicably shaky breath.

That was all it took. Her control broke and she wept. Great, racking sobs that horrified her even as the fear ebbed. Whatever happened now, even a prison cell, she wasn't alone. And he didn't tell her not to cry, but held her close, stroked her back and somehow lent her his own strength.

Slowly the sobs eased—she sniffled, and found a very large handkerchief pushed into her hand.

'It's perfectly clean,' he assured her.

She managed a watery laugh. Of course it was. She wiped her eyes and blew her nose. She became aware of Puck, standing on his hind legs, pawing at her gown, whining. 'It's all right, boy. Everything's all right now.'

Hugo cleared his throat. 'A slight exaggeration. John told me the charge was abduction. Of Kate and Sarah.'

She nodded. 'Yes. I don't understand. The only person who could have brought a charge of abduction is Cousin Wilfrid, but why would he bother? And the girls aren't heiresses, which is what the Runner said. Wilfrid of all people—'

'I'm afraid they are.'

'What? That's what the Runners said, but—'

The rest was smothered against his chest as he pulled her back into his arms. 'I'm sorry. This is my fault.'

'Your fault?' She looked up at him. 'Were you supposed to anticipate that Wilfrid would slip his moorings?'

He let out a frustrated breath. 'Yes. I suspected weeks—months ago that the girls were heiresses, but I said nothing to you. I couldn't. And then the day before I came out to Petersham I was told, point-blank, that they weren't, so—'

'What are you talking about? You're not making sense.'

He wasn't, either. Best to give her the pertinent information straight. 'Your great-aunt changed her will.'

'*Elinor*?'

He raked a hand through his hair. 'Yes. Your great-aunt, Miss Price—'

'Great-Aunt Elinor? She's died?'

'Yes. She called on me in the office. Not long after she called on you. Before she died. Asked a number of very nosy questions—'

'A talent of hers.'

He smiled briefly. 'Most of which I declined to answer, because they encompassed your private affairs. But I confirmed for her that the girls were with you because their father had left them penniless, and Price-Babbington had given instructions for them to be entered in orphanages.'

Althea frowned. 'There was no secret about that.'

'No. She'd gathered that from various other sources, but she wanted confirmation from me.'

'I don't see why that makes you think—'

'Althea, love, she had her own solicitor there.'

He told her the rest. Montague's subsequent visit, and the contents of the message that had brought him tearing back to London from Petersham. 'I'm sorry, Althea. I should have brought the three of you with me, or at the very least told you what was afoot, but I thought there must be some mistake.'

Althea's stomach turned over. 'Wilfrid must know.' She shut her eyes. Two penniless orphans were one thing. Two heiresses were quite something else. And he'd let them slip through his fingers.

Hugo spoke again. 'This is going to make them Wards of the Chancery Court. I'm sorry. I should have said something.'

She shook her head. 'Never mind that. This explains the abduction attempt.'

'*Abduction*?' He gripped her shoulders. 'What happened?'

She told him.

He swore. 'Price-Babbington has overreached himself with this. I know they removed Sarah, but John said Kate wasn't home, and Mrs Cable and Milly told me they lied—told the Runners they didn't know where she was.'

Althea bit her lip. 'I didn't tell them to say that, but she's only a baby. Surely—'

'Sweetheart, if we're to have the least chance of winning this, and of avoiding spending the night in a cell together—'

'They haven't arrested *you*, have they?'

'No, but if you think I'd let you spend the night in a cell by yourself, then you don't know me at all.' He gave her a gentle shake. 'Kate. We're going to have to produce her.'

She understood what he was saying, but—

'Abduction, Althea. It's serious. Especially when heiresses are involved, depending on how Birnie looks at it. I think if we promise to bring Kate tomorrow, then I can have you released into my custody. It shows good faith.'

Her stomach roiled. 'And you think Wilfrid will show good faith?'

He snorted. 'Not willingly. But I think we can force his hand. And if we can show that he hasn't acted in good faith? Show that he did not act in the girls' best interests? The magistrate won't like that. As for trying to snatch Kate at Petersham, if that's what it was about, he's sunk.'

'Will the magistrate care?'

'Yes, I think he will. I need to consult my law books for the precise wording, but a guardian must act in the best interests of his ward. And there's something else. Sarah is nearly fourteen. She is old enough for the court to give consideration to what she says. She can request a change of guardian.'

'But Wilfrid wouldn't bring her with him.' Althea knew that. He considered women, let alone girls, flibberty creatures, not to be permitted within spitting distance of any serious *men's* business, let alone a court of law.

Hugo's smile was close to a smirk. 'If the court requests that he bring her and he doesn't, then he is not merely showing bad faith, he'll be disobeying a court order. His solicitor, even an idiot like Montague, will advise against that.'

Her stomach twisted. 'But how *can* the court make that request? Sir Richard isn't even here. He wouldn't know about—'

He smiled. 'You're friendly with an influential countess. Not to mention Lord Martin Lacy. You changed your own will and set up trusts for the girls. You've been seeing to their education. You've demonstrated yourself to be a responsible guardian. I think we can count on Birnie being fully informed as to those particulars before he reaches for his after-dinner port this evening. I've sent a message to Lacy about the importance of having both girls present. Lady Martin assured me that he would run Birnie to ground for us and see to it.'

It took another half-hour before the magistrate on duty agreed to release Althea into Hugo's custody. Finally it was done, and he could escort her out onto Bow Street, Althea's hand on his arm and Puck at their heels.

Althea took a deep, shaky breath. 'I know I was lucky—no, privileged, because most other females would have been tossed into a cell, but I thought—'

He pressed his hand to hers as she broke off. 'Don't. You're safe now. Come. We'll find a cab and get you home.'

If he thought about Althea in a prison cell, he'd go insane. He couldn't imagine what it had been like for her.

* * *

The clatter of traffic between Bow Street and Soho was hideous, but Althea was only vaguely aware of it. The din was somewhere *out there*, beyond the circle of safety within the hackney cab, the reassurance of Hugo's large hand clasping hers.

The conditions of her release into his custody were stringent. He must remain with her at all times. She must not so much as step outside her house without his escort. If she defaulted, or failed to present herself at Bow Street with Kate at ten o'clock the following morning, she would be arrested when found and placed in prison. As would Hugo.

Desperate to control her panic, she focused on the practical. They had to collect poor Kate. The child would be frantic by now. What would Psyché Barclay have told her? That her aunt had been arrested for abducting her? That her sister had been taken? She pushed all that down.

'Kate may share my chamber tonight,' she said carefully. 'That leaves the girls' room free for you to use.'

He nodded. 'Thank you. If you permit, I will send John to collect some items from my lodgings.'

'Of course.'

At the Barclay house a servant informed them that the mistress was visiting Miss Selbourne's bookshop. Althea swallowed hard. She wanted nothing more than to get off the street, be somewhere private that she could fall to pieces. She took a breath. She could walk back down Compton Street to Kit Selbourne's shop. The strength of Hugo's arm under her hand, the sheer calm of his presence, his quiet voice as he thanked the servant, were more comfort than she could have expressed. She smiled her own thanks at Psyché Barclay's servant and accompanied Hugo blindly back down the street.

Kate was safe. She had to concentrate on that, on Hugo's steady conviction that they could get Sarah back. If they failed, if she lost Kate as well—

She couldn't think like that. She had to remain strong, steady, the sort of woman who could care for two orphaned girls. Her stomach roiled. Wilfrid would use every means at his disposal to discredit her. Her less than virtuous past, the fact that it looked as though she had lost her own fortune.

The shop was already shuttered for the evening, but Kit opened the door to let them in.

'She's here. Quite safe but very upset. I'll let her know you've arrived. We persuaded her to stay upstairs with my boys until you did.'

Althea gripped her hands. 'Thank you. I… Thank you.'

Kit squeezed Althea's hands. 'You're very welcome. Martin has gone to do what he can to ensure Birnie knows what's going on. He's also going to seek out someone from the Chancery Court, a school friend's father. Come. Sit down. You must be exhausted.' She beckoned to Psyché Barclay, who stood in the archway that led through to the circulating library. 'Psyché, sit Althea down and pour her a glass of wine.' She smiled at Hugo. 'And you. Thank you for bringing her back.'

She left them and her swift footsteps sounded on the stairs.

Psyché hugged Althea, guiding her through to the library. 'We brought her here because it seemed a little safer. And I'm afraid we sneaked her around through the back alleys. Your servants all knew where she was and, really, you couldn't have blamed them if they'd let it out when threatened with arrest. She told us some fellow tried to abduct her out at Petersham.'

Althea was nearly beyond words. 'Thank you. Yes. We…we think my cousin, the one who kicked them out, was behind that.' She gripped Psyché's hand. 'Thank you. More than I can say.'

Psyché shook her head. 'It was nothing. We're having supper here, all of us, to help you work out how to present your case tomorrow. Although,' she nodded at Hugo, 'you already have Mr Guthrie on hand.'

Scrambling feet sounded on the stairs, and a moment later Kate shot through the archway and hurled herself at Althea.

'You escaped!'

Althea's arms closed tightly around her as the child wept. 'Escaped?'

Psyché winced. 'We told her the truth. Anything else seemed pointless. One of Kit's boys promised her that Mr Guthrie would break her out of prison if necessary and that his father would help.' She gave Hugo an apologetic look. 'He's only fifteen. They've been up there working out the details with Kate.'

Althea gave a choking laugh as she guided Kate to the settee. Slowly she became aware that Hugo was sitting at Kate's other side, gently stroking her back. Her eyes burned, but she forced the tears back. Hugo's kindness threatened to undo her completely.

'Not quite an escape, Kate, love. I did a great deal of talking, as solicitors are wont to do, and persuaded a magistrate that he could either release your aunt into my custody or listen to me talk all night.'

He glanced up at Psyché. 'Do you happen to know where Lady Hartleigh's manservant is, ma'am? I need to send him to my lodgings.'

'He's here, Mr Guthrie, but if you require a change of clothes or a nightshirt, my husband said you were very welcome to borrow what you needed.'

He blinked. 'How very kind. Unfortunately I also need to consult my copy of *Blackstone's Commentaries on the Laws of England*.'

'I have a copy upstairs.' Miss Selbourne came through the archway. 'I'll take you up and we can bring them down if you wish.'

'*You* have a copy?'

Psyché gave a snort of a laughter as she poured another glass of wine. 'If it has a leather binding and pages in between, the odds are high that Kit has a copy somewhere.'

Miss Selbourne picked up a candle. 'I only wish! Come up and fetch the volume you need, Mr Guthrie.'

Hugo followed Kit upstairs into what he supposed was a dining parlour overlooking the street, wholly lined with bookshelves. He wondered if he could somehow invite himself back some time to explore this paradise properly. And why hadn't he ever thought of lining a dining parlour with bookshelves?

Unerringly, she went to a shelf by the window. 'Here we are. Which volume? I would assume the first, since it deals with the rights of persons, but—'

He stared in bemusement. It was one thing to have the books on her shelves, but for a female to be familiar with the contents of *Blackstone's Commentaries* was unusual to say the least. 'You are absolutely correct, Miss—' He broke off, still unsure how to address her.

She laughed, taking out the volume. 'Miss Selbourne is appropriate. If I am out somewhere official with Lord Martin I become Lady Martin, but here at home, or in the shop, I am Miss Selbourne for the most part.'

He took the volume she passed him. 'Is that confusing?'

'To me, no. Nor to Lord Martin. We know who I am.' Her smile was challenge incarnate. 'The sort of woman who knows her way around Blackstone's.'

Downstairs in the library Althea watched from the sofa, Kate snuggled against her, as Hugo opened the volume on the table, checking the table of contents.

'Won't the magistrates already know all this?' she asked.

He glanced up, flipping through the book. 'They do of course.' Here it was. *Chapter the Seventeenth: of Guardian and Ward.* 'But possession is involved here—your unspeakable cousin has Sarah—and there is the inescapable fact of your brother's will. We need to make our case, and make it in law. I want to be quite sure I have it all at my fingertips.'

He took a careful breath. What had Kit Selbourne said?

*'The sort of woman who knows her way around Blackstone's.'*

Althea was the sort of woman who could learn to find her way around Blackstone's. A woman with a spine of tempered steel, and a mind that thought for itself.

'Come and look.' He returned his attention to the page, as Althea—and Kate, clinging to her hand—joined him.

'Why does Cousin Wilfrid have Sarah?' Kate demanded. 'He didn't want us. I heard him say so.'

Hugo looked up sharply. 'Did you, sweetheart?'

Althea looked down at her. 'You never said anything about that.'

Kate wriggled closer. 'I didn't want to think about him at all.'

'What exactly did he say, Kate?' Hugo pulled a paper towards him, picked up a pencil. The child had a musician's memory—he'd heard her recite a half-heard conversation before.

'That he wasn't going to be saddled with the cost of two blasted little pauper bitches, and he wouldn't have tainted goods in his house corrupting his sons.'

'He said that in front of you?' Althea's voice remained even, but Hugo heard the bite of fury underneath. It found an answer in the fury simmering under his own outward calm.

Kate hung her head. 'Not exactly. I was hungry, so I'd gone downstairs to the kitchen to ask Mrs Minchin for something to eat. He was saying it to Cousin Mary—you know...his wife—in the parlour when I was on my way back, but the door was open a little bit and I heard him. Then he said he'd write to *"Frederick's lawyer fellow"*—that was you I think, Mr Guthrie—and tell him we'd be on the stagecoach the next week. He was washing his hands of us because there was little enough money as it was until the old lady died.'

Hugo met Althea's gaze. 'And he did write to me, and I met you.'

'Yes. And we weren't so scared any more.' Even with her tear-blotched cheeks, Kate gave him a trusting smile.

They must have been terrified, but he doubted even Sarah had fully understood the dangers that had awaited two young girls stepping off that stagecoach. Even now he wondered what might have happened to them had Wilfrid's letter gone astray. The girls' youth would not have saved them. Quite the opposite.

He pushed the pencil and paper towards the child. 'Write it down, Kate.'

She stared at him. 'Write what down?'

'What you just told us. And anything else you can remember that Wilfrid Price-Babbington said, either to you or about you.' Even if he didn't use it in tomorrow's hearing, it gave Kate something to do. Also, it might bring up a bit more evidence he could present to the magistrate.

'Even the rude words?'

He inclined his head, suppressing a grin. 'Certainly the rude words. Never tamper with the text in a legal document, sweetheart.'

She looked up at him very seriously. 'Why not?'

'Because you might change the meaning of what was said. It's important that the magistrate tomorrow knows *exactly* what your cousin said.' And what he'd meant.

'It doesn't make him sound like a very nice person, though.'

Hugo let the smile come. 'No. It doesn't, does it?'

*Pauper bitches.* It was an admission that Wilfrid Price-Babbington hadn't given a damn about the girls until they inherited money.

As the child settled into a chair and began to write, frowning in concentration, Hugo turned his attention back to *Blackstone's.*

He read slowly down the page, fiercely aware of Althea at his side, scanning the text with him.

'There. Is this what you need?' She looked up, her finger paused on the line that read: *at fourteen is at years of legal discretion, and may choose a guardian.*

Close, so close to him, her light scent enveloping him as it had every night at Petersham for nearly a week. It was oddly soothing for a change—it meant she was here, safe with him, not in prison. 'That's part of it. When does Sarah turn fourteen precisely?'

Althea bit her lip. 'Next month. Will it make a difference that she isn't quite fourteen yet?'

'I doubt it.' He reached out, laid his hand over hers and felt the slight tremor. 'We lawyers are very good at holding things up and stringing things out.'

She raised those elegant brows, even as her hand turned under his and clung. 'To everything there is a season, and a time for every purpose?'

He smiled. 'Quite so.' Hearing the airy sarcasm back in her voice lifted his heart, just as her fingers, warm and delicate in his, made it beat the faster. He pushed his mind back to *Blackstone's*. 'And there's more in here that I can use. Price-Babbington has made a mull of this.'

Kit Selbourne spoke. 'You may take those volumes along with you tomorrow, if you wish, Mr Guthrie.'

He looked up. It would help—

'There's no need.' Althea smiled at Kit. 'Thank you, though. Sir Richard Birnie has a set in his office.'

Hugo blinked. 'I suppose he would, but—you're sure?'

She shrugged. 'There wasn't a great deal to do in that office *except* look at the bookshelves. None of it looked frightfully inviting, but I do remember the name Blackstone. That was our coachman's name when I was a child.'

# *Chapter Twenty*

Hugo listened to the little house creak and settle into comfortable darkness around him. Sleep held off, out of reach in the shadows. The room, even in darkness, seemed full of the girls, brimming with their energy—a discarded ribbon on the dresser, along with several pretty crystal bottles. They didn't look new, but he knew they hadn't had them when they stayed with him, so Althea must have found them. Had they been hers? Something treasured that she had given the girls to help them feel at home? Loved? Secure?

He lay back with a sigh. Althea loved those girls. What if he couldn't persuade the courts that she was the right guardian for them? Her past and reputation wasn't going to help, and he had no doubt that Price-Babbington wouldn't hesitate to use it. And even if he had the time and means to dig up some scurrilous affair in the man's life, it was always different for men.

Men were expected to have affairs. Oh, there might be a little tut-tutting over it, but no one was going to declare a man an unfit guardian because he'd bedded a dozen women not his wife—even if he'd been married at the time. Whereas Althea, from all he understood, had indulged in a couple of reasonably discreet affairs once she'd been widowed.

He laced his fingers behind his head, reviewing his strategy for tomorrow's meeting at Bow Street. It was vital to show that Wilfrid was an unfit guardian because of the way he had treated the girls. Casting them out, not caring where they ended up, He had not acted in their best interests, and that was a basic tenet of guardianship. He had only taken an interest once they had become heiresses.

His mind caught on that. He didn't know the exact terms of Elinor Price's will. Robert Kentham had explained the gist, and given him a copy, of course, but he'd left it on his desk when he'd gone to call on Althea.

Who was the next heir if something happened to the girls? He could assume that if one of the girls died the other would inherit her sister's share. But what if something happened to both of them? The courts ensured that children left in ward were cared for by someone who could not inherit. Kentham would have seen to that, surely. If not, then the court would have no choice but to name another guardian.

Hugo let out a breath. He knew, as surely as he knew the colour of her eyes, the way her mouth curled into that delicious, wicked smile, what choice Althea would make if she could. She would refuse the bequest rather than lose the girls.

Staring into the darkness, Hugo called down every curse he could think of on the head of Frederick Price for leaving his daughters in such a mess.

Althea lay awake, unable to sleep with the lamp burning. But Kate, poor little Kate, even curled up in the same bed, with Puck snuggled against her, had begged for the light. Even with the lamp it had taken a long time and several stories for the child to doze off, her eyes red and swollen with tears.

She had heard Hugo come up to bed long after she had taken Kate upstairs. There had been a comfort hearing him move around the girls' room, hearing the bed creak under his weight. Before the girls came, she had learned to enjoy living alone, to savour her independence. Now she dreaded tomorrow, and the likelihood that Wilfrid would take Kate and Sarah from her.

Long ago she had decided that regrets were a waste of energy. You might come to the conclusion that something or other had been a colossal mistake. You acknowledged that and put it aside. If your mistake had hurt someone else, you tried to make amends. You did not waste time beating your breast over it. Or at least she didn't. Much. Sometimes, though, you couldn't help it.

This was one of those times.

Sitting up against her pillows in the lamplight, she wished bitterly that she had not indulged in those affairs. Not because she thought that she'd been wrong to do so. Those affairs had harmed no one, and after the cold mockery of her marriage she had wanted *something*. She had been a widow, for God's sake. Neither gentlemen involved had been married at the time. No one would have cared a finger-snap, if her idiot brother had not wanted to cover up his own misdoings by painting *her* as a feckless, irresponsible slut.

By having those affairs she had handed him all the ammunition he could have wanted. Society always enjoyed a good scandal and she had provided one. Ironic that the one person who might have resented her, Meg Rutherford, had become a close friend.

And Meg would have used her influence to facilitate her return to the *ton*.

*'Don't, Meg. And for heaven's sake, don't allow Rutherford to do so. Even if I wanted it, I can't afford it. If I am careful I have enough to live simply.'*

*'You truly don't want to come back?'*

*'Truly.'*

*'What about the truth? Doesn't that matter?'*

She had smiled. Meg was still young and naïve enough to believe that truth would always out.

*'Even that is no longer important. You know the truth. Rutherford knows. And a few others. People I am fond of. Who are fond of me. Why should I care what the rest think?'*

And she no longer had the energy to fight back.

Meg had scowled. *'Because lies can always come back to bite you.'*

Althea sighed. Perhaps Meg had not been so naïve, and she should have fought back against Frederick's lies. Instead she had removed herself from society, and the lies he had told to protect himself, and made a new life. She had found peace, contentment and just lately joy. But now those lies had come back to sink their teeth into everything that mattered, and tear it to pieces.

Beside her Kate tossed, muttered, her voice rising in panic.

'*Shh*, dearest.' She stroked the soft hair. 'It's a dream. Only a dream. You're safe.' A lie, but what else could she say?

But the nightmare held Kate fast as she thrashed, crying out. On the child's other side Puck sat up, pawed at her shoulder, whining.

Kate came awake on a scream—*'Sarah!'*—as the door flew open.

For a moment Althea thought the child was not quite awake, her eyes dazed and confused as she struggled against the bedclothes. Then her arms closed around the dog, now in her lap, and she folded over him, weeping.

That Hugo was now on the bed, holding Kate as she wept, seemed the most natural thing in the world.

'There now, Katie, love. Was it your old dream? It's gone now. You're safe.'

His voice, low, tender, made Kate sob even harder. 'It's not gone. It's worse. Because I did lose Sarah. She's gone! I ran and ran, but it was dark and I couldn't find her.'

Althea's arms tightened on the sobbing child. 'Only for now, Kate. We'll get her back. I promise you.'

Oh, God! What had she said? That was a promise she shouldn't make, couldn't be sure of keeping.

But between them the child's shuddering sobs eased.

On Kate's other side Hugo spoke. 'Listen, sweetheart. How old is Sarah?'

'Th...thirteen.'

'There you are.' He bent, pressed a kiss to Kate's temple. 'Nearly fourteen. And at fourteen she can choose her own guardian. It says so right in the law books. Do you really think she would choose your cousin Wilfrid?'

'No. But I'm not even *nearly* nearly fourteen. He might take me!'

Hugo's grim eyes met Althea's over Kate's head. 'Not once

I've finished with him, he won't.' Cold determination burned in his voice and eyes.

'Can you stay here with us? Like you used to?'

*Like you used to?*

Althea *felt* Hugo stiffen, knew exactly what he was thinking, heard the indrawn breath.

'Would you feel safer if he did, Kate?' She kept her voice casual.

'Yes. He used to tell me a story after.'

'That seems like a very proper thing to follow a bad dream.' Althea smiled at Hugo's slightly stunned, questioning gaze. 'Now, what story shall we hear from Mr Guthrie?'

By the time Hugo had wound his way through the tale of *Beauty and the Beast*, Kate was sound asleep between them. Althea had an arm around the sleeping child. Her head rested on his shoulder, her arm wedged against his side, and Kate herself was half on top of him. He suspected Althea was more than half-asleep, too.

So much for his skill as a storyteller. Damned if he knew how he was supposed to extricate himself, and he didn't mean from the bed. The dog at least had removed himself to the foot of the bed and lay on his back, snoring.

'She's had that dream before?' Althea murmured.

Not asleep then, although her head didn't move.

'Yes. I should have told you. She had it several times in the first week they stayed with me. After that—'

'She must have felt safe.' Althea sat up a little, but left her arm where it was. 'I don't think she's had it here before. What was it?'

Rage burned in his throat, but he kept his voice soft. 'She dreams that they get lost when they leave the stagecoach. It's very dark. At first they're together, but she becomes separated from Sarah in the darkness.'

'And when you heard her, you went in to them and comforted her.'

He squirmed. 'It's no more than anyone would do.'

A soft snort. 'Really? Can you see my cousin Wilfrid comforting a terrified child? Telling her a fairy tale to ease her back to sleep?'

He had no answer for that. 'Do you think we can shift her now? I… I ought not to be here.' No matter that it felt as though he were precisely where he ought to be, they had enough trouble without complicating it any further.

They tried. But when Hugo attempted to move the sleeping child, she stirred, muttering distressfully.

Althea let out a breath. 'I'll go and sleep in the other room. You stay here.'

She started to ease her arm free, and Kate cried out.

They stared at each other over the sleeping child.

'I think,' he said carefully, 'that we are sleeping together. Again.'

The movement of her throat as she swallowed did impossible things to his heart.

'Apparently so.' A moment's silence. 'Interesting pair of chaperons we've acquired.'

He smothered the escaping crack of laughter. 'Um, your head.'

Her eyes narrowed to glints of green. 'My head? Is something wrong with it?'

'What?' *Oh, Lord!* 'No. Not at all. It felt rather nice, er, where it was.' And his tongue felt as though it had tied itself in a Gordian knot, along with his heart.

'Where it was.'

He held his breath, unsure if he were about to be annihilated. Then, miracle of miracles…

'Like this?'

Her head rested on his shoulder again and the entire world seemed right and good.

'Yes. Yes, exactly like that.' The slightly astringent fragrance of her hair surrounded him. Chamomile. His mother had planted a chamomile lawn when he was a small boy. He'd loved to lie on it reading on hot summer afternoons. Warily, he lowered his cheek to those silken tresses, relaxed when she shifted closer.

'This is nice,' she murmured. 'Even without your new watch.'

* * *

Walking into the Bow Street Magistrates' Court the following morning, Althea half wished she'd woken up with a crick in her neck so that she could at least have something to regret about the night before. Had she lost her mind permitting that simple, unspoken tenderness between them? What if one of her servants had come in?

Fortunately Kate, ever an early riser, had stirred before the servants came up. Althea had awoken, her head still on Hugo's shoulder, to a very serious conversation between Hugo and Kate about the merits of a boiled egg and toast soldiers versus a poached egg on a slice of toast.

Now, with Kate clutching her hand as they walked into Bow Street, she wondered how it was that a man should be as unspeakably appealing discussing eggs as he was telling fairytales. He walked beside Kate now, holding her other hand, a quiet, protective presence.

'Will Sarah really be here?'

Althea hesitated.

Hugo said calmly. 'Perhaps not yet. We are a little early. But we know your cousin Wilfrid received the message that he must bring her this morning.'

Kate nodded solemnly. 'Because Lord Martin said so.'

Lord Martin had called during the consumption of toast soldiers and boiled eggs to say that, in addition to finding Sir Richard Birnie, he had spoken to a friend's father the previous evening.

*'Found him in the club after speaking to Birnie. Whittenstall is a decent chap, and he's appointed to the Chancery Court.'*

According to Lord Martin, Whittenstall had been more than a little annoyed that Bow Street had become involved in a case of wardship, which was within the purview of the Chancery Court.

*'Whittenstall has agreed to go along to Bow Street this morning to sort things out. He also agreed that both girls should be present, but particularly Sarah, and sent a note to Sir Richard about it.'*

Althea plastered a calm smile to her face and lifted her chin.

They had done everything that could possibly be done to prepare for this meeting. Please God, it would be enough.

Sir Richard was seated behind his desk and rose as they entered. He was not alone.

Sarah leapt to her feet from her place beside Wilfrid and hurled herself at them.

'Sarah!' Kate flung herself into her sister's arms, hugging her. 'You're safe!'

'Really! What an extraordinary thing for the child to say!' Wilfrid remained seated. 'I cannot imagine what you have been filling their ears with, Cousin Althea.'

Althea favoured him with a sweet smile. 'It was rather the other way around, Wilfrid. Until the girls turned up on my doorstep, I hadn't given you a thought in years. I believe you are acquainted with my solicitor, Mr Guthrie?'

Price-Babbington stared at Hugo, his eyes widening. 'I…er…yes. We have…ah…corresponded.' Turning to Sarah, he scowled. 'Kindly do not behave like a hoyden in here. Sit down, if you please, and conduct yourself as befits a young lady.'

Sir Richard spoke coolly. 'If this is for my benefit, Price-Babbington, I saw nothing untoward in Miss Price's behaviour. Only a very proper sisterly affection.'

Sarah bestowed a smile on the magistrate. 'May I sit with my sister, sir? I worried about her all night.'

Sir Richard eyed her closely. 'You may, but why would you have worried about her?'

'Because I knew she would be scared about what was happening, worrying about being taken away as I was. Especially after that horrid man tried to abduct her the other day.'

'I must protest, Sir Richard!' Wilfrid did rise now. 'Sarah was precisely where she ought to have been last night. Under my guardianship and protection. I have attempted to explain that to her, but I fear her mind has been poisoned against me!'

Sarah opened her mouth, caught the slight shake of Hugo's head, and shut it again.

Sir Richard frowned. 'We will come to all that. You will all please be seated. This should not take very long at all.'

Hugo frowned. That sounded as though the magistrate had already made up his mind.

'Your Honour, we should await Whittenstall from the Chancery Court, since we are dealing with a disputed guardianship.'

'So I have been given to understand, Mr… Guthrie, is it not?' Sir Richard inclined his head. 'I daresay that will prove useful on this occasion, but in future understand that I prefer to make my own arrangements in such matters.'

'Of course, Your Honour.' Hugo handed Althea to a seat. 'I felt that with the meeting set for this morning, and to avoid further distress to the young ladies—'

'As to that,' Price-Babbington fairly galloped into his speech. 'I have suggested to Sir Richard that all this may be very easily cleared up. I am willing to accept that there has been a misunderstanding, and if Lady Hartleigh relinquishes in writing, here and now, all claim to my wards, then I am prepared to withdraw the charge of abduction.'

Hugo narrowed his eyes. *What the devil?*

Sir Richard leaned forward. 'You see that this simplifies matters. What does your client say, Guthrie? Less upset for the young ladies, and your client avoids the very nasty charge of abducting two heiresses.'

'*No.*'

## *Chapter Twenty-One*

Althea had spoken before Hugo could even draw breath.

'It is a very generous offer, Cousin!' snapped Price-Babbington. 'And one that I shall not hold open for long!'

'I'm only surprised that you made it at all,' Althea began. Then she frowned. 'Or perhaps not. You didn't know Guthrie had become my solicitor, did you, Wilfrid? You seemed a little put out to see him.'

And Hugo understood that Althea had seen Hugo's miscalculation as quickly as he had himself. Price-Babbington had not considered that he might be here this morning. The idiot had assumed that Althea would be attempting to defend herself, or at best might have a solicitor who would know nothing about the background to the situation.

And yet he had been prepared to withdraw the charges… It dawned on Hugo that Price-Babbington had brought the charge as a ploy to frighten Althea into giving the girls up. The mud that would stick to her name when word got out would not have mattered to him in the slightest.

He spoke coldly. 'With respect, Sir Richard, Mr Price-Babbington has brought a very serious charge against my client. I believe Lady Hartleigh deserves the opportunity to clear her name. Then, assuming Whittenstall—'

He broke off as the door opened. A clerk ushered an elderly, black-clad gentleman into the room.

Sir Richard rose at once. 'Good morning, sir.'

The old man nodded to him. 'Birnie. Good morning.' He looked around, his gaze settling on Hugo. 'And I suppose you're old Hugh Guthrie's sprig. Good man, your father. I was sorry when I heard of his death. Now, what's all this fuss about an heiress?'

Whittenstall seated himself beside Sir Richard, pulled out a pair of eyeglasses and settled them on his nose. He peered over them at the girls. 'Which one of these is the heiress anyway?'

'Ah, both of them, sir.' Sir Richard shuffled through some papers. 'We haven't progressed quite that far. We're still on the abduction charge.'

'We *weren't* abducted!' Sarah burst out. 'Cousin Wilfrid refused to let us stay!'

'Eh?' Whittenstall frowned.

'Sarah.' Althea reached over Kate and patted Sarah's wrist. 'I think we need to allow Mr Guthrie to explain, and then answer any questions.'

'But—'

'Sarah.'

'Yes, Aunt Althea.' She bit her lip. 'I'm very sorry, Your Honour.'

Whittenstall nodded. 'Not at all, my dear. I'm sure all this is quite a shock.'

Sir Richard pulled out a paper. 'I have here, Guthrie, a copy of the last will and testament of Frederick Price, in which he very clearly names Wilfrid Price-Babbington as guardian to his daughters, Sarah and Catherine.'

'Yes, your honour. I am fully apprised of the terms. Although my late father drew up that will, it fell to me to enact it.'

'Then I fail to understand why, on receiving instructions to enter these girls in a good school, you should have taken them to Lady Hartleigh.'

Hugo caught Price-Babbington's eye and smiled at the man's panicked expression. No, the man had not expected him to be present.

'This is all a misunderstanding!' Price-Babbington blustered. 'My intention in writing that letter was to have both girls enrolled in some suitable school! An educational institution! I… I have offered to withdraw the charge of abduction already!'

'Perhaps this letter will enlighten you, Sir Richard.'

'That's my private correspondence!' Price-Babbington lunged at Hugo, snatching at the letter.

Puck growled, hackles up, but didn't move.

'Control that brute, Cousin!' Price-Babbington jerked back, his face white.

'He's sitting, Wilfrid. Perhaps you should follow his example?'

Hugo smothered a crack of laughter as he passed the letter to Sir Richard. 'And there's this. Miss Kate noted down a conversation between Price-Babbington and his wife.' He handed Kate's deposition to the magistrate.

Whittenstall rose slightly to lean over the desk and look at Puck. 'Nice little chap. Some sort of terrier, is he, ma'am?'

Althea raised her brows. 'It's possible, sir. A friend found him as a puppy, in the yard behind her shop, and gave him to me. I've never enquired very closely into his ancestry.'

Whittenstall nodded. 'Very wise. Breeding's not always the most important thing, eh, ma'am? These crossbreeds often have a deal of game about them. And an excellent nose for a rat, I daresay.'

Althea inclined her head gravely. 'So it would appear, sir.'

His jaw rigid, Hugo met Sir Richard's gaze. To the man's eternal credit there was only the slightest flicker at his jaw to show that he'd heard the exchange.

Turning to Whittenstall, Hugo said, 'I took the precaution of making a copy last night, sir, thinking it might speed things along this morning. I had no chance to have it notarised, but you may check it against the original I just gave Sir Richard.'

Whittenstall took the offered copy. 'Thank you, Guthrie. Much appreciated.' He adjusted his glasses and scanned the document, as Sir Richard did likewise with the original and Kate's evidence.

Sir Richard passed the latter across to Whittenstall without comment, but with an icy look in his eyes.

When Whittenstall had read that, the two men exchanged glances.

Whittenstall spoke first. 'Interesting. Birnie, might we have that clerk of yours back in? Helpful to hear an unbiased, chap-in-the-street sort of view on this.'

Duly summoned, the clerk looked enquiringly at Sir Richard.

Sir Richard held out the letter. 'Read this, if you please, Sutherland. And tell us what sort of institution you think is meant.'

'What?' Price-Babbington sputtered, half out of his seat. 'I have already told you that I meant—'

'Hold your tongue, sir!' Sir Richard Burnie picked up his gavel and banged it down—Puck barked. 'You will leave Sutherland to form his own conclusions.'

Price-Babbington subsided.

Sutherland read the letter carefully. He looked up, scowling. 'Exactly what did you want my opinion on, Sir Richard? Seems clear enough to me.'

Birnie gestured to Whittenstall. 'My learned colleague will explain.'

Whittenstall nodded. 'What type of institution do you think is meant, Sutherland?'

The clerk frowned. 'Says it right there. A charitable institution.'

'There are many charitable institutions in our fair city, my good man. Would you suppose that a school was intended, for example?'

Sutherland blinked. 'Wouldn't be my first guess, sir. Given what else this Price-Babbington chap writes about—' he broke off, glancing about. 'Are these the...children?' He gestured at Sarah and Kate.

'They are.'

'Right.' His expression became pugnacious. 'I'd say he meant an orphanage, your honour.' He flushed. 'Calls them *pauper brats*. Says he prefers not to have them raised with his sons—'

'I meant only that—boys of an impressionable age, you know.

They…they might fancy themselves in love or some such nonsense! It seemed safer for the girls if—'

'Are you telling us, Wilfrid, that your sons are not to be trusted around young ladies?' Althea enquired, her tone dripping sweetness. 'That says a great deal about their upbringing. And none of it good!'

'Thank you, Sutherland. That will be all for now. You've been very helpful.'

The clerk withdrew.

Sir Richard turned to Sarah. 'Miss Price.'

'Sir?'

'How did you and your sister reach London?'

'On the stagecoach, sir.'

'I assume that your cousin sent a servant to take care of you?'

'No, sir. The gig took us to the coaching inn. Vickers was supposed to go straight back, but he said the horse had a loose shoe and he took it over to the smithy and came back to wait with us for the coach.'

'I see. How old is your sister?'

'I'm eight, sir.' Kate clung to Sarah's hand. 'And Sarah is nearly fourteen.'

'Thank you, my dear. What happened when you reached London?'

'Why, Mr Guthrie met us. He said it was too late to make decisions that day so we dined at the inn, and then he took us back to his lodgings and slept on the sofa so we could have his bed.'

Sir Richard looked at Hugo. 'Did your reading of that letter concur with Sutherland's opinion?'

'Yes, your honour. I understood my instructions were to enter both girls in an orphanage.'

'And they remained in your lodgings while you made enquiries?'

'Yes.' He was going to have to tell the truth, and nothing but the truth. He hoped he could avoid the whole truth about *why* he had been unable to send the girls to an orphanage.

'But you took them to Lady Hartleigh instead.'

'Not immediately, sir. Since my father had acted for the family for many years, I knew a number of the girls' relatives. I wrote to everyone I could think of, even Lady Hartleigh.'

'Why *even* Lady Hartleigh?'

'I knew her to be estranged from the entire family, especially her brother, and thought there was little likelihood on those grounds of her being willing to house the girls. Also, I knew her finances to be straitened.'

'But she did!' Kate protested.

Unthinking, Hugo smiled down at her. 'Yes, she did, sweetheart. I was completely wrong.'

'Hmm. So you ignored your instructions from the girls' lawful guardian to enter them in an orphanage.'

'Yes.'

'Why was that?'

'I thought they would be happier with a family member. Even one in straitened circumstances.'

'Yet you failed to inform Mr Price-Babbington of your actions.'

Hugo frowned. 'On the contrary. I wrote again to each member of the family I had previously written to on behalf of the girls, *and* Price-Babbington, informing them that Lady Hartleigh had offered the girls a home.'

Sir Richard raised his brows. 'Naturally you wished them to know the girls were safe.'

Hugo hid a grin.

*Do be sure to stress my Christian charity, won't you? Especially to that insufferable prig Wilfrid!*

He took refuge in a half truth. 'Something like that. The only member of the Price family to respond in any way was Miss Elinor Price, but I assume that Mr Price-Babbington received his letter.'

Whittenstall drummed his fingers on the desk. 'That rather brings us to the nub of the matter. The girls' inheritances.'

'But we haven't *got* inheritances, sir,' Sarah told him.

Whittenstall frowned. 'Your cousin didn't tell you? I understood that he took you into his care yesterday.'

'I wouldn't call it *care*,' Sarah muttered.

'Leaving that aside, Miss Price, did your cousin not inform you of your inheritance?'

'No.'

'I felt it was better,' Price-Babbington said, 'given that Sarah was quite intransigent, to defer any mention of her good fortune until she was more amenable to her new situation.'

'I see.' Whittenstall's tone suggested he was seeing all sorts of things to which Price-Babbington might have preferred he remained blind.

'It falls to me then, Miss Price, to inform you that your Great-Aunt Elinor Price—'

'She called on us,' said Kate. 'And Aunt Althea said she was our great-*great*-aunt, and that she was surprised she was still alive. And Great-Great-Aunt Elinor heard her and said she was still alive because the devil wouldn't have her.'

From Whittenstall's face it was clear that he'd found his way through the morass of pronouns. Hugo didn't dare look at Birnie.

'Whether or not the devil changed his mind, Miss Kate, I'm sorry to tell you that your Great-Aunt Elinor died very recently. She has left you and your sister very handsome fortunes.'

'*Did* she?' Sarah stared at him. 'I didn't think she liked us. And Aunt Althea threw her out for being nasty.'

'Be that as it may, Miss Price, she left you and your sister ten thousand pounds each.'

Althea felt her jaw drop in unison with Sarah and Kate's gasps. *Dear God!* Even if they could stop Wilfrid's claim, all the girls' relatives would be offering them a home now. She swallowed hard. She ought to be glad for the girls—she was—not fighting back tears because she was going to lose them regardless.

She took a steadying breath, drew on the memory of Hugo's deep voice reciting a fairytale, and smiled. 'That was very kind of Elinor. You can thank her in your prayers tonight, girls.'

'Which brings us back to the question of guardianship.' Wilfrid looked smug. 'I am sure Althea must agree that a widow of straitened means is far from the best person to have charge of two wealthy orphans.'

'Must I, Wilfrid?' Althea kept her voice polite. 'I note you have not lost that irritating habit of telling everyone else what they must think.'

Whittenstall cleared his throat. 'That is a point, however. Guthrie, have you anything to say?'

Hugo rose. 'Yes. I would ask you to consider whether or not a man who put two unprotected young girls on a stagecoach bound for London, without making quite sure they would be met, is a fit and proper person to have charge of them. I will not go into detail about the dangers they faced had I been out of town or somehow not received that letter.'

'A…a mere oversight,' Wilfrid managed. 'Naturally I was expecting you to meet them or arrange for a substitute.'

Hugo looked him up and down. 'An oversight. I must also query the fitness of a guardian who declined to act for two orphaned children when they were destitute, sent them away from the only home they knew, lest they corrupt his impressionable sons, and snatched them back when they inherited a fortune. I would argue that he has not their best interests at heart and has thus disqualified himself as a suitable guardian.'

'And are you suggesting that *Althea*, with her tarnished reputation—' Wilfrid broke off, affecting a pious expression. 'I am grieved to raise this subject in front of innocent ears—perhaps the girls might be removed temporarily?'

'We're not going anywhere.' Sarah's mouth was a flat line and Kate's hand was tucked firmly in hers. 'Aunt Althea took us in when we had nothing, and she's not so frightfully well-off herself. She was the only one who wanted us. We're staying.'

Whittenstall glanced at Sir Richard, who nodded.

'Agreed.' The magistrate gestured to Wilfrid. 'If you have something to say, say it.'

Wilfrid shot Althea a vicious look. 'My cousin has been ostracised by the family since Lord Hartleigh's death. Not only did it transpire that she had managed to run through her own fortune, coercing her trustees to hand over capital sums, but she attempted to recoup her fortune by engaging in liaisons of an unsavoury nature with an uncounted number of wealthy gentlemen!'

She sat very still and straight, chin up. 'Are you implying, Wilfrid, that you can't count to *two*? Because that is the number. I had affairs with precisely two gentlemen. Both of whom were unmarried, as was I.'

'The number, my dear Althea, is irrelevant.' Wilfrid adopted a pious expression. 'A woman's reputation is a very lovely and fragile thing. Once gone, it is gone for ever.'

Althea shrugged. 'Unlike gentlemen? Who can wade through the muck, tell lies and whore as much as they please without consequence?'

Sir Richard leaned forward. 'You admit the affairs then, Lady Hartleigh?'

She snorted. 'Since I'm not a hypocrite, yes. However, for the past six years I have lived very privately and, believe it or not, chastely.'

Wilfrid sniggered. 'Not so chastely that Guthrie here hasn't been seen visiting your house at all hours. And last night he did not go home at all!' He turned to the magistrates. 'This is a plot! A plot to steal the money of two defenceless girls!'

'You can't have thought they were so very defenceless when you put them on that stagecoach,' Whittenstall remarked.

Sir Richard spoke. 'Guthrie, did you indeed remain at Lady Hartleigh's home last night?'

Hugo looked disgusted. 'I did. Your magistrate, Wilcox, had released Lady Hartleigh into my custody. I took that to mean that I should remain with her. In fact, he stipulated that I must do so. In addition,' he added, 'there had been an attempt by Price-Babbington to snatch Kate the day before. The child was—'

'I had nothing to do with those men!'

'What *men*, Cousin?' Althea's voice dripped malice.

'Thank you, Guthrie.' Sir Richard gave Wilfrid an icy glare. 'I think we can dispense with any further accusations of impropriety, sir.'

'Well, it's…it's all very fishy if you ask me,' said Wilfrid.

'No one did,' muttered Sarah.

Whittenstall cleared his throat. 'Ah, Miss Price, you are very nearly fourteen, I believe.'

'Yes, sir. Next month.'

'Fourteen is the age at which we consider a potential ward in Chancery old enough to have a say in who their guardian should be.'

Kate spoke up. 'Mr Guthrie said that last night. He found it in a law book with Aunt Althea.'

Whittenstall smiled. 'Did he now? That's good to know.' He looked back at Sarah. 'If I were to ask you next month whom you would prefer as your guardian, what would your answer be?'

'Aunt Althea,' Sarah said. 'She gave us a home rather than sending us to an orphanage. We'd rather stay with her. Are you going to make us go with *him* for a month until I turn fourteen?' She paled. 'You…you wouldn't separate us!'

'No.' Whittenstall shook his head. 'As your friend Mr Guthrie pointed out, we must have your best interests at heart. Separating you and your sister would clearly not be in your best interests. So you would prefer to remain with your aunt, despite her straitened circumstances, rather than live in your old home in comparative wealth and luxury?'

Sarah looked down at Kate, who nodded. 'Yes, sir.'

'Very well.' He looked at Althea. 'If—I repeat *if*—I award you guardianship of these girls—Did you say something, Price-Babbington?—then you must understand that there can be no allowance made from their fortunes to reimburse you.'

'That will not be necessary, sir. I am perfectly beforehand with the world these days.' Please God, he wasn't going to ask how she had achieved that.

'I am more than a little concerned about that fortune you ran through,' Whittenstall admitted. 'While you will not have control of the girls' money, you must be able to teach them prudence. That you dissipated your own fortune…' He shook his head, frowning.

Althea shut her eyes briefly. She *couldn't* say this in front of the girls. She glanced at them. 'Will you trust me?'

They stared, then nodded.

'I… I must ask you to leave the room briefly. Perhaps you could take Puck out for a stroll with Mr Guthrie?'

# *Chapter Twenty-Two*

Hugo made a protesting sound, but she turned to him, begging with her eyes. He was not proof against that, no matter that he wanted to take her into his arms and shelter her from everything. If she wanted the girls out, whatever she had to say must be bad.

He scowled. 'I don't like it, but if you ask it. Come, girls.'

They followed him out.

'Why did we have to leave, Uncle Hugo?' Kate demanded. 'And what's an *affair*?'

'Don't be silly, Kate.' Sarah scowled down at her. 'There's probably something about Papa that she doesn't want to talk about in front of us. Something awful he did.'

Hugo stared. How much else did the child know?

She met his startled, questioning gaze. 'Cousin Wilfrid wasn't exactly discreet about anything. He was furious that Papa left the estate so heavily mortgaged. I would have felt sorry for him if he hadn't been so horrid to us.' She touched Hugo's wrist. 'You should go back in.'

'And leave the pair of you to get yourselves arrested?'

The clerk, Sutherland, looked up from his desk. 'They'll be safe enough with me, sir. Got a lass of my own.'

'There. See?' Sarah grinned at him. 'We're perfectly safe. Kate?'

Kate held out the dog's leash. 'Take Puck. He growled at Cousin Wilfrid before. He might do it again.'

Somehow Hugo found himself with the dog leash in one hand and the other reaching for the doorknob.

'Well! I like *that*!' Wilfrid glared at Althea as the door closed behind Hugo and the girls. 'When I wanted them removed—'

'Oh, do hold your tongue, Wilfrid.' Ignoring him, she spoke directly to Sir Richard and Whittenstall. 'You must understand that my brother Frederick, the girls' father, was my principal trustee after our father's death. My godfather, our mother's uncle, had made me his heiress, and Frederick, as the boy, believed the money ought to have been left to him. Our father encouraged him in this belief. Both of them resented my inheritance bitterly.'

Wilfrid snorted. 'I hardly see how this—'

'Does Price-Babbington have anything to do with this, Lady Hartleigh?' asked Whittenstall.

She blinked. 'Nothing whatsoever, sir. He may already know the truth. I hardly care.'

Whittenstall nodded. 'May I ask why you wished the girls to leave? You did not scruple to speak of your past affairs in front of them.'

Althea swallowed. 'I did not wish them to hear what I must reveal about their father. They don't deserve that.'

Sir Richard looked at Wilfrid. 'You will remain silent, or you will be removed. And you will remember that anything said here in my court is confidential.'

He raised his brows as the door opened. 'Guthrie. What have you done with your charges?'

Althea's heart and stomach tangled into a vicious knot. 'Sir—'

Hugo let go of Puck's leash and the dog trotted straight to her, then leapt into her lap.

'The girls are in the outer office with your clerk, Sir Richard.'

He nodded. 'Continue, ma'am.'

Her arms closing around Puck, Althea groped for her thread of thought. She didn't want Hugo to hear any of this either. To know what a fool she had been! And yet… She met his eyes across the dog. Saw the unfathomable kindness that had found two young girls a home, saw the man who refused to judge.

In the face of that, she couldn't refuse to trust. She swallowed, and trampled down all her misgivings. 'After our father's death, Frederick was my trustee along with my godfather's solicitors. In time Frederick introduced me to his friend, Lord Hartleigh, who…courted me.' She swallowed. That was all any of them needed to know. 'We…married when I was just eighteen. I was encouraged to take some of the income from my fortune as extra pin money, and discouraged, indeed, forbidden by Hartleigh from taking any interest in the management of the capital. He considered it unbecoming in a female to interest herself in money matters beyond the household accounts. We lived in London much of the time, unless he wished to hunt or shoot. When he died in a riding accident I assumed that I would have more than enough to live on. I was amazed to learn that the capital was nearly gone. Apparently I had been requesting large sums for several years, and my trustees had acquiesced.'

*Would they understand? Could they?*

'But you had not requested those sums?' Hugo's swift understanding steadied her. His matter-of-fact tone suggested this might even be something that did not surprise him.

'No.' She fought to keep her own voice level, not to reveal the rage, the *hurt*, that seared at the memory of her brother's betrayal. 'Each time my brother informed the other trustees—'

'Who were they, Lady Hartleigh?' asked Sir Richard.

'What? Oh, my godfather's solicitors. Dunstable & Frome.'

Sir Richard made a note. 'Please continue.'

'Frederick gave them a letter supposedly from me, and they acquiesced. Eventually I discovered that these sums had been given to Lord Hartleigh who used them to pay off gambling debts.'

'So not only did *you* not run through your fortune, your brother assisted your husband in defrauding you?' Sir Richard's fist was clenched on the desk.

Althea fought to control her trembling hands. 'Yes. In fact, he was one of Hartleigh's creditors. I wrote to Frederick when I found out what had happened. I… I demanded that he restore my inheritance. He refused.'

'What a tarradiddle!' scoffed Wilfrid. 'This is to avenge herself on a dead man because he cast her off when she created a scandal!'

'That scandal was created by Frederick to discredit me when I threatened to tell the entire family what he had done.' She took a deep breath. 'I have the letters that I supposedly wrote requesting the release of the money. They are not in my handwriting, but Frederick's. I have Hartleigh's accounts, noting the amounts and their source, and to whom he owed gaming debts.' The bulk had been to Frederick, but he had not been the only one. That no longer mattered. All that mattered now—

'I did *not* fritter away my fortune, and you may be sure that I will do my very best to ensure that Sarah and Kate are taught to live within their means, and to ensure that they are not foolish enough to permit themselves to be cheated as I was.'

'Oh, *bollocks*, Althea!' Hugo erupted.

'Perhaps, Guthrie,' said Sir Richard, 'you might express your very understandable sentiments in more seemly terms.'

'Your pardon, Sir Richard.' Hugo turned to Althea, annoyance clear on his face. 'Don't you dare blame yourself for trusting your husband and your brother! *They* were the cheats. You said Hartleigh *forbade* you to take any interest in the management of your money?'

'Yes.'

Hugo turned to Wilfrid. 'Were you acquainted with Hartleigh?'

Wilfrid nodded, looking as though he would rather have been anywhere else. 'I… I was.'

'And was he the man to brook any disobedience from his wife?'

Wilfrid's smirk said it all. 'I should say *not*! Hartleigh had very proper ideas in that regard. Very proper.'

'I daresay.' Whittenstall's voice could have dried the Monday washing. 'Birnie, may I assume you are satisfied there is no charge of abduction for Lady Hartleigh to answer?'

'You may.'

Whittenstall nodded. 'Very well. Lady Hartleigh, the Court of Chancery is satisfied that you have acted in all ways in your nieces' best interests. The girls themselves wish to remain with you. So be it. You will continue as their guardian of nurture. The court will consider and appoint *suitable* trustees for their fortunes.' He looked at Hugo. 'Perhaps you might consider—'

'No.'

Althea stared. 'Why ever not? You didn't refuse when I appointed you as one of their trustees if something were to happen to me.'

'You have made a will in favour of your nieces, Lady Hartleigh? Appointed trustees?'

She flung Sir Richard an impatient glance. 'Of course I did. I had to ensure their safety as my idiot brother did not. Why not, Hugo?'

'I'm already trustee for part of their inheritance—'

She waved that aside. 'Not a very large part. I've little enough to leave them in comparison to Elinor's fortune, so—'

'Not quite true, ma'am.' Sir Richard rifled through the papers on his desk. 'Ah, here we are. Miss Elinor Price remembered you in her will also. I wondered at the wording when I read it, but it makes perfect sense now.'

He cleared his throat. '"*To my great-niece, Althea, Lady Hartleigh, née Price, only daughter of James Thurston Price and his wife, Anna, both deceased, having been defrauded by her husband and brother, the sum of fifteen thousand pounds to her absolute use and—*"'

'She knew?' Althea could barely breathe, her knees wobbled, and she was grateful for Hugo's steady hand under her elbow.

'I think so, Lady Hartleigh.' Sir Richard looked at her kindly. 'And you should know that she left it to your absolute use *if* you were still a widow when you inherited. Had you remarried the money was tied up so tightly that an ant couldn't have found a way to get near the capital.'

Althea didn't know if she was laughing or crying. 'She found out, and she trusted me.' It meant everything. After leaving her that day, Elinor had set to find out the truth and, finding it, had done her best to set things right.

'This is not *fair*!' Wilfrid glared around the room. '*I* was supposed to be Elinor Price's heir! She intended the money for my cousin Frederick, and after he died—'

'She found out that the fool had stolen his sister's fortune, gambled his own fortune away leaving his daughters destitute, and so she attempted to set things right.' Sir Richard Birnie leaned forward on his desk.

'None of that was *my* fault!'

'Cousin—' Althea felt a little bit sorry for him. 'If a loan would—'

'Lady Hartleigh,' Sir Richard interrupted, 'before you make that very generous offer, you should know that your great-aunt did not entirely disinherit your cousin. The residue of her fortune, some thirty thousand pounds, I believe, goes to him.' He smiled at her. 'He won't be a pauper.'

Althea looked at Wilfrid. 'You really are a toad, Cousin. You only wanted the girls back so you could ensure one of them married your heir.'

Wilfrid flushed. 'There's nothing wrong with keeping money in the family!'

'No? What about when it involves defrauding your sister?' Hugo rose from his seat beside Althea. 'Thank you for your time today, Sir Richard, Whittenstall. With your permission I will see Lady Hartleigh and *her wards* safely home.'

They walked. A breeze had sprung up, taking some of the heat from the air, and the day had cooled. The girls walked hand in hand, slightly ahead, with Puck trotting beside them.

'I'm rich again.'

Hugo smiled. 'Yes.' She'd said it a few times, as if she couldn't quite believe it. Her hand was safely tucked on his arm, and he hoped, he prayed, he was going to be able to keep it there.

'Not…not disgustingly rich, but *comfortable*.'

'Yes.'

'I shall stop at Mr Gifford's shop and see about that pianoforte for Kate,' she said.

'And what about something for yourself?' he asked. For a beautiful woman who had lived in fashionable society, she had the least acquisitive nature of anyone he knew.

'Me?' She shrugged. 'I have nearly everything I really need. I'm not going out to buy things for fun. I'm not *that* wealthy.'

He latched onto that first sentence. 'Nearly everything? Then there is something you want?'

They walked on a little way, crossed Denmark Street.

'It's not something I can buy,' she said at last. 'Hugo, may I ask you a question?'

'Certainly.'

'What did you wish to talk about that last morning at Petersham? Because there was something I wished to say to you, as well. And I… I wondered if we wished to say the same sort of thing to each other.'

He glanced down at her, saw the slight smile. 'Very likely. You understand why I couldn't say anything before I left?'

She scowled then. 'Yes. Your wretched professional ethics. I might love you for having them, but—'

'You love me?'

'Yes, of course, but they're still a damn nuisance.'

She loved him. His heart danced, and for a moment he floated along the pavement, his head somewhere on a level with the dome of St Paul's.

'You love me.' He said it again, scarcely able to believe it.

'Yes…' She sounded rather as though she were waiting for something.

'Ah. I love you, too, you know.'

She chuckled. 'Very well. When are you going to ask me to marry you?'

His head threatened to annoy St Paul's again, but he forced his brain to clear. 'When you have all your new financial affairs in order, and everything tied up in a trust. With proper trustees who can be trusted.'

'What?' She stared at him. 'Do you think I don't trust you?'

He looked down at her. 'I know you do. And because I'm

such a trustworthy fellow, we aren't going to so much as be betrothed until you have all that tidied up.'

'But—'

'I would have spoken months ago if not for believing the girls were going to become heiresses. If you think I'm going to take advantage of you when *you* have inherited a fortune, think again. Once we are officially betrothed you can't do anything with any of your property without my consent. Which I would give, but we aren't going down that road. You'll have this done before we're betrothed.'

She sighed. 'And, of course, neither you nor your partner can draw this up. I don't *know* any other solicitors!'

He grinned. 'Use that chap, Kentham, who drew up your aunt's will. At least we know he can be trusted to follow a lady's instructions. And I spoke to Lacy this morning very briefly when I saw him out, about him replacing me as the girls' trustee.'

'What? Why?'

'Because I can't be one of their financial trustees and be a guardian of nurture. Which I will be when we marry.' He laid his hand over hers. 'I'm sorry, sweetheart. More professional ethics.'

'Are we going to tell the girls now? Or does that have to wait, too?'

He chuckled. 'Kate already told me I should be buying you a ring when I bought the watch. I thought I'd ask their permission.'

She laughed. 'That sounds exactly right. When we reach home, Hugo, I'm going to kiss you. Will that be acceptable to your professional ethics?'

His fingers tightened on hers. 'That will be more than acceptable, sweetheart.'

# *Epilogue*

Hugo held Althea's hand as they walked towards the river in the deepening twilight. Under the sheltering trees the evening breathed the scents of night. The lantern he held in his other hand surrounded them in a little pool of light.

'This,' he said, 'has been the longest month of my entire life.'

They had married at St Anne's, Soho, that morning. A wedding breakfast had followed in their new home on the corner of Soho Square. Aunt Sue, having come up to town for the wedding, had remained there to look after the girls.

*'Take Althea away for a few days. Brighton or some such.'*

But when he had asked Althea if she might like to go to Brighton for their honeymoon, she had looked a little surprised.

'Brighton? Well, it's fun, of course. And if you would like that, then—'

'Where would *you* like to go?' he had interrupted.

'I thought your house at Petersham?'

'That would be *our* house,' he corrected. 'Are you sure you aren't saying that to please me?'

Now, turning onto the path along the river, with Althea's hand secure in his, and their wedding night before them, he smiled to himself, remembering her snort of laughter.

As she was laughing now. 'A long month?' she quizzed him.

'I admit that it surprised me that you suggested a walk after supper instead of going straight upstairs.'

He slipped his arm around her and his heart leapt as she snuggled closer. He felt the press of her cheek on his shoulder.

'Sweetheart, I've been waiting to be married to you, not merely to take you to bed. I've missed these evening walks.' He dropped a kiss on her hair, smiling at the soft laughter that shook her. 'Although,' he added, 'I've every intention of taking you to bed as well. Or letting you take me. And we won't be needing my new watch, either!'

* * * * *

# HISTORICAL

*Your romantic escape to the past.*

## Available Next Month

**Regency Christmas Weddings**
Christine Merrill, Liz Tyner & Elizabeth Beacon
**Their Convenient Christmas Betrothal** Amanda McCabe

..........................................................................................

**Compromised With Her Forbidden Viscount** Diane Gaston
**The Lady's Snowbound Scandal** Paulia Belgado

**Available from Big W and selected bookstores.**
OR call 1300 659 500 (AU), 0800 265 546 (NZ) to order.
Visit **millsandboon.com.au**

# This Christmas, could the cowboy from her past unlock the key to her future?

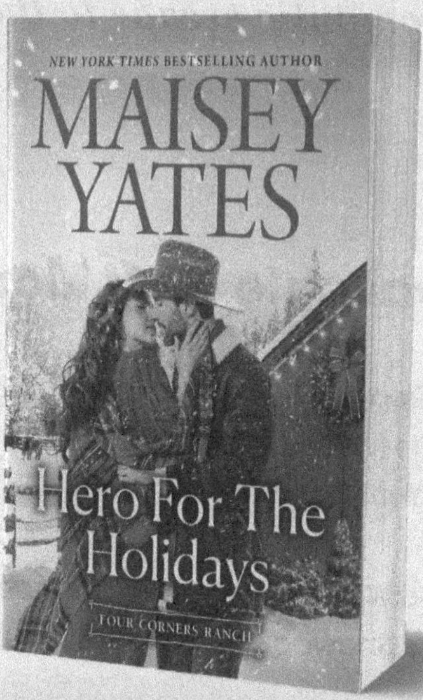


**Don't miss this brand-new Four Corners Ranch novel from *New York Times* bestselling author**

# MAISEY YATES

In-store and online November 2024.

MILLS & BOON

millsandboon.com.au